SAFARI OF SHADOWS

SAFARI OF SHADOWS

PREDATOR AND PREY ON
THE GARDEN ROUTE OF SOUTH AFRICA

R.D.D. SMITH

Modelbenders Press

Safari of Shadows: Predator and Prey on the Garden Route of South Africa

AI Disclaimer: All the text, characters, and plot were created by a human author. Therefore, it is all covered by copyright. AI contributions are described in the "AI Disclosure" section at the end.

Modelbenders Press books may be purchased for business and promotional use. For more information, please contact the publisher. Inquire with the author at **http://www.rddsmith.com/**

PRINTED IN THE UNITED STATES OF AMERICA

Interior and Cover Designed by Adina Cucicov at Flamingo Designs

The Library of Congress has cataloged the paperback edition:

Smith, R.D.D.
Safari of Shadows: Predator and Prey on the Garden Route of
South Africa
/ R.D.D. Smith–1ˢᵗ ed.
1. Action Adventure, 2. Travelogue, 3. Thriller
I. R.D.D. Smith   II. Title.

Paperback ISBN 978-1-938590-52-8
Hardback ISBN 978-1-938590-53-5
eBook ISBN 978-1-938590-51-1

FICTION BY R.D.D. SMITH

Dr. Monica Gray, Medical Thriller Series
The Surgeon in the Mirror
Against a Viral Threat
Savior of the War Torn
Beyond the Mind's Horizon
Echo

Global Runners Travelogue Series
Blood on the Equator (Ecuador)
Sebastian's Gold (Portugal & The Azores Islands)
Safari of Shadows (South Africa)

Short Stories
The Surgeon's Genie
Freyja $AI
Jack Hunter: One More Mission
Lauren Banister: Sacred Shadows
Guardians of Blackwood

Find his work at: www.rddsmith.com

In the breathtaking wilderness of South Africa, a running expedition becomes a deadly chase. What starts out as the adventure of a lifetime — traveling through South Africa's stunning coastlines and exploring the pristine wilderness of Kariega Game Reserve — turns into a fight for survival when the leader of Global Runners accidentally witnesses the brutal actions of Victor Malanga, one of South Africa's most dangerous crime bosses.

TABLE OF CONTENTS

CHAPTER 1

THE WAREHOUSE

Iron-black eyes surveyed the piles of animal pelts scattered across the concrete floor. Victor Malanga moved through the cavernous space with the casual ownership of a man accustomed to having dominion over all he surveyed. Beyond the corrugated metal walls, the industrial symphony of Cape Town's docklands created a constant backdrop. Malanga registered none of it, his razor-sharp mind too busy calculating profit margins with machine-like precision.

The warehouse air hung thick with competing scents: the metallic tang of blood, the musky odor of animal hides, and the ever-present smell of salt from the nearby ocean. Dust motes danced in the few shafts of sunlight that penetrated the grimy skylights, illuminating the true nature of his empire—row upon row of wildlife converted into commodities.

"Not enough." The words sliced through the stale air. "You're short this month."

Malanga's manicured finger pointed toward the tallest of the piles—impala pelts stacked like macabre pancakes, their once-sleek forms now flat and lifeless. His Italian leather shoes clicked sharply as he moved to inspect a row of curved buffalo horns arranged in a neat pile.

"I need ten more impala pelts." His voice remained level, almost conversational. He turned, gesturing toward the horns. "And five more of these."

Reggie Mbeki shifted his weight, his face betraying the first hints of anxiety beneath his practiced calm. At forty-three, his once-athletic frame had thickened around the middle, but he still carried himself with the alertness of a man who understood danger. Ten years as Malanga's lieutenant had taught him to recognize the warning signs—the slight narrowing of his boss's eyes, the too-casual stance that masked Malanga's coiled readiness.

"But, boss, the rangers are all over us now." Reggie kept his tone respectful but couldn't hide his frustration. "The herds have moved way deeper into the bush. It takes us twice as long to track them down and get them out now." He hesitated before adding, "We lost an entire team to some rangers last week. They grabbed everything we had—including all the pelts you wanted by today."

The mention of the anti-poaching rangers triggered a barely perceptible tightening of Malanga's jaw.

A grunt echoed from the warehouse entrance where Sipho Botha's silhouette filled the doorframe. The former rugby forward's presence alone typically ensured compliance from those who met him. His obsidian skin seemed to absorb the dim light, and the scar that ran from his left temple to his jawline gleamed slightly in the half-light. Then, there was his intimidating build; he was six-foot-six with more muscles than most people could ever dream of having, even most professional athletes. Sipho rarely spoke, instead acting as a silent sentinel waiting for Malanga's command—a slight nod or finger gesture that would signal it was time to transform verbal negotiation tactics into acts of physical persuasion.

"Your problem, Reggie, not mine." Malanga's voice dropped an octave, taking on the quiet menace that his associates had learned to fear more than shouting. "Get another team out there. Plenty of men need work." His lips curled into something approximating a smile. "Good work that pays well."

Behind the words hung the unspoken reality of the situation—failure wasn't an option. Malanga didn't fire people; they simply disappeared, their replacements already standing by. The criminal hierarchy of South Africa's smuggling networks functioned on brutal Darwinian principles.

"Yeah, sure thing." Reggie's voice caught slightly before he cleared his throat, trying to project more confidence than he felt. A thin sheen of sweat had formed along his hairline, despite the cool temperature inside the warehouse.

Malanga reached into the inner pocket of his tailored, charcoal-colored suit jacket and extracted a thick fold of American hundreds. The bills were bound by a platinum money clip engraved with the image of a leopard. One finger—adorned with a single, golden ring bearing a diamond that Malanga had certainly not bought at a jewelry store—flicked through the currency as he peeled away the exact sum he needed.

"For all this." He gestured dismissively at the assembled wildlife products—the tangible evidence of an ecosystem being dismantled for profit. Each pelt and horn represented not just an animal, but a piece of Africa's natural heritage being transformed into luxury items for foreign markets. "But I want more next week. Don't disappoint me."

Reggie nodded quickly. Relief washed over his features as he accepted the payment. "No problem. I'll get a new crew together today, have them out in the bush by morning."

Malanga smiled—a predator's expression that never reached his eyes—and patted Reggie on the cheek with cold familiarity. The gesture, borrowed from American gangster films he'd developed a fondness for, communicated both affection and ownership. "I know you won't let me down, Reggie."

Something flickered across Reggie's face—a fleeting expression of resentment quickly suppressed. After a decade of loyal service, he still received the same condescending treatment as the newcomers. The countless times he'd solved problems, covered their tracks, and expanded their business went unacknowledged. But like every ambitious lieutenant, he nursed his grievances silently, waiting for the day when patience might yield him a new opportunity.

Malanga caught the look but chose to ignore it. Ambition in subordinates was useful—until it wasn't.

He nodded toward Sipho, who cracked open the metal door, checking the street outside with practiced efficiency.

"Clear," Sipho rumbled, his deep bass voice reverberating in the cavernous space—one of the few times he spoke without explicit instruction.

The pair stepped out into the spring air of Cape Town's industrial district. The cool breeze offered momentary relief from the warehouse's oppressive atmosphere, carrying with it the mingled scents of sea salt and diesel fuel. They walked toward the narrow street where the silver Mercedes-Benz S-Class waited, its tinted windows reflecting the surrounding decay like a chromium anomaly—a bright spot of wealth amid the bleak ruins.

As they approached the vehicle, Malanga paused, glancing back at the nondescript building. From the outside, nothing suggested the bloody commerce within—just another anonymous warehouse in a city of thousands. The perfect cover for an operation that had made him millions while remaining invisible to most.

CHAPTER 2

SWEATING IT OUT

"One more, one more!"

Sheryl Diego gritted her teeth as she lay trapped beneath the loaded barbell while it hovered inches from her chest. Her muscles trembled with effort, lactic acid burning through her deltoids and triceps. The instructor's voice cut through her concentration—insistent, encouraging, and wrapped in an accent that sounded musical.

"Push!" he called, clapping his hands for emphasis.

Sheryl drew a sharp breath and focused. She'd started lifting weights once she turned twenty-one and had been at it for over fifteen years; her body knew what to do. She visualized the bar rising, channeled her frustration into power, and drove upward. Gradually, the barbell ascended until her arms locked out. With a satisfying clang, she racked the weight and exhaled forcefully.

"Nice! Didn't even touch the bar." The instructor grinned, extending a hand to help her up. "You're strong for an American."

Liam Visser stood about six feet tall, his skin bronzed from Cape Town's generous sunshine, his curly dark hair cut short on the sides. The sleeveless shirt he wore revealed arms mapped with veins—the physique of someone who practiced what he preached. The Cape CrossFit gym was his domain, a converted warehouse space where industrial fans fought valiantly against the smell of sweat and determination.

"Thanks." Sheryl stood and shook out her arms to disperse the tightness forming there. "That was exactly what I needed."

Morning light streamed through the high windows, illuminating a dozen other athletes moving through their own routines. The gym thrummed with energy—barbells dropped to the ground, jump ropes whipped against the rubber flooring, and encouraging shouts punctuated grunts of exertion. This morning, Sheryl had simply walked in, paid the drop-in fee, and declared herself ready for the 7 a.m. class. As the only visitor in a space filled with regulars, she'd received Liam's special attention.

"You've done this before," he observed, studying her form with professional appreciation.

"Every day back home. 6 a.m. religiously." Sheryl ran a hand through her long, blonde hair, which was already damp with sweat. "Try to hit gyms when I'm traveling, too."

She moved toward the heavy dumbbells, waiting for the push press portion of the workout. She was a bit taller than the average woman at five-foot-seven, and her athletic build reflected the years of disciplined training she had undergone—broad shoulders tapering to a narrow waist, defined arms suggesting functional strength rather than aesthetic sculpting. Her gray tank top bore the faded logo of a Utah fitness competition from three years prior.

Following her to the dumbbell rack, Liam asked, "Where's home?"

"Utah. Lots of hills, kinda like here." Sheryl selected weights that made Liam raise an eyebrow slightly. "Good training ground."

She settled into the workout, matching the regulars' rhythm. While many travelers would have taken their vacation as an excuse to abandon their fitness routines, Sheryl viewed her training as non-negotiable. Physical readiness wasn't just about looking good in hiking shorts—in her line of work, stamina could make the difference between a successful tour and a disaster.

The hour passed in a blur of movement and exertion. When the timer finally signaled the end of the workout, several members offered her high-fives as Sheryl toweled off. She'd proven herself—not an easy feat in a community as tight-knit as a CrossFit gym.

"Come back anytime, Ms. Diego," Liam called as she gathered her water bottle and phone. "We're doing power-lifting tomorrow."

Sheryl slung her small backpack over one shoulder. "Thanks, but I'll be on Table Mountain tomorrow. I'll be getting up early to prep everything for my group."

"Tour guide?" Liam's interest visibly piqued. Like many locals, he maintained a friendly rivalry with those who showed off his city to visitors.

"Expedition leader," she corrected with a smile that suggested the distinction mattered. "Adventure tourism."

"Maybe we should tag along that day," he suggested, a hint of flirtation coloring his voice. "See how the pros do it."

"Please feel free to join us. We start at seven sharp." Sheryl knew that few would actually take her up on the offer. Early morning hiking deterred all but the most dedicated.

"Maybe I will." Liam's grin widened as he slapped her hand in a final high-five. "Might learn something about my own backyard."

The brief connection lingered a moment longer than necessary, the touch an acknowledgment of a mutual attraction that neither would pursue. Sheryl had learned long ago that vacation romances complicated her professional life unnecessarily.

She pushed through the glass door and stepped into the cool morning air of the narrow street. The gym was not in a gleaming shopping center but wedged between industrial businesses in a working district of Cape Town. The street hosted an eclectic mix of electrical supply shops, plumbing wholesalers, and nondescript warehouses.

Sheryl turned left toward the primary thoroughfare that would lead back to her hotel. The neighborhood hummed as delivery vans double-parked, workers unloaded crates, and shop owners swept sidewalks. She inhaled deeply, filling her lungs with the mingled scents of the nearby harbor, brewing coffee from a corner café, and the indefinable essence of a city coming alive.

The training session had left her pleasantly tired but mentally alert. This heightened awareness—a professional habit refined over eight years of leading tourists through unfamiliar territories—allowed her to automatically catalog her surroundings. Two men emerged from a warehouse ahead, walking in her direction.

The contrast between them was striking. The smaller man moved like he owned the city, each step deliberate and controlled. His charcoal suit whispered of expense without ostentation—the kind of tailoring that announced wealth only to those who recognized quality. His face bore the sharp angles of ambition, and his eyes constantly scanned the world around him, assessing and then dismissing everyone he came across.

Beside him walked a human mountain—at least six and a half feet of solid muscle clad in loose-fitting clothes that did little to disguise his imposing physique. His expressionless face suggested a man accustomed to intimidating others with his mere presence. The bodyguard's watchful gaze swept the street with practiced efficiency.

Sheryl maintained her pace, deliberately shifting her attention as if admiring the architecture or planning her day—anything but acknowledging the men ahead. Years of traveling solo had taught her the trick of remaining invisible: you didn't make eye contact, didn't appear uncertain, and didn't show interest in other people's business.

The thin man's gaze flicked toward her as they approached—a reflexive assessment rather than genuine interest. He noted her blonde hair, fair skin, and the athletic build that all marked her as a foreigner. For a moment, confusion crossed his features. Then, his eyes caught the CrossFit sign behind her, and understanding replaced his apparent suspicion. He offered her a curt nod as they passed.

Sheryl suppressed the instinct to watch them go. Instead, her attention fixed on the warehouse door slowly swinging shut behind them. The building stood unremarkable among its neighbors—weathered brick, small windows set high on the walls, a loading dock on one side. A perfectly ordinary warehouse.

Just before the door closed completely, Sheryl caught a glimpse inside. The cavernous space contained piles of something on the floor—odd shapes arranged in clusters. A third man moved to block her view, his face transforming from neutral to hostile as he noticed her gaze. Their eyes locked for a fraction of a second before Sheryl snapped her attention forward and continued toward the main street, maintaining her casual pace through sheer willpower.

Her mind raced beneath the composed exterior. *What was that about?* The images were fragmentary—shapes on concrete, something organic about the arrangement. The man's reaction suggested something worth hiding.

As she walked the few blocks back to her hotel, Sheryl processed the mental snapshot she had taken. Street vendors had begun setting up along the sidewalk, displaying colorful wares for the day's tourists. Her eyes fell on a painting propped against a stall—a dramatic rendering of buffalo on the African plain, their magnificent horns sweeping upward in proud curves against a blood-orange sunset.

Recognition hit her like a physical blow. The shapes on the warehouse floor. Not random clutter but organized rows of animal parts—horns separated from the creatures that once carried them.

Sheryl stopped abruptly, earning an irritated "tsk" from the businessman walking behind her. She turned slowly, looking back toward the entrance of the small street she'd just left. Her professional instincts warred with her personal curiosity. Years of leading wilderness expeditions had cultivated a deep respect for wildlife and conservation efforts. Whatever operation ran from that warehouse, it definitely wasn't a legitimate business.

The thin man and his imposing companion had already disappeared into the morning bustle. Only the memory of that hostile stare from the warehouse worker remained, along with the disturbing image of severed horns arranged in neat rows.

The expedition leader calculated the risks versus benefits of getting herself involved in what she had seen. Her group would arrive tomorrow—two dozen adventure tourists expecting the trip of a lifetime, not potential danger. She had preparations to complete, routes to confirm, supplies to check. Whatever she'd witnessed wasn't her concern. Cape Town had authorities for such matters.

Yet, something about the scene nagged at her—the calculated precision of the arrangement, the obvious wealth of the thin man against the industrial setting, the immediate hostility she faced once the worker had realized what she had observed.

Standing at the intersection between listening to caution or her conscience, Sheryl considered her options. *What exactly had I seen, and what, if anything, could I do about it?*

CHAPTER 3

RECRUITING

The acrid smell of oil and metal hung in the air of Thabiso's Motorcycle Repair, a cramped shop tucked between a bakery and a cell phone store in Cape Town's Woodstock district. Fluorescent lights buzzed overhead, casting harsh shadows across the concrete floor stained with decades of grease and tire marks. Tools hung in meticulous order on a pegboard wall—a small rebellion against the chaos of the work itself.

Thabiso Mboko hunched over the disemboweled engine of a BMW R1200GS, his calloused fingers working with surprising delicacy among the gleaming components. His frame had retained its wiry strength, despite being in his early forties, though the years had etched fine lines around his eyes. Eyes that had seen too much through a rifle scope.

"How much do you make fixing motorcycles?" Reggie leaned against the workbench, watching Thabiso work. "It can't be enough to feed your family."

The question hung between them, weighted with implication. Reggie hadn't come for a motorcycle repair. Both men knew the real purpose behind this early morning visit.

Thabiso's shoulders tensed almost imperceptibly. "My wife works at the hospital. We make do." His voice carried a practiced casualness that didn't match the wariness in his eyes.

"Make do." Reggie snorted softly, rolling the words as if testing their inadequacy. "You should be doing better than that. You're a hero, brother. There aren't many with the talent you have."

Reggie straightened his posture, adjusting the cuffs of his shirt—a small habit that betrayed his nervousness, despite the confidence in his voice. Sweat gathered at his temples, even with the shop's ancient fan blowing stale air at his face. Malanga's deadline echoed in his mind. *A new team by tomorrow. In the field. Ready to work. No excuses.*

The mechanic's hands paused over the engine. "Listen, brother," Thabiso emphasized the word with subtle irony, "I know what you're offering. It's not for me. Too dangerous. Too much time away." He looked up, meeting Reggie's gaze directly. "I have two girls who need me. They're only ten and eight. What they need is a father who comes home to them every night."

Around them, the shop told its own story—framed photographs of two smiling girls in school uniforms perched on a shelf beside service manuals. A faded wedding picture hung beside Thabiso's military service commendation. These weren't decorations but reminders — anchors tethering him to a normal life.

"Thabiso," Reggie said and lowered his voice, leaning closer, "what they need is nice clothes, nice things, a good education." He gestured toward the photos. "They need opportunity. You can give that to them with what I'm offering. They could go away to school anywhere, get good jobs when they're old enough. Maybe work in the government. Maybe become college professors." He paused. "Isn't that more important to you than fixing rich men's toys?"

The pitch was well-practiced, but the desperation underlying it was new. Reggie had recruited dozens of men over the years, but never with such personal stakes. If he failed Malanga now, after ten years of service, after promising a team would be ready…

Thabiso had heard variations of this argument before. Reggie was a cousin of his wife's family — or perhaps the brother of a cousin; the exact connection was deliberately kept vague. Everyone in certain circles knew Reggie's line of work, knew who he worked for. And everyone with sense avoided getting entangled in the same web that had ensnared him. Men who entered Malanga's service rarely left it — at least not with breath still in their bodies.

Thabiso shook his head and turned back to the motorcycle, reaching for a torque wrench. The small gesture conveyed finality more clearly than words.

Reggie sighed, shoulders sagging as he weighed his options. Thabiso had been his best prospect — a former military sharpshooter with a legendary reputation. During his service, Thabiso had mastered every rifle the army possessed, developed skills in stalking and concealment that bordered on the supernatural, and accumulated a record of confirmed kills at distances that seemed impossible. He was exactly what a poaching team needed.

He was also stubbornly principled—a quality Reggie had once possessed himself, before necessity and ambition had worn it away.

Shaking his head in defeat, Reggie prepared to move on to his next candidate—a less skilled but perhaps more desperate man. The bell above the shop door jangled harshly, the rusty hinges protesting as the door swung open.

Both men turned toward the sound, their conversation forgotten.

The doorway darkened as if night had fallen prematurely. A massive silhouette blocked nearly all the light from the street, its edges sharp against the morning sun. Stepping into the shop, Botha ducked his head beneath the door frame. His massive frame seemed to compress the available space.

The enforcer's eyes, set deep in his scarred face, took in the scene methodically—Reggie's obvious disappointment, Thabiso's defensive posture, the half-repaired motorcycle. Botha's customary silence filled the room like smoke.

Then, in a move so unexpected that it caused both men to stiffen, he spoke.

"You have a new team?" The deep bass rumbled from his chest like distant thunder. "Boss sent me to help you find one."

The unspoken threat in those simple words charged the air. Botha didn't "help" with recruitment. He enforced decisions that were already made.

Reggie looked from Botha to Thabiso and back, trapped between two impossible positions. He needed to say yes—for his own survival. Yet, he had nothing to show for all the time he had spent convincing Thabiso. The sweat along his hairline doubled its production.

Noticing the hesitation, Botha shifted his gaze to Thabiso, studying him with the calculating assessment of a butcher evaluating livestock. After a long moment, he nodded once. "Yes, he is good. He will do."

Then, he jerked his thumb toward the door, the universal gesture of command. "Get in my truck. We're heading out now."

The color drained from Thabiso's face. "No, no. I'm just a mechanic. I have a family. I'm not interested." The words tumbled out, each one weaker than the last.

Botha remained impassive, unmoved by the protest. "Thabiso Mboko," he pronounced the name with precise enunciation, "you shoot like a god. This is the work for you. Get in the truck."

The familiar way Botha used his name sent ice through Thabiso's veins. They'd done their research. This encounter wasn't a casual recruitment attempt, but a targeted acquisition.

Reggie and Thabiso exchanged glances—Reggie's filled with apology, Thabiso's with accusation. Reggie hadn't intended for things to go down this way. Strong-arming family into service crossed a line he'd managed to avoid during his years with Malanga. But the situation had spiraled beyond his control. If he couldn't produce an alternative shooter immediately, Thabiso would be pressed into service, regardless of his wishes.

A bitter irony twisted in Thabiso's gut. He'd encountered Malanga's operation before, but from the opposite side of it. After his military service, he'd briefly joined anti-poaching units, using his skills to protect wildlife from men exactly like those now recruiting him. He'd been in firefights where his bullets targeted poachers, not animals.

He knew that distinction meant nothing to Malanga or his enforcer. All that mattered was that they needed a shooter, and they knew he had both the experience and the talent to fill that role. The rest was irrelevant.

Thabiso's mind calculated rapidly. This confrontation could proceed in only two ways: he could continue resisting and receive a beating severe enough to ensure compliance, or he could set down his wrench and accept the job. Either way, he would end up in that truck heading into the bush. Either way, his daughters could lose their father.

Slowly, deliberately, he laid the torque wrench down on the workbench. The metallic click seemed to finalize his decision. He wiped his hands on a rag, then reached for the shop keys hanging by the door.

"I need to lock up," he mumbled.

Botha nodded once—the gesture was that of a king granting a small mercy to a subject.

As Thabiso passed Reggie, their eyes met again. No words were exchanged, but the message in Thabiso's gaze was unmistakable—there would be retribution for this betrayal. Family or not, Reggie had crossed a line that could never be uncrossed.

Reggie's face crumpled momentarily, revealing the regret he normally kept hidden beneath his professional façade. He attempted to convey an apology through his expression, but the act felt hollow, even to him.

As the shop door closed behind them, the bell jangled with inappropriate cheerfulness. Through the window, Reggie watched as Thabiso climbed into the passenger seat of a faded Toyota Land Cruiser. Even from this distance, he could see how the mechanic's shoulders had already transformed—straightening, tensing, preparing. The soldier emerging from his civilian disguise.

Alone in the shop, Reggie noticed the family photographs still watching from their shelf. Two small girls smiled at a father who wouldn't be coming home tonight.

He turned away, unable to bear their innocent gaze. His phone vibrated in his pocket—likely Malanga checking on his progress. He would report success, of course. One problem solved, another created.

The cycle continued, the web expanding, drawing in another victim. And somewhere in the back of his mind, Reggie wondered when his own threads would finally snap.

CHAPTER 4

A GATHERING OF WAYFARERS

The Cape Red Hotel stood as an architectural fusion of contemporary European minimalism and subtle African influences. Sharp angles and clean lines dominated the interior, with vibrant accent colors punctuating the otherwise austere design. The lobby and bar had been meticulously crafted to coax guests from their private quarters into communal spaces—strategic lighting, comfortable yet stylish seating, and acoustics designed to facilitate conversation while still maintaining privacy. It was a social experiment disguised as elite hospitality.

Global Runners Travel had selected this particular establishment as their Cape Town headquarters for its prime location in the harbor district and its culinary reputation. In Sheryl's experience organizing adventure tourism, food ranked just below safety in importance—especially for Americans traveling abroad. They craved authentic local flavors but preferred them to be presented alongside recognizable dishes. That way, they could seek familiar comfort when cultural immersion became overwhelming. Portion size was equally crucial. You couldn't lead a group on a strenuous hike up Table Mountain only to reward them with modest servings. They needed to feast like the vacation-goers they were, guilt-free indulgence being an unspoken pillar of tourism.

The warm evening light filtered through the lobby's floor-to-ceiling windows as Sheryl entered, casting golden patterns across the polished concrete floor. Her trained eye immediately spotted Zuri Bicton—her assistant guide and logistics expert—holding court at a corner table surrounded by eager travelers. With her infectious laugh and encyclopedic knowledge of Cape Town, Zuri had already magnetized several early arrivals.

Zuri, a globe-trotting Brit with roots all around the world, had spent the past month in the city finalizing arrangements for this expedition. The tourists clustering around her—"runners" in company parlance—were clearly trying to extract insider information about the upcoming adventures, unwilling to let the journey unfold organically.

Pushing aside her lingering unease about the buffalo horns she'd glimpsed earlier, Sheryl slipped into her professional persona with practiced ease, approaching the group with open arms and a broad smile.

"Stanley! Madeline! You both look thinner than when I last saw you!" she exclaimed, embracing a silver-haired couple in their early sixties, whose matching hiking boots and moisture-wicking shirts identified them as seasoned adventure tourists.

"Ecuador. Last year," Madeline reminded her, returning the embrace with enthusiasm. Her Minnesota accent remained crisp, despite the South African chardonnay in her hand. "We've been training. Now that we know how hard you push us, we actually train for vacation." The woman's laughter rang out, though everyone present understood that it wasn't entirely a joke.

Stanley nodded solemnly. "Six months of conditioning. Lost fifteen pounds since Quito."

Zuri poked Madeline playfully in the side. "Please, that isn't difficult for you. If anything, I'm the one who has to train to keep up with you." Her subtle British inflection added charm to the compliment, eliciting appreciative chuckles from the group.

Sheryl glanced at her watch—a rugged outdoor timepiece that had survived adventures on six continents. "Dinner in thirty, upstairs in the Rhino Room. I need to get cleaned up first, so I'll see you all in a bit." With a parting wave, she made her way to the elevator, mentally reviewing the names of returning clients and trying to match them with faces.

When the elevator doors slid open, she was immediately engulfed in the enthusiastic embrace of Joan Lewis, another familiar face from past excursions

"Sheryl, where are you going? Dinner's about to start." Then, as she pulled away, Joan registered the casual clothes. "Oh! Right. Well, hurry up. We have so much to catch up on." Her midwestern warmth radiated through her words, though something in her voice seemed more strained than usual. "I brought photos from my last adventure to show you!"

Exactly thirty minutes later, Sheryl stood transformed before the assembled travelers in the Rhino Room. Her athletic frame was now draped in a vibrant shweshwe dress in bold blues and yellows, a conscious choice of local fashion. Her still-damp hair was pulled back, emphasizing her sun-weathered features.

Thirty expectant faces gazed up at their leader. The room hummed with anticipation and the low murmur of introductory conversations. The space itself was impressive—tall windows framed the twinkling lights of Table Mountain against the darkening sky, while tastefully displayed photographs of rhinos in their natural habitat adorned the walls.

"Thanks for trusting us with your vacation…again," Sheryl began, her voice carrying easily across the room without seeming forced. "You won't regret it. We've got a busy two weeks ahead of us. Zuri, Luke, and I—" she said as she gestured to her other two staff members, who stood at the periphery of the room, "—have personally checked every hotel, run every trail, and tested every activity. Tomorrow, we climb Table Mountain. The trail's steep, but trust me, it's worth it. You can't visit Cape Town without seeing the incredible views the mountain has to offer."

She paused, letting her gaze connect individually with both new and returning faces. "Saturday, we head out and start our trek around the southern coast. First up is Knysna with its amazing lagoon, then Featherbed Nature Preserve, the forests of Kranshoek, the Robberg Peninsula, the Bloukrans Bridge, and finally, the incredible wildlife of Kariega Game Reserve."

The excitement in the room mounted palpably with each destination she named. Eyes widened, partners squeezed each other's hands, and whispered exclamations peppered the crowd.

"If you're gonna do all this work," Sheryl continued with a knowing smile, "you need to fuel up. So, eat well tonight. Breakfast tomorrow will be quick so we can get to the mountain before the crowds and the heat."

With that encouragement, she gestured toward the buffet where servers were removing silver dome covers. Steam rose from traditional South African dishes arranged between more familiar international offerings.

The centerpiece was a massive potjie—a three-legged cast-iron pot containing a rich game stew that had been simmering for hours. Beside it stood trays of bobotie—spiced minced meat baked with an egg-based topping, its complex aroma of curry, turmeric, and bay leaves triggering appreciative murmurs. Golden-brown sosaties—marinated meat skewers—glistened next to colorful platters of chakalaka, a spicy vegetable relish whose vibrant colors matched the room's decor.

For those less adventurous, grilled steaks and seafood platters provided safe alternatives, though Sheryl always encouraged her groups to embrace local cuisine as part of the immersive experience.

As glasses of South African wines—robust pinotages and crisp chenin blancs—were distributed, the room transformed into a lively symposium of introductions and reconnections.

Around a large, circular table, Sheryl seated herself among a mix of newcomers and veterans, facilitating introductions.

Everyone took turns going around to announce where they were from and if they had been on any previous trips with the group.

"Hello. My name is Joan Lewis. I'm a forensic accountant from Wisconsin. Cape Town is the third excursion I've been on with Global Runners." She paused, then added more quietly, "Been looking forward to this trip for months." Her smile didn't quite reach her eyes, and Sheryl noticed how she checked her phone briefly before putting it away.

The next person, another woman, spoke up next with a warm smile on her face. "Wanda Mkhize. Hollywood, California. My father is from South Africa. I'm a stunt coordinator for movies. Not much work like that here in Africa, so I live in the US full-time."

"Cape Town born and raised," said a distinguished local man in his sixties who had been invited to join them. "Thomas Nkosi, university professor. I study tourism's impact on local communities." He smiled warmly. "I'm your cultural translator if you have any questions."

"Boulder, Colorado," chimed in a fit, young couple dressed in matching technical fabrics. "Tyler and Emma Wilson. Ultra-marathoners looking for new terrain to conquer." Their eager expressions and fit physiques marked them as the overachievers of the group—the ones Sheryl would need to rein in for their own safety.

As dinner progressed, more voices joined the chorus of introductions.

"Vancouver, Canada. Margaret Chu. Retired surgeon. My kids gave me this trip for my seventieth birthday, thinking

I might finally slow down." The elegant woman's wry smile suggested that was unlikely.

The younger woman next to Margaret spoke up. "Sabrina Chu. I'm her granddaughter. My parents sent me to keep an eye on her." She hooked a thumb at Margaret. "And also, as a college graduation gift."

"That's sweet," Sheryl interjected before letting the others continue.

"Austin, Texas. We're brothers, Derek and Sean Alvarez. We own a chain of food trucks. We came looking for new flavor inspirations." The younger brother was already enthusiastically photographing each dish before tasting it while the older one introduced them.

"Manchester, England. Kelly and Kim Donovan. We met Sheryl on the Inca Trail three years ago. Now, we plan our annual leave around her trips." Their deep tans showed they spent much of their free time outdoors.

Between introductions, conversation flowed naturally. Professor Nkosi became the center of attention when he explained the cultural significance of the dishes they were enjoying.

"The potjie," he explained, gesturing to his bowl of fragrant stew, "dates back to the early Dutch settlers who needed practical cooking methods on their treks. Using a three-legged pot allowed them to cook over open fires on uneven ground. The time people spent slow cooking their food soon became another opportunity for socializing—much like your American barbecues."

Emma from Colorado asked about the spices in the bobotie, which led to a detailed discussion of the dish's Cape Malay culinary influence—a fusion cuisine developed by slaves brought from Southeast Asia during colonial times.

"In many ways," the professor noted, "South African cuisine tells our complex history better than any textbook. Each dish carries a story of cultural collision and creative adaptation."

As the evening progressed, natural affinities began forming among the travelers. The ultra-marathoners from Colorado gravitated toward a former Olympic-hopeful from Chicago. The foodie brothers from Texas engaged the professor in an intense discussion of fermentation techniques. A photographer from Seattle compared equipment notes with an amateur wildlife photographer from London.

Sheryl observed these budding connections with satisfaction. Over the years, she'd witnessed how these initial conversations often predicted the support networks that would form during challenging moments of the journey ahead. The group was already coming together, their different backgrounds and experiences becoming complementary rather than divisive.

Later, as malva pudding—a sweet, spongy dessert soaked in caramelized sauce—was served alongside rooibos tea, Sheryl caught Zuri's eye from across the room. Her assistant gave a subtle nod of approval. The energy was good; the group dynamics were promising. Tomorrow, they would face their first physical challenge together, but tonight had accomplished the equally important task of establishing trust.

As coffee and dessert liqueurs circulated, Sheryl found herself seated beside Professor Nkosi, who spoke quietly while the room buzzed around them.

"Interesting group you've put together," he observed. "Diverse ages, backgrounds."

Sheryl nodded. "The best groups always are. Too much similarity breeds complacency."

"And what about you, Ms. Diego? What brings a woman from Utah repeatedly to the southern tip of Africa?"

The question caught her slightly off-guard. Before she could formulate a response, they were interrupted by Joan, who had a pressing question about appropriate footwear for tomorrow's climb.

The professor's query lingered in Sheryl's mind, unanswered but not forgotten. *What is it that keeps drawing me back to this place, where beauty and danger coexist?*

The evening wound down as jet lag began claiming victims among the travelers. As guests excused themselves to prepare for tomorrow's early start, the room gradually emptied, leaving only a few determined conversationalists nursing last drinks.

Standing at the panoramic window overlooking the harbor lights, Sheryl allowed herself a moment of quiet contemplation. Twenty-eight travelers and six staff, all under her care for the next fourteen days. Each with different expectations, different capabilities, different reasons for being here.

And somewhere out there in the darkness beyond the city lights waited the wild heart of South Africa—beautiful, unpredictable, and occasionally merciless to the unprepared. Just as it had always been.

CHAPTER 5

ASCENDING TABLE MOUNTAIN

"We're gonna climb that? Holy crap!" Madeline exclaimed, her voice betraying equal parts excitement and apprehension as she tilted her head back to take in the imposing silhouette of Table Mountain against the early morning sky.

The massive plateau dominated Cape Town's horizon, its sheer cliffs rising dramatically from the city below. In the soft morning light, the sandstone face took on a golden hue, deceptively gentle-looking, despite its formidable height.

Zuri patted Madeline on the back reassuringly. "It's not that bad. Luke and I have hiked it twice in the last month. The trail winds back and forth. It's not straight up." Her confident smile did little to diminish the mountain's intimidating presence.

The group had gathered at the Platteklip Gorge trailhead just after dawn. A light mist still clung to the lower slopes, promising to burn off as the sun climbed higher. The air carried a distinctive scent of something herbaceous, slightly sweet, and unmistakably wild.

"Two hours?" Stanley asked, repeating the estimated completion time while adjusting his hydration pack. His Minnesota accent stretched the vowels. "And it's not a race?"

"Not a race," Luke confirmed, his Cape Town accent lending authority to his words. Tall and lean with sun-weathered skin, he epitomized the outdoor guide profession. "We're here to hike, see some beautiful views, and get to know each other. Take time to talk. Find out who your neighbors are."

He gestured to the rocky path that zigzagged up the mountain. "This route's the oldest and most direct way to the top—the Platteklip Gorge Trail. It's been used since the 1600s. We've got about a thousand meters of elevation gain over about three kilometers. The terrain changes pretty dramatically as we climb through different ecological zones."

"Not a race. But still a run," Jack Hunter interjected, bouncing lightly on the balls of his feet. His muscular frame and calculated gaze marked him as more competitive than most. To him, this trip was only fun if it posed a challenge. Hiking and talking clearly weren't priorities on his agenda.

He wore technical trail-running gear that probably cost more than some people's monthly rent, and his restless energy suggested someone who found stillness uncomfortable. His eyes continuously scanned the trail ahead, plotting his route like a chess player anticipating his opponent's moves.

"I'll run a few steps with you," Rogerio volunteered, a Brazilian software engineer whose trim, athletic build belied his desk job. "Probably not the whole thing, but enough to get my legs and lungs pumping."

Jack nodded at the trail. "Then, let's go." Both men started off at an easy jog, leaving the pack of fellow tourists behind them. "It's only a few thousand feet of elevation gain. I do that in Seattle all the time," Jack called over his shoulder.

"It's the rate of the climb that's gonna get us," Rogerio replied, already noticing the immediate incline.

Looking back, both men could see that a couple of others had followed suit and decided to give running a try. The larger group was organizing for a more leisurely hiking party under Sheryl's guidance.

Rogerio called back to their guide, "Luke, tell us what we're seeing along the way. I'll stop for pictures and the view." Since Cape Town was his home territory, Luke was the best one to ask about such things. He and Zuri had worked together to plan all the outings on this vacation.

"Sure thing. You'll see the best spots for photos along the way. But we need to get a little more elevation first." Luke easily matched their pace, showing no signs of exertion, despite the increasing grade.

The trail quickly became steeper than anticipated, forcing the supposed runners to shift to a hiking stance on the more vertical sections. Large sandstone steps, worn smooth by countless feet over centuries, required careful foot placement. The morning dew made the rocks slippery here and there.

As they gained elevation, the surrounding vegetation changed noticeably. Luke spoke up between measured breaths, "this is fynbos all around us." He gestured to the dense, low-growing shrubs that lined the trail. "Just means 'fine bush.' Very prolific here and unique to the Cape Floral Kingdom—the smallest but richest of the world's six floral kingdoms."

Jack and Rogerio both nodded and gave incoherent acknowledgments, unable to speak clearly at the pace they had set.

Luke continued, seemingly unaffected by the climb. "See those plants with the silver-gray leaves? That's Leucadendron argenteum—its common name is silver tree. Endemic to these slopes. And those cone-shaped flowers are proteas—South Africa's national flower."

The botanically rich landscape bore little resemblance to anything the visitors had seen before. Unlike forest trails in North America or Europe, Table Mountain's slopes were covered with distinctive fynbos.

"The leaves and roots are very long and thin because the soil isn't rich and we have long dry spells," Luke explained. "So, the plants need to spread out to get enough nutrients to survive. Over 70% of the plant species here are found nowhere else on Earth."

As they rounded a bend, the trail briefly leveled out, providing everyone with momentary relief. The group's breathing became more labored as the elevation began to assert its influence. The air grew noticeably thinner with each step upward.

Still breathing easily, Luke pointed into the brush and called out the elusive wildlife that darted away from their approach. "There's a Cape skink. Oh, and a girdled lizard. Those are most common up here."

A small, bronze-colored reptile with intricate patterns scurried across the path, disappearing into the undergrowth with remarkable speed.

"Any snakes?" Rogerio managed between breaths, his earlier confidence now tempered by exertion.

"Not usually on the trail. But if you wander off into the bushes, you might find a Cape cobra or a puff adder."

"What? A cobra?" Jack exclaimed, his competitive stride faltering momentarily as he glanced nervously at the surrounding vegetation.

"Not on this trail. Too many people. Too many tourists," Luke said and chuckled reassuringly. "The snakes are smarter than to come out here." He navigated around a particularly large step on the trail. "But the tourists aren't smart enough to stay out of the brush. Every few weeks, we have an emergency rescue. Someone wanders into the bush, gets bitten, and needs antivenom."

"Do they ever die?" Jack asked, the bravado in his voice thinning along with the air.

Luke shrugged his shoulders without breaking stride. "Mmm. Sometimes. But not today."

The casual way he mentioned death made both tourists exchange nervous glances. This mountain wasn't a manicured and managed park.

The trail narrowed as it entered a section where the gorge walls closed in. The path here consisted of roughly hewn stone steps that seemed to stack endlessly upward. Each step required a substantial lift of the knee, creating a punishing rhythm that quickly burned through people's thigh muscles.

Just then, Rogerio jumped sideways and pointed frantically. "There's one! It's a snake!"

"Where?" Jack demanded as he froze in place. Both men watched a thin, black tail disappear into a bush ahead of them. They stopped in their tracks, hearts racing from more than just exertion.

Luke moved ahead calmly to examine the suspicious bush. After a brief investigation, he turned back to them with an amused expression. "No, guys. Just a lizard with a long tail. All good. That's a black girdled lizard—completely harmless unless you're an insect."

The trio returned to their hike, though their pace had slowed considerably since starting. The brief pause had allowed two others to catch up to them, making them a group of five.

"What stopped you guys?" Sheryl asked as she and Wanda joined them. Sheryl showed no signs of strain, despite the challenging ascent.

"Lizard snake," Rogerio explained sheepishly.

"What's that?" She directed the question at Luke, arching an eyebrow.

"Long, thin black girdled lizard. Not dangerous. Just startling," Luke clarified. "They're actually fascinating—they can detach their tails when threatened and grow new ones."

The group continued upward, the conversation providing a welcome distraction from burning quadriceps and labored breathing. The trail became increasingly technical, with loose rocks requiring careful navigation. A misstep here could result in a twisted ankle, or worse.

Taking the opportunity to question her local guide, Sheryl asked, "What do you know about Bebe Green Street? You know, where the Cape CrossFit gym is?"

"Warehouse district. Cheap rents," he answered, nimbly hopping from one stone to another. "Bit rough around the edges. Why?"

"Maybe cheap animal replica products?" Sheryl pressed, hoping to put her mind at ease about the glimpse she had caught into the warehouse.

Luke thought for a moment, his pace slowing as he considered the question. "Don't think so. We bring the cheap stuff in from China just like you guys do. Why do you ask?"

"Could there be poached animal parts in there?" Sheryl didn't know how to be more subtle, so she figured she would be as blunt as possible.

Startled, Luke slowed down further and stared at her. "I hope not. That area was barely safe to begin with. If poachers are operating there, the neighborhood's gotten way more dangerous. Not someplace you want to walk alone." His expression darkened. "Poaching's a massive problem here—rhino horn, elephant tusks, lion bones. The cartels are ruthless."

This information did nothing to reassure Sheryl. She lapsed into silence, considering what she'd seen and what it might mean. Finally, she said, "I'm sure I was mistaken."

Luke seemed eager to change the subject. He pointed ahead to where the gorge widened slightly. "Right there ahead of us. Good photo spot. We can stop for a breather and some pictures."

"Thank God!" Rogerio exclaimed, sweat pouring down his face. "Couldn't come at a better time."

The group emerged onto a natural stone platform that jutted out from the main trail. From this vantage point, Cape Town spread below them like a miniature model—the V&A Waterfront, the colorful houses of Bo-Kaap, and the azure Atlantic Ocean stretching to the horizon. The morning mist had completely burned off, revealing a crystal-clear view that seemed to extend forever.

The air at this elevation was noticeably cooler and fresher. As they caught their breath, a gentle breeze carried the faint scent of flowers from the surrounding fynbos. A single cloud passed overhead, temporarily casting them in shadow before moving on to reveal the warm South African sun.

Just as they were enjoying the respite, a flash of movement caught their attention. A small, antelope-like creature bounded effortlessly across the rocky terrain above them.

"Klipspringer," Luke identified with a smile. "Their name means 'rock jumper' in Afrikaans. They're perfectly adapted to these cliffs—can land on a surface the size of a coin."

The graceful animal paused, regarding the humans with mild curiosity before continuing its precarious journey across the near-vertical rock face.

As the rest of the hiking group caught up, their voices carried on the mountain air long before they appeared around the bend. The competitive runners' early lead had diminished considerably on the challenging terrain.

Looking up at the remaining ascent—still formidable, despite how far they'd come—Jack's earlier bravado seemed tempered by respect for the mountain.

"Halfway there?" he asked Luke.

The guide's knowing smile said everything he was thinking. "Not quite, mate. Not quite."

The mountain, it seemed, was teaching its first lesson in humility. And they still had a long way left to climb.

CHAPTER 6

THE SUMMIT

As the first Global Runner topped the final ridge, Zuri stood waiting next to a fluttering South African flag that marked the finish of the ascent. As the advance team, she'd used the cable car up the mountain to get everything prepared. Music—a blend of upbeat contemporary tracks interspersed with traditional African rhythms—pulsed from portable speakers set on a table overflowing with fresh fruit. The wind at this elevation was steady, carrying the scent of fynbos and the clean crispness that only mountain air possessed.

"Congratulations! You're the first one here." She raised her hand to high-five Anika, whose competitive nature had driven her ahead of the pack.

Anika slapped her hand before leaning forward, hands braced on her knees, her breathing labored but controlled.

"That was…" she paused to catch another breath, "excruciating…exhilarating. I'm glad to be done with it." Despite the exhaustion, there was unmistakable pride in her voice.

"You made good time. Sixty-nine minutes." Zuri glanced at her watch. "That took a lot of running. Is anyone behind you?" She looked down the path, expecting to see at least one more person ascending. The trail's final approach was visible from their position, winding up through the rocky terrain like a scar on the mountain's face.

Anika laughed, a short burst that turned into a cough. "Everyone's behind me. But if you mean close behind, then no. Haven't seen anyone else in the last half hour. One by one, everyone slowed to a walk. Luke was pacing a small group at the front last time I saw them."

"Well, there's fruit and water on the table. You can help me cheer on everyone else as they come up." Zuri gestured to the spread—watermelon slices, local cape gooseberries, bananas, and apples arranged in colorful abundance.

Anika had regained control of her breathing and was munching on a slice of watermelon, the juice running down her chin. "Sure." She was about to continue when she turned around and noticed the otherworldly panorama that lay before her. "Oh my God! That's amazing. The views along the way were great. But this one is unbelievable."

The city of Cape Town stretched out below, a patchwork of urban life nestled between the Atlantic Ocean and the towering mountains. To the right, she saw the glistening waters of Table Bay shimmering in the sunlight, dotted with ships and boats moving serenely across the waves. The iconic silhouette of Lion's Head rose proudly to the west, while the vibrant green of Signal Hill contrasted with the deep blue of the sea. Farther out, Robben Island—where Nelson Mandela had been imprisoned—lay quietly in the distance, a somber historical footnote amid the natural splendor. Enhancing the mood, multiple birds called out their beautiful songs.

It was Zuri's turn to chuckle. "I know, right? I've just been enjoying the view, waiting for all of you." Her casual tone belied the genuine pleasure she still took in the vista, despite having witnessed it several times during her planning trips.

Anika pulled her phone from a zippered pocket, instinctively reaching to capture the scenery, but she paused. "Pictures won't do it justice," she said, mostly to herself, but slid into photographer mode, anyway, carefully framing shots from different angles.

"The light changes constantly up here," Zuri advised. "If you wait till the others arrive, you'll have completely different lighting for your photos."

Anika nodded but continued shooting. "I'll take both. Different perspectives." Something in her methodical approach suggested she might be more than just an enthusiastic amateur.

As they stood staring at the scenery, eating fruit, and talking intermittently, they heard the voices of the next group approaching the top. The sounds of labored breathing and encouraging chatter drifted up from the trail.

"Come on, you've got this! Twenty more steps!" Luke's encouraging voice echoed against the rock face.

The next group crested the summit—Tyler and Emma, the ultra-marathoners from Colorado, along with Professor Nkosi and, surprisingly, Margaret Chu, the seventy-year-old retired surgeon from Toronto.

"Dr. Chu!" Zuri exclaimed. "You're putting these youngsters to shame!"

The elegant, older woman straightened her hiking shirt and smiled broadly. "I've climbed Kilimanjaro twice. This hike was just a morning stretch." Her breathing was remarkably controlled for someone of her age who had just completed such a strenuous ascent.

Tyler and Emma immediately began stretching routines that looked choreographed, their movements synchronized after years of training together. "The trail surface was more technical than we expected," Emma commented, her voice betraying no fatigue. "But the gradient was manageable."

"Speak for yourself." Professor Nkosi laughed, his academic composure momentarily abandoned as he gratefully accepted a bottle of water from Zuri. "I teach about these mountains; I don't usually climb them."

Luke arrived with them, looking as fresh as if he'd just taken a casual stroll. "Perfect conditions today," he observed, glancing at the sky. "Sometimes, the clouds roll in so fast up here that by the time everyone arrives, the view's completely gone."

"The tablecloth," Professor Nkosi explained to the others. "That's what we call it when the clouds cover the mountain like that." He gestured expansively. "It's part of what makes Table Mountain so iconic."

The newly arrived group turned their attention to the panoramic vista, their conversations falling silent as the majesty of the scene registered. Emma quietly slipped her hand into Tyler's, a rare public display that spoke volumes about the impact of the moment.

Over the next forty-five minutes, more groups of two and three arrived at the summit. The Alvarez brothers from Austin came up arguing good-naturedly about which local South African ingredients they should try to incorporate into their food trucks. Stanley and Madeline arrived with Rogerio, all three looking exhausted but triumphant. Joan arrived with a small cluster of hikers, though she seemed more subdued, working on her phone even at this elevation.

Each group repeated the same sequence of reactions—exhaustion, amazed surprise, and silent contemplation of the vista. It was exactly why the guides had planned this event as the opening of their vacation adventure: the shared challenge created instant bonds, while the reward of the view cemented the experience as unforgettable.

Sheryl was among the last to arrive, accompanying the final stragglers and ensuring no one was left behind—a core principle of her leadership style. Her face brightened seeing the entire group spread across the plateau, some sitting on rocks enjoying the fruit, others taking photos, all visibly affected by the accomplishment and the view.

"Everyone accounted for?" she asked Luke as they reached the flag.

"All present and relatively unscathed," he confirmed. "A few blisters to treat tonight, but nothing serious."

Sheryl nodded with satisfaction and clapped her hands to gather everyone's attention. "Congratulations, everyone! You've just climbed one of the world's most iconic mountains. Not bad for your first day in South Africa."

This statement elicited cheers and a spontaneous round of applause.

"We'll have about forty-five minutes to enjoy the summit before we need to head back down. There's a small exhibition center just over there—" she said and pointed to a stone building nearby, "—with info about the flora and fauna of the mountain. And, of course, plenty of spots for those Instagram-worthy photos."

As the group dispersed across the plateau, Jack approached Sheryl with an unexpected question. "That warehouse district you mentioned to Luke on the way up—is it near the harbor?"

Sheryl's expression flickered with surprise. "Yeah, just off the main dock area. Why do you ask?"

Jack hesitated, seeming to measure his response. "Just curious. I do some wildlife photography work back in Seattle. I've heard stories about the poaching problems here."

Before Sheryl could respond, they were interrupted by Derek, who thrust his phone between them. "You guys have to see this! Sean and I just found an actual dassie! Isn't it the cutest thing ever?"

The screen showed a short video of a rock hyrax—known locally as a dassie—a small, furry mammal that resembled a guinea pig but was, surprisingly, a distant relative of elephants. The creature was sunning itself on a rock, seemingly unconcerned by the human attention.

"They're all over the mountain," Luke joined in, appearing at Sheryl's side. "They've gotten used to tourists. Just don't try to feed them—they have a nasty bite."

Jack seemed ready to continue his previous line of questioning, but Sheryl had already moved away, drawn into a conversation with Professor Nkosi about the geological formation of the mountain.

The casual interaction left Jack thoughtful, his gaze following Sheryl as she moved through the group. There was something deliberate in his attention, a focus that went beyond normal tourist curiosity.

Across the plateau, Sheryl was speaking with Luke in hushed tones. "I keep thinking about what I saw in that warehouse," she admitted. "It's been bothering me since yesterday."

Luke looked uncomfortable. "Look, I know that area. If you saw what you think you saw, it's best to just forget about it. Those operations have protection from people you don't want to cross."

"What do you mean, 'protection'?"

Luke glanced around to ensure that he wasn't overheard by anyone else. "Let's just say that certain officials find it profitable to look the other way. It's complicated, Sheryl. This isn't Utah."

Their conversation was interrupted by Zuri announcing that it was time to prepare for the descent. They would be taking the cable car down rather than hiking—a welcome relief for most of the group, whose legs were already protesting the morning's exertion.

As the group made their way toward the cable car station, the camaraderie of shared achievement was palpable. New friendships were forming, inside jokes already established, the collective experience of the climb binding them together exactly as planned.

As the cable car descended, offering spectacular spinning views of the mountain and city, Sheryl made a decision. Tonight, after the group dinner, she would return to Bebe Green Street. She needed to know if what she'd glimpsed was real or if her imagination was manufacturing threats where none existed.

Either way, she needed certainty. Thirty-four people were in her care, and uncertainty was a luxury she couldn't afford.

SUSPICIONS

The long tables of the hotel's restaurant buzzed with excited conversation as the Global Runners assembled for dinner. Unlike their welcome meal, which had been characterized by polite introductions and hesitant small talk, tonight's gathering hummed with the energy of shared experience. The morning's climb up Table Mountain had transformed them from strangers into comrades.

Sheryl watched from near the entrance as the group settled into their seats beneath soft amber lights. The rooftop terrace overlooked the yacht basin, where expensive vessels bobbed gently in the evening waves, their masts creating a forest of vertical lines against the darkening sky. Behind them, the silhouette of Table Mountain was clearly visible, now looking deceptively benign in the twilight.

"Quite a view, isn't it?" Professor Nkosi appeared at her side, a glass of red wine in his hand. "I think you Americans might be getting spoiled with the scenery on this trip."

Sheryl smiled. "I don't think the human eye can ever get spoiled by too much beauty. Though I admit, coming from Utah, I have high standards for natural wonders."

"Ah, Utah—red rock country. I lectured at the University of Utah once. Magnificent landscapes." He sipped his wine. "But different from here. Our wilderness has teeth."

Something in his tone made Sheryl glance at him. "What do you mean?"

The professor's expression turned serious. "South Africa's beauty comes with dangers—some natural, some man-made. We locals learn to navigate both." He seemed about to say more but was interrupted by Joan, who was calling him over to settle a debate about local wildlife.

Sheryl checked her watch discreetly. She had planned her evening carefully—dinner with the group, then a quiet exit while everyone was engaged with dessert and the local musicians scheduled to perform until 9:00. That would give her roughly two hours to investigate the warehouse and return before anyone noticed her extended absence.

The meal progressed pleasantly, with servers bringing out platters of Cape Malay cuisine—fragrant bobotie, yellow rice with raisins, and sosaties accompanied by various chutneys. Wine flowed freely, and stories from the morning's climb were exchanged with increasing embellishment and laughter.

"I swear that dassie was posing for us," Sean insisted, showing his phone's gallery of photos around the table. "Look at this one—he's literally giving us 'Blue Steel!'"

"You should've seen Margaret powering up that last section," Emma added, raising her glass toward the elderly doctor. "She made the rest of us look like amateurs."

Dr. Chu smiled modestly. "Age and treachery will always overcome youth and skill."

Sheryl joined in the conversation, laughing at the right moments, asking questions to keep discussions flowing, but her mind was elsewhere. She'd secured a rental car that afternoon—a nondescript black sedan. It was waiting in the hotel's parking structure, the keys already in her pocket.

Across the table, Luke was busy talking to the Alvarez brothers, but Sheryl noticed his eyes occasionally drifting to her, a slight furrow in his brow. Earlier, when she'd mentioned feeling tired and possibly turning in early, he'd given her a long, assessing look that suggested he wasn't convinced.

Jack sat further down the table, seemingly absorbed in conversation with Tyler and Emma about training programs for ultra-marathons. Unlike Luke, he showed no particular interest in Sheryl's movements, which was a relief. Jack's military background and current security work made him particularly observant—the last person she wanted tracking her activities.

When the servers began clearing the main course dishes, Sheryl caught the eye of the hotel's event coordinator she'd briefed earlier. The woman nodded subtly, confirming that the local musicians were ready to begin on schedule. *Perfect.*

As the dessert course was being served, Sheryl leaned over to speak quietly with Zuri.

"I've got a splitting headache coming on. Would you mind taking over for the rest of the night? Everything's already been arranged—you just need to welcome the musicians after dessert."

Zuri looked concerned. "Of course. Do you need anything? I have painkillers in my room."

"No, I took something already. I just need to lie down in a dark room for a while." Sheryl stood, touching shoulders and murmuring quiet apologies as she made her way around the table. "Please, everyone, enjoy the rest of the evening. Zuri will take good care of you."

A chorus of well-wishes followed her as she moved toward the exit, maintaining a slightly pained expression while walking steadily. As she passed behind Luke, she felt rather than saw his posture stiffen slightly. She continued without pausing, but a sixth sense told her that he was watching her.

Sheryl moved quickly through the hotel lobby, retrieving a small backpack she'd stashed earlier behind the front desk under the pretense of holding some supplies for tomorrow's activities. She slipped into a restroom, changed from her dinner attire into dark jeans and a black, long-sleeved shirt, then exited through a side door that led directly to the parking structure.

The night air had cooled considerably, carrying the scent of salt from the nearby ocean. She moved purposefully through the parking levels until she reached the rental car—a dark Toyota with no distinguishing features. As she settled into the driver's seat and started the engine, she allowed herself a moment of doubt. What she was doing was potentially dangerous and definitely outside her job description.

"But not outside your experience," she reminded herself aloud, thinking of her years as a park ranger in Canyonlands National Park, where she'd dealt with everything from armed poachers to drug runners using remote trails. And the adventure races she competed in had taken her through some of the world's most challenging terrain, often requiring quick decisions under extreme pressure.

Still, this time was different. She was deliberately courting trouble in a foreign country; with powerful people who Luke had already warned her about.

She programmed the address of Bebe Green Street into her phone's navigation system and pulled out of the parking garage. The streets of Cape Town were still busy with evening traffic, providing welcome anonymity as she made her way toward the harbor district.

Luke lingered at the dinner table only long enough to avoid suspicion. He mumbled something about checking on tomorrow's arrangements before heading toward the hotel entrance. Once in the lobby, he scanned the room quickly but saw no sign of his target. Moving to the front windows, he caught a glimpse of a black sedan pulling onto the main road. Just before it disappeared out of sight, he saw Sheryl sitting in the driver's seat.

He swore under his breath. He'd recognized the look in her eyes at dinner—he'd seen it often enough in his conservation officer days when tracking poachers. It was the expression of someone on a mission.

Luke had a pretty good idea of where she was headed. After her questions about the warehouse district and her reaction to his warnings, her sudden "headache" seemed way too convenient.

He pulled out his phone, hesitated for a moment, then put it away without making a call. If she was just being paranoid, calling in concerns to his contacts in local law enforcement would be an overreaction. Better to follow her himself and pull her back if necessary.

Luke slipped out to the employee parking area where his personal vehicle was parked—a well-used Land Rover Defender that had seen him through years of conservation work before he'd switched to tourism. Within minutes, he was following the same route Sheryl had taken, staying far enough back to avoid detection but close enough not to lose her in the evening traffic.

"What are you playing at, Sheryl?" he muttered as he drove. If she was heading where he suspected, she had no idea what she was walking into.

Jack excused himself from the dinner table shortly after noticing both Sheryl and Luke's departures. His years in special operations had hard-wired him to notice patterns, and two key people leaving within minutes of each other—both with flimsy excuses—triggered his instincts.

He hadn't planned on following them. In fact, he'd told himself repeatedly that he was here for a different job. But old habits died hard, and curiosity—mixed with a genuine concern for their safety—propelled him to the lobby just in time to see Luke hurrying toward the staff parking area.

Jack considered his options. He could return to dinner and mind his own business, or he could satisfy his curiosity and make sure nothing was amiss. The decision took only seconds.

He moved quickly to the front desk. "Excuse me," he said to the concierge, "I need a ride immediately. It's rather urgent."

A minute later, Jack was in the back seat of a taxi, instructing the driver to follow the Land Rover that had just pulled out of the staff lot. The driver, a middle-aged man with a bored face, merely raised his eyebrows in the rearview mirror.

"I'm not getting involved in anything illegal, sir," he said calmly.

Jack smiled reassuringly. "Nothing illegal. Just making sure my friends don't get into trouble."

The driver seemed satisfied with this explanation and skillfully maneuvered into traffic, maintaining a discreet distance from Luke's vehicle.

Jack sat back, considering the situation. Sheryl had been asking pointed questions about the warehouse district during their hike. Luke had seemed unusually evasive. And now, both of them were heading somewhere in a hurry, separately, while the celebration dinner for the trip's first milestone was still in progress.

His instincts kept telling him that something was definitely off.

INTO THE SHADOWS

The warehouse district near the harbor was significantly quieter than Sheryl remembered it being from her gym visit yesterday. Most of the legitimate businesses had closed for the evening, leaving the area largely deserted, except for the occasional security guard or late-shift worker.

Sheryl drove slowly, the car's headlights illuminating the empty loading zones and chain-link fences. She recognized the uneven pavement where she'd nearly twisted her ankle when she'd walked this route. Just ahead was the nondescript building with the faded green door—the place where she'd glimpsed what looked like African buffalo horns in neat rows.

She parked the car a block away, positioning it for a quick exit if necessary. From her backpack, she retrieved a small flashlight and slipped it into her pocket.

As she approached the warehouse on foot, staying close to the shadows cast by adjacent buildings, she noted that, unlike her previous visit, there were no vehicles parked outside. The loading bay doors were firmly closed, and no lights were on.

Disappointed but not deterred when she tried to open the door and it didn't budge, she circled the building carefully. There had to be some evidence of what she'd seen—something to confirm that she wasn't imagining things. She found a narrow alley between the back of the warehouse and the neighboring building.

The back of the warehouse featured a rusty fire escape and a small door that appeared to be used as a service entrance. Unlike the loading bay area, this door showed signs of recent activity—the surrounding ground was marked with multiple footprints, and crumpled cigarette butts were scattered nearby.

Sheryl crouched behind a dumpster, weighing her options. Breaking and entering was definitely crossing a line she wasn't comfortable with. But perhaps there was another way to gather evidence.

Her deliberation was interrupted by the sound of an approaching vehicle. She pressed deeper into the shadows, her heart rate accelerating when the engine cut off and she heard car doors slam shut.

Footsteps crunched on gravel, and male voices became audible—two men approached. A moment later, light spilled into the alley as the service door opened. Sheryl carefully positioned herself to see what was happening without being seen herself.

Two men entered the warehouse—one she recognized immediately as the man she'd seen before. The other was younger, thin, and more nervous, and he was carrying what appeared to be takeout food containers. They left the door slightly ajar behind them, a wedge of yellow light cutting across the alleyway. Either they hadn't noticed that the door wasn't closed all the way, or they just didn't care.

Sheryl's mind raced. Now was her chance to confirm her suspicions, but it required getting closer—much closer than was safe. She hesitated, calculating the risks.

Ultimately, her need to know won out. Moving with the careful deliberation she'd learned in her ranger days—placing each foot silently in front of the other, testing her weight before committing to each step—she approached the partially open door.

Voices became clearer as she drew nearer, and the men had switched to English.

"Victor said midnight. Not before." The voice was gruff and impatient.

"I know, I know. But I'm telling you, someone's going to notice this place and what we have here."

Sheryl froze, her blood turning to ice water in her veins. Did that refer to her?

"Victor's handling it," Reggie said dismissively. "Now, shut up and eat. We've got a long night ahead of us."

Sheryl eased closer to the door, risking a quick glance inside. What she saw confirmed her worst suspicions. The warehouse interior was dimly lit, but she could clearly make out stacks of animal pelts and crates along one wall. One crate was open, revealing what were unmistakably rhinoceros horns packed in straw.

Her sharp intake of breath must have been audible, because both men suddenly went silent. Sheryl began backing away immediately, but her foot caught on an uneven section of pavement, causing her to stumble slightly. The sound, though slight, echoed in the quiet alley.

"What was that?" The younger man's voice was tense.

"Check it out," Reggie ordered.

Sheryl didn't wait to hear more. She turned and moved as quickly and quietly as possible back the way she'd come, her heart pounding in her ears. She'd seen enough—more than enough. Now, she needed to get back to her car and away from here before—

A figure stepped out of the shadows directly in her path, blocking her escape route.

She froze, adrenaline surging through her veins, and her body instinctively shifted into a defensive stance.

"It's me," Luke hissed, his voice barely audible. "Come on, we need to get out of here now."

Before she could respond, the service door behind them banged fully open, flooding the alley with light.

"Hey!" Reggie's voice echoed between the buildings. "Stop right there!"

Luke grabbed Sheryl's arm. "Run!"

They sprinted down the alley together, the sound of pursuing footsteps close behind them. As they reached the end of the narrow passage, Sheryl risked a glance back and saw Reggie, now joined by the younger man, both of them giving chase—and Reggie was pulling something from his waistband that looked like a gun.

"This way," Luke urged, pulling her to the right, away from where she'd parked her rental car. "My vehicle's closer."

They rounded the corner of the building, the footsteps behind them growing louder. Sheryl's ranger training kicked in—run, find cover, create distance. But the open area between warehouses offered little concealment.

A sharp crack split the air—the unmistakable sound of a gunshot. Luke cursed, pulling her harder. "Keep moving!"

They zigzagged between parked delivery trucks, using them as cover. Luke's Land Rover was visible now, maybe thirty yards ahead. Another shot rang out, this one pinging off metal somewhere to their left.

"These guys are serious," Luke panted as they ran. "What did you see in there?"

"Animal pelts, rhino horns. All crated for shipping," Sheryl managed between breaths. "They mentioned someone named Victor."

Luke's expression darkened. "Victor Malanga. If he's involved, this operation is big."

They were within ten yards of the Land Rover when another figure emerged from beside it—tall, imposing, moving with purpose.

"Get down!" the figure shouted.

Luke reacted instantly, pulling Sheryl behind a stack of pallets. A moment later, two more shots rang out in quick succession—but they weren't aimed at Sheryl and Luke. Instead, they were directed back toward their pursuers.

In the chaos, Sheryl recognized the shooter as Jack, his stance and handling of the weapon unmistakably military. Where he'd gotten the gun, she had no idea, but his presence was a relief.

Their pursuers scrambled for cover. Jack moved with precision, taking carefully aimed shots that didn't hit the men but kept them pinned down.

"To the car—now!" Jack called as Luke and Sheryl made a final dash to the Land Rover.

Luke fumbled with his keys, finally getting the door unlocked. "Get in!"

Sheryl climbed in, Luke behind the wheel, both of them ducking low as another shot whizzed past.

"What about Jack?" Sheryl asked, unwilling to leave him behind.

"Three, two, one—" Luke counted down, and on cue, Jack sprinted toward them, diving into the back seat as Luke gunned the engine.

The Land Rover roared to life, tires squealing as he executed a perfect J-turn and accelerated away from the warehouse.

"Everyone okay?" Jack asked from the back seat, calmly ejecting the magazine from his weapon and checking it.

"Where did you get a gun?" Sheryl demanded, her voice shaking slightly with residual adrenaline.

"My client provided it. Local source," Jack replied matter-of-factly. "Registered and legal, if you're worried."

"I'm more worried about the people shooting at us," Luke cut in, navigating the Land Rover through back streets, taking a circuitous route away from the harbor. "And the fact that we've just pissed off Victor Malanga's crew."

"You followed me," Sheryl said, the realization of what their presence meant just now dawning on her.

"You weren't exactly subtle," Luke replied. "Headache? Really?"

"And you followed both of us," she said to Jack.

He shrugged. "Professional habit. Good thing, too."

Sheryl leaned back against the seat, the full impact of what had just happened washing over her. She'd gone looking for evidence and found it—but also found herself in the crosshairs of what appeared to be a large poaching operation.

A small detail dawned on her. "How am I going to get my car back?"

Luke replied, "Really? That's your concern? I can send one of the staff to get it in the morning…when it's daylight out…not the middle of the night."

"Okay. And we need to contact the authorities," she said firmly.

Luke's laugh was bitter. "With what? What proof do we have?"

"I saw rhino horns in that warehouse."

"Your word against theirs. And now, they know we're onto them."

They rode in tense silence for several minutes, each processing the implications of the night's events.

"They mentioned midnight," Sheryl finally said. "Something's happening at midnight. A pickup, maybe?"

Sheryl looked between the two men—Luke, visibly tense and conflicted; Jack, calmly assessing the situation with professional detachment. She thought about the group of travelers back at the hotel, unaware of the danger that could now disrupt their vacation.

"We need to be smart about this," she said finally. "Just an anonymous tip to the local police or rangers or whoever. Let them do what they want about it."

Luke sighed in resignation. "Fine. Hopefully, those two didn't get a good look at our faces. Malanga isn't someone to be taken lightly. He's dangerous—and he has people everywhere."

"Does Cape Town still have pay phones?" Jack asked.

As if answering the question, Luke pulled to the curb next to the nearest building. "Courtesy of Africa Telkom." He waved at a phone booth mounted to the wall, looking exactly like the defunct devices in America.

Frowning at Sheryl as he slipped out of the car, Jack said, "Stay here."

In a moment, he was back. "There. Anonymous report of gunfire and suspicious activity at that address. It's in the police's hands now. Can we get back to our vacation?"

"Thanks," Sheryl said. Then, seeking to explain her behavior, she added, "You know, I used to be a park ranger in America. We dealt with poachers, drug runners, and all kinds of weirdos."

Neither of the men answered.

As they drove the short distance back to the Cape Red from the harbor, Sheryl found herself studying the lights of anchored boats creating tiny constellations on the water's surface. Just twenty-four hours ago, her biggest concern had been making sure everyone had the right hiking boots for Table Mountain.

"This wasn't in the brochure," she murmured.

Jack chuckled quietly from the back seat. "The best adventures never are."

So focused on their escape and conversation, all three failed to notice the vehicle that slid into a parking space across the street from the hotel. The two men inside watched as the trio's vehicle entered the parking garage.

"Who are they?" the driver asked.

"Americans. Maybe with that bus." The passenger pointed to the large tour bus parked prominently in the side lot. "It says 'Global Runners' on the front window."

"What do we do now?"

"We'll come back in the morning and see who boards that bus. Then we report back to the boss."

CHAPTER 9

UNWILLING ACCOMPLICE

The night pressed down on the valley bushveld like a heavy blanket. Thabiso sat rigid in the passenger seat of the battered pickup truck, his hands gripping the R5 rifle as if it were both a lifeline and a curse. The weapon felt wrong in his hands—heavier than it should be, the weight of compelled service rather than his choice.

The night vision scope attached to the rifle gave the landscape an eerie green glow, transforming the familiar African plains into something alien. Beside him, the driver—a hard-faced man who had introduced himself only as Duma—periodically adjusted the cheap night vision goggles strapped to his face, cursing softly when they slipped or failed to focus properly.

"See anything yet?" Duma asked, his voice grating in the stillness of the night.

Thabiso swallowed hard. Twenty minutes ago, he'd watched a pair of white rhinos through his scope — a mother and calf moving slowly through the brush, unaware of the human predators nearby. His finger had trembled against the trigger guard, but he'd lowered the rifle and shaken his head.

"Nothing," he'd lied, feeling a small victory in the deception.

Now, the truck jolted over the uneven terrain, its headlights off to avoid detection by anti-poaching patrols. They were somewhere on a private reserve in the Eastern Cape — Thabiso wasn't sure exactly where. They'd driven for hours until they reached this remote location.

Through his scope, Thabiso now spotted a small herd of kudus, their distinctive spiral horns visible even in the green wash of night vision. The antelopes moved with grace, unaware of how valuable those horns were to certain collectors. Again, he lowered the rifle.

"Just some birds," he muttered. "Nothing worth shooting."

Duma grunted skeptically but kept driving, following some mental map of likely animal pathways that Thabiso couldn't discern.

How did it come to this? Thabiso thought, his mind circling back to the same questions that had haunted him since being forced into the truck outside his motorcycle shop. His life had been simple — fixing bikes, raising his daughters with his wife in their small apartment, saving for a better future. Now, he was here, hunting endangered animals for a criminal he'd never even met face-to-face.

A family of warthogs scurried across the path ahead, and Thabiso deliberately shifted his aim away from them. Their tusks would fetch a good price, but he couldn't bring himself to fire.

"I need to get home," he said aloud, not really expecting a response. "My daughters. They won't understand why I'm gone."

Duma kept his eyes on the terrain ahead. "Everyone's got family. Malanga pays well. Do the job, you go home with money. Simple."

But Thabiso knew it wasn't so simple. The man named Botha had made that clear when he'd towered over Thabiso in his shop. One job would become many. One night would become a lifetime. Once Malanga had you, he owned you. The former soldiers Thabiso had met during his own military service—the ones who'd turned to poaching for quick money—none of them had ever managed to walk away.

The truck crested a small rise, giving them a better view of the sprawling plains below. In the distance, Thabiso could make out a small herd of impalas, their distinctive profiles clear through his scope. He watched them for a moment, admiring their alertness, the way the dominant male stood guard while the others grazed.

"Nothing there," he said, lowering the rifle again.

Duma slowed the truck, suspicion evident in the set of his shoulders. "You were good in the army. Best shot in your unit, they said. How is it you see nothing when I can see shapes moving even with these crappy goggles?"

Thabiso's heart rate increased. "Bad luck. Wrong place."

"Or maybe you don't want to see," Duma said, his voice taking on a dangerous edge. "Maybe you think if you don't shoot, we go home empty-handed, and Malanga blames me instead of you."

"No, I—"

"Shut up, and look again," Duma hissed, cutting the engine and pointing toward a stand of acacia trees about three hundred meters away. "There. Tell me what you see."

Thabiso raised the rifle again, adjusting the scope slightly. His breath caught in his throat. A magnificent sable antelope stood in the shadow of the trees, its curved horns sweeping back almost a meter in length. The animal was beautiful, majestic—and worth a fortune in certain markets.

He lowered the rifle slowly. "Just some bushes moving in the wind."

Duma stared at him for a long moment, then reached into his jacket and pulled out a phone. "Maybe I should call Botha now. Tell him that his new shooter is blind. I wonder what he'd do to your family while they're waiting for you to return."

The threat hung in the air between them, as tangible as the rifle in Thabiso's hands. He thought of his wife, Maria, and their daughters. The image of Botha standing in their small apartment made his blood run cold.

"I'll do better," Thabiso said, his voice hollow. "Just…give me time. The animals are hiding tonight."

Duma put the phone away with deliberate slowness. "One hour. Then, we will either have results, or I will make the call."

The truck moved forward again, traversing the savanna in irregular patterns, following game trails and water sources where animals might gather. With each passing minute, desperation grew in Thabiso's chest. He needed to find some way out of this situation, some path that didn't end with either dead endangered animals or threats to his family.

Through his scope, he spotted a leopard drinking at a small watering hole, its spotted coat distinctive even in the green haze of night vision. The big cat would bring a substantial payment—its skin, teeth, and claws all valuable. Thabiso found himself raising the rifle, then deliberately shifting his aim to the right, where nothing stood.

"Water, but no animals," he reported, lowering the rifle again.

Duma's patience was visibly wearing thin. His knuckles whitened on the steering wheel as he guided the truck around a stand of thorny bushes. Then, suddenly, he stiffened.

"There," he said, pointing ahead and slightly to the left. "Big one."

Thabiso raised his rifle, already preparing another excuse, when he saw what Duma was pointing at. An African buffalo—a massive bull with a formidable set of horns—stood grazing in a small clearing approximately one hundred meters away. Even through Duma's inferior night vision equipment, an animal that size would be unmistakable.

"I see it," Thabiso admitted, unable to deny the obvious.

"Then, shoot," Duma said flatly, cutting the engine. "Or I make the call."

Thabiso positioned the rifle, settling the stock against his shoulder, feeling the familiar posture his body remembered from his military days. The buffalo was in perfect range, unaware of their presence, the night vision scope giving Thabiso a clear shot, despite the darkness.

His finger hovered over the trigger. He thought about missing deliberately, but he knew Duma would recognize an intentional miss from this range. The man might not be a marksman, but he'd been poaching long enough to know the difference.

I'm sorry, Thabiso thought, addressing the animal, his family, himself—he wasn't sure which.

The rifle cracked, the sound shockingly loud in the night's stillness. Through the scope, Thabiso watched the buffalo stagger, then collapse. A clean kill, at least—a small consolation for what he'd just been forced to do.

"Good," Duma said, already reaching for the machete and saw stowed behind the seats. "Now, we'd better work fast."

They approached the fallen buffalo on foot, the massive animal's bulk impressive even in death. Thabiso felt hollow as he watched Duma begin the grim work of removing the horns, the poacher's movements efficient from practice.

"Hold this," Duma ordered, handing Thabiso the flashlight.

Blood glistened black in the artificial light. Duma slit the animal's abdomen open to make it easier for the predators that would clean up after them. Then, he set to work on the horns, sawing through bone and tissue. The buffalo's eyes, still open, seemed to stare accusingly at Thabiso. Once, he had protected animals like this when he worked with an anti-poaching unit after leaving the military. Now, he was on the wrong side of that equation.

"Faster," Thabiso urged, scanning the horizon. "The sun will come up soon."

"Almost done," Duma grunted, working the saw vigorously. "These big ones, the horn base is thick. Good money, though."

With a final effort, Duma separated the horns from the buffalo's skull, wrapping them quickly in a tarp before carrying them back to the truck. Thabiso followed, the rifle slung over his shoulder, feeling as if he were walking through a nightmare.

They tossed the bloody package into the truck bed, where it landed with a dull thud. Duma seemed pleased, checking his watch as he climbed back into the driver's seat.

"Good timing. We'll be out of the preserve before dawn." He started the engine, executing a tight turn to head back the way they'd come. "You did well. Maybe next time you won't wait so long to find a target."

Thabiso said nothing, staring straight ahead as the truck bounced over the uneven ground. The eastern horizon showed the first faint lightening of pre-dawn, stars beginning to fade against the gradually brightening sky.

"Your family—they live in Cape Town, yeah?" Duma asked conversationally as he drove.

The question sent ice through Thabiso's veins. "Why?"

Duma shrugged. "Just making conversation. Botha likes to know these things about his people. Where they live, who they care about. Makes for more…loyal employees."

The message couldn't have been clearer if Duma had spelled it out. Thabiso's family was known to them, their safety contingent on his cooperation. Whatever faint hope he'd harbored of refusing future "jobs" withered at the implied threat.

As the truck sped back toward civilization, carrying its bloody cargo, Thabiso stared at the horizon. He had become the very thing he once fought against. And for what? To protect his family from men who would go to any lengths to ensure that he cooperated.

The irony wasn't lost on him. He'd shot the buffalo to save his family, just as he would likely kill again for the same reason. The circle of coercion was complete, and he saw no way to break it.

But as the first genuine rays of sunlight broke the horizon, Thabiso caught a last glimpse of the fallen buffalo, now just a dark shape in the growing light. Birds were already gathering around the carcass, nature's cleanup crew beginning their work.

"Next time will be easier," Duma said, misinterpreting Thabiso's silence as remorse.

Thabiso nodded slightly, not trusting himself to speak.

CHAPTER 10

SHADOWS AT CAPE POINT

Morning sunlight glinted off the Atlantic as the Global Runners tour bus wound its way along the coastal road. Through the large panoramic windows, passengers oohed and aahed at the Twelve Apostles—massive buttresses of sandstone and granite that towered over the coastline, standing sentinel between mountain and sea. The bus climbed steadily toward Chapman's Peak Drive, arguably one of the most spectacular marine routes in the world.

Sheryl stood at the front of the bus, microphone in hand, her professional demeanor giving no hint of the previous night's confrontation at the harbor.

"We're approaching one of the greatest engineering marvels of South Africa," she announced, gesturing toward the winding road ahead. "Chapman's Peak Drive hugs the near-vertical face of the mountain for about nine kilometers, with 114 curves carved into the rockface. It's known locally as 'Chappies,' and you'll soon see why it's considered one of the most beautiful drives in the world."

The bus rounded a particularly dramatic curve, revealing a sweeping vista of Hout Bay and the cobalt blue Atlantic stretching to the horizon. A collective gasp rose from the group, followed by the clicking of cameras.

Momentarily losing herself in the awe she saw on her clients' faces, Sheryl smiled at their reactions. But beneath her tour guide persona, her mind kept replaying fragments from the previous night—the warehouse, the rhino horns, the gunshots. She'd barely slept, awakening every hour to check that her room's door was securely locked.

The tour group had accepted her explanation that she'd gone for an evening walk to clear her head after dinner, hoping that the fresh air would help her headache. Luke had backed her story, claiming he'd spotted her and joined her for a stroll along the waterfront. Jack had said nothing, but his knowing eyes had followed her throughout breakfast.

Zuri approached from the back of the bus, handing Sheryl a bottle of water. "You look like you could use this," she said quietly. "Everything okay?"

"Just a bit tired," Sheryl replied as she accepted the water gratefully. "Didn't sleep well."

Zuri nodded sympathetically. "Yeah, headaches are the worst. But this drive always wakes people up."

As if on cue, the bus navigated another hairpin turn, the road seemingly suspended between mountain and sea with nothing but air below. The view was heart-stopping—sheer cliffs plunging hundreds of meters into crystalline waters.

"Perfect timing to hand off tour guide duties," Sheryl said, returning the microphone to its holder. "I need to double-check our permits for the nature reserve."

Zuri took over seamlessly, pointing out a pod of dolphins visible in the waters far below. As the group's attention turned seaward, Sheryl moved to a vacant seat near the middle of the bus, pulling out her tablet to review the day's logistics.

"Impressive country," came a softly accented voice from across the aisle.

Sheryl looked up to find a woman with short blonde hair and striking green eyes watching her. Anika Elsen— the Belgian woman who'd been noticeably quiet during the group introductions and subsequent activities. She wore hiking clothes that looked both expensive and well-used, suggesting an experienced traveler rather than a tourist with new gear.

"It certainly is," Sheryl agreed. "Have you visited South Africa before, Anika?"

"Twice for work, but never for pleasure," Anika replied, her accent melodic but hard to place precisely—it didn't sound like any other Belgian accent Sheryl had heard before. "And never with time to see places like this."

"What kind of work brings you to South Africa?" Sheryl asked, taking the opportunity to learn more about one of her more reserved clients.

Anika's expression remained pleasant but became slightly more guarded. "I'm a procurement manager for a multinational corporation. Very boring compared to what you do."

"Which corporation?" Sheryl asked casually.

"One that generates many spreadsheets," Anika replied with a small smile. "And requires confidentiality agreements. Truly not worth discussing when there's all this to see." She gestured toward the window, where the landscape was transitioning from coastal cliffs to the more rugged terrain of the Cape Peninsula.

Sheryl recognized the deflection but didn't press for more information. In her experience, clients either opened up over the course of a trip or maintained their privacy—forcing conversation rarely helped either way.

"Are you an intense runner?" Sheryl asked instead, noting Anika's athletic build.

"Not competitively," Anika replied, and she relaxed slightly at the change of subject. "But I enjoy trail running when I can. It clears the mind."

"It does," Sheryl agreed. "Today's route in the Cape Point Nature Reserve is spectacular—challenging in spots, but with views that make every step worthwhile."

"I'm looking forward to it." Anika studied Sheryl for a moment. "You seem…preoccupied today. Not sleeping well in a new place?"

The question caught Sheryl off-guard. *Is my unease that obvious?* "Just juggling logistics," she said lightly. "Making sure everything runs smoothly. Lots of spreadsheets in my business, too."

Anika nodded but looked unconvinced. "In my experience, people who are good at their jobs make them look effortless. You strike me as someone very good at your job, Ms. Diego."

There was something in Anika's tone—an undertone of assessment, almost—that made Sheryl wonder if the woman was more observant than she'd initially given her credit for.

Sheryl excused herself and moved back to the front of the bus as they approached the entrance gates to the reserve. The bus slowed, then pulled into the visitor parking area. Clusters of tourists were already gathered around, some boarding the funicular that carried less adventurous visitors up to the lighthouse.

As their vehicle crested the last hill overlooking the Cape of Good Hope, Luke gestured toward the dramatic view where two oceans appeared to meet at Africa's southwestern edge. "What you're seeing is one of maritime history's most significant landmarks," he explained. "Portuguese explorer Bartolomeu Dias first rounded this cape in 1488, opening the vital sea route between Europe and Asia that would transform global trade and exploration. Though it's a common misconception that this is where the Atlantic and Indian Oceans meet—that actually occurs at Cape Agulhas about 150 kilometers east—the Cape of Good Hope earned its name from the relief that sailors felt upon reaching it after surviving the treacherous waters that had already claimed countless ships. Originally named 'Cape of Storms' by Dias, it was later renamed by King John II of Portugal to encourage maritime traffic, though its reputation for dangerous conditions persisted well into the modern era. Today, beyond its historical significance, this reserve protects a remarkable ecosystem containing over a thousand native plant species found nowhere else on Earth."

"We'll do this the proper way," Sheryl said with a smile once Luke was finished introducing the area they would be exploring today. "First, we'll hike up to the lighthouse for some group pictures. Then, it's down to the Cape of Good Hope. Altogether, there are about two hours of spectacular views ahead of us. The bus will meet everyone at the parking area at the bottom when we're done."

As the bus came to a stop, Sheryl gathered her permits and stepped out into the bright morning sun. She made her way to the ranger station, breathing deeply, trying to clear her mind of everything but the day ahead.

The ranger on duty—a tall woman with close-cropped hair and a friendly face—checked Sheryl's permits efficiently while asking a few routine questions about the size of the group and their planned route.

"Everything's in order," the ranger said and stamped the permits once she was satisfied that there was nothing out of place. "Just remind your group to watch out for baboons. They can be aggressive if they think you have food."

"Will do," Sheryl promised, tucking the approved permits into her backpack.

As she turned to head back to the bus, movement near a park vehicle caught her eye. Two men stood talking beside a Land Rover with the Cape Point logo on its door. One was a ranger. The other, his back to Sheryl, seemed out of place for a tourist spot. Something about the set of his shoulders, the stance, it felt familiar, like she'd seen him before. As if sensing her gaze, the man turned slightly, revealing his profile.

Sheryl's heart stuttered. It was the man from the warehouse, the one who was shooting at her.

She quickened her pace, keeping her head down, willing him not to look in her direction. *What is a wildlife trafficker doing chatting with a ranger at Cape Point?* The implications weren't good. *If they have connections within the park system…*

Sheryl climbed back onto the bus, forcing a smile for her waiting group.

"All set!" she announced with false brightness. "We're cleared for the coastal trail. Please, before leaving the bus, make sure you have water, sunscreen, and appropriate footwear. And remember—no food in your outer pockets. The baboons here could teach New York pickpockets a thing or two."

The group laughed, then gathered their daypacks and water bottles. Sheryl moved to where Luke was organizing trail maps.

"Problem?" he asked quietly, noticing her tense expression.

"The guy from the warehouse is here," she murmured while pretending to check a map. "Talking to a ranger by the administration building."

Luke's fingers stilled momentarily on the maps. "You sure?"

"Positive."

Luke nodded almost imperceptibly. "I'll tell Jack. Act normal, get the group moving. Maybe it's a coincidence."

"You believe that?" Sheryl asked.

"No," Luke admitted. "But panicking won't help. Let's just focus on getting through today."

Sheryl nodded and turned back to the group with forced enthusiasm. "All right, runners! Grab your gear, and let's hit the trail."

Chattering excitedly about what kinds of animals and plants they'd see, the group filed off the bus. Jack was among the last to exit. His movements were unhurried, but his eyes scanned the surroundings with professional skill.

Luke intercepted him at the door, speaking in a low voice that Sheryl couldn't hear. Jack's expression didn't change, but he adjusted the position of his daypack, making Sheryl wonder if he was carrying his weapon.

The group reassembled as Sheryl led them toward their starting point for the lighthouse climb. As they crossed the parking lot, Sheryl noticed a silver sedan with tinted windows parked near the exit. A man sat in the driver's seat, his features obscured, but from what she could tell, his posture was alert, scanning the crowd.

Sheryl felt a chill run along her body, despite the warm morning sun. *Not a coincidence, then. We're being followed.*

"You saw them, too?" Jack asked quietly, materializing beside her as the shuttle navigated a particularly scenic stretch of road.

Sheryl nodded. "He was talking to a ranger. And there's another guy in the car."

"I know." Jack's voice was calm, but his eyes were hard. "The sedan pulled in right after our bus. They're not trying to be subtle."

"What do they want?" Sheryl whispered. "We didn't take anything, didn't get evidence—"

"We saw them," Jack interrupted. "We can identify them. And they don't know what else we might've seen or heard at the warehouse."

Luke joined them, positioning himself so that their conversation wouldn't be overheard by the rest of the group. "The guys in the sedan are definitely watching us."

"So, what do we do?" Jack asked.

"Not much we can do," Luke admitted. "We're in a national park with more than two dozen tourists counting on us. Can't exactly bail on them."

"We stick to public areas," Sheryl decided. "Stay with the group. There's safety in numbers."

CHAPTER 11

THE QUIET ONE

After several group photos, the group turned their attention toward the primary destination for the day.

Forcing enthusiasm into her voice, Sheryl called, "Everyone ready? The trail follows the coastline all the way to Cape Point. We'll take it easy, with plenty of stops for photos."

The group set off along the coastal path, the terrain immediately demanding their attention with its uneven surfaces and dramatic drop-offs. The trail hugged the cliff-side, which offered them breathtaking views of what people commonly thought of as the meeting point between the Atlantic and Indian Oceans.

Jack positioned himself at the back of the group, while Luke stayed near the front with Sheryl. Between them, the tourists spread out according to their comfort levels, most stopping frequently to photograph the spectacular scenery.

Anika kept pace just behind Sheryl, and she moved with the efficient stride of someone accustomed to challenging terrain. When they paused at a particularly scenic overlook, she moved alongside Sheryl.

"We're being followed," she said quietly, not looking at Sheryl but out toward the horizon.

Sheryl tensed. "What?"

"The silver sedan. Two men. They're not tourists or rangers." Anika's voice remained conversational, as if discussing the weather. "They've been following us since Cape Town."

"I don't know what you're talking about," Sheryl replied carefully.

Anika's green eyes flickered toward her briefly. "You don't need to explain. But heads up—they're not just following the bus. One of them has broken off on foot. He's paralleling our route along the service track."

Sheryl resisted the urge to look up toward the maintenance path that park employees used. "How do you know that?"

A slight smile touched Anika's lips. "Analysts notice details. Numbers, patterns. Things that don't add up." She adjusted her backpack. "Just thought you should know."

Before Sheryl could respond, Anika moved away, stopping to photograph the ocean that spread before them.

Luke appeared at Sheryl's elbow. "Everything okay?"

"I'm not sure," Sheryl replied, briefly relaying what Anika had told her.

Luke frowned as he scanned the side path without being obvious about it. "She's right. There's a guy up there, keeping pace with us."

"How does she know they've been following since Cape Town?" Sheryl wondered.

"Good question." Luke's expression was thoughtful. "She might be more than she seems."

The group continued along the trail, the path growing steeper as they approached the lighthouse perched atop the point. The day had warmed considerably, the sun beating down on the exposed coastal route. Several of the less fit group members were struggling with the climb, requiring frequent rest stops.

Joan seemed particularly affected by the heat and exertion. During one rest break, she sat heavily on a boulder, dabbing her forehead with a towel while checking her phone again.

"You okay?" Wanda asked, offering her an extra water bottle.

"Just tired," Joan said, forcing a smile. "And worried about…" She gestured vaguely at her phone. "Financial stuff. Bad timing for a vacation, really."

"Hey, that's exactly when you need a vacation most," Wanda said. "Whatever's waiting back home will still be there next week. Right now, just try to focus on having fun and taking in all the beauty around us." She gestured at the sweeping ocean vista to emphasize her point.

Joan nodded, but her trembling hands betrayed her continued anxiety as she tucked her phone away into her pocket.

During one such pause, Jack made his way to where Sheryl and Luke stood conferring over the map.

"We've got company on both sides now," he reported quietly. "One on the service path, and another guy I don't recognize has joined the trail behind us."

"So, what do we do?" Luke asked.

"Not much we can do," Jack admitted. "We're pretty exposed here. Best bet is to reach the point where there's more people around."

Sheryl nodded. "We're about forty minutes from the end. I'll pick up the pace for anyone who can handle it."

She addressed the group, encouraging those who felt strong enough to continue at a brisker pace, while Luke would stay with those needing more time. The group naturally divided, with about half choosing to push ahead with Sheryl.

Jack and Anika were among those who stayed with Sheryl, and they made good time up the increasingly rough path. Joan, despite her obvious fatigue, chose to stay with the faster group—whether from stubborn determination or a sense that something was wrong.

Jack maintained a position at the rear, occasionally glancing back down the trail, while Anika kept pace just behind Sheryl. Joan walked between them, but she didn't talk. Instead, she seemed focused on the demanding trail and barely looked away from her feet.

They reached the official Cape of Good Hope Point without incident, where everyone took pictures of the ocean, the cliffs, and each other.

"Everyone has thirty minutes to explore," Sheryl told her group. "Then, we'll regroup at the bus."

Joan found a bench and sat down heavily, finally allowing herself to rest while the others scattered to various viewpoints.

Her phone came out again, and she stared at the screen with growing distress.

Sheryl moved to a less crowded viewing area. Jack joined her a moment later.

"Our shadow stayed on the service path," he reported. "He's watching from the ridge to the east. The other one's still with Luke's group on the trail."

"What do they want?" Sheryl asked. Her frustration was evident, despite her attempt to appear casual.

"Information, most likely. They want to know if we've contacted anyone, if we're working with someone. Or they're waiting for an opportunity."

"For what?"

Jack's expression was grim. "To eliminate a problem."

The reality of their situation hit Sheryl with renewed force. These weren't just opportunistic criminals they'd encountered—they were an organized operation with resources and reach. And Sheryl and her group had walked right into the middle of it.

"What about the rest of the day?" she asked, focusing on the most immediate concerns.

"We stay in public, stick to the schedule. Boulders Beach will be crowded with tourists—good for us. After that, we need a better plan than just hoping they'll lose interest."

The second half of the group arrived, Luke looking relaxed but with his eyes constantly scanning their surroundings. He gave Sheryl and Jack a subtle nod, indicating nothing had happened on the trail.

After the photos, they boarded their bus for the short drive to Boulders Beach, home to a famous colony of African penguins.

The mood had lightened, the group chattering excitedly about their hike and the spectacular views they had seen.

Through the bus windows, Sheryl spotted the silver sedan pulling onto the road behind them. Still following. Still watching.

At Boulders Beach, the group dispersed along the wooden boardwalks that protected both visitors and the penguin colony. The small black and white birds waddled comically across the sand and rocks, occasionally diving into the turquoise waters to feed.

Under different circumstances, Sheryl would have delighted in the scene. Today, she found herself constantly looking over her shoulder, searching for shadows among the crowds of tourists.

Joan seemed to find some peace watching the penguins, her phone nowhere to be seen as she leaned against the boardwalk railing. For the first time all day, her face showed genuine relaxation instead of worry lines.

"They're pretty amazing," she said to no one in particular, watching a penguin awkwardly navigate the rocks. "Makes you realize that there are more important things than quarterly reports and retirement projections."

Wanda joined her at the railing. "See? I told you that this trip was a good idea."

Joan smiled—the first real smile Sheryl had seen from her all day. "Maybe you're right. At least penguins don't send nasty emails about overdue payments."

Sheryl found Jack standing at the far end of one boardwalk, ostensibly photographing the penguins but positioned with a clear view of the parking area.

"Still there?" she asked, pretending to point out a particularly photogenic penguin.

"Parked by the exit. They don't even seem to care if we know they're there anymore." Jack lowered his camera. "They want us to know we're being watched."

"Intimidation?"

"Partly. Also, reconnaissance. Seeing if we meet with anyone interesting."

The realization made Sheryl feel exposed, vulnerable. Not just for herself, but for the entire tour group, who had no idea of the danger potentially surrounding them.

Luke approached, leading a small cluster of tourists excited about a penguin that had wandered particularly close to the boardwalk.

"Our Belgian friend's been watching the watchers," he murmured to Sheryl as the tourists photographed the penguin. "Very systematic about it. Almost professional."

"What do you think her story is?" Sheryl asked.

"Not sure," Luke replied. "But I don't think she's just a procurement manager."

As the afternoon waned and the group reassembled for the return journey to Cape Town, Sheryl felt the weight of uncertainty pressing down on her. The bus wound its way back along the peninsula, retracing the spectacular coastal route now bathed in the golden light of late afternoon.

In the gathering dusk, the Twelve Apostles cast long shadows across the road as the bus approached Cape Town. The city lights twinkled in the distance, Table Mountain a dark silhouette against the deepening blue sky.

Sheryl moved through the bus, checking on her clients, answering questions about the evening's dinner arrangements. Everyone seemed content, tired in that satisfying way that came from a day spent outdoors in beautiful surroundings.

Besides the four of them, no one else knew about the sedan following them. None of the others had noticed their shadows on the trail. None of them realized that their tour leader was now caught in a dangerous game with people who wouldn't hesitate to eliminate problems.

As the bus pulled into the Cape Red Hotel driveway, Sheryl caught sight of Anika watching her with those observant green eyes. The Belgian woman gave her a small nod—not friendly exactly, but somehow acknowledging a shared awareness.

Joan stirred awake as they stopped, looking around with momentary confusion before remembering where she was. Her hand went automatically to her phone, checking for messages, and Sheryl saw her face fall slightly at whatever she found there.

The sedan drove past the hotel entrance without stopping, but Sheryl had no doubt they would be back. This problem wasn't over. It was, she feared, only beginning.

The shadows were lengthening, not just across the landscape but across their future. And somewhere in those shadows, Victor Malanga was watching, waiting, planning his next move.

CHAPTER 12

WAVES AND WHISPERS

The afternoon sun glinted off the turquoise waters of Muizenberg Beach, its famous colorful beach huts creating a cheerful backdrop against the sweeping shoreline. Known for its gentle, rolling waves, the beach provided ideal conditions for first-time surfers—which most of the Global Runners group certainly were.

"Remember what Josie taught us," Sheryl called out while gesturing to their surf instructor, who stood nearby. "Pop up quickly, bend your knees, and keep your eyes on the horizon—not your feet!"

The group was divided into smaller clusters along the beach, each practicing the awkward motion of transitioning from lying on their boards to standing in one fluid movement. Results varied dramatically.

"I think I've got it!" called Margaret, the retired surgeon from Toronto, who had surprised everyone with her natural balance. She demonstrated a perfect pop-up on the sand, looking decidedly more graceful than most of her younger companions.

Beside her, the Alvarez brothers from Austin were having considerably less success. Derek had managed to tangle himself in the ankle leash three times already, while Sean kept overbalancing and tumbling sideways into the sand, sending both brothers into fits of laughter.

"If my clients could see me now," Anika joked as she wobbled dramatically on her board before intentionally flopping onto the sand. The group chuckled, and the tension from the previous day's events was momentarily forgotten in the sunny, light-hearted atmosphere.

Jack moved with unexpected grace for such a solidly built man, his military training evident in the control he had over his body. He executed the pop-up flawlessly, drawing appreciative nods from the instructors.

"Done this before?" Sheryl asked as they prepared to enter the water.

Jack shrugged. "Had to learn some water stuff during training back in the day. Different waves, but yeah, same basic idea."

Joan stood at the water's edge, looking uncertain with her rental board under one arm. The forensic accountant had been quietly observing the others, and the relaxation she had allowed herself to feel at the beach yesterday was nowhere to be found today.

"You sure about this?" she called to Wanda, who was already waist-deep in the water. "I mean, what if I can't get back up? I'm not exactly built for athletic stuff."

"That's the whole point!" Wanda laughed. "Besides, the worst thing that happens is you get wet. Pretty sure that's unavoidable, anyway."

Joan managed a nervous smile but waded in slowly.

With boards under their arms, they joined the colorful array of surfboards dotting the sea. Several other tourist groups were also taking lessons, creating a festive, international atmosphere.

"All right, Global Runners!" Josie called out, her South African accent thickened with enthusiasm. "Remember, start by catching the wave on your belly. Only try standing once you feel the board being pushed forward. And if you fall—which you will—fall sideways, never forward or back!"

What followed was an hour of spectacular wipeouts, unexpected successes, and more laughter than Sheryl had heard from the group since their arrival. Joan, despite her initial reluctance, caught a small wave and stood for nearly five seconds before tumbling into the water with a triumphant whoop.

"Did you see that?" she called to Wanda, spitting out seawater but grinning widely. "I actually did it! I rode the wave!"

"That was awesome!" Wanda cheered while paddling over. "You looked like a natural out there!"

The ultra-marathoners from Colorado, Tyler and Emma, turned the activity into a friendly competition, counting each other's successful rides with good-natured trash talk.

Even Professor Nkosi, who had initially declined to participate, eventually allowed himself to be coaxed into the water by Luke, riding a small wave all the way to the shallows on his first attempt.

"It's just physics and balance," he explained with a modest smile as the others applauded.

Sheryl caught a perfect beginner's wave, the sensation of gliding across the water's surface bringing a genuine smile to her face. For a few precious moments, the threats and dangers faded, replaced by the simple joy of trying something new.

As the afternoon progressed, even the most uncoordinated participants managed at least one successful ride. The instructors organized a final challenge—attempting to get as many of the group as possible riding the same wave.

"On my signal!" Josie called as a promising swell approached. "Paddle, paddle, paddle… now!"

Nearly twenty members of the group caught the wave, a chaotic, joyful mess of wobbling riders. Some fell immediately, others managed a few seconds of standing upright, and a lucky few—including Jack, Margaret, and surprisingly, Sean Alvarez—rode all the way to the shallows.

Joan caught the wave on her belly and ride it nearly to shore, laughing so hard that she could barely breathe. When she finally stood up in the shallows, her usually anxious expression had been replaced by something resembling wonder.

"I can't believe I just did that," she said to no one in particular. "Wait till I tell my sister. She always said I was too nervous for my own good."

"That's enough to join our wall of fame!" Josie declared, pointing to a board near the surf shop covered with photos of group rides. "Not a record-breaker, but definitely impressive for beginners!"

The group made their way back to shore, exhausted but exhilarated, wetsuits and rash guards dripping as they trudged up the sand toward the surf shop to change and shower.

"Free time until five o'clock," Sheryl announced. "Explore the beach, or take a walk along the boardwalk to the St. James tidal pools. Just remember sunscreen!"

As the group dispersed, Sheryl found herself standing next to Anika, who had participated in the surfing with quiet competence, never drawing attention to herself but successfully riding several waves.

"Good lesson?" Sheryl asked while wringing water from her hair.

"Very much," Anika replied with a small smile. "Though, I suspect it's as much about building group camaraderie as actual surfing skills."

"That's the idea," Sheryl admitted. "Shared new experiences create bonds. Makes the whole tour memorable for everyone."

Anika nodded thoughtfully. "Smart approach. And useful to have everyone focused on learning something new rather than…other distractions."

Before Sheryl could respond to the subtle reference to their followers, Anika had moved away, heading toward the changing rooms with her towel slung over her shoulder.

Joan lingered near the water's edge, still glowing from her surfing success but gradually returning to her usual worried state.

"Everything okay?" Sheryl asked, approaching her when the woman showed no signs of moving away from the water.

Joan quickly turned toward Sheryl, showing that she had been on her phone once again. "Oh, just…work stuff." She forced a smile. "Nothing that can't wait till I get back, right? I mean, what's the worst that could happen in two weeks?"

The forced cheerfulness in her voice didn't hide the genuine anxiety underneath, but Sheryl decided not to push. Everyone deserved their small escapes from reality.

While laughter and conversation drifted up from the beach, a figure in a maintenance uniform made his way toward the row of parked tour buses. Reggie pulled a set of slender tools from his pocket as he approached the Global Runners bus, glancing around to ensure no one was watching before tripping the door latch.

Seconds later, he slipped inside, closing the door behind him. The bus was empty; everyone having joined the group on the beach for their surfing lesson. Perfect timing.

Moving efficiently through the vehicle, Reggie headed first for the small glovebox where he knew guides typically kept important documents. The simple lock yielded easily to his tools.

Inside, he found exactly what he was looking for—a folder containing copies of passenger information. He quickly photographed Sheryl Diego's details with his phone—Utah driver's license, passport, emergency contact information. Standard tourist documentation, nothing suspicious.

He continued his search, methodically checking the storage compartments where passengers had left their daypacks while surfing. Most contained predictable items: sunscreen, water bottles, cameras, changes of clothing.

When he reached Jack's bag, however, Reggie paused. The reinforced fabric and multiple secure compartments spoke of something beyond the average tourist's needs. He unzipped the main pocket carefully.

Inside, he found a second bag, this one secured with a small lock. Reggie smiled slightly, removing another set of tools from his pocket. Thirty seconds later, the lock clicked open.

Two passports lay inside—one bearing the name Jack Hunter with unusual stamps from over a dozen countries, the other for Jarrod Turner with fewer stamps but similar photos. Beneath them, a leather card case contained business cards: "Hunter Security International—Specialty Missions Worldwide."

Reggie photographed everything, his expression hardening. Not an ordinary tourist, then. Potentially private security, maybe even competition from another smuggling operation. Malanga would want to know immediately.

As he continued his search, his hand encountered something heavy and metallic. He carefully withdrew a compact pistol, well maintained and loaded. Definitely not standard tourist equipment. After photographing it, he returned it exactly as he had found it—no sense alerting Jack that his belongings had been searched.

The last item of interest came from the front compartment where the tour leaders kept their planning materials—a complete printed itinerary for the fourteen-day tour. Reggie carefully removed one copy, noting the detailed schedule of locations, accommodations, and activities.

Kranshoek Forest on day six, Knysna Heads on day eight, Kariega Game Reserve for the final four days—all locations where Malanga had operations or connections. All places where the group would be increasingly isolated from authorities and assistance.

Reggie slipped the itinerary into his pocket and exited the bus as casually as he had entered, making his way to a service vehicle parked at the far end of the lot. Once he got inside, he sent the photographs and a brief message to Malanga, then started the engine.

There was no need to follow the tour bus anymore. Now, they knew exactly where the group would be and when. They could prepare accordingly, choosing the perfect moment to address the problem these nosy tourists presented.

As Reggie drove away from Muizenberg Beach, the sounds of laughter and splashing continued below. The Global Runners group enjoyed their day in the sun, blissfully unaware that their entire journey had just been mapped out by a predator.

CHAPTER 13

VINEYARD SHADOWS

The sleek BMW X7 cut through the morning mist as it sped along the N2 highway toward the Langeberg Mountains. Reggie adjusted the climate control, enjoying the luxury of the vehicle—a stark contrast to the utilitarian truck he usually drove for operations. Beside him, Botha's massive frame filled the passenger seat, his expression impassive as he stared through the windshield.

"We'll beat them there by at least two hours," Reggie said after glancing at the navigation screen. "Their bus left Cape Town thirty minutes ago."

Botha grunted in acknowledgment, his massive hands resting on his knees. The man rarely spoke, but when he did, people listened.

Reggie pulled the stolen tour itinerary from his jacket pocket and placed it on the center console in between them. "Today, they're doing the Langeberg Meander, with a stop at our vineyard for wine tasting and lunch."

The irony wasn't lost on either of them. Of all the vineyards in the region, the tour company had chosen the one owned by Malanga himself—one of his few legitimate businesses, at least on paper.

Reggie reached for his phone and hit the speed dial. The call connected through the car's Bluetooth system after just two rings.

"Talk to me," Malanga's smooth voice filled the vehicle.

"We're heading to the vineyard," Reggie reported. "The tour group should be there around eleven. They'll be running through the property before lunch and wine tasting."

"And you're sure about what you found?" Malanga asked, his tone measured.

"Yeah, boss. One tourist is Jack Hunter. He's carrying two passports and a gun. His business card says 'Hunter Security International.' Looks professional, not amateur."

The line went silent for a moment, only the faint sound of papers being shuffled coming through the speakers. Reggie exchanged a glance with Botha, whose dark eyes had narrowed slightly.

"Hunter Security," Malanga finally said. "I know that name. They do investigation work for mining operations, including De Beers. Interesting coincidence, considering today's meeting."

Reggie tightened his grip on the steering wheel. "You think they know about the diamonds?"

"That's what worries me," Malanga replied. "The timing is…problematic. The courier from Venetia Mine will arrive at the vineyard at two o'clock, just as this tour group's finishing their tasting."

The Venetia Mine in the Limpopo Province was South Africa's largest diamond mine, producing nearly 40% of the country's annual diamond output. A contact inside had been diverting small quantities of uncut stones to them for months, and today was to be their largest exchange yet—stones worth over three million dollars on the black market.

"Want us to redirect the tour group?" Reggie asked as the BMW entered the Huguenot Tunnel. The car's headlights illuminated the concrete walls rushing past.

"No," Malanga decided after a brief pause. "That'd draw attention. Besides, the exchange happens in the private cellar. The tourists will be stuck in the tasting room and terrace."

Reggie nodded, even though Malanga couldn't see him. Still, the feeling of unease wouldn't go away, so he suggested, "We could cancel the diamond meet."

"Absolutely not," Malanga's voice hardened. "This shipment's been arranged for weeks. Our inspector's flying in specifically for this meeting. The exchange happens today."

The silence that followed was heavy with implications. Malanga's legitimate businesses—the vineyard, his import-export company, his stake in the Cape Town warehouse—all served the crucial purpose of laundering money from his more profitable illegal enterprises: wildlife smuggling, stolen diamonds, occasional arms shipments. The vineyard in particular served as a perfect meeting place for transactions, with its remote location and respectable cover.

"This isn't a coincidence," Malanga finally said, and his voice was tight with controlled anger. "First, they show up at the warehouse, now at my vineyard? On the exact day of a major transaction? Someone's watching us."

"Or it really is just bad luck," Reggie said, though he didn't believe it himself. "Tour companies book these stops months in advance."

"I don't believe in luck," Malanga replied coldly. "Not this kind."

"We'll keep our eyes open and keep the groups separated."

The BMW rounded a curve, revealing a patchwork of vineyards, olive groves, fruit orchards, and lavender fields nestled between the mountain slopes that all made up the Langeberg region. Under different circumstances, Reggie might have appreciated the beauty of it.

"Sipho," Malanga said suddenly. "You there?"

Botha leaned slightly toward the speaker. "Yes, boss."

"I want you with me during the exchange. If this tour group is somehow connected to law enforcement, I want to know before they make a move."

"Understood," Botha replied.

The call ended, leaving Reggie and Botha in silence as they continued toward the vineyard. The property came into view in the distance—Ashford Estates, with its Cape Dutch architecture gleaming white against the green backdrop of vines and mountains. From this distance, it looked like any other upscale wine estate in the region, pristine and inviting.

Only those who knew what happened beneath its immaculate surface understood that the vineyard produced more than just award-winning shiraz and chenin blanc. Its cellars had witnessed transactions worth millions, and its soil had occasionally concealed evidence that needed to disappear.

"The woman from the warehouse," Botha said suddenly, breaking his long silence. "She saw the rhino horns?"

Reggie nodded. "And the pelts. She was there with two men—one of them had to be this Hunter guy. He's probably the one who shot at us."

Botha's massive hands flexed slightly. "If they're law enforcement…"

"Then, they're either really brave or really stupid to show up at the boss's vineyard," Reggie finished for him.

The BMW turned off the main road onto a smaller paved lane lined with London plane trees. A discreet sign marked the entrance to Ashford Estates. As they approached the security gate, Reggie couldn't shake the feeling that today would end badly for someone.

Whether it would be the mysterious tour group or themselves remained to be seen.

CHAPTER 14

WINDING TRAILS

The Global Runners tour bus climbed steadily through the Cape Winelands. They had departed Cape Town before dawn, the early morning fog still clinging to the harbor as they pulled away from the hotel. Now, as they emerged from the Huguenot Tunnel into the bright morning light, gasps of appreciation rippled through the group.

"Ladies and gentlemen, welcome to the Langeberg region," Sheryl announced into a microphone while standing at the front of the bus. "Those mountains you see on either side form part of the Cape Fold Belt, some of the oldest mountains on Earth."

The scenery was spectacular—rugged peaks rising dramatically above lush valleys where vineyards stretched in geometric patterns across the slopes. Morning sunlight high-lighted the contrast between the cultivated lands and the wild, craggy heights above.

"Those neat rows you see climbing up the hillsides are some of South Africa's finest vineyards," Luke added into his own microphone, pointing to the meticulously tended vines. "The combination of the Mediterranean climate, diverse soils, and altitude creates perfect conditions for winemaking."

Sheryl moved through the aisle, checking on her travelers as the bus negotiated the winding road. Most were captivated by the scenery, their phone cameras clicking furiously at each new vista. Near the middle of the bus, she paused beside Kelly and Kim, the couple from Manchester who had been quiet during the first few days of the tour. From what Sheryl could remember about them from their last trip together on the Inca Trail, they preferred keeping to themselves, but they at least socialized during the daily excursions. This time, however, they seemed content to talk only to one another.

"How are you both enjoying the trip so far?" Sheryl asked.

Kelly, a petite woman with shoulder-length, auburn hair and sharp features, looked up with a bright smile on her face. "It's absolutely brilliant! And I'm especially excited about today's stop. I adore South African wines."

Kim, a tall, lean woman with brown hair and a big smile, nodded enthusiastically. "Kelly's quite the expert, actually. She traveled here frequently for business and developed quite the palate."

This sudden enthusiasm from the previously reserved couple surprised Sheryl. "Oh? What business brought you to South Africa?"

"Mining," Kelly replied, her eyes bright. "I've worked for De Beers for nearly a decade. Spent lots of time at Venetia Mine in Limpopo, but we entertained clients throughout the wine regions."

From across the aisle, Anika glanced up from her book, her attention caught by the mention of De Beers. Though her face remained impassive, something sharpened in her green eyes.

"Venetia Mine." Margaret leaned forward from the seat behind them. "Isn't that South Africa's largest diamond mine?"

"The very one," Kelly confirmed with a hint of pride. "I was in quality control for seven years before moving to client relations. We'd often bring important buyers to the vineyards—combine business with pleasure."

"Any particular vineyard you would recommend?" Margaret inquired.

"Ashford Estates," Kim answered before Kelly could speak. "We've heard their shiraz is exceptional."

"That's exactly where we're headed," Sheryl confirmed. "It's our main stop after this morning's run."

Kelly's smile widened. "Perfect! I've always wanted to visit. Their wines have quite the reputation."

Joan, seated a few rows back, listened to the conversation with careful attention. Something about the Donovans' sudden shift from quiet observers to enthusiastic wine experts struck her as oddly timed.

As the conversation continued, Anika appeared absorbed in her book, but her attention remained fixed on the Donovans when no one else was looking. Occasionally, she made subtle notes in the margin of her book, her handwriting tiny and precise.

The bus turned onto a narrower road, passing beneath avenues of oak trees that formed a tunnel of dappled light. Beyond them, olive groves gave way to more vineyards, the vines heavy with ripening fruit.

"We'll arrive at our starting point in about fifteen minutes," Sheryl announced. "Remember to bring water and sunscreen. The route takes us through some beautiful terrain before ending at the actual winery, where lunch and wine tasting await us."

As the group began preparing their running gear, Jack watched the interactions around him with quiet observation. His gaze lingered briefly on Anika, noting how her attention kept returning to the suddenly talkative Donovans.

"Beautiful country," he commented, moving to sit beside Luke in an empty row.

"The best," Luke agreed, but his tone was distracted. He, too, had been watching the interactions among the passengers.

"Interesting how some people come alive in certain environments," Jack observed casually. "The Donovans seem pretty excited about wine."

Luke nodded. "Everyone has their passions."

"And their secrets," Jack added softly, his eyes meeting Luke's briefly before returning to the view.

Joan, gathering her running gear, overheard the exchange and felt a rush of anxiety run through her. She decided to stay alert during the run and vineyard visit. Not because she expected trouble—this trip was supposed to be a relaxing vacation, after all—but because something unusual was afoot.

Forty minutes later, the Global Runners group assembled at a trailhead nestled between two vineyard properties. The morning had warmed considerably, but a pleasant breeze kept the temperature comfortable as Sheryl outlined the route.

"Today's run is about seven kilometers of moderate trail," she explained while pointing to a map displayed on her tablet, which was directed out toward everyone else for the group to see. "We'll follow this ridgeline through the nature preserve, then descend through olive groves and vineyards to finish at the estate's hospitality house. The route's well-marked with these blue trail blazes."

Zuri distributed electrolyte gels to each runner. "For those who prefer a shorter option, there's a cutoff point here," she said and indicated a fork in the trail. "That reduces the distance to about four kilometers, still with beautiful views."

The group stretched and chatted excitedly as they prepared to set off. Kelly, dressed in pristine running gear that looked barely used, positioned herself near the front of the group. Kim, less athletically inclined, opted for the shorter route with several other members.

Joan found herself in an unusual position—torn between her natural caution and a growing desire to push herself beyond her comfort zone. The surfing lesson had awakened something in her yesterday, a sense that maybe she was capable of more than she'd allowed herself to believe.

"You doing the full distance?" asked Wanda, who was jogging in place nearby.

Joan hesitated for a moment, then nodded with determination. "Yeah, I think so. Time to stop playing it safe all the time."

As they set off along the trail, the runners quickly spread out according to their abilities. The path climbed steadily through the ever-present fynbos before cresting a ridge that offered spectacular views in all directions. Mountains rose majestically to the north and east, while to the south and west, the landscape descended in a patchwork of farms, vineyards, and small villages.

Anika, normally content to run in the middle of the pack, increased her pace until she drew alongside Kelly, who was surprising everyone with her strong pace near the front of the group.

"Beautiful morning for a run," Anika commented. Her breathing sounded controlled, despite the uphill section they were currently on.

Kelly glanced sideways, sizing up the blonde woman beside her. "Gorgeous. Though, I may have started too ambitiously." She laughed lightly, and a slight sheen of sweat glistened on her forehead.

"The view makes it worthwhile," Anika replied as they reached a particularly scenic outlook. Both women paused for a moment, ostensibly to appreciate the landscape.

"You mentioned that you work for De Beers," Anika said casually as they resumed running. "That must be fascinating."

"It is," Kelly confirmed, picking her way carefully along a rocky section of trail. "Diamonds are uniquely captivating— almost magical when they're transformed from rough stones to finished gems."

"I've always been curious about the security at such places," Anika continued. "Must be pretty intense."

Kelly's stride faltered slightly. "Extremely. Multiple checkpoints, body scans, the works. Venetia is like a fortress."

"Yet, I've read about occasional thefts," Anika countered. Her tone remained conversational, but her expression was serious. "Impressive, given the security."

"Inside jobs, usually," Kelly replied, her voice cooler. "Someone with access and knowledge of the systems."

"Like someone in quality control?"

Kelly shot Anika a sharp look, and her pace increased suddenly. "Exactly. Which is why those positions require extensive background checks and constant monitoring."

Joan, running about fifty meters behind them, couldn't hear what was being said but noticed their body language — Kelly's sudden increase in pace as if desperate to get away, the way Anika seemed so serious and determined to keep the conversation going.

The trail descended into a sun-dappled forest, where dew still glistened on ferns and moss-covered logs. The path narrowed, forcing the two women ahead of her to run single file, with Kelly taking the lead. Joan took advantage of the change in terrain to close the gap slightly, her curiosity overriding her usual caution.

The trail eventually opened onto a breathtaking view of the estates below — white Cape Dutch buildings nestled among perfectly aligned rows of grapevines, with mountains providing a majestic backdrop.

"Almost there," Kelly observed, her earlier warmth returning as she pointed toward the estate. "I can practically taste the shiraz already."

Anika smiled politely. "Looking forward to it. Will your partner join us for the tasting?"

"Oh, yes," Kelly laughed. "Kim never misses a chance to sample fine wine, especially when someone else is driving home afterward."

As they continued down the trail toward the vineyard, several runners caught up to them, and the conversation shifted to more general topics. Sheryl appeared among them, looking pleased with the group's progress.

"Beautiful route, isn't it?" she asked as they approached the final kilometer.

"Spectacular," Anika agreed. "I've worked up a real taste for that wine now."

The trail widened as it approached the vineyard property, transitioning from wild landscapes to the disciplined beauty of cultivation. Workers moved through the vines, checking leaves and fruit, occasionally glancing up to watch the colorful procession of runners descending toward the estate.

As the group reassembled on the manicured lawn behind the main building where tastings were held, those who had taken the shorter route greeted the arriving runners. Kim handed Kelly a bottle of water, whispering something in her ear that made her nod sharply.

"Our Belgian seems pretty interested in the diamond experts," Jack said quietly to Luke.

"I noticed that, too," Luke replied. "Think it's just curiosity?"

Jack's eyes narrowed slightly as he watched Anika discreetly adjust a small device in her ear—easily mistakable for a wireless earbud but likely something more sophisticated.

"No," he said. "I don't think it's curiosity at all."

The group began moving toward the tasting room, where white-clothed tables were prepared for their lunch and wine sampling. As they walked, Jack maneuvered himself closer to Sheryl.

"Stay alert," he murmured. "Something's happening here beyond just a wine tasting."

Sheryl's smile remained in place for anyone watching, but her eyes reflected immediate understanding. "Coincidence?" she whispered back.

"There's no such thing," Jack replied. "Not in my line of work."

As they approached the entrance to the tasting room, a well-dressed man stepped forward to greet them, his smile professional and welcoming.

"Welcome to Ashford Estates," their host announced, his eyes scanning each face with particular attention to Sheryl, Jack, and Luke. "We're delighted to host Global Runners today."

Behind him, through the open doors, the elegant space awaited them with gleaming glasses and bottles of award-winning wines. And somewhere beyond, unseen but present, Malanga prepared for a transaction that had nothing to do with wine.

CHAPTER 15

FACETS OF DECEPTION

Ashford Estates' private cellar lay beneath the main tasting room. Unlike the bright, airy space above, the cellar embraced shadows and secrets—stone walls lined with oak barrels, dim lighting that made the aging bottles gleam like precious gems, and a temperature carefully maintained for optimal wine preservation.

Malanga adjusted his tailored jacket as he descended the stone steps to this inner sanctum. He carried himself with the confident bearing of a successful businessman—his tight hair precisely cut, skin lean and taught across his jaw, a Rolex Yacht-Master gleaming on his wrist.

"Everything ready?" he asked Reggie, who waited at the bottom of the stairs.

"Yeah, boss. The inspector showed up five minutes ago—Swiss guy, just like you expected. He's been cleared, and he's waiting inside for you." Reggie lowered his voice. "No sign of our diamond courier yet."

Malanga checked his watch—thirteen minutes until the scheduled meeting. "And our tourists?"

"Still at their tasting. Botha's keeping an eye on them, especially the guides."

Above them, the tour group had progressed to the final wine of their tasting—Ashford's limited-production dessert wine, served with artisanal chocolates. The atmosphere was relaxed, conversations flowing as freely as the wine. Only a few participants remained fully alert to the undercurrents beneath the pleasant surface.

Anika returned her wine glass to the table after barely taking a sip. Her thoughts were entirely focused on Kelly, who sat three tables away, engaged in animated conversation with Margaret. Kim had disappeared ten minutes earlier, claiming she needed to find a restroom.

Across the room, Jack maintained his position near the room's entrance, seemingly enjoying the décor and listening to all the conversations happening around him but actually monitoring everyone entering or leaving. His eyes met Anika's briefly, a silent acknowledgment passing between them.

Sheryl circulated among the guests, acting as the perfect tour leader—attentive, knowledgeable, ensuring everyone's needs were met.

Anika checked her watch. Rising casually, she approached the sommelier. "Where are the restrooms?" she asked with a polite smile.

"Down the hall to your left, ma'am," he replied, then gestured toward a corridor that led away from the tasting room.

Instead of following his directions, Anika took a different turn once out of sight, moving quickly down a service hallway she'd noted earlier. It would lead toward the storage areas and, she hoped, provide access to the cellar where the exchange would likely occur.

At the end of the corridor, she encountered a locked door. Drawing a slim case from her pocket, she extracted specialized tools and made quick work of the lock. When the door swung open, she found concrete steps descending into cooler air—a utility access to the cellar.

Anika moved silently down the stairs, hyperaware of every sound echoing in the stone passage. At the bottom, another corridor branched in two directions—one leading toward the main area on the left, the other toward what appeared to be storage rooms on the right.

Voices echoed faintly from the left. Anika pressed herself against the wall, straining to hear.

"—verification process takes only minutes," a man was saying, his accent distinctly Swiss-German. "My equipment's highly portable but precise."

"Mr. Malanga wants thoroughness," came Reggie's voice in response. "The provenance has to be untraceable."

"Naturally," the Swiss man replied. "Discretion's my trademark."

Anika edged closer, peering around a stack of empty wine crates. Through a partially open door, she could see into what appeared to be a tasting room more luxurious than the one upstairs — leather chairs, a polished wooden table, and sophisticated lighting focused on the table's center.

A heavy man in his sixties with silver hair sat at the table, arranging what looked like specialized equipment — a loupe, digital scales, and what Anika recognized as a portable spectrometer for gemstone analysis. Malanga stood nearby, swirling amber liquid in a crystal glass. Reggie remained by the door, vigilant.

But where are the diamonds? And where is Kelly — or Kim?

A soft sound behind her made Anika freeze. Footsteps — approaching from the corridor she had just traversed. With nowhere to hide, she made a split-second decision, slipping through another door into what proved to be a small storage room filled with wine crates. She left the door slightly ajar, allowing her to observe the corridor.

Kim appeared, moving with purpose rather than the casual demeanor she'd maintained throughout the tour. In her hand was a small black bag, held with the careful attention one might give to something extraordinarily valuable.

She paused at the entrance to the private tasting room, knocked twice, and was admitted by Reggie. The door closed behind her.

Once she was sure the coast was clear, Anika tiptoed out of her hiding place until she was standing next to the door leading to the meeting room. She knelt down, then activated her phone's recording function, positioning it to capture audio through the space between the door and the ground.

As a security agent for De Beers, she needed evidence before making any move. Diamonds were valuable, but prosecutable evidence was priceless.

"Mr. Heller, let me introduce Ms. Donovan," Malanga's voice came clearly through the door. "She's got something quite special from Venetia."

"A pleasure," the Swiss man—Heller—responded. "I understand we have mutual interests in exceptional stones."

"Absolutely." Kim's voice sounded different—more confident, less the affable wine enthusiast and more the confident thief. "Should we get started?"

The sound of small stones falling onto a metal plate carried through the room. Anika strained to see through the crack but could only glimpse a portion of the room, mostly people's feet while they sat at the table.

"Impressive," Heller remarked after a moment of silence. "These match the description exactly. Twenty-seven stones, primarily Type IIa, exceptional clarity."

"The color grade's better than what we discussed," Kim noted, still all businesslike. "Which should bump up our valuation."

"Let me verify," Heller replied. "The equipment doesn't lie."

Anika needed visual confirmation of who all had attended the meeting. She eased the door open a centimeter, wincing as it emitted a faint creak. No one seemed to notice as they were focused on the examination taking place.

From her new angle, she could see Kim now standing beside Heller, who was bent over the testing equipment. On the table between them lay a black velvet cloth, and upon it, sparkling even in the subdued light, were rough diamonds—uncut, unpolished, yet unmistakably valuable. Anika's trained eye estimated their total weight at approximately two hundred carats—consistent with the Venetia theft.

"All twenty-seven stones are authentic," Heller announced after several minutes of testing. "Premium quality, no artificial treatments or enhancements." He looked up at Malanga. "Should we finalize our agreement?"

Malanga nodded, glancing at Reggie. "Get the case."

Reggie disappeared briefly into an adjoining room, returning with a metal attaché case. He placed it on the table and entered a combination to unlock it.

Anika had seen enough. She now had audio of Kim presenting stolen diamonds and the buyer confirming their authenticity. All she needed was to document the financial transaction, and her case would be complete.

But as she shifted position for a better view, her elbow nudged the door open even further. She held her breath, waiting to see if she was detected.

The crew in the next room were so focused on their exchange that they hadn't heard the slight creak of the door moving. The exchange continued its course.

As the attaché opened, Anika was surprised to realize that it was mostly empty. It wasn't filled with the bundles of cash she'd expected.

Malanga reached into the case and extracted a single computer memory stick. Extending it toward Kim, he said, "Two million in cryptocurrency. Untraceable. The addresses and keys are all on the stick. Easy for you to transfer."

Kim frowned at him. "Two million? We were expecting at least three."

"Ms. Donovan, I might be able to sell them for three. You, however, can get only two for your services. Unless you know someone offering a better price?"

"Fine, two. And how am I supposed to verify there's actually something on that stick?" She waved her hand around the cellar. "From here in a stone cellar?"

"Trust," Malanga responded. "Simple trust."

"Yeah, trust. Okay, I can work with that. I'm gonna walk out of here with the diamonds and the memory stick. I'm sure you trust me. Once I get back to the hotel with Wi-Fi access, I'll verify that the currency's on the stick, and I'll transfer it to my account. Then, once that's done, you can pick up the diamonds."

"You think I'm stupid? Once you have the stick, I'll never see you again." Malanga's face was flushed with anger at Kim's arrogant smirk.

"Trust, Mr. Malanga. You can trust me exactly as much as I can trust you. Besides, I'm a stranger here in your country. I'm defenseless. You can always send your guys after me if I try to run." Kim held the criminal's gaze as she waited for him to decide. Her heart was racing inside her chest. She felt the sweat rising on her skin. It was a dangerous game she was playing with a man like Malanga, but that's how she liked it. "My friends are waiting for me upstairs. What's it gonna be?"

Realizing that he couldn't simply take what he wanted without attracting the attention of dozens of American tourists when Kim failed to reappear, Malanga tipped his head slightly in her direction to admit defeat. "Fine. You've got two days. We'll find you at your next stop."

Kim breathed a sigh of relief. She scooped the diamonds back into their bag and lifted the memory stick from the table. Both disappeared into her backpack. "Nice doing business with you. We'll get the crypto verified tonight if we can. You can have the diamonds any time after that."

With the agreement sealed, each party turned toward the door through which they had come and dispersed. No one had noticed that the door leading to the meeting room was cracked open when it had once been closed.

DEADLY INTRUDER

The late afternoon sun slanted through tall windows at the Protea Hotel in Knysna, washing the lobby in amber light as the Global Runners tour group dispersed to their rooms after the check-in process was complete. The hotel's polished wood, elegant furnishings, and spectacular views of the lagoon contrasted sharply with the tense expressions of three particular guests who lingered near the elevators.

Looking at Luke and Jack, Sheryl asked, "Why would Anika ask all of us to meet her in the conference room?"

Luke only shrugged, while Jack remained silent as they entered the room to see the intense woman waiting for them.

Anika paced the perimeter of the room once they all had arrived, her frustration evident in every step. "I had them," she said. Her voice was tight with barely controlled anger. "I had the evidence, the recording, visual confirmation of the diamonds. And then—" She stopped abruptly, collecting herself. "And then, I lost them."

"What are you talking about?" Sheryl asked.

"Sorry." Producing her business card, Anika said, "I'm actually with De Beers Diamonds. Security office. I'm here because the Donovans are here. We suspect—no, we know—they're here to sell diamonds they've stolen from our mines. My job is to catch them and their buyer."

"Wow! That explains a lot about your behavior." Then, looking at the two men in the room, "And you wanted to tell Luke and me about this because we're leading the tour." She nodded her head toward Jack. "But why's he here?"

Jack spoke for the first time. "I'm actually her backup. In case things get more violent than she can handle."

"I don't need your help. But the company insisted." Anika scowled at Jack, asserting her confidence in her abilities.

Jack merely shrugged at this.

"Well, you didn't lose anything," Sheryl suggested. "You identified both thieves, confirmed they had the stolen diamonds, and documented the attempted sale. That's huge progress."

"Progress isn't enough," Anika replied before finally taking a seat. "I want to get Malanga and the Donovans. Now, I have to wait for another rendezvous."

Luke leaned forward, his elbows resting on the table. "Malanga will be back. We just have to keep our eyes open and be ready for him."

"And the Donovans?" Sheryl asked, turning to Anika.

"They're trapped," Anika explained. "They can't leave the tour without raising suspicion, especially after today. And they wouldn't dare to double-cross Malanga by disappearing before they deliver the diamonds to him."

Jack spoke up. "There's something else. Kim has the crypto, which she will transfer as soon as she can. You won't be able to get that back after she does."

Sheryl looked at Anika for a reaction.

Nodding in acknowledgement, Anika said, "That money doesn't belong to De Beers. So, not my problem."

Jack showed his surprise. "You'd let the Donovans keep the cryptocurrency, even after they're arrested?"

"That's a police problem to solve."

A knock at the door interrupted her. They fell silent as Sheryl moved to answer it.

"Excuse me," the hotel manager said pleasantly, "I wanted to confirm that the conference room works for your needs?"

"Perfect, thank you," Sheryl replied with a warm smile that betrayed none of the tension in the room. "We're just finalizing tomorrow's itinerary."

After the manager left, Jack stood up. "We should continue this discussion later. Too many ears in a hotel, and we can't be sure which ones are friendly and which ones aren't."

As they exited the conference room, they encountered several of their tour group in the lobby, proudly displaying wine purchases from the day's excursion.

"Sheryl!" Madeline called, holding up a bottle of Ashford Estates' Shiraz. "What do you think? Worth the splurge?"

"Absolutely," Sheryl confirmed with professional enthusiasm. "That's one of the region's finest."

"Did you notice how secretive they were about the private cellar?" Stanley added. "Seemed almost suspicious how they hustled us away when Thomas asked for a tour."

Sheryl maintained her smile while exchanging a brief glance with Jack. "High-end vineyards often keep their special reserves under tight security. Just part of the mystique they want to uphold for their clients."

The conversation continued for several minutes as the tour guides performed their expected roles, answering questions about the day's excursion and tomorrow's plans. Finally, they extracted themselves with promises to meet everyone for dinner at seven.

As Sheryl made her way to her room on the third floor, the weight of multiple pressures settled on her shoulders. What had begun as a simple, two-week trip to South Africa had become dangerously complicated, complete with poaching, diamond thieves, international buyers, and a ruthless businessman all converging at once. And somewhere in that mix, Malanga had realized that their group had witnessed more than he would have liked.

Her room offered a welcome respite—spacious and elegant, with a balcony overlooking the lagoon, where evening lights twinkled on the water. After the intensity of the day, the prospect of a hot shower and a moment of solitude was deeply appealing.

Sheryl placed her key card on the desk, checked that her room service coffee order for the morning was correctly filled out, and then headed to the bathroom. The marble and glass enclosure was luxurious, with plush towels and high-end toiletries arranged precisely on the counter.

She turned the shower to its hottest setting, allowing steam to fill the room while she unpinned her hair and began to undress. The day's tension eased from her muscles as she stepped under the powerful spray, letting the water sluice away the dust and strain of the day's hike.

Twenty minutes later, wrapped in the hotel's plush robe, Sheryl emerged from the bathroom while still toweling her damp hair. The room had grown dim as sunset deepened outside, and she moved toward the bedside lamp.

A faint sound—barely perceptible—made her freeze mid-step.

It had come from the door: a soft click, like the door had been opened and closed in quick succession. Sheryl's senses, honed by years as a park ranger in dangerous terrain, shifted instantly to high alert. *Something's wrong.*

She reached slowly for the light switch, keeping her movements deliberate and controlled. As soft illumination flooded the room, her breath caught in her throat.

Less than ten feet away, coiled on the carpet between her and the door, was a puff adder—one of Africa's deadliest snakes. Nearly three feet long with a thick, heavy body patterned in chevrons of brown and black, it was unmistakable. It adjusted its position, head raised slightly, black eyes fixed on her with primordial focus.

Sheryl remained absolutely still, her ranger training kicking in automatically. Any sudden movement would trigger the snake's defensive strike. Puff adders were responsible for more fatalities than any other African snake—not because they were the most venomous, but because they were common, well-camouflaged, and disinclined to flee when threatened.

How the hell did it get in here? The thought flashed through her mind, followed immediately by the answer. *Malanga.*

The snake's body tensed slightly, its head bobbing in the characteristic warning that preceded a strike. Unlike the rattlesnakes Sheryl had encountered in Utah, the puff adder gave no audible warning—just the silent, deadly focus of a predator.

She assessed her options in seconds. The door was beyond the snake. Her phone was on the nightstand behind her. The bathroom offered potential refuge, but she'd have to turn her back on the adder to reach it.

The snake's body shifted again, its muscles tensing visibly beneath its patterned scales.

"Easy," Sheryl whispered, the word barely audible. Not that the snake would respond to her voice or understand what she was saying, but the sound helped steady her own nerves.

With glacial slowness, she edged sideways, moving parallel to the threat rather than away from or toward it. The puff adder's head tracked her movement, its tongue flicking rapidly to taste the air.

Four feet to her right stood a heavy floor lamp with a marble base. If she could reach it without triggering a strike…

The snake's head bobbed more pronouncedly—the final warning. Sheryl knew what was coming.

The strike was blindingly fast—a blur of motion as the adder launched forward, its head extending nearly two-thirds of its body length toward her exposed legs. Sheryl pivoted sharply, the heavy hotel robe swinging out as she twisted away from the attack. The snake's fangs caught in the thick terry cloth, momentarily tangling in it.

Sheryl used the precious seconds to lunge for the lamp, yanking its cord from the wall and gripping it by its metal stem. The adder reoriented immediately, frustrated by its failed first strike. Its body inflated slightly as it huffed air in a threatening display—the behavior that gave the species its name.

"Come on, then," Sheryl muttered, adjusting her grip on the makeshift weapon.

The second strike came from a different angle as the snake attempted to circle around her. This time, Sheryl was prepared, swinging the lamp base in a defensive arc that intercepted the adder mid-strike. The impact sent the snake skidding across the carpet, but it recovered with unsettling speed, immediately coiling to strike again.

Sheryl's heart pounded, adrenaline sharpening her senses to hyperawareness. The lamp was heavier than she'd expected, already straining her arms as she kept it positioned between herself and the snake. She couldn't maintain this defense indefinitely.

The third strike was more determined—a full commitment that sent the adder sailing through the air directly at her. Sheryl swung the lamp like a baseball bat, connecting solidly with the snake's body and sending it crashing into the wall. The impact stunned the reptile, giving Sheryl the opening she needed.

With a controlled but powerful movement, she brought the heavy base of the lamp down directly on the adder's triangular head, pinning it to the carpet. The snake's body whipped violently, powerful muscles struggling against the crushing weight. Sheryl held firm, applying steady pressure, despite the sickening sensation of the creature's death throes beneath her hands.

"Die, you bastard," she hissed through clenched teeth, maintaining the pressure until the violent thrashing gradually subsided to weak twitches, and finally, stillness.

Even then, she didn't immediately release the pressure. Adrenaline still coursed through her system. Her breathing was ragged in the sudden quiet of the room. Sweat had soaked through her robe, even with the air conditioning.

A sharp knock at the door made her jerk in surprise.

"Sheryl?" Luke's voice called out. Concern was evident in his tone. "Everything okay in there? I heard noises."

"Just a minute," she called back, her voice remarkably steady despite what had just happened.

Keeping the lamp base firmly pressed on the snake's crushed head, she used her foot to drag a side table closer, then wedged the lamp beneath it to maintain the pressure. Only then did she cautiously approach the door, checking the peephole before opening it.

Luke stood in the hallway, his expression shifting from concern to alarm as he took in her disheveled appearance. "What happened?"

"Come in," she said tersely, closing the door behind him immediately. "And watch your step."

Luke's eyes widened as he spotted the dead snake pinned beneath the lamp. "Jesus Christ," he breathed. "A puff adder? In your room?"

"Courtesy of our new friend, Malanga, I'm guessing," Sheryl replied, then moved to retrieve her phone from the nightstand. "Or, more likely, his enforcer."

Luke crouched to examine the snake without touching it. "This isn't a coincidence or accident. These snakes don't just wander into hotel rooms on the third floor."

"Exactly." Sheryl quickly dialed Jack's room. When he answered, her instructions were brief. "My room. Now." She hung up without elaboration.

"How did you—" Luke gestured at the dead reptile.

"I dealt with plenty of rattlesnakes in Utah," Sheryl explained while running a hand through her still-damp hair. "Different species, same basic tactics."

"Still," Luke said and shook his head in admiration, "not many people walk away from a surprise encounter with a puff adder."

"I got lucky," Sheryl admitted, the post-adrenaline crash beginning to make her hands tremble slightly. "If I'd stepped out of the bathroom and straight onto it in the dark…"

She didn't need to finish the sentence. Both of them knew the outcome would have been very different.

A soft knock announced Jack's arrival. Luke let him in while Sheryl quickly changed in the bathroom, emerging in jeans and a T-shirt moments later.

Jack took in the scene with a professional assessment. From the small black case he'd brought, he extracted a digital camera and began documenting the snake from multiple angles.

"How'd it get in?" he asked while photographing the area near the door.

"That's what I'd like to know," Sheryl replied. "The door was locked. Balcony, too."

Jack moved to examine the door lock, then the balcony access. "No signs of forced entry. Someone either has a key or great lock-picking skills."

"Hotel staff?" Luke suggested.

"Maybe," Jack acknowledged. "Malanga's got connections everywhere. Wouldn't surprise me."

"This was a message," Sheryl stated flatly. "Malanga's showing us he can reach us anywhere."

Jack completed his examination of the room before returning to the snake. With gloved hands, he carefully removed the improvised trap and examined the crushed head.

"Mature female," he noted. "And recently fed, based on the bulge. Someone had been keeping this snake for a while before they released it in your room."

Luke said with certainty, "This is very personal intimidation. Calculated to inspire fear without leaving evidence that could lead back to them."

"Except they didn't count on you having experience with venomous snakes," Jack added, looking at Sheryl with a new-found respect.

"We need to move to new rooms," Luke added. "All of us. Right now."

Jack carefully placed the dead snake in a plastic bag from his kit. "I'll dispose of the body. Snake venom stays active even after death."

As they coordinated their next steps, Sheryl calculated what this escalation meant for their operation. Malanga had moved beyond passive observation to actively threatening their lives.

"What about the rest of the group?" Luke asked, voicing the concern that had already occurred to Sheryl. "If Malanga's willing to target us directly…"

"The ordinary tourists should be safe," Jack replied. "Targeting them would draw too much attention to the situation. He wants to scare us off, not create an international incident."

"Still, we need to be more careful," Sheryl decided.

As Luke left, Jack paused at the door. "You handled this well," he said quietly. "Not everyone would've kept their cool."

Sheryl offered him a grim smile. "Wildlife was never the most dangerous part of being a ranger," she replied. "It was always the people."

After they departed, Sheryl stood alone in the center of the room, surveying the aftermath of the attack. The lamp lay on the carpet, a dark smear marking where the snake's head had been crushed.

Tonight marked the beginning of a deadlier game—one with rules Malanga had played before. But Sheryl hadn't survived years in the wilderness by being easily intimidated.

She began gathering her essential belongings for the room change, her movements efficient and purposeful. Malanga had made a critical miscalculation. He had revealed his willingness to escalate without knowing his prey. That mistake would cost him dearly.

CHAPTER 17

PATHS AMONG THE ORCHARDS

The late morning light streamed through the tall windows of the converted barn with exposed beams and stone floors that served as the Joubertsdal Estate's welcome area. By 9:30 a.m., after a short bus ride, the runners had assembled in the courtyard, many still nursing coffee from breakfast and comparing notes on their historic location.

"Everyone ready to hit the trail?" Sheryl asked, scanning the group with professional attentiveness while discreetly checking for any signs of the Donovans' nocturnal activities. The couple stood near the back of the group, appearing tired but present.

"This place is incredible," Margaret commented, stretching her calves against a stone wall. "The estate must date back a century."

"Two," Luke replied, consulting a small information card. "The farmhouse furniture was imported from England in 1792. The Joubert family preserved most of the original estate."

Sheryl clapped her hands twice to gather everyone's attention. "Today's route is really special. We'll be running through active orchards, across the estate's hills, and around its retention pond before circling back. About five miles total, but with some challenging elevation changes."

Jack stood slightly apart from the group, appearing to adjust his running shoes while actually surveying the estate grounds. Since the incident the previous night, the team had maintained heightened vigilance, though they'd seen no further signs of Malanga's presence.

"This property's been continuously farmed for over 150 years," Sheryl continued, pointing toward the neat rows of trees stretching to the eastern hills. "We'll start through the fruit orchards, which were just harvested last week."

Anika positioned herself near the Donovans, her Belgian tourist persona firmly in place, despite the previous day's revelations. Her attention never strayed far from Kelly, whose backpack most likely contained the crypto memory stick.

Luke stepped forward with a laminated map. "Important safety note—we're in wild country here despite the cultivated appearance. That means we need to respect any wildlife we encounter. Baboon troops occasionally move through these orchards. They're generally peaceful if not provoked, but keep your distance. And, please, do not try to feed them, no matter how cute you may find them."

"Are they dangerous?" Joan asked, looking concerned. Her experience with African wildlife was limited to nature documentaries.

"Only if threatened," Luke assured her. "Just give them space, and don't make direct eye contact with them, which they consider an act of aggression."

Joan nodded, though her worried expression suggested she was mentally calculating the various ways this run could go wrong.

With her instructions delivered, Sheryl led the group out of the courtyard and onto a well-maintained dirt path that wound between the first rows of almond trees. The morning air carried the mingled scents of rich soil, orchard blossoms, and the faint sweetness of fermenting fallen fruit. Despite the tensions simmering beneath the surface of their expedition, the sheer beauty of the setting was undeniable.

The runners spread out naturally as they found their pace. Tyler and Emma quickly took the lead, their competitive instincts driving them forward. Behind them, the group stretched into small clusters based on ability and social connections formed over the previous days.

Joan found herself in the middle of the pack, settling into a steady rhythm that felt manageable. Unlike the surfing adventure where she'd surprised herself with unexpected boldness, this morning, she was content to play it safe.

About half a mile in, the path began a gentle ascent through rows of almond trees, their branches partially bare after the recent harvest. Sunlight filtered through the remaining leaves, casting dappled patterns on the ground. Sheryl maintained a moderate pace with the runners in the middle, keeping the faster runners in sight while ensuring the slower participants weren't left too far behind.

Jack caught up with her, his breathing controlled, despite the incline. "Beautiful morning," he commented casually, though his eyes continued their systematic scan of their surroundings.

"Almost makes you forget yesterday," Sheryl replied quietly.

"Almost," Jack agreed. "Anything from our diamond smugglers?"

Sheryl answered in a voice low enough that nearby runners couldn't overhear. "Anika said they were agitated at breakfast."

"Speaking of whom," Jack said and nodded ahead where Anika had accelerated to join Kelly and Kim, who were running side-by-side through the orchard.

Anika fell into step beside Kelly, her breathing deliberately heavier than necessary as she established her presence. "Magnificent trees," she commented between breaths. "Some must be decades old."

Kelly seemed startled by Anika's sudden appearance but quickly composed herself. "Yes, quite lovely," she agreed, her English accent more pronounced.

"Did you sleep well?" Anika inquired innocently. "I found my room rather warm."

"Fine, thanks," Kim answered curtly, increasing her pace slightly as if to pull ahead.

Anika matched the acceleration effortlessly. "I was thinking about our vineyard tour yesterday," she continued, watching the couple's reactions closely. "Such interesting cellars they had at Ashford Estates."

Kelly stumbled slightly, recovered, and shot her partner a warning glance. "We didn't see much of the cellars," she replied carefully.

"No? I thought perhaps you'd arranged a private tour," Anika pressed, her tone conversational.

Before either Donovan could respond, a sharp exclamation from up ahead diverted everyone's attention. The lead runners had stopped at a bend in the path, pointing toward something among the trees.

"Look there—a baboon!" Stanley called back excitedly, gesturing toward a clearing between the rows of trees.

The group converged gradually, maintaining a respectful distance as they observed the solitary male baboon methodically inspecting the ground beneath the trees. His dark brown fur caught the morning light as he moved with unhurried purpose, occasionally stooping to retrieve fallen fruit that had escaped the harvest machinery.

"Magnificent specimen," Professor Nkosi murmured. "A lone male, probably separated from his troop."

"Is that normal?" Madeline asked, slightly nervous, even though the creature seemed calm and disinterested in the humans observing it.

Luke nodded, keeping his voice low. "Males sometimes forage independently. He's after the refuse from the harvest."

The baboon seemed unconcerned by their presence, maintaining its deliberate search pattern through the orchard. His powerful hands deftly handled the fruit with surprising delicacy.

"Perfect photo opportunity," Sheryl suggested, "but please, keep your distance."

As the group spread out along the path to observe and photograph, Sheryl noticed the Donovans hanging back, exchanging what appeared to be heated whispers. Anika had positioned herself nearby, pretending to adjust her shoe while clearly monitoring their conversation.

Jack materialized beside Sheryl again. "Our friends seem upset," he observed quietly.

"Something's shifted since yesterday," Sheryl agreed. "Anika thinks they're planning an exit."

Jack's response was interrupted as Luke approached, gesturing for them to continue the run. "We should keep moving," he suggested, loud enough for nearby runners to hear. "Let's leave our friend to his breakfast."

The group gradually reformed, continuing along the path that now climbed more steeply into the hills. The orchard rows gave way to natural vegetation—the distinctive shrub land ecosystem unique to the Cape region. Proteas and ericas dotted the hillside with splashes of color among the silver-green foliage.

As they crested the hill, the vista opened dramatically before them. From this elevation, they could see the entirety of Joubertsdal Estate spread below—the historic homestead, the geometric patterns of the various orchards, and beyond them, the glittering surface of the retention pond reflecting the morning sky.

"Worth… the… climb," Rogerio gasped between labored breaths as he reached the summit, his hands braced on his knees.

"Absolutely incredible," Margaret agreed, her face flushed with exertion but beaming with appreciation of the view.

The path followed the ridgeline for several hundred yards before beginning its descent toward the eastern orchards. The gradient was challenging enough that conversation momentarily ceased as runners focused on their footing on the rocky trail. The silence was broken only by the rhythmic sounds of heavy breathing and the multitude of footfalls on packed earth.

As the path leveled out again, entering a grove of peach trees, conversation resumed. Sheryl found herself flanked by Madeline and Stanley, Global Runners' longtime clients who had developed a keen eye for group dynamics through multiple expeditions.

"Something's different with this tour," Madeline commented between breaths, her voice low. "It's more…intense."

Sheryl maintained her professional demeanor. "South Africa's got a distinct energy than Ecuador," she replied smoothly. "More complicated history, more dramatic landscapes."

"It's not the country," Stanley persisted, though he sounded slightly winded. "It's the group. That Belgian woman and the Donovans, there's something going on there, a weird sort of energy between them like they can barely stand to be around each other."

"And you," Madeline added, giving Sheryl a knowing look. "You and Jack and Luke seem…distracted all the time."

Sheryl managed a laugh that sounded more natural than she felt. "That's just good tour management. We've been working together to make sure everyone has the best experience possible."

Before they could press further, the path curved sharply, revealing the retention pond—a man-made lake spanning nearly two acres, bordered by reeds and water plants. A wooden boardwalk extended partway across one side, offering views of waterfowl and the occasional lazy fish that sent ripples across the otherwise placid surface.

The runners paused along the shoreline and boardwalk. Some stretched or took photographs. Sheryl used the opportunity to confer with Jack and Anika, the three of them clustering near a wooden bench that offered a view of both the pond and the surrounding area.

"They're making a move tonight," Anika reported, her voice barely above a whisper. "I overheard Kim tell Kelly that they 'can't wait any longer' and 'need to contact him today.'"

"Meaning Malanga?" Jack asked, taking a drink from his water bottle while scanning the group.

"Most likely," Anika confirmed. "My guess is they'll try to negotiate a handover."

"Which puts us in a tough position," Sheryl noted. "If the Donovans leave the tour to meet Malanga, we lose our best lead."

Jack's expression hardened slightly. "Or it creates an opportunity. If we know when and where they're meeting…"

"We could potentially catch both parties together," Anika completed his thought, a glimmer of professional excitement in her eyes. "Malanga with the stolen diamonds, the Donovans handing them over."

"It's risky," Sheryl cautioned, watching as more runners gathered for the last leg of the journey. "Malanga's already shown that he's willing to escalate to violence."

Their conversation halted as Derek and Sean approached, both looking invigorated by the run.

"This place is unbelievable," Derek enthused, gesturing toward the landscape. "Like running through a painting."

"The chef at the homestead mentioned they'll be serving fresh-picked peaches with lunch," Sean added with clear anticipation. "Apparently, there'll also be local cheeses, wines, and desserts." He rubbed his hands together with a devilish smile in anticipation.

With the break concluded, Luke called the group back together to begin the last segment of their run. The path followed the pond's contour before cutting across a lavender field—a recent addition to the estate's agricultural portfolio. The sweet, herbaceous scent released by their passage added another sensory dimension to the already rich experience.

As they approached the homestead, now visible through a stand of old oak trees, the runners naturally accelerated, drawn by the promise of the finish line. The path widened to accommodate their spread-out formation, eventually depositing them back in the courtyard where they had begun nearly an hour earlier.

Runners arrived in waves—the Wilsons first, followed by Sheryl, Jack, and most of the group. The Donovans were among the last to return, both looking more fatigued than the moderate run should have caused.

Joan finished with the latter group, breathing hard but smiling with satisfaction. The run had been challenging but manageable, and she felt a quiet pride in completing it with no major struggles. It was a minor victory, but for someone still learning to push beyond her comfort zone, it felt significant.

"Wonderful course," Luke announced to the assembled group, many now stretching or drinking from water bottles. "You've earned your lunch. There'll be sausages and roasted corn on the lawn, and you'll find barbecue on roosterkoek bread and samosas up on the patio. Local producers have wine, cheese, and juices for you to sample and purchase if you like."

As the sweating, flushed-faced tourists dispersed, Sheryl caught a significant glance from Anika, who subtly tilted her head toward the Donovans. They were already walking away, heads bent close together in conversation.

"The game's moving faster now," Jack commented quietly as he stood beside Sheryl, watching the retreating figures of the diamond thieves.

"Then, we'd better keep pace," Sheryl replied, her thoughts already turning to the potential confrontation that seemed increasingly inevitable. The peaceful beauty of the Joubertsdal Estate had provided a temporary respite, but beneath its serene surface, dangerous currents continued to gather strength.

CHAPTER 18

SONGS OF THE WINELANDS

Sheryl circulated among the group, ensuring that everyone was enjoying themselves.

"This spread is extraordinary," Margaret commented as she selected a samosa from the buffet. "I'd expected good food on this tour, but everything's exceeded my expectations."

"Joubertsdal's known for its farm-to-table approach," Luke explained, pouring glasses of the estate's own chenin blanc for those interested. "Most of what you're eating was harvested within a kilometer of where we're standing."

Jack nodded as Anika approached casually.

"Any activity from our friends?" Jack asked quietly, nodding toward the Donovans, who were seated at the far end of the table.

"Normal, nothing notable," Anika replied before sipping her wine.

Their conversation paused as Albert Joubert, the estate's sixth-generation owner, approached the center of the terrace. In his early sixties, with his tanned skin and the confident bearing of a man firmly connected to his land, Joubert embodied the blend of European ancestry and African identity that characterized the Cape Winelands.

"Friends, welcome to our family home," he announced, his English carrying the distinctive melodic cadence of Afrikaans heritage. "For 150 years, the Joubert family has cultivated this land, learning its secrets, respecting its challenges, and celebrating its gifts. Today, we're pleased to share not only our produce and wine with you but also something equally precious—the cultural wealth of our region."

He gestured toward the stone steps leading up to the festival building, where a group of fifteen men and women had quietly assembled. Dressed in coordinated outfits of black fabric with decorative African accents, they arranged themselves in a semicircle facing the lunch gathering.

"I'm honored to present the Zolani Youth Choir from the nearby township of Ashton," Joubert continued. "They'll share traditional songs that tell the story of our shared land—songs of hardship and hope, of struggle and celebration."

An expectant hush fell over the lunch gathering as a woman stepped forward from the center of the choir. With quiet dignity, she addressed the tourists.

"*Molweni.* Greetings," she said, her voice rich and resonant even without speakers. "I'm Nomvula Khumalo, director of the Zolani Choir. Today, we bring you songs from our hearts—songs in Xhosa, Zulu, and Sotho that have sustained our people through many seasons of history."

Nomvula returned to her position, and without any instruments playing, the choir began. The first notes emerged softly—a single voice singing a haunting line that seemed to float on the midday air. One by one, other voices joined, building harmonies of such unexpected complexity and beauty that several of the tourists visibly straightened in their seats, all of their earlier conversations forgotten.

The opening song swelled with overlapping call-and-response patterns, punctuated by the distinctive clicking consonants of Xhosa. The sound was unlike anything most of the tourists had ever heard—ancient and immediate, the clicks adding percussion to the melody.

"'*Qongqothwane*,'" whispered Luke to those seated nearby. "'The Click Song,' made famous internationally by Miriam Makeba. It tells of a small bird that brings good fortune."

The lyrics flowed across the terrace:

"Igqira lendlela nguqongqothwane
Sebeqabele gqithapha le ntaba
Sebeqabele gqithapha…"

The harmonies built and receded like ocean waves, creating patterns of sound that seemed to bypass intellectual understanding and connect directly to something more primal. Even those who couldn't understand a word of it nodded in time, expressions of wonder spreading across faces.

"It's extraordinary," Joan whispered to Rogerio beside her. "I've never heard anything like it."

As the first song concluded, a spontaneous burst of applause erupted from the tourists. The choir members smiled but immediately began their second piece—this one more rhythmic and celebratory. A male voice led with a powerful opening line, the rest of the choir answering in perfect synchronization.

> *"Shosholoza, ku lezontaba*
> *Stimela siphume South Africa*
> *Wen' uyabaleka*
> *Wen' uyabaleka*
> *Ku lezontaba…"*

"This is '*Shosholoza*,'" Luke explained quietly. "Originally sung by workers in the mines and railways. It describes a train moving through the mountains."

Several tourists had taken out their phones to record the performance, transfixed by the choir's ability to create such textured soundscapes using no instruments. The singers moved subtly as they performed, their bodies swaying in gentle unison, hands occasionally rising to emphasize particular phrases.

Madeline leaned toward Stanley, her eyes bright with emotion. "I'm getting chills," she whispered. "You can feel the history in every note."

At a nearby table, the Donovans appeared genuinely moved by the performance, momentarily distracted from whatever plans they had been formulating. Kelly discreetly wiped a tear from the corner of her eye as the song reached a particularly poignant passage.

The choir transitioned to a third song—this one slower, more solemn, with complex harmonies that seemed to layer one atop another like geological strata. The song began with a solo female voice before the full choir joined in sustained chords.

"Thula Sizwe, ungabokhala
Ufik' uJesu, sizoyigqoba
Inkululeko, sizoyithola
Thula Sizwe, ungabokhala…"

"'Thula Sizwe'—'Be Still, Nation,'" Professor Nkosi translated quietly for those nearby. "A freedom song from the apartheid era. It promises that liberation will come."

The choir's timing was impeccable, their breaths choreographed to maintain the unbroken flow of sound. What initially seemed simple revealed itself as extraordinarily complex when listeners tried to follow individual voices weaving through the harmonies.

As the song progressed, the choir moved into a foot-stomping rhythm, transforming the solemn opening into a declaration of determination. The tourists instinctively leaned forward, drawn into the emotional journey of the piece.

Derek turned to his brother, Sean, speaking in a hushed tone. "I feel like I'm hearing the entire history of this country in song."

Sean agreed. "It's like it's taking us through all the generations."

The choir concluded the song with voices gradually fading until only a single soprano remained, her pure tone holding the last note before dissolving into silence. The hush that followed was profound—a moment of collective reflection before applause erupted, several guests rising to their feet in appreciation.

Nomvula stepped forward again. "Our final song is 'Bawo Thixo Somandla'—a prayer to the Almighty that's been sung in our communities for generations. It asks for divine guidance and protection during difficult journeys."

The choir members arranged themselves in a tighter formation, and when they began, the sound was a shifting tapestry of harmonies that created a peaceful space in the open air.

"Bawo thixo somandla
Wena kanye nguwe
Ulidwala labantu
Abantu abadiniweyo…"

"It's asking for guidance through mountainous terrain," Luke whispered to those near him. "Pretty fitting for our journey."

Sheryl, standing at the edge of the gathering, found herself unexpectedly moved. Despite the tensions and dangers surrounding their expedition, this moment of cultural connection reminded her why she'd been drawn to this work—the opportunity to experience authentic expressions of humanity anywhere in the world.

As the notes of the prayer song faded into the afternoon air, the tourists rose in a standing ovation. Many faces showed traces of tears, and the applause continued for nearly a minute, punctuated by calls of "Bravo!" and "Magnificent!"

Nomvula acknowledged the response with gracious dignity. "Thank you for receiving our songs with open hearts. Music has always been how we tell our stories, how we remember our struggles, and how we celebrate our joys. We're honored to share these traditions with visitors who've come so far to know our land."

As the formal performance concluded, the atmosphere shifted to animated conversation. Tourists approached choir members with questions and compliments, while estate staff refreshed wine glasses and brought out platters of locally made ice cream and oliebol.

Luke explained the linguistic features of Xhosa to an intrigued group of tourists. "The clicks you heard are actual consonants in the language," he explained. "There are three main types: the dental click, like the sound of disapproval or 'tsk'; the lateral click, which sounds like calling a horse; and the alveolar click, which is the sharpest sound."

"I had no idea language could include such sounds," Margaret commented. "It's fascinating how different human communication can be."

"Yet, the emotions in the music came through clearly, even without understanding the words," the professor added. "That's the universal language at work."

Joan approached one of the younger choir members, a woman about her own age. "Thank you," she said simply. "That was beautiful."

The woman smiled warmly. "Music is the bridge between our hearts," she replied in accented English. "It speaks what words cannot say."

The songs had spoken of guidance through mountains and protection during difficult journeys. As the shadows lengthened across the Joubertsdal Estate, Sheryl suspected that they would need both before the night was over.

LOW TIDES

Morning sunlight glinted off the broad expanse of the Knysna Lagoon, transforming the rippled surface of the water into a dazzling mosaic of gold and turquoise. Breakfast at the second hotel on their route had been a lively affair, with runners energized by anticipation of the day's route. According to Luke's briefing, they would experience one of the most dramatic coastal runs of their South African journey — crossing the lagoon via an old railway line before following the shoreline to the famous Knysna Heads, twin sandstone cliffs that guarded the narrow channel where lagoon met ocean.

The group assembled at the starting point, just a hundred meters from the hotel. Many hats and sunglasses glinted in the bright coastal light, and water bottles were securely fastened to running belts. The railway causeway stretched before them—a long, narrow path across the lagoon's shimmering waters, offering a perspective of Knysna few visitors experienced.

"Remember what I mentioned at breakfast," Luke called out as the group prepared to depart. "Depending on the tide, some sections of the path may be underwater. Nothing dangerous, but expect wet feet at a minimum!"

As the runners moved forward in their usual formation, Kelly hung back, apparently adjusting the laces on her trail shoes. Her partner, Kim, stood nearby, scanning the gathered tourists with unusual attentiveness. Their behavior hadn't escaped notice—Professor Nkosi observed them with curiosity while pretending to apply sunscreen to his arms.

"Everything all right over here?" Luke asked while approaching the Donovans.

"Fine, thanks," Kelly replied with forced brightness. "Just making sure these laces won't come undone when they get wet. Kim's phone's acting up, too—she's trying to get a signal before we lose coverage."

Kim held up her mobile with an apologetic smile. "Trying to check in with my sister back home. Time zones make it tricky."

Luke nodded and moved on, but not before noticing Kim's phone screen—not displaying a calling interface but what appeared to be a messaging app with a text that began, "Confirmed for today…"

The runners proceeded along the railway causeway in single file, the wooden ties and rails providing a rhythmic counterpoint to their footfalls. On either side, the lagoon spread outward—a fifteen-square-kilometer expanse of protected water surrounded by forested hills and wetlands, home to over two hundred species of fish and countless birds.

The causeway gave way to shoreline, where the path narrowed and undulated with the natural contours of the lagoon's edge. As Luke had predicted, the advancing tide had already submerged sections of their route, requiring runners to splash through ankle-deep water in some places.

At one such crossing, Kelly stumbled slightly, grabbing Kim's arm for support. What appeared to be a momentary loss of balance served as cover for a whispered exchange, their heads close together for several seconds before they separated, continuing forward with renewed purpose.

"Spectacular location," Madeline commented to no one in particular as the group rounded a bend, revealing their first unobstructed view of the Knysna Heads. Waves crashed against the rocky bases, sending spray skyward in ephemeral displays that caught the morning light.

"One of the most treacherous harbor entrances in the world," Luke called back, pointing toward the channel. "The currents between the Heads have claimed over thirty ships. Only skilled local captains attempt passage."

The path climbed as they approached the Western Head, zigzagging upward through coastal vegetation. The group naturally spread out along the ascent, each runner finding their comfortable pace for the challenging gradient.

Professor Nkosi noticed the Donovans accelerate unexpectedly, moving from near the back to somewhere in the middle of the pack. They positioned themselves behind Tyler and Emma and in front of the foodie brothers, who were too busy discussing local oyster varieties to pay attention to those ahead of them.

In this pocket of relative isolation, Kelly removed her phone from her running belt, consulting it briefly before showing something to Kim. She nodded once, decisively, before Kelly returned it to her belt pouch.

The group continued climbing until they reached a magnificent viewpoint atop the Western Head. Even the most serious runners paused here, the landscape demanding appreciation—the full expanse of the lagoon to the north, the rugged coastline stretching away to the west, and directly below, the powerful convergence of lagoon and ocean through the narrow channel.

"Five-minute water break," Luke announced. "The descent to the cave is steep—watch your step, maybe slow down a little."

The descent from the Western Head proved as challenging as promised. Several runners adopted a cautious side-stepping technique on the steepest sections, while the more confident bounded downward with controlled momentum.

Near the bottom, the path leveled out, revealing a dramatic sea cave carved into the base of the cliff by centuries of waves. During high tide, the cave would be partially submerged, but the current water level allowed the group to enter the cool, echoing space.

"This cave's got a fascinating history," Luke explained as runners gathered inside the natural chamber. "Local legend says it once sheltered escaped slaves in the 1800s. More recently, it was used by smugglers during apartheid to move contraband past customs."

The Donovans exchanged a glance at this information, a micro-expression of interest passing between them before they resumed their neutral demeanors.

Emerging from the cave, the path turned northward, following the eastern edge of the lagoon through a landscape of weathered rocks and hardy coastal vegetation. Sections of the trail now required careful navigation as the rising tide had submerged portions, creating knee-deep wading zones that slowed progress but added to the adventure.

During one such crossing, where runners needed to wade through thigh-deep water around a rocky outcropping, Nkosi noticed Kim deliberately drop behind most of the group. As the professor watched while navigating the deep section, he saw Kim produce her phone again, quickly photograph something on the distant shore, and zoom in to examine the image before pocketing the device.

The final kilometer of the run followed a more established trail through coastal forest before emerging onto a pristine, private beach. Protected from prevailing winds by surrounding cliffs, this secluded cove featured crystal-clear water and fine white sand. It was the perfect conclusion to their morning exertion.

"Welcome to East Head Beach," Luke announced as the group gathered on the shore. "The restaurant's just up those stairs for anyone ready for refreshments. For those looking to cool off, the lagoon waters here are perfect for swimming."

Most of the runners immediately moved toward the water, eager to cool their overheated bodies after the challenging route.

Others headed for the shade of umbrellas that had been set up along the beach, while a few walked toward the wooden staircase leading up to the restaurant perched on the cliff above.

After approximately twenty minutes, when most of the group had either settled on the beach or gone upstairs for refreshments, Kim and Kelly exchanged a look before beginning their ascent to the restaurant. Their timing seemed deliberate—occurring just as Luke was organizing an impromptu swimming race among the more competitive tourists.

The East Head Café occupied a prime position atop the cliff, its expansive deck offering unparalleled views across the lagoon to Knysna town and the distant mountains beyond. Known for excellent seafood and local wines, it was popular with both tourists and residents, its tables typically filled with diners appreciating what many considered the finest view in the region.

Inside, the restaurant featured nautical-themed décor—weathered wood, blue and white color schemes, and vintage photographs of the lagoon throughout its history. Large windows maximized the panoramic vistas, while ceiling fans circulated the sea-scented air.

The Donovans entered casually, pausing at the host station, where a young woman greeted them with professional courtesy.

"Looking for the group buffet?" she inquired.

"Actually," Kim replied with practiced nonchalance, "I think we're meeting friends upstairs. In the private dining area."

The hostess consulted her tablet briefly. "Ah, yes. The Eagle's Nest reservation. They're already seated. Please, follow me."

She led them past the main dining area, where several of their fellow tourists were already enjoying cold drinks, through a discreet door marked "Private Function Room," and up a narrow staircase to the restaurant's uppermost level. This exclusive space, known locally as the Eagle's Nest for its commanding position, featured a separate deck and floor-to-ceiling windows offering a view of the Knysna Heads, the channel, and the open ocean beyond.

At the top of the stairs, the hostess paused before a heavy wooden door. "Your party's inside. Enjoy your lunch."

"Thank you," Kelly replied.

The hostess descended, leaving them alone on the small landing. Kim reached for the door handle but hesitated, turning to her partner first.

"Ready?" she asked quietly.

Kelly straightened her shoulders, all pretense of casualness falling away. "A million reasons to be," she answered, her accent suddenly crisper, more pronounced.

Kim nodded once, her expression hardening into something far removed from the affable persona she'd maintained throughout the tour. With deliberate movement, she opened the door, revealing the private dining room beyond—and the three men who awaited them.

Seated at a table positioned to capture both the spectacular view and clear sightlines to the door sat Malanga, impeccably dressed as usual. To his right stood Botha, whose massive arms were crossed over his chest, his expression impassive. The third man, positioned near the side entrance that led to the private deck, was Reggie. His calculating gaze assessed the Donovans as they entered.

"Ms. Donovan," Malanga greeted them, his cultured voice carrying just a hint of amusement. "Good to see you again after the vineyard. Please join me. We have much to discuss about your…investment portfolio."

As Kim closed the door behind them with a decisive click, the sounds of laughter and conversation from the tourists below faded away, replaced by the subtle but unmistakable tension of a high-stakes negotiation about to begin.

CHAPTER 20

FRACTURED NEGOTIATIONS

"Please sit," Malanga said, though his tone made it clear it wasn't really a request. He nodded to Reggie, who closed the balcony door and took up a position beside it, effectively controlling the room's second exit.

Kim remained standing, her jaw set with determination. "We need to talk about your payment."

Malanga's eyebrows rose slightly. "My payment was exactly as we agreed. Two million in cryptocurrency, fully transferable and untraceable."

"That's where you're wrong," Kelly said, her Manchester accent clipped with anger. "We accessed the wallet last night. There's only one million on that drive, not two."

A moment of silence stretched between them before Malanga smiled—a haughty expression that held no humor. "Ah. You discovered the adjustment."

"Adjustment?" Kim's voice rose with indignation. "You mean theft. You promised two million and delivered half that amount."

"I delivered what those diamonds are actually worth in the current underground market," Malanga replied evenly, settling back in his chair with the relaxed confidence of a man entirely in control. "Given the increased scrutiny from De Beers security and the heightened risk, one million is quite generous."

Kelly's face flushed with fury. "We had an agreement. Two million for the diamonds. You can't just change the terms after the fact."

"Can't I?" Malanga's tone turned dangerous. "You're in my country, selling stolen merchandise through my channels. I believe I can adjust the terms as I see fit."

Kim stepped forward, her fists clenched. "This is robbery. You're getting diamonds you can sell for three million while only paying pocket change for them."

Botha shifted his stance slightly, tensing at Kim's aggressive movement. Malanga held up one finger—a subtle command for his bodyguard to remain in place, for now.

"Miss. Donovan, I suggest you moderate your tone," Malanga advised. His voice dropped to a dangerous register. "And I suggest you honor our agreement. You received a generous payment as promised. Now, I'm here to collect what I purchased."

"What you underpaid for," Kelly corrected sharply. "Those diamonds are worth three million, and you know it."

"*Were* worth three million," Malanga countered. "In legitimate markets, to legitimate buyers. But you brought them to me because no legitimate buyer would touch them. The risk premium for stolen De Beers merchandise is significant."

Kim shook her head defiantly. "Not three-to-one significant. You're trying to steal from us."

"I'm trying to complete a business transaction," Malanga replied, and his patience was clearly wearing thin. "You have the cryptocurrency. I want the diamonds. Simple exchange, as agreed."

"No." The word came out flat and final. "We're keeping the diamonds until you pay what you promised. Two million, not one."

The temperature in the room seemed to drop several degrees. Malanga's relaxed posture shifted to something more predatory, while Botha's arms unfolded, ready to act.

"That's not how this works," Malanga said softly. "When I make a purchase, I complete the transaction. Always."

"Then, you should have paid the right amount," Kim shot back.

Malanga sighed with theatrical weariness. "Very well. Since you insist on making this difficult..." He nodded once to Botha.

The bodyguard moved with surprising speed for his size. Before Kim could react, Botha's fist drove into her sternum with blunt force—not a wild punch but a calculated strike to incapacitate her without visible external damage.

The sound that escaped Kim was part gasp, part cry of pain as her ribs gave way under the impact. She doubled over, clutching her chest, face contorted in agony as she struggled to draw breath.

"Kim!" Kelly screamed, lunging toward her partner. Her cry echoed through the room, loud enough to penetrate the floor below, where other diners paused momentarily in their conversations, glancing upward with curiosity.

Malanga remained seated, adjusting his cufflinks with apparent indifference to the scene unfolding before him. "Ms. Donovan, please control yourself. Hysterics will only complicate an already unfortunate situation."

Kelly helped Kim into a chair, her hands trembling as she supported her partner's weight. Kim's breathing came in shallow, pained gasps, each inhalation triggering a wince.

"You broke her ribs," Kelly hissed. Fury now replaced her initial shock. "Over a business disagreement?"

"I honor my commitments, Ms. Donovan," Malanga replied in a suddenly glacial tone. "Always. When I promise consequences for disrespect, I deliver those as well." He leaned forward slightly. "Now, the diamonds. Immediately."

Kim, still struggling to breathe normally, managed to speak through clenched teeth. "Kelly...don't..."

But the fight had gone out of Kelly. Faced with Botha's looming presence and Kim's obvious pain, her defiance crumbled. "They're...they're in the hotel safe," she admitted reluctantly.

"No, they're not," Reggie interjected from his position by the door. "You wouldn't risk leaving them where hotel staff might discover them. You have them with you."

Malanga's eyes narrowed. "Mr. Mbeki is correct. You're too wise to do something with such obvious risks. Where are they?"

Kelly's shoulders slumped in defeat. With trembling hands, she reached into a hidden pocket in her running hydration vest, extracting the same small, black pouch that Kim had shown at the vineyard.

"Excellent," Malanga said with satisfaction as Kelly placed the pouch on the table. "You see how much simpler things are when you just stick to our arrangement?"

Reggie stepped forward to collect the pouch, examining the contents with a jeweler's loupe to confirm the diamonds' authenticity. "Twenty-seven stones, the same that we tested at the vineyards," he confirmed.

"Outstanding." Malanga rose from his chair and straightened his jacket. "Our business is now truly concluded. The cryptocurrency payment remains yours—consider it fair compensation for your…cooperation."

Kim had recovered enough to sit upright, though her face remained pale with pain. "You're a thief," she whispered.

"I'm a businessman," Malanga corrected. "One who honors his commitments and expects others to do the same." He moved toward the balcony door. "Mr. Mbeki, shall we?"

The sound of rapid footsteps on the stairs outside caught everyone's attention. Reggie quickly secured the diamond pouch in an inner pocket while Botha moved toward the main door.

"Our time here is concluded," Malanga stated, gathering his composure. "I suggest you attribute Ms. Donovan's condition to an unfortunate fall. Medical assistance without police involvement would be in everyone's best interest."

The footsteps outside grew louder, followed by what sounded like a brief altercation with the hostess—a female voice insisting on access, the hostess protesting about private reservations.

"Ms. Donovan," Malanga added as he moved toward the balcony exit, "I trust you understand that further attempts to contact me or interfere with my business would be inadvisable. Enjoy the remainder of your tour."

The door handle turned just as Malanga and his associates slipped through the balcony exit, using the service staircase to disappear onto the service road below. Botha was the last to leave, pulling the door shut behind him as the main entrance burst open.

Anika rushed into the room with a determined expression. Her stance and alert assessment of the space showed that she wasn't just a busybody tourist. Quickly scanning for threats, she positioned her body to respond to potential danger.

"Where are they?" she demanded while taking in the scene: Kim hunched over in pain, Kelly standing protectively beside her, the balcony door still swinging shut.

Without waiting for an answer, Anika crossed to the balcony and yanked the door open, revealing the empty service stairs beyond. Malanga and his men had already vanished.

"Damn it," she muttered, returning her attention to the Donovans. "What happened here? I heard screaming."

"Kim fell," Kelly responded automatically, the lie sliding into place, despite her distress. "She hit the railing and hurt her ribs."

Anika's expression made it clear she didn't believe this explanation, but before she could challenge it, more footsteps sounded on the stairs. Moments later, Sheryl and Luke appeared in the doorway, both slightly breathless.

"What happened?" Sheryl asked, quickly assessing the situation. "We heard a commotion."

"Kim's injured herself," Anika replied. Her tone conveyed far more than her words. "Apparently from a fall."

The aftermath unfolded exactly as Malanga had predicted. Medical transport was called, police took their statements about the "accident," and the Donovans maintained their story, despite clear evidence of violence having taken place.

The transaction was complete, but justice remained elusive. And somewhere in the shadows of the South African criminal underworld, Malanga continued his operations, richer by millions of dollars in stolen diamonds and confident that his message about the consequences of crossing him had been clearly delivered.

CHAPTER 21

SUSPENDED BETWEEN WORLDS

Dawn broke over Plettenberg Bay in a cascade of coral and gold, illuminating the coastline in soft, forgiving light. The Plett Quarter Hotel buzzed with pre-run energy as members of Global Runners gathered in the lobby. Absent from the morning assembly were the Donovans, who remained in Knysna under medical observation.

Joan arrived in the lobby precisely five minutes before the scheduled departure, her punctuality a hallmark of her midwestern upbringing.

"Morning, Joan," Sheryl greeted her. "Sleep well?"

"Well enough," Joan replied with a slight smile. "Though, I could've done without the 3 a.m. call from my bank."

Sheryl raised an eyebrow. "Everything okay?"

Joan waved dismissively, but something tightened around her eyes. "Just an automated fraud alert. Someone tried accessing my account from Johannesburg. They didn't get in, but the call sure ruined my sleep."

Before Sheryl could inquire further, the lobby doors swung open, admitting a woman who moved with a confident stride. Her wild curls had been corralled into a messy bun, and her running gear featured splashes of impractical but infectious neon orange.

"Good morning!" she announced to the room at large. "Sorry if I'm cutting it close. Had to make sure my GoPro batteries were charged for today's zipline action," Wanda announced as she found her place in the group next to Joan and the Alvarez brothers.

"You're right on time," Luke assured her after checking his watch. "We're heading out in three minutes."

Wanda grinned with excitement. "Perfect. I can't wait for today."

Joan observed the other woman with an expression that hovered between amusement and mild disapproval when Wanda's hip rammed into hers in an excited gesture, perhaps with more force than was intended. "Someone's enthusiastic," she murmured to Madeline, who stood nearby.

"Thank goodness for that," Madeline replied. "After yesterday's drama, we could use some positive energy."

The group departed promptly at 7:30 AM, jogging at an easy warm-up pace from the hotel through the outskirts of Plettenberg Bay. The route soon led them away from beachfront developments and onto a tree-lined path marking the entrance to Harkerville Forest—a 250-acre sanctuary of indigenous trees representing one of the largest remaining patches of true Afromontane Forest along the Garden Route.

Luke assembled everyone at the trailhead for final instructions. "Today's run is six kilometers through moderate terrain. The first half climbs gradually through the forest to an escarpment overlooking the ocean. From there, we'll follow the cliff edge before descending to meet our zipline guides." He gestured to the canopy rising above them. "You'll be seeing this forest from above later. There are four ziplines that we'll be trying out that cross the gorge, with the longest span being nearly seven hundred feet."

Wanda's eyes lit up with anticipation. "Now we're talking," she said, bouncing slightly on her toes.

As the group moved deeper into the forest, the atmosphere shifted perceptibly. Sunlight filtered through the canopy in dappled patches. The air grew richer, heavy with the scent of damp earth and yellowwood trees. Birdsong echoed through the branches—the trills of forest canaries, the distinctive call of Knysna turacos, and the sounds of woodpeckers creating a natural symphony.

The trail began its gradual ascent, meandering between massive tree trunks and across small streams bridged by moss-covered logs. Conversation diminished as runners focused on negotiating roots and rocks that punctuated the path, each person finding their own rhythm.

Joan maintained a steady, economical pace near the middle of the pack. Unlike some who attacked hills with bursts of effort, she took her time and made sure that her breathing was controlled and her footfalls were precise and deliberate.

About two kilometers into the forest, the group encountered a massive yellowwood tree that stood like an ancient sentinel beside the path. Its trunk measured at least three meters in diameter, with gnarled roots spreading outward and covering the earth around it.

"This old giant is estimated to be over seven hundred years old," Luke explained as runners gathered around its massive circumference. "One of the few that escaped the colonial logging operations. At its peak, Knysna exported ship timber throughout the British Empire."

"I feel like I should whisper," Margaret commented, gazing upward at branches that disappeared into the canopy far above. "It's like being in a church somehow, like I'm witnessing a miracle."

"Beautiful wood," Joan observed while running her fingertips over the textured bark. "My ex-husband would've asked how much he could get for it, as if he could cut it down himself, instead of appreciating its beauty." Something in her tone suggested this difference in values hadn't been limited to forestry.

The group continued upward, the trail growing steeper as it approached the escarpment. Wanda showed no signs of fatigue. She moved with the fluid confidence of someone entirely comfortable in her body, and she occasionally broke into a faster-paced jog. Soon, the trail opened before her, but she decided to pause and wait for the others, barely breathing hard.

"You run professionally?" Jack asked when he caught up, his question casual but his assessment professional.

"Rock climb, mostly," Wanda replied. "Plus, my job forces me to be in pretty good shape." She grinned. "Can't exactly do a convincing rooftop chase scene if you can't catch your breath."

"Stunt work sounds dangerous," Joan commented after arriving at their resting spot with measured breaths.

"Physically hard," Wanda corrected. "Everything's planned, rehearsed, and safety-checked." She gestured toward the trail ahead. "Shall we?"

When they finally emerged onto the cliff edge, the view snatched away whatever breath remained after the climb—the Indian Ocean stretched endlessly beyond two dramatic cliffs, waves breaking far below against jagged rocks.

"Wow, I can't believe how beautiful it is," Rogerio declared, his hands on his knees as he recovered from the ascent.

Wanda assessed the trail ahead of them, noting the aggressive descent and frequent switchbacks of the mountain bike trail they'd be following.

The group stretched into a line to proceed once everyone had made it. Ahead, the trail emerged once more from the trees, revealing an open park that served as the operating base for SA Zip-Adventures.

"The longest zipline crosses nearly the entire gorge," Luke explained, gesturing toward a deep ravine that cut through the forest below, opening to the sea. "You'll hit speeds up to eighty kilometers per hour with nothing between you and a two-hundred-meter drop but a harness and cable."

"Outstanding," Wanda enthused, already scanning the distant cables visible between the trees.

"Is it safe?" Joan asked, peering somewhat dubiously at the distant lines.

"Completely," Luke assured her. "The system's rated for weights far exceeding any of ours, with multiple safety features. The company's operated for fifteen years without a single serious incident."

Joan positioned herself at the platform's edge, gazing not at the ziplines but at the ocean beyond.

Sheryl approached to offer her a water bottle. "You're looking contemplative."

Joan seemed to consider the question before shaking her head. "Just the universe reminding me that planning only gets you so far. Sometimes, life throws unexpected challenges—or opportunities—your way." She capped her water bottle with a decisive twist. "Anyway, enough about that. We've got flying to do, don't we?"

Staff in matching forest-green uniforms greeted them with professional enthusiasm, holding clipboards with liability waivers and harnesses awaiting distribution.

After completing paperwork and a brief safety orientation, the group was divided into smaller cohorts of six, each assigned to a guide. Wanda, unsurprisingly, volunteered immediately when the lead instructor asked for the first participants. Joan, somewhat unexpectedly, joined the initial group along with Nkosi, Rogerio, and the Alvarez brothers.

"Honestly, at this point, I just want to get it over with," Joan explained when Madeline expressed surprise at her eagerness.

The first platform stood about fifteen meters above the forest floor, accessed via a wooden staircase that ended in empty space. The initial zipline stretched 120 meters across a relatively shallow section of the gorge—a "warmup" run, according to their guide, designed to acclimatize participants to the sensation before the more dramatic crossings to follow.

"Who wants to go first?" the guide asked of the first group after demonstrating the proper body position and braking technique.

"Is that a real question?" Wanda laughed, already stepping forward. "See you on the other side, guys!"

The guide checked her harness connections, attached her trolley to the cable, and gave last instructions before stepping back. Wanda flashed a megawatt smile to the group, offered a theatrical salute, and launched herself from the platform with an exuberant whoop that echoed through the gorge.

The others watched as she zipped across the open space, her form textbook-perfect—body streamlined, legs raised at the best angle for maximum speed. Upon reaching the opposite platform, she executed a flawless landing, turning immediately to wave encouragement to those waiting.

"She's definitely done this before," the guide commented with a nod of appreciation.

Joan volunteered to go next, approaching the edge with calm determination rather than Wanda's exuberance. She listened attentively to the guide's reminders, took a deep breath, and stepped deliberately off the platform.

Her journey across the gap lacked Wanda's athletic flair, but that didn't matter to Joan. It only mattered that she had done it at all. Upon landing, her expression transformed into one of surprised delight.

"That was actually…fun," she admitted, sounding almost bemused by the discovery.

The remaining four completed their crossings with varying degrees of enthusiasm and technique, ranging from Rogerio's white-knuckled determination to Derek's unexpected talent at filming himself while flying through the air.

From the second platform, the true scale of the zipline course became apparent. The gorge deepened dramatically, with subsequent lines crossing increasingly vertiginous drops. The fourth line—dubbed "The Abyss" by the operation's marketing department—traversed the gorge's widest point nearly two hundred meters above the boulder-strewn stream below.

"This is where visitors either find religion or lose their lunch," their guide joked as they approached the platform. "You'll reach maximum speed here—about eighty kilometers per hour if you position yourself correctly."

Wanda, predictably, couldn't wait. "Any chance I could hang upside down on this one?" She asked, her expression hopeful.

"Absolutely not," the guide replied firmly. "Safety protocols apply to everyone, even stuntwomen."

Wanda shrugged, then secured her helmet camera to capture what promised to be the most spectacular crossing. "Worth a try."

When her turn came, she approached the edge with theatrical reverence, making a show of peering into the depths below. "If I don't make it," she announced to the others with mock solemnity, "tell my stunt director I stuck the landing, anyway."

Once again, Wanda nailed the form, and her journey across went as smoothly as possible. Her landing was so precise that it drew applause from the waiting staff on the opposite platform.

Joan shook her head with reluctant admiration. "She's something else, isn't she?"

Unlike Wanda's, Joan's crossing had a quality of surrender to it—not fighting the experience but allowing it to happen, her body relaxing into the harness as the wind rushed past her face. Her landing was not technically perfect, but she still had a huge smile on her face when she was done.

"That was…" she began, then seemed at a loss for words.

"Freeing?" Wanda suggested with knowing recognition.

"Exactly," Joan agreed, something shifting behind her eyes. "Like all the spreadsheets and paperwork and worries just…" She made a gesture of release with her hands.

"That's why people pay good money to do things like this." Wanda grinned. "Temporary escape from gravity—and everything else weighing us down."

Throughout the four crossings, the group's confidence and enjoyment visibly increased, with even the most hesitant participants finding unexpected pleasure in the activity.

When every zipline was completed, they settled onto wooden benches with plates of local cheese, fresh bread, and dried fruits in front of them. Conversation bubbled with the peculiar bonding energy that followed such a shared adventure. Even Joan participated more actively, her earlier preoccupations seemingly set aside in the afterglow of adrenaline.

"I haven't felt that kind of freedom since…" She paused, searching for the comparison. "Since I drove away from my divorce lawyer's office five years ago."

"Liberation comes in many forms," Nkosi observed philosophically. "Physical experiences like ziplines just make the sensation more immediate and undeniable."

"Some people chase that feeling their whole lives," Wanda added, having already finished her lunch. "In my profession, we call it a 'wire high'—that clarity that comes when you're suspended between earth and sky with nothing but your skill and equipment keeping you alive."

Joan considered that as she absently toyed with her water bottle. "I've always been the risk-averse person—the one who runs the numbers before making a move. Today felt like… stepping outside that mold."

"Did you like the view from out there?" Wanda asked with curious intensity.

"Strangely, yes," Joan admitted. "Though, it contradicts my self-image as the responsible one."

Wanda laughed. "The responsible ones often make the best daredevils—they just need permission to try."

Wanda found herself walking alongside Joan, the unlikely pairing of professional risk-taker and cautious accountant continuing their earlier exchange.

"So, what's next on your bucket list after flying through a South African gorge?" Wanda asked.

Joan seemed to consider the question seriously. "I've always wanted to see the Northern Lights. Something about a natural phenomenon that can't be scheduled or controlled appeals to me."

"The universe laughs at our schedules," Wanda agreed. "That's what makes the best adventures—you can prepare for them, but you can't script them."

"A philosophy that would've served me well these past few months," Joan murmured, almost to herself.

By mid-afternoon, as Sheryl had promised, the group returned to the Plett Quarter Hotel. The day's exertion and excitement had created a collective mood of satisfied fatigue, with many tourists planning to enjoy the hotel's amenities before dinner. Joan excused herself immediately, citing the need to make some calls during American business hours, her earlier lighthearted mood giving way once more to preoccupation.

As she disappeared into the elevator, Wanda watched her go with thoughtful attention. "Interesting woman," she commented to Sheryl. "There's a lot more going on there than she lets on."

"Most people have hidden depths," Sheryl replied neutrally.

"Today was fun, but I'm already looking forward to tomorrow's adventures. What're we doing?"

"Robberg Peninsula," Sheryl answered. "One of the most dramatic coastal trails in South Africa—a narrow isthmus with ocean on both sides, seal colonies, ancient caves, and if we're lucky, dolphins or even whales visible from the cliffs."

"Perfect." Wanda's eyes lit with anticipation. "I'll make sure my camera batteries are fully charged." With a casual wave goodbye, she headed for the stairs rather than waiting for the elevator, taking them two at a time.

Sheryl watched her go, mentally filing away observations about both Wanda and Joan. As the afternoon light softened toward evening, casting long shadows across Plettenberg Bay, Sheryl contemplated the state in which they all currently existed: suspended between what they knew and what remained hidden, between safety and danger, between the controlled environment of a tourist experience and the unpredictable realities of the criminal world that had begun to intersect with their journey.

CHAPTER 22

DIVERGING PATHS

The rooftop terrace of the Plett Quarter Hotel offered a spectacular sunset view over Plettenberg Bay. Most of the tour group had gathered for pre-dinner drinks, the day's zipline adventures providing animated conversation as servers circulated with trays of wines and canapés.

Sheryl stood slightly apart from the main gathering, appreciating the vista but actually conducting a headcount—a habit that had intensified since the incidents at Ashford Estates and the East Head Café. Everyone appeared accounted for except the still-absent Donovans, Anika, and Jack, the latter two having requested a brief meeting in the hotel's small business center adjacent to the lobby.

After ensuring Luke had the group well in hand, Sheryl made her way downstairs. The business center—a modest room with a conference table, two computer workstations, and a printer—offered the privacy they needed for conversations that couldn't risk being overheard by curious tourists.

She found Anika and Jack already waiting, their expressions suggesting the conversation had begun without her. Anika stood near the window, her arms crossed, while Jack occupied a chair at the table, his posture relaxed but attentive.

"Sorry I kept you waiting," Sheryl said before closing the door firmly behind her.

"Not at all," Anika replied, her tourist persona entirely absent. The woman who stood before Sheryl now was clearly the professional De Beers security agent—focused, direct, and visibly impatient. "I was just explaining to Jack that we need to leave the tour group for a day."

"I figured as much," Sheryl acknowledged, taking a seat across from Jack. "The diamonds?"

Anika nodded crisply. "First, we need to grab the Donovans before they disappear with whatever payment they got from Malanga. Second, recover the stolen diamonds, which are presumably now in Malanga's possession." She began pacing the small room with controlled energy. "I can't do either while maintaining my cover with the tour group."

"The Donovans' 'accident' creates a natural opportunity," Jack added. "We can say Anika's leaving to help them out."

Anika stopped pacing and leaned against the conference table. "The point is, we need to move now. The Donovans finished their deal with Malanga, but they're vulnerable—Kim's injury gives us both a way to limit their movements and a reason for law enforcement to get involved."

"And the police already have them on their radar after the accident," Jack added.

Anika nodded. "I've contacted a Detective Molefe in Knysna. He'll meet us at the hospital where the Donovans were treated. Once they're in custody, we can search for more proof about Malanga's involvement."

"What about the diamonds themselves?" Sheryl asked. "They're with Malanga now, right?"

"That's phase two," Anika confirmed. "Once we've got the Donovans secured, we'll find Malanga."

Sheryl considered the implications. "That's fine with me. You have our schedule. You can rejoin us at any point on the tour."

Anika gathered her small backpack, which Sheryl now noticed contained more tactical equipment than tourist essentials. "We'll contact you as soon as we know what's happening with the Donovans."

With brief handshakes and nods, they parted with Anika and Jack heading for the hotel's side entrance where their rental car waited and Sheryl returning upstairs to focus on her actual job.

CHAPTER 23

LOCAL ASSISTANCE

The drive from Plettenberg Bay to Knysna took about forty minutes along the N2 highway, winding through forested hills and across lagoon bridges. Sunset had given way to dusk, the sky deepening to indigo as Anika navigated the rental car aggressively.

"You're annoyed that the company didn't trust you to handle this alone," Jack said.

A small smile flickered across her face, despite her attempt to maintain a professional distance. "Fine. I'll admit that my professional pride was wounded. Now, can we talk about the Donovans?"

Jack settled back in his seat. "The Donovans, yeah. They've been on De Beers' radar for nearly six months, right? Since the initial inventory problems at Venetia?"

"Eight months," Anika corrected. "The thefts were sophisticated—small quantities of high-value rough stones, mostly Type IIa diamonds with exceptional clarity potential. Kelly manipulated the security system using her position in quality assessment to bypass several safeguards, but not all of them."

"And Kim?"

"External logistics. She arranged transportation and buyer contacts through her import export business connections." She navigated around a slower vehicle with precision. "What wasn't clear until recently was their connection to Malanga."

"Malanga's main business has been wildlife products," Jack noted. "Diamonds are fresh territory for him."

"Not uncommon in sophisticated smuggling operations," Anika replied. "The infrastructure for moving contraband works for different products."

They reached the outskirts of Knysna as full darkness settled over the Garden Route. The town's lights reflected in the still waters of the lagoon, creating an almost mirror-image effect that belied the tensions simmering beneath the surface.

Knysna Private Hospital occupied a modern, three-story building on the eastern edge of town. Despite the late hour, the facility remained well lit and active, its small emergency department serving the surrounding communities. Anika parked in the visitor section, and they proceeded to the main entrance where Detective Sergeant Molefe awaited them.

Molefe cut an unassuming figure in plain clothes—medium build, closely cropped hair, and observant eyes that assessed them as they approached. Only the subtle bulge of a service weapon beneath his jacket and his alert posture hinted at his law enforcement role.

"Ms. Elsen," he greeted Anika with a brief handshake. "And Mr. Hunter. I'm curious about your story."

"Thanks for meeting us, Detective," Anika replied. "Has there been any change in the Donovans' status?"

Molefe's expression tightened slightly. "That's our first problem. They're no longer here."

"They've been discharged?" Jack asked.

"Not officially," Molefe confirmed, leading them toward a side corridor away from the main reception area. "According to hospital records, Ms. Donovan was scheduled for additional imaging to check the extent of her rib fractures. She never showed up for the procedure. When staff checked their room, they found it empty. Personal stuff gone, the bed hadn't been touched since last night's rounds."

Anika's posture stiffened. "They left with no formal discharge or medical clearance?"

"Sometime between midnight and 5 a.m., based on what staff saw," Molefe confirmed. "I've already put out alerts with border control, airports, and car rental agencies, but they've got about a fifteen hours' head start on us."

"Damaged ribs would limit their mobility," Jack observed. "They couldn't have gone far without significant pain for Kim."

"Unless they decided escape was more important than comfort," Anika countered. "Did they leave any clues as to where they were going?"

"Nothing obvious," Molefe replied, "though I've only done a quick look at their room. Maybe you'd like to see it? Your familiarity with them might reveal stuff I missed."

He led them to an elevator and up to the second floor, down a quiet corridor to a room marked 214. The space had the antiseptic uniformity of hospital accommodations worldwide—a single adjustable bed, visitor chair, small bathroom, and minimal storage. The bed had been stripped of linens, presumably by housekeeping after discovering the patient's departure.

Anika moved methodically through the space, examining the bedside table, bathroom counter, and closet area with professional thoroughness. "No documentation left behind," she noted. "No medication containers, papers, or personal stuff. They were careful."

Anika completed her inspection, finding nothing of investigative value. "They're running, which confirms they're guilty but makes our recovery efforts harder." She turned to Molefe. "I need to fill you in completely on the diamond theft case. What they stole, the confirmed deal with Malanga, and the evidence we've gathered thus far."

Molefe gestured toward the door. "Let's continue this conversation somewhere more appropriate. My office is nearby."

Twenty minutes later, they were seated in Detective Molefe's modest office at the Knysna Police Service headquarters—a space that reflected its occupant's personality with neatly organized files, minimal personal effects, and a large map of the region dominating one wall.

Anika had provided a comprehensive briefing on the Venetia Mine theft, including Kelly's position in quality control that had allowed her to bypass security, the gradual accumulation of rough diamonds over several months, and the estimated value.

"The Donovans used the Global Runners tour as a cover for their planned deal with Malanga," she explained, displaying the documented proof she had collected on her tablet. "We think their meeting at the café resulted in the diamond transfer, though we guess Malanga underpaid them."

"Which would explain the fight that resulted in Kim's injuries," Molefe noted. "The medical report showed impact trauma consistent with a direct blow, not a fall like they claimed."

"Exactly," Anika agreed. "I was there when Malanga paid them with crypto on a memory stick during their first meeting at the winery. He claimed it was two million. They didn't believe him. Hence, the second meeting after they'd confirmed the contents of the stick. I'd guess something went wrong with that deal."

Molefe leaned back in his chair, processing the information. "So, we've got confirmed diamond theft from Venetia Mine, smuggling of said diamonds into the Western Cape, and a deal with a known wildlife trafficker." He made notes in a small notebook.

"The Donovans are flight risks with resources to leave the country," Anika emphasized. "And Malanga now has diamonds worth millions."

"I've already put out a watch notice on the Donovans," Molefe assured her. "Their passport info is flagged at all border crossings and airports. As for Malanga…" He paused, a thoughtful expression crossing his face. "That's both a challenge and an opportunity."

"How so?" Jack asked.

Molefe turned to the wall map, indicating a location near the Knysna waterfront. "Malanga keeps an office here in Knysna—a legitimate business front for Ashford Estate's wine. It's one of several properties he owns throughout the region."

"You've had him under surveillance?" Anika asked with professional interest.

"Of course. Everyone knows who he is. But we need actual evidence in order to convict him," Molefe acknowledged. "He's careful. Previous investigations haven't given us enough evidence for warrants. However…" He tapped the map thoughtfully. "The diamond connection changes things. This is something big we haven't had before."

"You think the diamonds might be at his Knysna office?" Jack asked.

"It's possible they're moving through that location," Molefe replied. "Malanga typically moves contraband quickly, using a network of couriers and temporary storage locations."

Anika exchanged a look with Jack. "We need to get there—now."

"Agreed." Molefe nodded. "I can set up surveillance of the office location while processing an expedited warrant request based on the info you've provided."

"How long for the warrant?" Jack asked.

"Under normal circumstances, twenty-four hours," Molefe admitted. "However, given the value of the assets and flight risk, I might be able to rush it through a magistrate I know. Maybe by morning."

"And until then?" Anika pressed.

"Observation only," Molefe stated firmly. "I get your urgency, Ms. Elsen, but procedural violations could mess up the entire case. South African courts do pay close attention to proper evidence gathering, you know."

Anika's frustration was evident, though she didn't let it out. She knew Molefe was just doing his job. "Every hour increases the chance that the diamonds move beyond our reach."

"I know," Molefe said. "Which is why I'm suggesting that we start surveillance immediately, while I work on the warrant. If we see clear evidence of more criminal activity, it could give us grounds for immediate action."

Jack nodded. "Reasonable compromise. Where exactly is this office?"

Molefe indicated a position on the Knysna Quays—an upscale waterfront development featuring shops, restaurants, and office space catering to both tourists and legitimate businesses. "Second floor, above an art gallery. The location has multiple access points—main entrance from the waterfront promenade, service entrance at the rear, and potential water access via a private dock."

"Good choice of location," Jack observed.

"Malanga's nothing if not thorough," Molefe agreed. "His legitimate operations provide excellent cover for his smuggling activities. The wine business justifies all of his international shipments, frequent travel, and financial transactions that might otherwise trigger scrutiny."

"I'd like to see the location," Anika stated, her tone making it clear it wasn't a request.

Molefe checked his watch. "It's nearly 9 p.m. The commercial areas of the waterfront will be busy with evening diners and shoppers—good cover for reconnaissance, but Malanga's people might still be there."

"We should be able to blend into the tourist traffic," Jack pointed out.

Molefe considered this point briefly before nodding. "All right. We'll do a discreet drive-by, followed by a walking assessment if conditions permit. But I have to emphasize that it's observation only unless we see undeniable proof of a crime being committed. My department's been building a case against Malanga for nearly two years. I won't jeopardize it, even it means recovering millions of dollars' worth of diamonds."

"Understood." Anika nodded, though her tone suggested less than wholehearted acceptance.

As they prepared to leave, Molefe's phone rang. He answered, listening intently before responding with brief professional acknowledgments. When he hung up, his expression shifted subtly.

"Interesting development," he told them. "A hotel in George reported a couple matching the Donovans' description checking in about three hours ago. The desk clerk recognized them from the alert bulletin and contacted us after they'd gone to their room."

"George?" Jack questioned. "That's moving away from any international departure options."

"But closer to regional airports with connections to Johannesburg," Anika noted. "They could be planning a multi-hop exit."

"I can send officers to confirm their identity," Molefe said. "If it's them, we'll have them within the hour."

"And the USB drive?" Anika pressed.

"Will be secured as evidence and documented," Molefe assured her. "Assuming it's recovered during the search."

Anika nodded. "How far is George from here?"

"About sixty kilometers," Molefe replied. "Do you want to go there instead of the waterfront?"

Anika and Jack exchanged a brief look, weighing their options.

"No," Jack suggested. "The Donovans can be easily handled by your officers. Our primary concern is the diamonds."

"Agreed," Anika confirmed after a moment's consideration. "We'll stick with the Knysna waterfront reconnaissance as planned."

Molefe nodded his approval of their decision. "I'll go to George to oversee the capture. You can meet my recon team at Malanga's office here in Knysna."

As they left the police headquarters, the detective offered one final observation. "You should know that Malanga's network extends into unexpected places. His financial resources have bought influence throughout the region—not just with criminals, but sometimes with people who should be beyond influence."

"You're suggesting official corruption?" Anika asked directly.

"I'm suggesting discretion in who you trust with operational details," Molefe replied carefully.

The implication hung in the air as Anika and Jack drove toward the waterfront, the glittering lights of Knysna's tourist district reflecting off the dark waters of the lagoon—beautiful and inviting on the surface, but concealing unpredictable currents beneath.

CHAPTER 24

DISAPPEARING CRYPTO

The modest hotel on the outskirts of George presented an unremarkable façade—three stories of beige stucco with a small, illuminated sign and a parking lot half-filled with rental cars and tourist minibuses. Located about sixty kilometers inland from Knysna, the town of George served primarily as a transportation hub for the Garden Route, housing the region's main airport and serving as a connection point to South Africa's interior.

Molefe observed the building from across the street, his expression revealing nothing as he coordinated positions with the local George Police Service officers who had joined the operation. Four uniformed officers and two plainclothes detectives had taken positions covering all potential exits, while hotel management had quietly provided access to the building's security systems and room information.

"Room 317," Molefe confirmed over his secure radio. "Third floor, east wing. Front desk confirms two guests matching subject descriptions checked in at 17:45 using passports consistent with the Donovans' identities. No departures observed since check-in."

"Copy that," responded Detective Constable Kani, who was positioned in the hotel lobby in casual attire that allowed her to blend with other guests. "Elevator and main stairwell under observation. Service stairwell secured."

Molefe checked his watch—just past 22:30. The timing was deliberate, selected to maximize the chance that the subjects would be in their room but not yet asleep. Hotel staff had confirmed a room service delivery about ninety minutes earlier, suggesting the Donovans were still there.

"All units in position and ready," came the final confirmation from the tactical team leader.

Molefe gave a single nod, though no one could see it. "Proceed with standard arrest protocol. Subjects may be injured but aren't considered dangerous."

With casual efficiency that belied the relative rarity of such operations in the quiet town of George, the officers moved into position. Two uniformed officers secured the elevator on the third floor while two plainclothes detectives approached Room 317 from opposite ends of the hallway. Detective Constable Kani joined them, positioning herself slightly behind and to the side of the door, ready to enter once access was gained.

Detective Molefe arrived last, taking command position with clear sightlines to both the room entrance and the hallway beyond. He gave a final nod of readiness, and the senior detective stepped forward to knock firmly on the door.

"Hotel services, Ms. Donovan," he called in a neutral tone designed to avoid triggering suspicion. "We've got a nightcap and chocolates for you."

A moment of silence followed, then shuffling sounds could be heard from within the room. The security peephole darkened briefly as someone looked through it from inside, followed by a muffled conversation too quiet to make out clearly.

"Just a moment, please," came a quiet voice—Kim Donovan's accent unmistakable even through the door.

Molefe raised three fingers, silently counting down for his team. As the lock disengaged from inside and the door opened, he gave the "go" signal.

"South African Police Service," the lead detective announced clearly, pushing the door wider as he displayed his identification. "Please stay where you are."

Kim Donovan stood frozen in the doorway, her expression cycling rapidly from confusion to recognition to resignation. She was dressed in casual clothes—khaki shorts and a matching shirt. Her movements appeared stiff, consistent with the rib injury reported from the East Head Café incident.

"What's going on?" she asked, her tone suggesting she already knew the answer.

"Kimberly Donovan, we're placing you under arrest on suspicion of theft, smuggling of restricted goods, and customs violations," Molefe stated formally, stepping into the room as the other officers secured the doorway and hallway. "You have the right to remain silent. Anything you say can be used against you in court. You have the right to an attorney…"

As Molefe continued reciting the required rights, his practiced eye surveyed the hotel room's interior. Kelly Donovan sat rigidly on the edge of one of the twin beds, her expression a careful, blank mask. On the small table between the beds was a laptop computer and, beside it, incongruously prominent, a red USB drive.

"…Do you understand these rights as I've explained them to you?" Molefe concluded.

Kim nodded stiffly. "I understand, but there's been some mistake. We haven't done anything wrong."

"We'll sort that out at the station," Molefe replied evenly. "Detective Constable Kani will now explain the procedure to your partner."

As Kani moved to the bedside to formally arrest Kelly, Molefe signaled to the evidence technician who had accompanied them. "Secure the electronic devices and any other potential evidence. Priority on any storage media or financial documentation."

The technician nodded, immediately putting on gloves before approaching the table where the USB drive sat. Its placement seemed almost deliberately obvious—directly in the center of the wooden surface rather than connected to any device.

Kim protested, her voice tightening. "This is all a misunderstanding."

"Both of you will have the chance to make statements once we've finished processing you at the station," Molefe replied, maintaining professional detachment.

As the officers secured the pair—applying handcuffs with consideration for Kim's injury—the evidence technician had begun documenting and collecting items from the room. The laptop was powered down using forensic protocols that preserved potential evidence.

"We'll need your personal stuff as well," Detective Kani informed the couple as she conducted a methodical search of Kelly's handbag. "Phones, wallets, ID, room key cards."

Throughout the process, the Donovans maintained a curious blend of concern and composure. They offered no resistance to the arrest procedures, yet both repeatedly emphasized their innocence in careful tones that struck Molefe as somewhat rehearsed.

"We were just resting after our accident," Kelly explained as Kani secured her personal items in evidence bags. "Kim fell at the restaurant in Knysna. Remember? We planned to rejoin our tour group tomorrow once she felt stronger."

"All of that can be addressed in your formal statements," Molefe reiterated, his attention caught by a signal from the evidence technician, who had stepped aside to examine the USB drive using a secure tablet.

"Sir," the technician said quietly, "preliminary scans show the drive is completely empty. Factory-reset with no recoverable data."

Molefe's expression remained neutral despite this unexpected development. "Continue your evidence collection and documentation. We'll do a full forensic analysis at the station."

As the Donovans were escorted from the room—Kim moving with careful deliberation that emphasized her injury—Molefe remained behind briefly with the evidence technician.

"Nothing at all on the drive?" he confirmed once the others were out of earshot.

"Completely wiped, sir," the technician replied, displaying the tablet screen that showed the drive's empty memory allocation table. "If there was ever anything on it, it's been professionally erased—not just deleted, but overwritten multiple times based on the disk health metrics."

Molefe considered this information, his detective's instincts sharpening. "The drive's placement was too obvious. They wanted us to find it."

"I think so," the technician agreed. "Now, we have to find where the data went that they didn't want us to find."

"Check the laptop thoroughly," Molefe instructed. "Focus on recently accessed sites, especially financial platforms or cryptocurrency exchanges. And pull their phone records as soon as we get the clearance."

As they finished securing the scene and prepared for transport to the George Police Station, Molefe made a brief call to update Anika and Jack, who had remained in Knysna observing Malanga's office.

"We've got the Donovans in custody," he reported succinctly. "No resistance during arrest. However, the USB drive we found in their room appears to have been wiped clean."

"Completely empty?" Anika's voice carried clear frustration, even over the phone.

"Professional-grade erasure," Molefe confirmed. "If it contained cryptocurrency access codes like you suspected, they're not on it anymore."

"They've transferred the funds," Jack's voice joined the call. "Standard procedure in cryptocurrency transactions—move the value from the delivery wallet to personal wallets immediately, then start breaking the trail through multiple conversion transactions."

"Can it be traced?" Molefe asked.

"Maybe," Anika replied, though her tone suggested limited optimism. "Depends on which cryptocurrency was used and how sophisticated their conversion path was. Blockchain transactions leave records, but following them requires specialized expertise and often international cooperation."

"I'll submit requests for financial forensics support from our cybercrime division," Molefe decided. "Meanwhile, we'll proceed with a standard interrogation once we've processed them at the station."

After concluding the call, Molefe joined the rest of the team at the transport vehicles. The Donovans had been placed in separate police cars to prevent the coordination of stories before formal questioning. Both maintained neutral expressions, though Molefe noted Kim's occasional wince when she moved a certain way.

The short drive to the George Police Station proceeded without incident, passing through the quiet streets of the small city where few pedestrians remained at this hour. The station itself was illuminated against the night sky, its concrete architecture softened somewhat by landscaped native plants.

Photographs, fingerprints, documented inventory of personal possessions, and medical assessment of Kim's injury to ensure proper care during detention were all completed to cover their bases. Throughout these procedures, both women maintained their calm assertion of innocence, neither becoming confrontational nor requesting legal representation—a behavior pattern Molefe found intriguing given the circumstances.

By midnight, preliminary processing had been completed, and the Donovans were placed in separate interview rooms while the evidence team began their technical analysis of the seized devices. Molefe took a moment to review the case notes before beginning formal questioning, focusing particularly on the timeline of events leading to the East Head Café incident and their subsequent disappearance from the hospital.

Kani joined him in the small observation room that connected to the interview suites. "Technical division has started analysis of their phones and laptop," she reported. "Preliminary findings suggest heavy internet activity about three hours after they checked into the Knysna hotel."

"Cryptocurrency transactions?"

"Multiple encrypted connections to financial platforms," Kani confirmed. "They're still working to identify specific destinations, but the timing and pattern are consistent with a money transfer."

Molefe nodded, adding these details to his interview plan. "I'll start with Kim Donovan. Her injury might make her more willing to talk, especially if she thinks cooperation could get her more comfortable accommodations."

The interview room presented a deliberately neutral environment—a simple table with chairs, overhead lighting bright enough for clear video recording but not harsh enough to constitute discomfort, and minimal distractions. Kim Donovan sat with a carefully controlled posture. Her expression was composed, despite the circumstances.

"Ms. Donovan," Molefe began after formal introductions and confirmation that the interview was being recorded, "I'd like to clear up some details about your recent activities, particularly what happened at East Head Café in Knysna and where you went afterward."

The discussion moved from the supposed incident at the café, through the hospital visit, and the move to George. Molefe also asked about Anika's accusations of smuggling and selling diamonds.

Kim answered every question calmly and without hesitation, as if she'd already planned out how she'd explain all of it.

Molefe was getting frustrated by the alternative explanations for everything, especially as he started to realize that, without the cryptocurrency, they had no real evidence of criminal activity. He could see the opportunity for a conviction slipping through his fingers.

As Molefe left the George Police Station, the night sky had cleared, revealing the brilliant southern stars that somehow appeared more numerous and brighter over the Garden Route than in South Africa's urban centers. The beauty provided a stark contrast to the complex criminal web they were untangling—a web that stretched from the diamond fields of the northern provinces to the coastal tourist havens of the south, connecting international smuggling and organized crime beneath the surface of South Africa's picture-perfect destinations.

The Donovans had successfully converted their payment to virtually untraceable cryptocurrency, but their freedom had been cut short. Though, without concrete evidence, the Donovans would soon walk away free. Meanwhile, the diamonds themselves—the physical evidence that could conclusively link Malanga to international smuggling operations—remained at large, possibly in transit at that very moment through Malanga's Knysna office.

As Molefe's vehicle accelerated onto the N2 highway for the return journey to Knysna, he knew that the next few hours would likely determine whether his and Jack and Anika's parallel investigations ended in partial success or complete failure.

CHAPTER 25

SURVEILLANCE ACCELERATED

The commercial district of Knysna after business hours presented a study in contrasts—the waterfront area still animated with tourists enjoying dinner and entertainment, while just two blocks inland, office buildings stood dark and deserted. This transitional zone between the tourist hotspot and the everyday business center provided ideal cover for surveillance operations, offering multiple vantage points with plausible reasons for lingering after hours.

Anika adjusted her position in the small coffee shop across from the Thesen Office Park, where Malanga Imports occupied a second-floor suite overlooking the Knysna Lagoon. The café had reduced its staff for the evening lull but remained open until 10 p.m., catering to the occasional tourist who wandered away from the more vibrant waterfront. With phone in hand and several notebooks spread across her table, Anika presented the perfect image of a business traveler catching up on work while enjoying a cappuccino.

Her phone's earbud crackled softly with Jack's voice. "Northeast corner still clear. No movement at the service entrance for the past forty minutes."

Jack had positioned himself in the rental car parked in the adjacent lot, offering sightlines to both the main and service entrances of the building. His cover—a man waiting to pick up someone working late—had already withstood cursory scrutiny from a passing security guard who had merely nodded and continued his rounds.

"Understood," Anika murmured. "Any word from Molefe?"

"Brief update. Molefe's tech guys said there were multiple data transfers from their computer. They think it was the crypto being moved."

Anika suppressed a frown. The Donovans had successfully moved their payment—not unexpected, given the ease of cryptocurrency transfers, but frustrating nonetheless. It meant that their only avenue to closing the case and prosecuting everyone involved would be irrefutable proof that Malanga had the diamonds in his possession.

Detective Molefe had provided the address of Malanga's office as a courtesy, expecting them to coordinate with his surveillance team already in position. Instead, upon arrival, they had decided to establish independent observation posts, reasoning that creating their own vantage points might provide them with a unique opening.

"Movement at the main entrance," Jack's voice interrupted her thoughts. "Silver Mercedes sedan approaching drop-off zone."

Anika casually adjusted her position, angling her chair to improve her view of the building's entrance while maintaining her businesswoman cover. The vehicle that pulled up matched Malanga's preferred mode of transportation—late model, darkly tinted windows, deliberately understated luxury that projected wealth without drawing excessive attention.

The driver's door opened first, revealing Botha, who surveyed the area with professional thoroughness before opening the rear passenger door. Malanga emerged, impeccably dressed as always, in a tailored suit that somehow remained unwrinkled, despite the late hour. A moment later, Reggie exited from the opposite side, carrying a slim briefcase and what appeared to be takeout food containers.

"Confirmed visual on all three primary subjects," Anika murmured, her pulse quickening, though she projected a calm demeanor. "Entering main lobby now."

"They wouldn't bring the diamonds to the office," Jack theorized, "unless they're planning an immediate move or transfer."

"Or they think it's the safest location precisely because it seems too obvious," Anika countered. "Either way, this is our first concrete lead on their location."

The three men disappeared into the building, Botha holding the door while scanning the street one final time before following the others inside. A light came on in the second-floor corner office about two minutes later.

"Second floor illuminated," Jack confirmed. "Matches known location of Malanga Imports suite. I'm repositioning for a closer look."

Anika watched through the café window as Jack exited his vehicle and casually crossed the street, phone to his ear as though taking an important call. He found a position in the shadow of a closed boutique that offered a clear view of the illuminated windows while remaining outside the building's security camera coverage.

"I see three distinct figures moving in the space," he reported after a moment.

Anika made a show of gathering her materials and settling her bill, establishing her imminent departure from the café in case anyone was observing her movements. "I'm coming to join you. It's time to decide on what to do next."

The official plan had been surveillance only—hopefully documenting Malanga's movements while awaiting Molefe's return with warrants and police support. However, the unexpected appearance of all three subjects, potentially with the diamonds in their possession, presented them with an opportunity that might not return.

Anika crossed the street via a different path than Jack had taken.

"Thought we were waiting for Molefe," Jack commented quietly as she joined him in the shadows, though his tone suggested he'd anticipated her decision.

"Change of plans," Anika replied. "The diamonds are almost certainly inside. This might be our only chance before they're moved beyond our reach."

Jack nodded once. "You should know I'm armed," he stated simply, indicating the concealed holster beneath his light jacket.

"Useful, though hopefully unnecessary. Our objective is evidence recovery, not a shootout."

"Agreed. Entry?"

Anika surveyed the building's access points, weighing their options against any potential risks. "Main entrance is likely unlocked. I didn't see them unlock or relock the doors when they entered. Service entrance would trigger alarms. Timing suggests they're settling in for a meeting rather than an immediate exit."

"The direct approach, then," Jack concluded.

They moved with purposeful confidence toward the main entrance—not hurrying, which might trigger suspicion, but walking with the assured stride of people with legitimate business in the building. The lobby featured minimal security after hours—the single desk normally staffed during business hours now stood vacant, with a visitor sign-in screen that no one monitored.

The door yielded to Jack's pull, confirming their assumption about easy access. Inside, the air conditioning maintained a cool environment that carried faint traces of cleaning products and coffee from the day's activities. A directory board showed Malanga Imports occupied suite 207, matching their intel.

They bypassed the elevator, opting instead for the stairwell that would allow a quieter approach. The staircase had concrete steps with metal railings, illuminated by always-on fluorescent fixtures that cast harsh shadows. Their footsteps, despite how carefully they walked, echoed slightly in the enclosed space.

On the second-floor landing, Anika paused, listening intently for any sounds that might indicate others being aware of their presence. Hearing nothing unusual, she eased the door open a few centimeters, revealing a carpeted hallway with offices on both sides. Light spilled from beneath a door at the far end, accompanied by the muted sounds of conversation—too distant to distinguish words, but clearly multiple male voices engaged in discussion.

They moved along the hallway with practiced stealth. As they approached the illuminated office, the conversation became clearer—Malanga's cultured tones contrasting with Reggie's more clipped speech patterns, while Botha's deep bass rumbled occasional monosyllabic responses.

"The dealer requires visual confirmation before finalizing arrangements," Malanga was saying as they reached the door.

"We could use the secure video link here," Reggie suggested. Then, Anika could hear the distinctive sounds of someone unpacking containers—likely the takeout food they had brought.

"Yeah, agreed. Set it up," Malanga replied.

The door stood slightly ajar—not enough to see through but sufficient to hear the conversation. Anika positioned herself on one side, Jack on the other, both listening intently.

"Two million is the floor for negotiation," Malanga continued. "Given the exceptional clarity of the larger stones, we should be able to command closer to two-point-five."

"Even after fees and laundering costs, that's still a million profit," Reggie noted with satisfaction. "Not bad for three days' work."

"Good profit margins on this new business," Malanga agreed.

The sound of a briefcase opening was followed by Malanga's satisfied exhale. "Beautiful specimens. The two larger stones alone would fetch over a million in legitimate markets."

Anika and Jack exchanged significant glances—confirmation that the diamonds were present in the room, likely displayed on the conference table Malanga had been preparing when they first observed the office from outside before entering the building.

"Sipho," Malanga's voice carried the easy authority of someone accustomed to unquestioned obedience, "run out and check the building perimeter again."

"Yes, sir," Botha's deep voice replied, followed by heavy footsteps approaching the door.

Anika and Jack had seconds to decide—retreat and risk losing their opportunity, or commit to immediate action. A rapid series of hand signals between them confirmed their mutual decision. Jack positioned himself opposite the door, prepared to intercept Botha, while Anika moved slightly further down the hallway to avoid immediate detection.

The door swung open, and Botha's frame filled the doorway. He stepped into the hallway, beginning to turn toward the stairwell—and froze as he registered Jack's presence in his peripheral vision.

The struggle that followed exemplified the choreographed precision of trained fighters. Botha pivoted with surprising speed for his size, his massive hands already forming fists as he recognized the threat in front of him. Jack moved simultaneously, closing the distance to negate Botha's considerable reach advantage.

The first exchange happened in near silence—Botha's powerful right hook missing as Jack ducked beneath it, countering with a swift strike to the larger man's solar plexus. The blow would've incapacitated an average opponent, but Botha merely grunted, his abdominal muscles absorbing much of the impact.

"Intruders!" Botha called out in a controlled voice that clearly carried into the office.

His warning delivered, Botha shifted to offensive tactics, launching a series of powerful strikes that forced Jack into defensive moves. Though outweighed by at least forty kilograms, Jack's military training was evident in his economy of motion—deflecting rather than blocking, using Botha's momentum against him when possible.

Anika didn't hesitate, using the distraction to slip past the struggling men and into the office. Inside, she found exactly what they had expected—a modern conference room dominated by an oval table, where the black velvet pouch containing the diamonds lay open, its contents glittering under recessed lighting.

Reggie reacted immediately, lunging across the table toward the diamonds, but Anika was faster. She feinted left before pivoting right, using her momentum to drive a precisely aimed strike to Reggie's descending arm. The blow connected at the brachial plexus—a nerve bundle that, when struck correctly, temporarily paralyzed the arm.

As expected, Reggie's arm went momentarily numb, his fingers unable to close around the pouch. He recovered quickly, however, shifting to place himself between Anika and the table. "You've made a serious mistake," he snarled, all pretense of sophistication abandoned.

"De Beers security doesn't make mistakes," Anika stated. "I'm taking those diamonds, Mr. Mbeki."

Reggie's response was physical rather than verbal—a rapid combination of strikes revealing an experienced street fighter. Anika parried the first two blows before absorbing a glancing hit to her shoulder. She countered with a sequence that blended Krav Maga and traditional boxing, driving Reggie backward with unexpected power from her compact frame.

In the hallway, the confrontation between Jack and Botha had escalated. The confined space limited Botha's ability to fully use his strength, while Jack's more technical approach created slight advantages. A particularly well-executed leg sweep sent Botha staggering into the wall, creating the opening Jack needed.

His hand moved efficiently to his concealed holster, drawing and presenting his sidearm in a single fluid motion. "Stay down," he commanded, his voice carrying the unmistakable authority of someone who wouldn't issue the instruction twice. "Hands where I can see them."

Botha, despite his imposing physicality, recognized the new situation immediately. He slowly raised his hands, though his expression promised future retribution if the opportunity presented itself.

Inside the office, Anika had maneuvered Reggie into a position that left the diamond pouch accessible. A quick feint drew his attention high while she executed a sweeping leg movement that compromised his balance. As he staggered, she delivered an elbow to his sternum—forceful enough to disrupt his breathing without causing lasting damage.

Reggie collapsed into a chair, gasping for air as Anika secured the diamond pouch with her left hand. Only then did she register the fact that Malanga was nowhere in the room.

A quick visual sweep confirmed that the office had a second exit, likely connected to adjacent suites. The door stood slightly ajar, evidence of Malanga's hasty but silent departure while she had dealt with Reggie.

Jack appeared in the doorway, his weapon still trained on Botha, who had moved to a kneeling position in the hallway as instructed. "Status?" he inquired tersely.

"Diamonds secure," Anika confirmed while holding up the velvet pouch. "But Malanga's gone."

Jack's expression tightened minutely. "The building's got multiple exits. He could be anywhere by now."

With the immediate situation secured, Jack asked, "Next steps?"

The answer echoed from the first-floor hallway. "Knysna Police! Who's here? Identify yourselves!"

Jack quickly holstered his pistol and pulled his shirt over it. No need to upset the legitimate authorities. He called out, "De Beers security agents in the conference room upstairs!"

He heard several pairs of feet climbing the stairs.

Botha had remained hyperaware of the situation. Seeing that Jack had holstered his pistol and become distracted by the arrival of the police, Botha bolted to his feet, pushed Jack aside, and ran for the same door that his boss had used. He was gone in a second.

Jack shouted, "Malanga's goon is running out the back exit!" The first of the police officers ran past Jack and followed Botha out the back door. The others gathered around the remaining three in the conference room.

Eyeing them suspiciously, the officer said, "I assume you two are the De Beers agents who Molefe said would be joining us. But you didn't do that, did you? You decided to take matters into your own hands." He was clearly unhappy with the events that had unfolded.

Anika held out her De Beers credentials. "But we recovered my company's stolen diamonds, which is what I was sent here to do. Malanga was here preparing to move them."

"You've got proof of that?" the officer asked, scanning the room for the well-known, but missing, crime kingpin.

Anika pointed to Reggie. "This is one of his guys."

Reggie's brow furrowed. "I'm not one of his 'guys.' I'm a legitimate employee of Malanga Imports. This is our office, and you're trespassing. We'll press charges."

The officer rolled his eyes. "Oh, please. We know who you are and what this office is. But let's say, just for one second, that we believe your little innocent act. Why are the stolen diamonds here?"

Reggie countered, "I don't know anything about that. She brought those with her."

"Sure, she did," the officer replied.

"I've done my job—recover the diamonds, catch the Donovans," Anika decided. "Malanga's a local law enforcement problem. He's lost both his payment to the Donovans and the diamonds. That's a success in my book."

Jack nodded in agreement.

Anika and Jack exchanged a look of professional acknowledgment. The mission had evolved significantly from their initial assignment, but the core objective had been achieved—the stolen diamonds recovered, one key suspect detained, and evidence linking the operation to an international smuggling network collected.

Malanga's escape remained the single significant failure—a dangerous loose end that would require future vigilance. Not a perfect operation, but in the complex world of international crime, perfection was rarely an achievable goal.

The real question now was what Malanga's next move would be—and how his wounded pride might lash out at those who had interfered in his business.

CHAPTER 26

SEAL MOUNTAIN

Morning arrived in Plettenberg Bay with perfect clarity—the kind of South African day that reminded visitors why the Garden Route deserved its reputation as one of the world's greatest coastal journeys. From the breakfast terrace of the Plett Quarter Hotel, the ocean stretched to the horizon in gradients of blue, while the distinctive shape of the Robberg Peninsula jutted into the sea like the prow of a massive stone ship.

Sheryl studied the peninsula through binoculars as she sipped her coffee, mentally tracing the hiking route they would follow that morning. The narrow finger of land extended into the Indian Ocean, its rocky spine rising dramatically from the water, creating sheer cliffs on the seaward side while sheltering a perfect crescent beach in its embrace. Even from this distance, she could make out the dark specks of seals gathered along the rocky shore of the peninsula.

Predictably, it was Madeline who approached Sheryl's table first, concern evident in her expression. "Any news about Kim's recovery?" she asked, setting down her plate of fresh fruit and yogurt. "Stanley and I thought about sending flowers."

"That's thoughtful of you," Sheryl replied, maintaining the established narrative. "From what Anika told me before she left, Kim's scheduled for another imaging visit."

"And Jack went with Anika, why?" Madeline pressed gently.

"You know, maybe Jack's hoping to be more than friends with Anika," Sheryl said and winked. It wasn't the cover they'd planned, but it was more interesting.

"Oh, juicy," Madeline said with a smile, always eager for some gossip. Before she could inquire further, Luke joined them, a welcome distraction clutched in his hands in the form of detailed trail maps for their morning hike.

As other tourists gathered around to examine the route, Sheryl ticked off names to make sure everyone was awake and ready for the adventure ahead of them.

"The complete circuit is about nine kilometers," Luke said, tracing the path with his finger. "We'll start at the car park here, climb to the ridge that forms the peninsula's spine, and follow it out toward the point. Along the way, we'll encounter five distinct ecosystems—coastal fynbos, aeolian dunes, a freshwater wetland, rocky shores, and the remarkable 'island' formation at the peninsula's center."

"Island?" Nkosi inquired with academic interest. "On a peninsula?"

Luke smiled. "A geological curiosity. During the last ice age, when sea levels were lower, the central section of Robberg was an actual island, separated from the mainland by a narrow channel. As sea levels rose, sand accumulation created a natural isthmus connecting it to the peninsula. Today, that connection forms a magnificent beach known as 'the Gap,' with ocean on both sides."

"How tough is the hike?" Margaret asked while adjusting her sun hat.

"Pretty challenging," Luke admitted. "There are some steep sections with wooden steps, and parts of the trail run close to cliff edges. But the pace is leisurely, with plenty of stops for wildlife observation and photography."

"Speaking of wildlife," Rogerio interjected, "the name Robberg means 'seal mountain,' right? Will we see them?"

"Thousands of them," Luke confirmed enthusiastically. "The Cape fur seal colony at Robberg is one of the largest in South Africa—between six and ten thousand animals depending on the season. We'll observe them from the cliffs during our hike, and this afternoon's boat trip will bring us much closer."

The detailed briefing continued as everyone finished breakfast, excitement building for what promised to be an exhilarating day.

An hour later, the group assembled at the nature reserve's entrance—a modest collection of stone buildings housing interpretive displays, restrooms, and a small shop selling refreshments and souvenirs. A wooden signboard displayed trail information, wildlife notices, and tide tables, while a three-dimensional topographic model offered visitors a preview of the terrain they were about to hike.

With Luke taking the lead and Sheryl positioned at the rear to ensure that no one fell behind, the group began their ascent up the initial section of trail—a well-maintained path that climbed steadily through the vegetation.

As they climbed, the expansive views opened progressively—first Plettenberg Bay itself, with its perfect crescent of a white sand beach, then the wider coastline stretching eastward toward the distant Tsitsikamma mountains. Cargo ships could be seen on the horizon, following the busy shipping lanes between South Africa's industrial centers.

"Amazing to think this peninsula's been a navigation landmark for seafarers since the late 1400s," Luke explained during a brief water break. "Portuguese explorers named it Cabo Talhado—the 'Sharp Cape'—because of how dramatically it cuts into the ocean. It appears on navigational charts dating back to 1576."

"Was there ever human habitation here?" Nkosi asked, his academic interests engaged.

"Archaeological evidence suggests human presence dating back 120,000 years," Luke confirmed. "There's a cave system on the peninsula's southern side with some of the oldest Middle Stone Age deposits in South Africa. We'll see the cave entrance during our hike."

The path continued upward until it reached the spine of the peninsula, where it leveled out along a narrow ridge offering views in both directions—to the north, the protected waters of Plettenberg Bay; to the south, the uninterrupted expanse of the Indian Ocean stretching toward Antarctica. Here, the full force of the offshore winds became apparent, and several hikers adjusted caps and secured loose items against the steady breeze.

"Perfect conditions for the resident black eagles," Luke pointed out, gesturing toward a pair of raptors soaring on thermal updrafts along the cliffs. "They nest in the crevices of the southern cliffs and hunt dassies that live in the boulder fields below."

The group spread out naturally along the ridge path, each finding their comfortable pace. Tyler and Emma maintained their positions at the front, their competitive spirits evident even in this non-running activity. Behind them, the Alvarez brothers kept a steady pace, occasionally stopping to photograph striking views or unusual plants.

Sheryl noticed Joan was walking alongside Nkosi and Margaret. Their conversation appeared animated, with Joan gesturing toward the ocean periodically as though making specific points.

As the ridge path continued, the dramatic geology of the peninsula revealed itself more fully. Ancient quartzite formations, contorted by millions of years of geological pressure, created sculptural outcroppings that seemed to defy gravity. In places, the trail navigated between massive boulders that formed natural gateways, while in others, wooden boardwalks carried hikers across particularly sensitive or hazardous sections.

After about three kilometers, the group reached the Gap. Here, a natural bridge of white sand had waves breaking on both sides simultaneously—a rare feature that drew appreciative comments from the hikers.

Luke gathered everyone for a brief explanation. "This formation shows the dynamic nature of coastal processes. The sand we're standing on is continuously being deposited and eroded by waves. During certain extreme storm conditions, the ocean can actually wash completely across this section, temporarily returning the western portion to its ancient island state."

Ahead, the trail climbed again, ascending wooden steps embedded in the rock to regain the height of the peninsula's central ridge. As they approached this climb, Madeline fell into step beside Sheryl, her expression suggesting she had been waiting for a moment to speak privately.

"I don't mean to pry," she began carefully, "but Stanley and I have been part of three Global Runners tours now, and something feels tense about this one."

Before Madeline could pursue the conversation further, they reached the wooden staircase, where single-file ascent prevented continued discussion. Sheryl made a mental note to be more conscious of her distracted thoughts around her guests.

At the top of the stairs, the path continued along the rocky spine of the peninsula's western portion, gradually narrowing as it approached the Point—the furthest extension of land into the ocean. Here, the first distant barking of seals became audible, carried on the breeze as they neared the tip of the peninsula.

"We're approaching the main seal colony," Luke announced as the group paused at a particularly spectacular viewpoint. "From here, we'll descend slightly to an observation area built specifically for viewing the colony without disturbing them."

As they rounded a bend in the trail, the full spectacle came into view—the rocky shore below teeming with thousands of Cape fur seals in various states of activity. Some basked motionless on sun-warmed rocks, others engaged in noisy territorial disputes, while hundreds more could be seen swimming and playing in the churning waters around the Point. The cacophony of barks, growls, and splashes rose from below, creating a soundtrack that perfectly matched the wild setting.

"Incredible," Nkosi murmured, already adjusting his camera settings for optimal wildlife photography. "Is this their peak season?"

"Near peak," Luke confirmed. "We're approaching breeding season when the colony will grow even larger. The dominant bulls have already established territories, and females will soon start getting pregnant."

The observation area featured rustic wooden benches positioned to offer unobstructed views of the colony while keeping human visitors at a non-disruptive distance. The group settled gratefully onto the few seats, many reaching for water bottles and snacks while continuing to watch the endlessly entertaining activities of the seals below.

After about ten minutes of rest and wildlife observation, Luke signaled it was time to continue. "We'll complete the circuit by following the path along the northern side of the peninsula," he explained. "It's more sheltered from the wind. We should reach the archaeological cave site in about forty minutes."

The northern path offered a striking contrast to the exposed southern route. Here, the peninsula sheltered them from the prevailing winds, creating microclimates that supported more diverse vegetation. In protected hollows, dense thickets of milkwood trees formed miniature forests, their gnarled branches creating natural canopies above the trail. Small freshwater seeps supported pockets of wetland plants, attracting colorful sunbirds that darted among the flowers.

This side of the peninsula also offered views back toward the mainland—the developed waterfront of Plettenberg Bay, the estuary of the Keurbooms River, and the forested hills that surrounded the coastal settlement. Several hikers commented on the remarkable contrast between the wild, primeval nature of Robberg and the comfortable civilization visible just across the bay.

The trail descended slightly to reach a cave opening set into the cliff face. A wooden platform built outside the entrance provided enough space for Luke to gather the group for an in-depth explanation about the cave's history.

"This is Nelson Bay Cave," he explained, "one of the most important archaeological sites on South Africa's southern coast. Like I said earlier, excavations here have revealed a continuous record of human occupation spanning over 120,000 years—from the Middle Stone Age through to colonial times."

"Are those shell middens?" Nkosi asked, pointing to visible layers of white material in the cave walls.

"Exactly," Luke confirmed. "Those represent thousands of years of seafood consumption by the cave's inhabitants. Archaeologists have identified distinct layers corresponding to different periods and cultures, allowing them to track changes in diet, tool-making technology, and social organization over massive time spans."

The group spent several minutes examining the cave entrance and the interpretive signage that explained its significance. As they prepared to continue the last leg of their journey, Madeline once again found an opportunity to speak privately with Sheryl.

"I hope I didn't seem nosy earlier," she said. "It's just that Stanley and I have grown quite fond of Global Runners over our three tours. We notice when things seem…different."

"I appreciate your concern," Sheryl replied sincerely. "I hope you're enjoying this one as much or more than your previous two."

Madeline nodded thoughtfully. "It's outstanding, and we've barely begun. I can't wait to see what's ahead."

Luke called for the group's attention, announcing the last stretch of trail back to the reserve entrance. The rest of the hike followed a gradually ascending path through coastal fynbos, eventually rejoining their original route for the final approach to the car park. As they completed their circuit, a sense of collective achievement permeated the group.

"Amazing morning," Derek commented as they reached the reserve entrance. "Those seals are gonna be even more incredible up close this afternoon."

"The boat trip offers a completely different view," Luke confirmed. "You'll be looking up at the cliffs we just stood on, with seals swimming all around the boat. It's one of the most popular activities in Plettenberg Bay for good reason."

The group returned to their transportation for the short drive to the waterfront restaurant where lunch had been arranged—an open-air establishment overlooking the bay, with the distinctive shape of Robberg Peninsula visible across the water. Tables had been reserved on the covered deck, offering welcome shade after the exposed conditions of their morning hike.

As servers distributed prepared plates of local seafood specialties, conversation flowed easily among the tourists.

The lunch break provided Sheryl with an opportunity to check her phone for updates from Jack or Anika, stepping away from the group briefly with the excuse of confirming their afternoon boat reservation. The message waiting for her from Jack was brief but significant:

"Donovans arrested in George. Recovered the diamonds. M got away. Returning today."

The news brought about mixed feelings—yes, progress had been made, but there were still loose ends that could interfere with the rest of their trip. She sent a brief response to Jack before returning to the group, her smile firmly in place, despite the tensions that continued to simmer beneath the surface.

CHAPTER 27

SEAL SHOALS

The group assembled at the small harbor where their boats waited. The vessels—inflatable twelve-person zodiacs—were lightweight and easily launched from the sandy beach.

Jon Steyn, a local with three decades of experience piloting boats along this coastline, greeted them at the gangway. "Welcome aboard the Seal Seekers Tour," he announced as the group settled onto cushioned seats. "We'll be spending about ninety minutes exploring the waters around Robberg Peninsula, with special focus on the seal colony you saw this morning. Safety briefing first, then we'll get going."

The briefing covered standard maritime safety procedures—location of life jackets, man-overboard protocols, and seasickness management—before addressing wildlife viewing guidelines. "We get as close as we can without disturbing the animals," Steyn explained. "That said, the seals are naturally curious and often approach the boat on their own. Please don't try to touch them, no matter how close they come. They are still wild animals, and as such, they can be very unpredictable."

With the briefing complete and all passengers seated, the boats' trailers were attached to a large farm tractor, which rushed toward the sea, giving each the momentum it needed to glide into the ocean as the trailers dipped below the waterline.

"Well, that's a new way to launch a boat," Sheryl commented once they were afloat.

"I wonder how we get the boats back onto the shore after the tour?" Joan wondered aloud.

Sheryl noticed that Joan had positioned herself at the vessel's bow, her camera ready. After ensuring the rest of the group was comfortably settled, Sheryl moved to join her.

"Different perspective from this morning," she commented, gesturing toward Robberg, which appeared even more impressive from sea level.

"Hmm?" Joan seemed to return from distant thoughts. "Oh, yeah. Amazing how big those cliffs are from down here. We were pretty badass hiking all of that."

As the zodiacs rounded the eastern tip of the peninsula and began following its southern coastline, the first seals came into view—sleek forms swimming through the swells or lounging on exposed rocks. Steyn reduced speed, allowing for better observation as they approached the main colony area.

"Ladies and gentlemen, we're entering the heart of the Robberg Marine Protected Area," he announced over the sound of the engine. "In addition to the Cape fur seals, keep watch for dolphins, which frequently hunt in these waters, and possible whale sightings—we've had southern right whales visiting the bay this week."

The scale of the seal colony became increasingly apparent as they approached—thousands of animals covering virtually every available rocky surface, with hundreds more visible in the water. The cacophony of barks and growls that had been audible from the cliff tops that morning now surrounded them, creating an immersive wildlife experience that drew exclamations of delight from everyone.

"Look at that big bull defending his rock," Steyn pointed out, indicating a massive male seal posturing aggressively toward younger challengers. "He'll be nearly three hundred kilograms, and those teeth aren't just for show—the dominance battles can be pretty fierce during breeding season."

As if to demonstrate, two younger males began a confrontation nearby, rearing up and slashing at each other with impressive displays of agility, despite their bulk. The group watched, fascinated by this glimpse into the social structure of the colony.

The captain skillfully maneuvered their boat parallel to the rocky shoreline. As predicted, curious seals began approaching the vessel, swimming alongside it and occasionally popping their heads above water to examine the human visitors.

"They're so playful," Margaret commented as a particularly acrobatic youngster performed a series of underwater somersaults clearly visible in the crystal-clear water beside the boat.

"Incredibly intelligent animals," Luke confirmed. "Studies suggest their cognitive abilities rival those of many primates. They're also remarkably adaptable—these colonies have survived centuries of human presence on this coastline, despite periods of intensive hunting in colonial times."

All three boats continued their circuit around the peninsula, offering continuously changing perspectives of both the wildlife and the dramatic geology they had hiked earlier. Several times, the captains cut the engines completely, allowing the vessels to drift quietly and passengers to get nice photographs of the scenery or the curious seals that approached.

Soon, excited calls from the ocean side drew everyone's attention. A pod of bottlenose dolphins had appeared, their dorsal fins cutting through the water as they approached the vessel with apparent curiosity.

"Common bottlenose dolphins," Steyn announced. "A resident pod that frequents these waters. They often hunt the same fish as the seals, though there's limited competition due to slightly different feeding preferences."

The appearance of these new marine mammals temporarily redirected everyone's attention, cameras pivoting to capture the graceful cetaceans as they performed synchronized dives around the boats. Several passengers clapped in delight when a mother and calf surfaced simultaneously just meters from the boat, offering a perfect photo before disappearing beneath the surface once more.

The boats completed the circuit of the peninsula and began the return journey to the harbor, the late afternoon light casting a golden glow across the landscape.

As the boats approached the beach from which they had launched, Joan asked Steyn, "Are we gonna have to wade ashore? I wasn't prepared to get that wet today."

Steyn chuckled and, with a big smile, responded, "No, ma'am, I'll get you on shore completely dry. You might want to take a seat, though." Then, raising his voice to the crowd, he said, "If everyone would please brace themselves in their seats, it's time to go ashore."

Sheryl had her butt down and her feet braced. Several of the others were looking questioningly between their boat captain and the beach. Then, Steyn pressed the throttle all the way forward; the staff members driving the other boats followed suit, and the zodiacs leapt into the oncoming waves.

Passengers scrambled for their seats as the boats gained speed, the bows pointed straight at the point where they'd originally launched.

Margaret turned to the Alvarez brothers. "Umm, are they really gonna crash this boat into the shore?"

"Yep! That's how the Navy does it. That's why we're using zodiacs."

At that moment, the boats reached the edge of the water and the beginning of the sandy beach. With their gathered momentum, they continued forward as if they were made for land travel. The zodiacs slid smoothly across the sand until the accumulated friction caused them to stop abruptly, snapping everyone forward.

Steyn announced, "Welcome ashore! I hope you enjoyed your adventure!"

There was spontaneous applause for the unexpected excitement. Everyone rose to slide over the inflatable sides of the crafts and drop to the sand.

Smiles and animated conversations began immediately as they filed toward their awaiting bus back to their hotel, where preparations for dinner were already underway.

As twilight settled over Plettenberg Bay and the silhouette of Robberg Peninsula faded into deepening shadows, Sheryl found herself grinning at the memories she had gained that would last her a lifetime. However, once she was inside her room for the night and preparing for bed, she had a nagging feeling that Malanga wouldn't take the loss of his diamonds so easily.

CHAPTER 28

BORDERS AND CONTRASTS

Sheryl stood on the resort's main deck, watching the mist perform its slow dance across the property while mentally reviewing the complex logistics of the day ahead. Today's Bloukrans Pass run was one of the tour's unique experiences—a journey between provinces that revealed South Africa's stark contrasts in a singular, seven-kilometer stretch.

The dining area hummed with conversation as runners assembled for the morning meal—a generous buffet of fruits, homemade breads, boerewors sausage, and the spiced tomato relish known as chakalaka. Large windows overlooked the Indian Ocean, where the morning mist was gradually burning off to reveal the perfect arcs of surfing waves rolling toward shore.

"Morning, everyone," Luke greeted the group with enthusiasm. "Hope you all slept well! We've got a unique experience ahead today—a run that'll take us across one of South Africa's most significant provincial boundaries."

"Any news from our missing friends?" Madeline inquired as Sheryl joined their table with a coffee in hand. "We were wondering if Kim and Kelly will rejoin us before the trip ends."

"I got a message last night," Sheryl confirmed, offering up the partial truth. "Anika and Jack will rejoin us tomorrow. The Donovans have changed their itinerary based on medical advice—Kim's ribs need more recovery time than our activity schedule allows."

"That's unfortunate," Stanley commented, "though probably wise. There are some tough activities ahead of us, and I would hate for her to get hurt even more than she already is."

Sheryl nodded in agreement, inwardly reflecting on how readily people accepted narratives that aligned with their expectations. No one questioned the cover story because accidents on hiking trails happened all the time.

Luke called for everyone's attention, thankfully before Sheryl had to answer any more questions. "Today's run takes us through the Bloukrans Pass along a quiet, little-used road, and the official boundary between the Western and Eastern Cape Provinces."

The group nodded without really understanding why this information was significant.

"We'll drive to the starting point at the top of the pass. From there, we'll descend through indigenous forest into what locals call 'the Fairy Glen'—a misty green valley of quiet solitude."

"Sounds magical," Margaret commented.

"It really is," Luke assured her. "After the descent, we'll cross the provincial boundary—which you'll notice immediately from the change in road maintenance—before starting the climb back up the opposite side of the pass."

"How steep are we talking?" Rogerio asked, ever concerned with gradients.

"About 150 meters of elevation loss, followed by 180 meters of gain over the seven kilometers," Luke replied. "Challenging but doable, especially since we're taking it at a relaxed pace and you can stop and walk at any point. The paved road surface makes for easier running, despite the incline."

With breakfast concluded and everyone's running gear assembled, the group boarded their bus to head to the starting point. The morning mist had dissipated, revealing a crystalline blue sky that promised perfect running conditions. As they traveled, the landscape shifted subtly—the manicured tourist-friendly environments giving way to more authentic, rural South Africa, where small settlements and subsistence farming became more prevalent.

"We're moving into areas less frequented by international visitors," Luke explained as they passed through a small town where locals went about their morning routines with barely a glance at the passing tour vehicle. "The Eastern Cape has a distinct character from the Western Cape—less economically developed but culturally rich, especially in Xhosa traditions."

The bus began climbing a winding road that ascended through increasingly dense vegetation. Massive yellowwood trees created a natural canopy. Their branches were draped with old man's beard lichen that swayed gently in the breeze. Glimpses of the valley below revealed a landscape that seemed to belong in a fantasy novel—mist-filled hollows between forested hills, occasional clearings where sunlight pooled like liquid gold, and the distant silver ribbon of a river winding its way toward the coast.

They reached the starting point—a small gravel pullout at the highest point of the pass, where an interpretive sign provided information about the indigenous forest and the historical significance of the route. While Luke distributed snacks and confirmed everyone had adequate sun protection, Sheryl took a moment to absorb the view—the forested valley spreading below them, the road they would follow visible in sections as it descended through the canopy.

"This pass has been a critical transportation route for centuries," Luke informed the group as they assembled for their final briefing. "Originally, it was an elephant migration path, then it was adapted by indigenous peoples, colonists, and eventually modern transportation planners. The current road follows basically the same route that ox wagons used in the 1800s."

With those instructions, the group began their descent into the valley. The initial gradient was gentle enough to allow comfortable conversation, though it would steepen considerably as they progressed. The air carried the distinctive scents of indigenous forest—rich humus, aromatic leaves, and the faint sweetness of nectar from flowering plants that thrived in the moist environment.

"It's like running through a movie set," Wanda commented as they rounded a curve where sunlight filtered through the canopy in dramatic shafts. She had her GoPro mounted on a head strap, recording the experience from a runner's perspective. "I half expect mythical creatures to come out from behind those trees."

As they descended deeper into the valley, trunks rose up like columns to support a living ceiling far above, and dappled light created ever-shifting patterns on the road's surface. The running group naturally spread out according to individual pace.

"This section of forest is one of the most intact patches of Afromontane vegetation remaining in South Africa," Luke explained to the middle of the pack that included Sheryl, Joan, and the Alvarez brothers. "Some of these yellowwood trees are over eight hundred years old, which means they were already mature when the first European ships landed at the Cape."

"How'd they survive the colonial logging operations?" Joan asked, showing unexpected interest in environmental history.

"Mostly accessibility," Luke replied. "This valley was too steep and remote for efficient timber extraction with 19th-century technology. By the time modern equipment made it possible, conservation awareness had developed enough to protect these remnants."

The descent continued, the gradient occasionally requiring careful attention to footing, despite the paved surface. The forest gradually thinned as they approached the valley floor, opening to reveal stunning views into the broader landscape. Here, the full sensory experience of the pass revealed itself—the auditory richness of flowing water and birdsong, and the ever-changing play of light and shadow as clouds drifted overhead.

"We're approaching the provincial boundary," Luke announced as they reached a particularly scenic point where the road leveled briefly. "Perfect spot for a water break and some photos before we cross."

The group gathered at a small roadside clearing that offered unobstructed views in both directions—back toward the Western Cape they had descended from, and forward toward the Eastern Cape that awaited them.

"The boundary we're about to cross represents more than just administrative division," Luke explained as they rested. "It marks significant historical, cultural, and economic transitions within South Africa."

"Is that why the road surface changes?" Derek asked. "Different provincial maintenance?"

Luke smiled. "You'll see for yourselves in about half a kilometer. But yeah, the contrast in road quality reflects broader economic disparities between the provinces. The Western Cape has South Africa's highest GDP per capita and gets substantial tourism revenue, which funds better infrastructure. The Eastern Cape faces greater economic challenges, with higher unemployment rates and less favorable historical developments."

As they resumed their run and approached the actual boundary—marked by a bridge across a small stream—the change Luke had referenced became immediately apparent. The smooth asphalt surface they had been running on gave way to a patchwork of repairs, potholes, and uneven sections that required more attentive footing.

"Whoa," Rogerio commented, deliberately placing his feet to avoid the holes. "There's literally a line in the road."

"Welcome to the Eastern Cape," Luke confirmed with a knowing nod. "What you're experiencing isn't just about road maintenance budgets—it reflects the entire colonial and apartheid history of South Africa."

As they continued their journey, now beginning the gradual ascent that would complete their circuit, Luke provided context for the dramatic transition they had just experienced.

"The Western Cape was the first area colonized by Europeans, starting in the 1650s," he explained. "It got disproportionate development investment for centuries and remains the province with the most favorable infrastructure and economic boost. The Eastern Cape, by contrast, was historically Xhosa territory—the frontier zone where colonial expansion met indigenous resistance."

"So, these differences go back hundreds of years?" Stanley asked.

"Absolutely," Luke confirmed. "During apartheid, parts of the Eastern Cape were designated as Bantustans—supposedly independent homelands that actually functioned as labor reserves for white South Africa. The economic legacy of that system still persists, despite democratic reforms that have been introduced since 1994."

As if to illustrate his point, they passed a small settlement visible from the road—modest dwellings constructed from a mixture of traditional materials and modern components, where women carried water from a communal tap and children played in yards decorated with colorful laundry hanging to dry.

"The Eastern Cape has produced many of South Africa's most significant political leaders," Luke continued while they ran. "Nelson Mandela, Oliver Tambo, Steve Biko, and Thabo Mbeki all came from this province. Their experiences of rural poverty and inequality shaped their political consciousness and, ultimately, the nation's path to democracy."

The ascent grew steeper as they progressed, requiring more focused effort from the runners. Conversation naturally diminished as breathing became more deliberate, though the group maintained a comfortable pace appropriate to the challenging terrain. The landscape opened further as they climbed, offering views across valleys and ridgelines extending toward the distant ocean.

"Almost halfway up," Luke encouraged as they rounded a particularly demanding switchback. "Perfect timing for a second water break if you want."

The group gathered gratefully in a small widening of the road that featured a rustic wooden bench, likely positioned by thoughtful locals familiar with the pass's demands. As the runners rehydrated and caught their breath, Sheryl noticed Rogerio checking his phone.

"No signal?" Sheryl asked casually.

"Spotty at best," he confirmed, returning the device to his pocket. "Though, maybe that's a blessing. You know, living in the moment and all that."

"The provincial contrasts extend to telecommunications infrastructure, too," Luke noted, overhearing their exchange. "Western Cape has nearly complete coverage, while Eastern Cape still has significant gaps, especially in rural areas like this one."

The final kilometers of ascent challenged even the fittest members of the group, with gradients that would be respectable on alpine mountain passes. The road wound upward in a series of switchbacks, each turn revealing new perspectives on the landscape they had traversed. Vegetation shifted again as they climbed, transitioning from valley flora to hardier species adapted to the wind-swept upper slopes.

Tyler and Emma maintained their customary positions at the front. Behind them, the group had spread out considerably, each runner finding their own comfortable rhythm for the sustained climb. Sheryl maintained a position near the middle, keeping both the leaders and trailing runners within sight as much as the winding road allowed.

When they finally crested the pass, emerging onto a plateau that marked the completion of their ascent, a collective sense of achievement permeated the group. Runners arrived in stages, each receiving congratulations from those already present as they completed the challenging circuit.

"Incredible run," Madeline declared, her face flushed with exertion but her expression delighted. "That forest section felt enchanted."

"The contrast in road surfaces was even more dramatic than I expected," Stanley added. "Like crossing between different decades of development."

Luke had arranged for their bus to meet them at this upper viewpoint, where a small picnic area provided the perfect setting for post-run refreshments. A simple but satisfying spread awaited them—fresh fruit, nuts, locally made jerky, and traditional South African rusk biscuits perfect for dipping in hot tea or coffee from insulated containers.

As the group milled about, enjoying their well-earned snacks, Luke expanded on the provincial distinctions they had experienced during their run.

"The Western and Eastern Cape provinces represent two distinct cultural and economic models within South Africa," he explained, gesturing toward the respective territories visible from their elevated position. "The Western Cape has a Mediterranean climate perfect for wine production, strong tourism infrastructure, and a diversified economy."

"And the Eastern Cape?" Derek asked.

"The Eastern Cape is predominantly Xhosa in culture and language," Luke continued. "It has a more challenging climate for agriculture, less developed tourism infrastructure, and faces greater socioeconomic challenges."

"Yet, the natural environment seems equally magnificent," Margaret observed, gesturing toward the stunning landscapes surrounding them.

"Absolutely," Luke agreed. "The Eastern Cape contains some of South Africa's most pristine wilderness areas and extraordinary coastlines. What it lacks isn't natural resources or cultural wealth, but rather the historical advantages of colonial investment and contemporary economic development."

As the group boarded their transportation for the next leg of their journey, Sheryl reflected on what the group had seen today. The Bloukrans Pass had, indeed, offered a perfect metaphor for South Africa itself—a country of extraordinary beauty marked by sharp divisions, where history had carved boundaries more significant than lines on a map.

CHAPTER 29

INTO THIN AIR

The afternoon sun hung high over Bloukrans Bridge, its rays illuminating the massive concrete structure against a backdrop of pristine, blue sky. At 216 meters above the river below, the bridge stood as both an engineering marvel and the site of one of the world's most extreme adrenaline-inducing activities—the highest commercial bungee jump on the African continent and fifth highest in the world.

The Global Runners tour group had arrived after lunch, having spent the morning traversing the historic pass that wound through the gorge's natural splendor. Now, they faced a different challenge, one that wasn't about physical endurance but the more primal fear of stepping into empty space.

"Welcome to Bloukrans Bridge Bungy," announced their guide, a young South African man named Maseko, whose smile and enthusiasm relieved the tension of the experience. "Today, you'll have the chance to experience either our scenic Skywalk, which takes you beneath the road deck to a viewing platform at the center of the arch, or, for the more adventurous, the full bungee jump experience."

The group gathered at the facility's reception area. Inside, video screens displayed footage of previous jumpers, their expressions cycling through terror, exhilaration, and euphoria in rapid succession.

"I can't believe we're actually considering this," Margaret murmured, watching as one particularly enthusiastic jumper executed a swan dive into the void.

Beside her, Sabrina Chu practically vibrated with nervous energy as she watched the jumpers on screen.

"I'm definitely doing it," Sabrina declared, though her voice carried a tremor that belied her confident words. "I've been following Face Your Fears Friday on social media for months. This'll be my ultimate post."

Sabrina represented a new generation of adventure tourists—driven not just by personal challenge but by the social currency of shareable experiences. Her phone case featured a collage of social media logos, and she'd already documented every aspect of her South African journey with meticulous attention to lighting and composition.

Luke gathered the group for a final briefing before they committed to their chosen activities. "Both options require signing waivers," he explained. "The Skywalk is accessible to almost everyone with basic mobility. It's completely safe, though admittedly unnerving for those with a fear of heights. The bungee jump has some physical restrictions — minimum weight of thirty-five kilograms, maximum 150 kilograms, and certain medical conditions are disqualifying."

"How many people actually change their minds at the edge?" Nkosi inquired, his academic curiosity showing.

"About one in twenty gets to the jump platform and decides not to go through with it," Maseko answered with practiced casualness. "Totally normal and nothing to be ashamed of. We never pressure anyone to jump if they're uncomfortable. But we will encourage you several times before we let you out of the harness." He smiled and chuckled wickedly.

As waivers were signed and medical questionnaires completed, Sheryl observed the group's natural division into thrill-seekers and cautious observers. Wanda, predictably, completed her paperwork with enthusiastic efficiency, already discussing camera angles with Maseko for optimal documentation of her jump. Tyler and Emma, ever the competitive ones, debated whether tandem or sequential jumps would provide the better experience.

More surprising was Joan's quiet request for a bungee application. Then again, she had seemed to enjoy their time ziplining.

Sabrina Chu alternated between confident proclamations about her imminent jump and nervous glances at the bridge visible over the edge. "I've been practicing visualization," she informed anyone within earshot. "My coach says if I can see myself doing it successfully, my body will follow."

Sheryl signed her own bungee waiver. As tour leader, she made a point of participating in all available activities—both to assess their quality and safety, and to encourage more hesitant clients.

After completing the administrative tasks, the group was led along a purpose-built walkway that extended beneath the road surface of the bridge. The Skywalk allowed visitors to experience the full majesty of the gorge from a unique perspective, regardless of whether they intended to jump.

The walkway itself represented an impressive feat of design—a metal mesh pathway with solid railings that provided both security and unobstructed views. As they progressed further beneath the roadway, the immensity of the gorge revealed itself in panoramic splendor—sheer rock walls descending to the river far below, indigenous forest clinging to impossible gradients, and occasional birds of prey soaring on thermals rising from the valley floor.

Most tourists moved along the walkway with cautious appreciation, maintaining a firm grip on the railings, despite the structure's obvious security. Sabrina Chu, however, approached each section with a curious blend of theatrical terror and determined enthusiasm—gasping at particularly dramatic viewpoints while simultaneously ensuring her phone captured both the vista and her reaction to it.

"I'm literally shaking," she narrated into her device. "216 meters above the ground, about to take the biggest jump of my life!"

The walkway culminated at the center of the bridge's arch, where a viewing platform allowed a 360-degree appreciation of the spectacular setting. Here, jumpers would separate from those choosing only the Skywalk experience, following a dedicated path to the jump platform positioned at the highest central point of the bridge.

Maseko gathered the six committed jumpers—Sheryl, Wanda, the Wilson couple, Joan, and a visibly trembling but determined Sabrina—for their safety briefing, while the remainder of the group continued enjoying the views under Luke's guidance.

"The jumping process is straightforward but must be followed exactly," Maseko explained, his tone shifting from casual to serious. "You'll be fitted with a full-body harness system secured by multiple redundant attachments. Our jump masters will guide your body position for optimal safety."

As he continued explaining technical details and safety protocols, Sabrina's complexion had taken on a distinctly greenish tinge. "I think I might be sick," she whispered to Sheryl, who stood beside her.

"Totally normal," Sheryl assured her quietly. "The anticipation's often worse than the actual jump. Focus on your breathing—slow inhale through the nose, gentle exhale through the mouth."

Sabrina nodded gratefully, attempting to follow the breathing guidance while maintaining her social media persona. "Just got our safety briefing," she narrated to her phone, voice quavering slightly. "About to get harnessed up for the jump of a lifetime!"

The preparation area hummed with efficient activity as the jump team fitted each participant with their equipment—ankle harnesses secured with multiple fasteners, safety checks performed and verbally confirmed by two separate staff members, and final weight measurements to ensure proper bungee cord selection.

Wanda, naturally at ease in this environment, chatted enthusiastically with the jump master about the technical aspects of the cord system. "I've done similar setups for film stunts," she explained. "Though, it's usually with more safety rigging that gets removed in post-production."

The Wilsons had opted for tandem jumping—a specialty of the Bloukrans operation that allowed couples to experience the plunge while being physically connected. Their competitive nature had transformed into unusual tenderness as they prepared, exchanging private words of encouragement that suggested the activity had touched something deeper than their usual athletic pursuits.

Joan, seeming to have gotten her breathing under control and no longer looking as green, listened intently to instructions, confirming each safety check with quiet acknowledgment.

Sabrina, meanwhile, had progressed from nervous chatter to silent terror, her social media narration abandoned as the reality of the imminent jump overwhelmed her carefully cultivated online persona. When the jump master called for the first volunteer, she took an involuntary step backward.

"I'll go first," Sheryl offered, recognizing the value of demonstration for nervous participants. "Always helps to see a successful jump before taking your own leap."

Maseko nodded in approval. "Excellent. If you'll follow me to the platform, we'll get you set up."

The jump platform extended from the central point of the bridge—a small, rectangular stage with nothing but transparent barriers between jumpers and the yawning abyss below. As Sheryl stepped onto this precipice, the full psychological impact of the activity became apparent. Despite her extensive adventure experience, she could feel her accelerated heartbeat and heightened awareness of what she was about to do.

"We'll have you stand at the edge with your toes slightly hanging over," Maseko instructed, guiding her to the jumping position. "Arms outstretched like wings for your initial descent. When I count down from five and say 'bungee,' you'll push forward from your ankles—don't jump up, jump forward into space."

Sheryl nodded, positioning herself as directed. The view from this position was both magnificent and terrifying—the entire gorge spread below, the river a distant, silver ribbon, and absolutely nothing between her and a 216-meter drop except the bungee cord secured to her harness.

From the preparation area, she could hear Wanda's encouraging whoop and see the other jumpers watching with expressions ranging from excitement to horror.

"Ready?" Maseko asked, completing his safety check.

"Ready," Sheryl confirmed, focusing on the horizon rather than the dizzying drop immediately before her.

"Five, four, three, two, one...BUNGEE!"

Sheryl pushed forward as instructed, the momentary resistance of her conscious mind dissolving as gravity claimed her. The initial sensation was one of pure freefall—the rush of air, the visual blur of the gorge walls, and the indescribable feeling of complete surrender to natural forces.

The fall lasted about four seconds before the bungee cord reached its extension limit and began its rebound cycle.

As she bobbed at the end of the cord, the world slowly stabilizing around her, Sheryl found herself suspended in the heart of the gorge—a unique perspective few humans ever experienced. Birds flew below her position, the river glistened in dappled sunlight, and the ancient forest revealed patterns invisible from above.

After allowing her several moments to enjoy the suspended sensation, the retrieval system activated. Unlike many bungee operations that pulled jumpers back to their starting point, Bloukrans employed a unique retrieval method where a staff member was lowered to secure the jumper before both were winched back to the platform.

The retrieval technician—a muscular, young man with a ready smile—descended smoothly to her position. "Beautiful jump," he commented professionally as he secured the retrieval harness around her torso. "Perfect form."

As they began their ascent, suspended together in the center of the gorge, he leaned closer under the guise of adjusting her harness. His next words, delivered directly into her ear in a voice too low to be captured by any recording devices, sent an entirely different kind of chill through her body.

"Mr. Malanga wants you to know that this jump could've ended very differently," he murmured, his friendly expression unchanged, despite the menacing content of his message.

"You've been spared today, but this is a warning to stop meddling in his business."

Sheryl maintained her composed expression, offering no visible reaction that observers might notice. The retrieval continued normally, the winch system drawing them steadily upward toward the platform, where the other jumpers waited their turns.

Her mind, however, raced through the implications. Apparently, Malanga had connections reaching even into legitimate tourism businesses. The threat confirmed both his awareness of their location and his willingness to escalate beyond the violence displayed at the East Head Café.

As they reached the platform and the technician released her from the retrieval harness, she scanned his features carefully, committing them to memory while maintaining the expected expression of post-bungee exhilaration.

"Amazing experience!" she exclaimed for the benefit of the waiting jumpers, her voice betraying none of the strategic calculations now unfolding in her mind. "Absolutely worth facing the fear."

"Who's next?" Maseko called cheerfully while the retrieval technician disappeared into the preparation area, his message delivered and his jobs for both the bungee company and Malanga complete.

"I'll go," Wanda volunteered immediately, already moving toward the platform before she even finished speaking.

Sheryl joined the others in the waiting area, accepting congratulations while surreptitiously examining each staff member for threatening looks suggesting they might also have heard from Malanga. The operation appeared to function normally—safety protocols followed meticulously, staff focused on their assigned responsibilities—yet, somehow, within this legitimate business, Malanga had placed at least one mole.

Wanda's jump proceeded flawlessly—her stunt background evident in the perfect swan dive she executed from the platform, transforming the plunge into a performance of controlled elegance. Her retrieval completed with no noticeable issues or signs of discomfort, which suggested the threat had been specifically targeted at Sheryl rather than a general intimidation of the group.

The Wilsons followed with their tandem jump, their competitive nature manifesting in synchronized movements as they plunged into the abyss together. Their shared experience seemed to generate a unique bonding moment, both emerging from the retrieval with expressions of wonder rather than their usual achievement-oriented satisfaction.

Joan approached her jump with a nervous determination. Standing at the precipice, she paused momentarily, her eyes closed as though accessing some internal dialogue. When she opened them again, her expression had transformed from one of anxious concentration to serenity.

"Ready," she stated simply and, at Maseko's countdown, stepped deliberately into empty space without hesitation.

Her descent was neither flamboyant like Wanda's, nor technically perfect like the Wilsons', but carried a quality of personal significance that transcended the physical activity. When she returned to the platform after her retrieval, something in her demeanor had shifted subtly—a lightness that hadn't been present before.

"Better than balancing spreadsheets?" Sheryl asked lightly as Joan rejoined them.

"Infinitely," Joan replied with unexpected warmth. "Somehow, your worries don't matter when you're plunging into thin air."

Sheryl was glad that Joan had been relieved from some of the stress she carried with her. Sabrina Chu had watched each preceding jump with increasing trepidation, her social media narration growing progressively less confident.

"It's totally okay if you've changed your mind," Maseko assured her as she approached the platform with visible reluctance. "Many people discover their actual limits differ from what they imagined."

"No, I'm doing this," Sabrina insisted, though her voice quavered. "I didn't come all this way to back out now."

"Your social media followers will respect whatever you choose," Sheryl suggested gently. "Either decision can make a powerful story."

Sabrina shook her head determinedly. "I need to do this. For myself, not just the social cred." She squared her shoulders and stepped onto the platform, though her complexion had paled considerably.

Maseko guided her through the position with patience, adjusting her stance at the edge while providing reassuring commentary. "Remember, just fall forward; don't jump up. The equipment does all the work—you just need to surrender to the experience."

Sabrina stood frozen at the precipice, her body visibly trembling as she stared into the vast empty space before her. The seconds stretched into a full minute as she attempted to override her instinctual resistance.

"I can't," she finally whispered, tears welling in her eyes. "I thought I could, but I can't."

"That's totally okay," Maseko assured her without a hint of judgment. "But it's a beautiful day. Perfect for a jump. Most people don't get such good weather." The fact that he hadn't moved her back from the edge showed clearly that he had hope for her.

Sabrina looked at his smiling face. "It is a perfect day, isn't it?"

"Mhmm," he agreed.

"Okay, I can do it. Just push me." She glanced over her shoulder and waved at her aunt as the count reached the end.

"…BUNGY!" Maseko called out and pushed the young woman from the firm platform into open air.

A scream leapt uncontrollably from Sabrina's lips as she hung for a split second before plunging into the gorge.

Everyone watched as the last member of the group dangled at the end of the cord, 216 meters below.

"Holy cow! I couldn't do that," Rogerio exclaimed.

When Sabrina had been winched back onto the bridge support, she raised both hands in triumphant celebration. "I did it! I can't believe it. I was so terrified. But I did it anyway."

As they rejoined the non-jumping members of the tour group at the platform, animated conversations erupted—jumpers describing their experiences, non-jumpers sharing their congratulations, everyone processing the emotional intensity of the activity in their own ways.

Sheryl used this moment to send a brief message to Jack, whose planned return with Anika now carried increased urgency given Malanga's threat. The text was simple: "Malanga knows we're here. He sent a threat through one of the jump staff."

The response came quickly: "Understood. Arriving tonight."

As they reversed their path through the Skywalk, the emotional arcs of the activity were evident in each person's demeanor. The jumpers carried the distinctive, energetic afterglow of people who had just undergone an adrenaline-inducing experience.

"The photos and videos will be available for purchase in about fifteen minutes," Maseko announced as they reached the main building.

While the group browsed through jump footage and souvenir options, Sheryl began coordinating their next move.

Luke approached her with some concern in his expression. "Everything okay?" he inquired quietly. "You seem more intense than usual."

Sheryl considered how much to share with Luke, but in the end, she decided she couldn't risk any of her clients overhearing. "Just residual adrenaline from the jump," she replied, matching his discreet tone. "When Jack and Anika rejoin us tomorrow, we should discuss our plans, what we've been doing."

Luke nodded, understanding the subtext requiring no further elaboration.

As the group prepared to depart, having collected their souvenirs, Sheryl observed Joan standing slightly apart, gazing through the panoramic windows at the bridge they had just jumped off of. Something in her expression suggested the bungee jump represented more than what it seemed.

"Meaningful experience?" Sheryl inquired, joining her at the window.

Joan nodded thoughtfully. "There's something profound about voluntarily stepping into empty space," she replied. "Trusting that something you can't fully see or control will protect you." She turned from the view to meet Sheryl's gaze directly. "It shows what matters and what doesn't."

Sheryl smiled and hugged Joan. "I'm glad it helped."

CHAPTER 30

THE UNEXPECTED TREASURE

Finished with the day's adventures, the tour bus wound its way along the coastal highway, passing through landscapes that shifted subtly as they moved deeper into the Eastern Cape province. Vegetation became slightly more arid, the hillsides populated with indigenous aloes whose architectural forms created striking silhouettes against the sky. Occasional glimpses of the Indian Ocean appeared between headlands, the water changing color with the angle of the sun—deep cobalt in open water, translucent turquoise in protected coves.

"We're now approaching Cape St. Francis," Luke announced as they rounded a bend that revealed a sweeping vista of the coastline ahead. "This area represents one of

South Africa's most significant fishing communities, especially known for its calamari industry."

"I thought calamari was mostly Mediterranean," Derek Alvarez commented.

"Common misconception," Luke replied. "The Cape waters host Loligo vulgaris reynaudii—the Cape Hope squid, which is considered among the finest calamari in the world. We'll learn much more about it during our special presentation this evening."

They arrived at their accommodation—the Cape St. Francis Resort,—where check-in proceeded efficiently, allowing tourists time to refresh in their rooms before the evening's activities.

As sunset approached, Luke gathered the group for a short walk to the aptly named Sunset Rock—a dramatic natural formation that extended into the ocean, providing an unobstructed view of the sun's descent.

"Perfect timing," Sheryl commented as they arrived at the rocky outcropping. The sun hung just above the horizon, its light diffused by thin clouds into spectacular arrays of amber, crimson, and violet that reflected off the ocean's surface.

The group settled onto natural stone seats, conversation diminishing as the natural spectacle commanded their attention.

"The Dutch called this region 'Cabo das Tormentas'—the Cape of Storms," Luke explained quietly as they watched the sun's final descent. "But on evenings like tonight, it's hard to imagine the fierce weather that gave it that name."

As darkness gathered and the first stars appeared above them, the group made their way back to the resort for dinner.

Rather than the resort's main restaurant, they were directed to a specially arranged private dining room overlooking the illuminated pool area. Here, a demonstration kitchen had been set up at one end of the space, with dining tables positioned to allow clear views of the culinary presentation to come.

"Good evening, travelers," greeted a woman standing confidently behind the preparation counter. Chef Nomsa Khumalo's crisp white jacket contrasted with her warm smile as she welcomed them into her domain.

"Tonight, we explore the story of Cape St. Francis through its most famous product—calamari," she continued, gesturing to an impressive array of culinary equipment and seafood specimens arranged before her. "But this isn't just a cooking demonstration. It's a journey through history, culture, economy, and sustainability."

As the group settled at their tables, servers circulated with glasses of sauvignon blanc from a nearby Eastern Cape vineyard—a crisp wine specifically selected to complement the seafood to follow.

Chef Nomsa began by displaying a whole, unprocessed squid—about thirty centimeters in length, its pearlescent skin catching the light as she handled it with clear respect.

"Loligo vulgaris reynaudii," she announced, using the scientific name with practiced ease. "Our Cape Hope squid. Before we discuss cuisine, we must understand the remarkable creature itself."

What followed was part biology lesson, part culinary demonstration, as she systematically dissected the specimen with practiced precision. Her commentary blended scientific detail with practical knowledge gained through decades of working with the local fishing industry.

"Note the ten appendages," she pointed out. "Eight arms and two feeding tentacles that extend dramatically to capture prey. The beak—yes, squid have beaks—is located centrally among the arms, leading to the digestive system."

With deft movements, she separated the mantle—the main portion of the body—from the head and tentacles, then demonstrated the extraction of the internal quill—a transparent cartilaginous structure that served as the animal's skeletal support.

"This internal 'pen' was historically used as an actual writing implement," she noted. "The term 'squid' itself may derive from an old word for an ink-dropping pen, referencing the ink sac we see here."

The dissection continued with the removal of the ink sac—performed with surgical precision to avoid rupturing the delicate membrane—followed by the separation of edible portions from internal organs. Throughout, Chef Nomsa maintained an engaging narrative that balanced technical information with cultural context.

"In many cultures, every part of the squid is used," she explained. "The ink for risotto nero in Italy, the tentacles grilled in Mediterranean cuisine, the mantle stuffed in Greek dishes or sliced for Japanese sashimi. Here in South Africa, our approach blends these global influences with our unique local preferences."

With the anatomy lesson complete, she transitioned to the historical narrative that explained Cape St. Francis's emergence as a calamari epicenter. As she spoke, her hands continued working—cleaning, slicing, and preparing the demonstrated specimens for cooking.

"For generations, local fishermen viewed squid mainly as bait," she explained. "They'd catch it to use for targeting more valuable species like kob, red steenbras, and geelbek. The squid itself was considered incidental—useful but not commercially significant."

She paused to adjust the temperature on the induction cooktop where olive oil was heating in a well-seasoned pan. "That changed in the late 1960s and early 1970s, when British visitors recognized the exceptional quality of our local squid. Having experienced calamari in the Mediterranean, they immediately understood its commercial potential."

The aroma of garlic and herbs filled the room as she added the prepared ingredients to the hot oil. "From that recognition emerged our modern calamari industry. By the mid-1980s, Cape St. Francis had established itself as the epicenter of South African squid fishing, with export markets developing first in Europe, then globally."

As she continued her narrative, servers presented the first tasting course—delicate strips of calamari prepared using minimal intervention, dressed simply with olive oil, lemon, and fresh herbs. The presentation emphasized the natural sweetness and tender texture that distinguished the Cape Hope squid from its counterparts in other regions.

"The exceptional quality comes from several factors," Chef Nomsa explained as guests sampled this introductory offering. "Our cold, nutrient-rich Benguela Current provides ideal feeding conditions. The squid grow more slowly here than in warmer waters, which allows them to develop a better texture for eating. And our traditional handling methods result in less damage to the squids' delicate flesh."

The culinary demonstration progressed through several preparations, each highlighting different cultural influences on its preparation. Between courses, Chef Nomsa expanded on the socioeconomic aspects of the local industry, her narrative bringing to life the complex ecosystem of boats, crews, processing facilities, and export logistics that supported the community.

"The chokka boats you may have noticed in the harbor represent the backbone of the local economy," she explained while demonstrating a traditional Cape Malay preparation that incorporated fragrant spices and coconut milk. "These specialized vessels typically carry crews of twelve to twenty men, who spend between five and twenty days at sea depending on conditions and catch rates."

"How do they actually catch the squid?" Joan inquired, showing unexpected interest in the technical aspects of the industry.

Chef Nomsa brightened at the inquiry. "Great question! Unlike many commercial fishing operations that use trawl nets, local fleets mainly use jig fishing."

She set down her cooking utensils to demonstrate using the jig she lifted from the table. "Jigs are specialized lures, often cylindrical with multiple upward-facing hooks. The fishermen lower these on lines into the water, then use a specific motion—" she said as she mimicked a particular wrist action,"—that makes the jig dance in a way that attracts squid."

"Is it mechanized now?" Nkosi asked.

"Some larger operations use mechanical jigging machines," she acknowledged. "But most of our local boats still use traditional hand-jigging techniques. The fishermen develop incredible sensitivity to the presence of squid on their lines. They can feel the difference between a squid investigating the jig and one that's taken it."

As servers presented the next tasting course—calamari prepared with a distinctive South African braai flavor—Chef Nomsa shifted her narrative to the human dimension of the industry.

"The life of a calamari fisherman is challenging," she noted, her tone reflecting personal familiarity with the community she described. "Many crew members come from impoverished backgrounds in the Eastern Cape. The work's physically demanding, the hours unpredictable, and the income dependent on successful catches."

She described the living conditions aboard the chokka boats—cramped quarters shared by the entire crew, limited freshwater for washing, and the constant humidity that made being comfortable difficult. Despite these hardships, positions on the boats remained sought after because of the potential earnings when catches were good.

"During peak season, a successful trip can earn a crew member more than they might make in months of land-based work," she explained. "This payout creates a boom-and-bust cycle that defines many fishing communities, including ours."

The socioeconomic narrative provided context for the subsequent discussion of sustainability—both environmental and economic—that Chef Nomsa wove into her presentation. As she demonstrated a contemporary fusion preparation that incorporated indigenous Cape herbs with classical techniques, she explained the careful management required to maintain the natural resource.

"Squid populations are especially vulnerable to overfishing because of their short lifespans—typically only twelve to eighteen months," she noted. "A single generation experiences its entire lifecycle within that period, which means overfishing in one year can significantly impact the following year's population."

She described the seasonal fishing closures, catch limits, and marine protected areas that had been established to ensure the long-term viability of the industry. These conservation measures, initially resisted by some fishing operations, had gradually gained acceptance as their benefits became apparent in sustained catch rates.

Throughout the presentation, Sheryl noted the engaged attention of the tour group—even those who she might have thought to be disinterested in culinary or fishing topics. Chef Nomsa's skillful blending of technical information, cultural context, and sensory experience had created an engaging portrait of the region.

Joan, in particular, seemed unusually engaged, asking several thoughtful questions about the economic structure of the industry and the financial arrangements between boat owners, captains, and crew members.

"The traditional share system creates both opportunity and risk," Chef Nomsa explained in response to one of Joan's queries. "Crew members get a percentage of the catch value rather than fixed wages. This incentivizes everyone to work efficiently, but it also means income can fluctuate dramatically with seasonal variations and market conditions."

As the culinary demonstration approached its conclusion, Chef Nomsa presented a final tasting—a contemporary preparation of calamari that incorporated elements from South Africa's diverse culinary traditions. The dish featured tender tubes stuffed with a mixture that included local morogo spinach, aromatic Cape Malay spices, and indigenous herbs, served with a sauce that balanced European technique with African flavors.

"This represents my personal philosophy about our culinary heritage," she explained as servers distributed the carefully plated portions. "We keep our traditional knowledge and techniques while still embracing new ideas from other countries. That reflects both where we've come from and where we're going."

The appreciative murmurs and expressions as guests sampled this final offering suggested she had, indeed, achieved her culinary objective. Even those who had initially expressed skepticism about squid as a featured ingredient found themselves won over by the thoughtful progression of the story.

As the formal demonstration concluded and the evening transitioned to the more conventional dining experience, with additional courses being served on the buffet, conversations flowed naturally around the tables.

Chef Nomsa drifted from group to group during this portion of the evening, answering individual questions and sharing additional insights that hadn't fit into her presentation.

As guests lingered over dessert and coffee, the conversations had evolved from the specific topic of calamari to broader reflections on the economy, ecology, and culture that defined Cape St. Francis.

"Amazing how a single product can define an entire community's identity," Nkosi said to those at his table. "The calamari industry here functions much like wine does in Stellenbosch — not just an economic activity but a cultural identity."

"And similarly vulnerable to both environmental and market forces," Margaret added. "The boom-bust cycle she described reminds me of resource-dependent communities everywhere."

Sheryl circulated among the tables. When she reached Joan's table, she found the usually reserved woman engaged in animated conversation with Luke about the financial structure of small-scale fishing operations.

"The share system creates natural alignment between individual and collective interests," Joan was explaining, her professional expertise evident in her analysis. "But it also concentrates risk at exactly the level least able to absorb economic shocks."

"You seem really interested in the economic aspects," Sheryl observed as she joined their conversation.

Joan nodded, a glass of local dessert wine cradled thoughtfully in her hands. "I've spent decades analyzing how financial systems either support or undermine community resilience. The calamari industry here presents a fascinating case study in balanced and imbalanced risk distribution."

As the group gathered their belongings and prepared to depart, the conversations continued—a sign of successful educational tourism where experiences catalyzed deeper understanding. Chef Nomsa stood at the exit, personally thanking each guest for their participation and attentiveness during her presentation.

When Sheryl reached her, the chef clasped her hand warmly between both of her own—a gesture that appeared merely hospitable but allowed for a moment of direct communication.

"Safe travels," she said, her emphasis subtle but unmistakable. "In South Africa, many currents run dangerously beneath calm waters."

CHAPTER 31

FROM SUNRISE TO SAFARI

Dawn arrived at Cape St. Francis with theatrical precision—the sky transforming from indigo to lavender to radiant gold as the sun breached the horizon over the Indian Ocean. Most tourists remained soundly asleep in their comfortable resort accommodations, but the Global Runners group had already assembled in the parking lot.

"Morning, everyone," Sheryl greeted them, her voice matching the hushed quality of early daybreak. "Our sunrise run takes us through three different ecosystems—coastal forest, dune fields, and beach. A nice sampling of what the Eastern Cape's got to offer."

The group had dressed lightly for the warm climate, expecting both their bodies and the sun to raise the temperature over the next hour.

"We'll follow the trail through the nature reserve first," Luke explained, indicating the wooden boardwalk that led into the light coastal thicket. "The route eventually opens onto dune fields, then loops back along the beach past the lighthouse. Total distance is about eight kilometers, with pretty much no elevation change."

With final route instructions delivered and water bottles secured, the group began their morning journey. The initial section led them through indigenous coastal forest—a dense tangle of milkwood trees, candlewood bushes, and wild olive trees forming a canopy over the narrow trail. Bird life awakened around them, filling the air with calls ranging from the liquid warble of Cape robin-chats to the distinctive cackle of hadeda ibises.

"This coastal forest system's remarkably tough," Luke explained as they jogged at a comfortable pace along the winding path. "Some of these milkwood trees are estimated to be over five hundred years old, having survived centuries of coastal storms."

The trail gradually transitioned from forest to dunes, the vegetation growing sparser as sandy soil replaced the richer humus of the woodland. Here, the specialized plants that had adapted to harsh coastal conditions created a different kind of beauty—restios with their architectural forms catching first light, groundcovers spreading in geometric patterns across the sand, and the occasional burst of vivid color from flowering succulents.

As they crested a large dune, the full spectacle of daybreak revealed itself—the endless expanse of the Indian Ocean spread before them, its surface gilded by early sunlight. Several runners paused briefly to absorb the view, their phones emerging to capture the moment before continuing their journey.

The dune section required more effort, the soft sand challenging their stride efficiency, but the reward came as ever-changing vistas as they followed the undulating terrain. Eventually, the trail descended to the beach itself—a vast expanse of pristine sand that stretched toward the iconic lighthouse visible in the distance.

"The Cape St. Francis Lighthouse's been guiding ships along this treacherous coastline since 1878," Luke shared as they approached the distinctive white tower. "It stands twenty-eight meters tall, and its light is visible from nearly thirty nautical miles at sea."

The beach section offered firmer footing than the dunes, allowing for more conversational pacing. Tyler and Emma maintained their customary position at the front, with a brisk tempo. Madeline and Stanley kept steady middle-of-the-pack positions, while Nkosi had struck up a running conversation with Rogerio, both men discussing the distinctive geology along the coast.

Sabrina Chu was absolutely glowing on the morning run, her confidence noticeably bolstered by her successful bungee jump the previous day. She jogged alongside Margaret, occasionally filming brief segments of their progress with her ever-present phone, but spending more time simply experiencing the environment than documenting it.

"Nothing quite like running on a beach at sunrise," Margaret commented to no one in particular, her expression reflecting genuine appreciation for the experience.

As they completed their circuit and approached the final stretch of beach leading toward the finish line, Luke indicated a staffed station set up near the water's edge — a white-clothed table with a small array of breakfast items and, notably, a champagne bucket.

"Our traditional sunrise run refreshments," he announced as they gathered at this impromptu spot. "Mimosas on the beach to celebrate this gorgeous morning."

The group gathered in clusters, sipping their mimosas and commenting on the beautiful course.

"To South African sunrises," Sheryl proposed, raising her glass in toast. "And to new adventures ahead at Kariega Game Reserve."

The group echoed her toast, the shared morning experience and anticipation of their upcoming safari boosting their growing camaraderie. Conversation flowed easily as they enjoyed their light refreshments, many reflecting on highlights of their Garden Route journey thus far.

"The bungee jump was definitely my personal breakthrough," Joan shared, her previous timidity replaced by quiet pride. "When I finally jumped, I wasn't thinking about what's waiting for me back at home at all — just the incredible feeling of dropping into the air."

"That's the essence of adventure travel," Stanley observed sagely. "The moments that matter most are rarely the ones you plan."

As they finished their beach snack and prepared to return to the resort for a proper morning meal and departure preparations, Sheryl received a message on her phone. The brief text from Jack confirmed their schedule: "Arrived safely. Will meet group at resort as planned."

The timing aligned perfectly with their itinerary—the sunrise run complete, allowing just enough time for breakfast and checkout before beginning their journey to Kariega, where the safari portion of their adventure would begin.

By mid-morning, the tour group had completed checkout and assembled in the resort's entrance area, the luggage organized for loading onto their bus. The familiar faces of Jack and Anika among them generated warm greetings and questions about the Donovans' situation.

"Kim's recovering well but really can't continue the tough schedule we've got ahead of us," Anika explained, maintaining their cover story with ease. "They've both decided to cut their trip short and will unfortunately miss the safari portion of our journey."

"We're sorry to hear that," Madeline responded with genuine concern. "Please, pass along our best wishes when you're in contact with them again."

Jack nodded an acknowledgment, his expression appropriately regretful while betraying none of the actual circumstances regarding the Donovans' current accommodations in police custody. His brief eye contact with Sheryl communicated everything that needed to be said without the need for words.

With the group reunited—minus the Donovans—they boarded their bus for the long drive. The route would take them further into the Eastern Cape province, transitioning from coastal environments to the distinctive bushveld that characterized the region's interior.

"We've got about three hours of driving ahead of us," Luke announced once everyone had settled. "We'll break the journey with a stop at Nanaga Farm Stall—a local institution that is an authentic slice of Eastern Cape culture."

As they departed Cape St. Francis, Sheryl found a moment for discreet conversation with Jack and Anika, using the privacy created by their seating arrangement near the front of the bus.

"Mission successful," Jack confirmed quietly. "Diamonds secured and en route to De Beers. The Donovans are in custody, facing multiple charges, but without the cryptocurrency as definitive proof of their payment, I think it'll be more difficult to get a conviction if they get the right lawyer."

"And Malanga?" Sheryl inquired, keeping her voice below the ambient noise level of the bus.

"Still running free," Anika acknowledged, her frustration evident. "He's gone to ground, but our guess is that his business has been significantly disrupted. Both the wildlife trafficking and diamond smuggling networks have lost money and product."

"He's already made a point of demonstrating his reach when he had that guy at the bridge threaten me."

Jack nodded. "Classic intimidation tactics. His power's been diminished, so he's compensating with empty threats."

"I've officially completed my mission with the diamond recovery," Anika added. "De Beers security has green lit my

continued vacation with the group. So, I'm just a tourist from here on."

Their conversation shifted to details about the remainder of the tour, with particular attention to the more remote environment of the game reserve. The transition from populated coastal areas to the isolated bushveld presented both challenges and advantages.

As they completed their conversation, the landscape outside had transformed noticeably. The coastal vegetation gave way to a distinctly different greenery—the Eastern Cape's valley bushveld, characterized by dense thickets of spekboom, euphorbia trees with their distinctive candelabra shapes, and aloes that punctuated the landscape.

About ninety minutes into their journey, they approached the promised refreshment stop. A simple roadside sign announced "Nanaga Farm Stall" with little embellishment, though the crowded parking area suggested it was a major tourist stop.

"Nanaga's an old Eastern Cape institution," Luke explained as they pulled into the parking area. "What began as a simple farm stand selling local produce has evolved into a regional landmark, particularly famous for its meat pies and pineapple juice. You'll find some meats unique to Africa in their bakery."

Inside, the farm stall revealed its true popularity—a bustling hive of activity centered around a bakery counter where staff in green aprons efficiently served a continuous stream of customers. The air carried the intoxicating aroma of freshly baked bread, roasting meats, and the distinctive scent of coffee.

"Nanaga began in the 1970s as a simple roadside stand selling excess produce from the family farm," Luke elaborated as the group explored the space. "It remains family-owned, and it's an essential stop for anyone traveling between Port Elizabeth and Grahamstown. The building dates from the mid-1980s, though it's been expanded several times to accommodate its growing popularity."

The tourists dispersed throughout the space, many gravitating toward the bakery counter, where glass cases displayed an impressive array of savory pies, sweet pastries, and the signature roosterkoek—round bread rolls cooked over open coals and served with farm-fresh butter and preserves.

"I'd recommend the warthog pie," Luke suggested to those seeking lunch options. "And their milk tart's considered among the best in the Eastern Cape for those with a sweet tooth."

The stop provided not just refreshments but a glimpse into everyday Eastern Cape culture.

After about twenty minutes, sufficient time for refreshments and exploration of the souvenir section, the group reassembled for the final push to the game reserve.

As they continued eastward, the landscape changed to rolling hills covered in dense bush and occasional glimpses of valleys cutting through the terrain. The human footprint became progressively less evident, with farmhouses and cultivated fields giving way to larger tracts of semi-wild bushveld.

"We're entering what historically was known as the frontier zone," Luke explained while they traveled. "This region marked the contested boundary between European colonial expansion and indigenous territories for nearly a century. The landscape bears witness to that history—European-style farm-houses standing near traditional Xhosa homesteads, mission churches alongside sacred indigenous sites."

The educational narrative continued as they approached their destination, Luke skillfully transitioning from historical context to practical information about their upcoming safari experience.

"Kariega Game Reserve encompasses about ten thousand hectares of pristine Eastern Cape landscape," he explained. "Unlike the more famous Kruger region, Eastern Cape reserves come from reclaimed agricultural land that's been carefully restored to its natural state, with indigenous wildlife reintroduced over the decades."

The anticipation within the vehicle was palpable as they turned onto a gravel road marked by a simple wooden sign bearing the Kariega logo. The transition from public thoroughfare to private reserve was marked by a staffed security gate, where rangers checked their reservation details before welcoming them with warm smiles.

"Kariega welcomes the Global Runners," the senior ranger announced as the gate swung open. "Your safari adventure begins now."

The change in environment was immediate and dramatic. Where the public road had been bordered by fencing and occasional farmhouses, they now entered a wilderness where the boundary between road and bush blurred organically. The bus slowed to a game-viewing pace, allowing an assessment of the landscape that would be their home for the rest of their vacation.

They'd traveled barely five hundred meters past the entrance when excited murmurs rippled through the vehicle. A small herd of impalas had emerged from the bush beside the road—an elegant antelope species with distinctive lyre-shaped horns, their reddish-brown coats gleaming in the midday sun.

"Our first wildlife sighting," Luke confirmed with clear satisfaction. "Impalas are often called the McDonald's of the bush—they're everywhere, and they're on every predator's menu. But don't let their abundance diminish your appreciation of their remarkable adaptation to this environment."

Cameras emerged as the group photographed this first authentic safari experience—the beginning of what would undoubtedly become thousands of wildlife images captured during their stay. The impalas, accustomed to vehicles, continued their graceful browsing with only occasional glances toward the bus.

As they drove deeper into the reserve, the wildlife sightings increased in frequency and diversity. A pair of giraffes appeared silhouetted against the sky as they crossed a ridgeline ahead, their characteristic profiles unmistakable, even at a distance. A family group of nyalas—males with their magnificent spiral horns and distinctive white stripes across their backs, females with their smaller builds and reddish-brown fur—emerged from a thicket to observe the vehicle with calm curiosity.

"The nyala represents one of Africa's most sexually dimorphic antelope species," Luke explained as cameras clicked rapidly. "The males and females look so different they were initially classified as separate species by early naturalists."

The excitement of these initial wildlife encounters created a festive atmosphere in the vehicle—the tangible beginning of the safari experience they had traveled thousands of miles to experience.

After about twenty minutes, they crested a final hill to reveal their destination—Kariega Main Lodge, positioned on an elevated ridge with commanding views across the reserve. The architecture reflected the traditional African safari aesthetic updated for contemporary sensibilities—thatched roofs over stone walls, expansive viewing decks, and careful integration with the natural environment through indigenous landscaping.

Staff members awaited their arrival on the broad entrance steps, a welcoming party that included both hospitality personnel and rangers who would guide their safari activities. As the vehicle came to a stop, a tall man stepped forward from the group—his ranger uniform and confident stance marking him as someone intimately connected to this wilderness.

"Welcome to Kariega," he announced, his voice carrying the distinctive cadence of the Eastern Cape. "I'm Pieter Pretorius, head of conservation and anti-poaching operations here at the reserve. My brother, Luke, has told me about your adventures along the Garden Route, but now, your real African experience begins."

The family resemblance between the brothers was clear, despite their different professions—Luke's more polished appearance contrasting with Pieter's rugged look.

As the group gathered their immediate belongings, Pieter continued his welcome speech. "Kariega represents a conservation success story—land that was degraded by generations of agricultural use, now restored to wildlife habitat. Everything you'll see during your stay here exists because of deliberate rewilding efforts spanning decades."

The arrival process unfolded with the efficiency of a well-managed safari operation—drinks appearing on trays, luggage directed to appropriate chalets, and brief orientation information delivered with enthusiasm rather than a rehearsed script.

"You've arrived in time for our lunch service," the hospitality manager informed them. "After you've refreshed yourselves, please join us on the main deck for a buffet of local specialties. Your first game drive departs at 16:00, when the animals become more active as the day cools."

As the tourists were escorted to their accommodations—luxury chalets positioned to maximize privacy and comfort—Sheryl remained briefly with Luke, Jack, and Anika to greet Pieter more personally.

"Good to finally meet in person," Pieter said after shaking hands with each of them. "Luke's kept me updated on your experiences. Impressive work with the diamond recovery."

"There's still unfinished business with the wildlife trafficking, though," Jack noted.

Pieter nodded, his expression shifting to professional seriousness. "Unfortunately, you've arrived during an active period. We've recorded multiple poaching intrusions in the past week—primarily targeting rhino, but there's also been evidence of snaring operations focused on bushmeat."

"Malanga's people?" Sheryl asked.

"Almost certainly," Pieter confirmed. "We've identified at least two distinct groups operating in the region. One led by an individual known as 'Thabiso'—a former professional soldier turned poacher. The second focuses on high-volume bushmeat and opportunistic trophy animals for Asian markets."

"They lost their diamonds, thanks to us," Anika noted. "That may increase pressure on the poaching portion of their operation to bring in revenue."

"Probably accurate," Pieter agreed. "We've enhanced security accordingly—additional ranger patrols, drone surveillance of the boundary fence, and increased coordination with neighboring reserves."

This reality check tempered their idyllic arrival with the awareness of ongoing conservation challenges. For tourists, Kariega represented a carefully managed wilderness experience; for Malanga's operation, it represented exploitable resources for illicit markets.

"We should continue this conversation after lunch," Pieter suggested, aware of the other staff members within potential earshot. "I can update you on specific intelligence during this afternoon's game drive. I'll be personally guiding one group today."

With nods of agreement, they separated to attend to their respective responsibilities—Sheryl and Luke to oversee their clients' comfortable transition to safari life, Jack and Anika to relax into pure tourist mode, and Pieter to arrange the afternoon's safari experience and intelligence briefing.

As Sheryl walked to her assigned chalet, the juxtaposition of their circumstances struck her with particular clarity.

Here in this seemingly pristine wilderness, far from the urban complexities of Cape Town or the tourist infrastructure of the Garden Route, they had perhaps moved closer to the central threat of their antagonist. The remote bushveld might feel removed from Malanga's shadowy urban operations, but in reality, they'd entered the production zone of his wildlife trafficking business—the source that fed his international smuggling channels.

The distant call of a fish eagle echoed across the reserve—a sound quintessentially African, representing both the wilderness they had come to experience and the natural resources under threat from poaching.

For now, however, Sheryl decided the runners deserved the authentic safari experience they'd traveled so far to enjoy—the wonder of Africa's wildlife, the beauty of its landscapes, and the unique perspective that only immersion in this environment could provide. The magic of Kariega would take center stage.

CHAPTER 32

A CONSERVATION RENAISSANCE

As Pieter led the afternoon game drive through Kariega's rolling landscape, his passion for the reserve's history and conservation mission on full display. The collection of vehicles followed a winding dirt track that ascended a gentle rise, offering panoramic views across the ten-thousand-hectare property. He brought the lead vehicle to a stop at this strategic viewpoint, allowing the group to absorb the sweeping vista of river valleys, acacia-dotted savannas, and dense thickets that characterized the Eastern Cape bushveld.

"What you're seeing now," Pieter began, gesturing toward the seemingly pristine wilderness spreading before them, "is actually one of South Africa's most remarkable ecological restoration stories. Less than thirty years ago, this entire landscape looked completely different."

The tourists, who had already been thrilled with sightings of nyalas, zebras, and a distant elephant bull during their drive, turned their attention to Pieter's narrative with interest.

"Kariega's history mirrors the broader transformation of the Eastern Cape," he continued. "This land's experienced multiple dramatic shifts in its ecological character—from pristine wilderness, to frontier battleground, to agricultural degradation, and finally to a conservation rebirth."

Sheryl noticed how Pieter's storytelling differed from Luke's more polished presentation. Where Luke crafted narratives optimized for tourist engagement, Pieter spoke with the direct authenticity of someone whose life was bound to the land he described.

"Originally, this entire region supported vast populations of wildlife," he explained, pointing toward distant ridgelines. "Historical accounts from the early 1800s describe herds of elephants, buffalos, and antelopes so numerous they darkened the landscape. Predators—lions, leopards, cheetahs, and hyenas—maintained the ecological balance. The indigenous San and Xhosa people lived within this system, using resources sustainably for thousands of years."

He shifted position slightly, indicating different sections of the landscape as his narrative progressed through time.

"European colonization changed everything. The frontier wars between the Xhosa kingdoms and European settlers raged across these valleys for nearly a century. When the dust settled, the land was divided into European-style farms—primarily sheep and cattle operations that required clearing indigenous vegetation and eliminating predators."

Nkosi raised his hand with a question. "When did the transition from farming to conservation begin?"

"The agricultural phase lasted about 150 years," Pieter replied. "By the mid-1900s, many of these farms had become ecologically compromised. Overgrazing degraded the soil, erosion scarred the hillsides, and native vegetation struggled to recover under continuous livestock grazing."

He pointed toward a distant section where a different vegetation pattern was barely discernible. "That area belonged to the Van Rensburg farm, beginning in 1867. By the 1980s, it could barely support fifty head of cattle. The combination of poor agricultural practices and the Eastern Cape's challenging climate had exhausted the land's productive capacity."

The convoy of vehicles began moving again, descending toward a riverine area where massive yellowwood trees created a natural canopy over a crystal-clear waterway. Pieter continued his historical narrative as they traveled.

"Kariega's conservation story began in 1989, when the first parcels of marginal farmland were purchased for what started as a small real estate development project. The initial property was just 660 hectares—a tiny fraction of what you see today. Initially, the owner wanted to sell ranch homes to a few dozen buyers. But that project failed to attract interest, and one of the few who did show up was a conservationist who planted the idea of a preserve in the owner's head. The vision was radical for its time: remove all agricultural infrastructure, reestablish native vegetation, and eventually reintroduce the wildlife that'd been absent for generations."

As if to punctuate his point, a family of warthogs emerged from a thicket beside the road—two parents and four tiny piglets trotting in characteristic single file, their tails held vertically like antennas. The vehicle paused as cameras captured this charming sight.

"These warthogs are one of our earliest restoration successes," Pieter noted. "Native to the region but eliminated during the farming era, they've built sustainable breeding populations throughout the reserve."

The drive continued into an open savanna area, where giraffes browsed peacefully on acacia trees, their elegant forms silhouetted against the afternoon sky. Nearby, zebras grazed alongside red hartebeest. These different species comfortably shared the same grassland.

"Our restoration philosophy centers on rebuilding complete ecosystems rather than simply stocking photogenic animals," Pieter explained, as they observed this multi-species gathering. "Each reintroduction is carefully planned to restore ecological functions and relationships. Herbivores modify vegetation through their feeding patterns, creating habitats for smaller species. Predators regulate herbivore populations, preventing overgrazing."

"How do you determine which species to reintroduce and when?" Jack asked.

"We follow historical records to identify native species, then assess habitat readiness before each species," Pieter replied. "The sequence matters tremendously. We begin with habitat engineers like elephants and buffalo that create conditions for other species. Predators come later, once prey populations are established."

He directed their attention to subtle landscape features that revealed the reserve's agricultural past—a distant stone wall barely visible through vegetation, the faint outline of an old farm road now largely reclaimed by nature, a non-native eucalyptus stand marking a former homesteading site.

"Complete ecological restoration requires both addition and subtraction," he continued. "We reintroduce native species while simultaneously removing human-introduced elements—invasive plants, agricultural infrastructure, artificial water sources that distort natural movement patterns."

The vehicles turned onto a different track that led toward a massive earthen dam—one of several water retention structures visible throughout the reserve. A pod of hippos occupied the deeper section, their eyes and ears visible above the water surface like living periscopes.

"Some modifications we maintain deliberately," Pieter noted while indicating the dam. "The Eastern Cape's rainfall patterns are increasingly unpredictable due to climate change. These water management systems help wildlife survive extended dry periods while we gradually transition toward more natural water distribution."

As they circled the dam, Pieter pointed out less obvious conservation interventions—erosion control structures on hillsides, carefully managed burn patterns in grassland areas, and replanted thickets of spekboom, a succulent plant with carbon-sequestering properties.

"Spekboom is our secret weapon in both ecological restoration and climate action," he explained with enthusiasm. "It can capture up to ten times more carbon than an equivalent area of Amazon rainforest. It prevents soil erosion, provides food for multiple species, and thrives in our challenging climate."

The drive continued through increasingly varied habitats, each revealing different stages of Kariega's conservation practices. In a secluded valley, they encountered multiple white rhinos—massive yet delicate creatures grazing peacefully in the late afternoon light.

"Our rhino population is both our greatest conservation success and our most significant security challenge," Pieter acknowledged, his tone shifting. "We began rhino reintroduction in 2002 with three individuals. Today, despite the poaching pressure we still fight against, we maintain a growing population through intensive protection efforts."

Sheryl noticed the subtle change in his demeanor when discussing rhinos—a combination of pride in his team's conservation success and the weight of responsibility for their protection. The anti-poaching mission was clearly personal for him.

"What restoration challenges are unique to the Eastern Cape?" Nkosi inquired.

"Several significant ones," Pieter replied, and his smile signified that he appreciated the question's depth. "Unlike the Kruger region, our wildlife populations were completely eliminated, not just reduced. This meant reintroductions started from zero, requiring careful genetic management to prevent inbreeding."

The vehicles began climbing again, following a ridge that offered views across multiple valleys and habitat zones. Pieter continued his explanation as they ascended.

"We also faced extensive soil degradation from generations of farming. Restoring soil health requires multiple actions—strategic animal reintroductions to increase organic matter, vegetation management to prevent erosion, and sometimes direct remediation of severely compromised areas."

He indicated a distant section where the vegetation was clearly different than the other areas they had seen thus far. "That area suffered extreme erosion from sheep farming. We've spent fifteen years rebuilding its soil through planting spekboom, controlling the herbivore populations, and careful managing water sources. It's now supporting wildlife that would've been impossible a decade ago."

As they reached the ridge top, the true scale of Kariega's operation became apparent. The reserve stretched in all directions, its boundaries barely discernible where it met neighboring conservation areas.

"Our most important recent development's been connectivity with adjacent reserves," Pieter explained. "Wildlife doesn't recognize property boundaries. By removing internal fencing and coordinating management with neighboring conservancies, we've effectively created a much larger functional ecosystem."

He pointed toward the distant hills that marked the expanded boundaries. "This landscape connectivity is critical for species requiring extensive territories, like elephants, lions, and particularly leopards. It also creates genetic diversity that strengthens the resilience of different populations of animals."

The conversation shifted to the reserve's community engagement efforts when Madeline inquired about relationships with surrounding populations.

"Conservation can't succeed as an island," Pieter acknowledged. "Kariega operates extensive community programs focused on education, employment, and shared economic benefit. We maintain a foundation that supports local schools, healthcare initiatives, and skill development courses."

He described their eco-ranger training program that prepared local youth for conservation careers, agricultural mentorships that helped nearby communities implement sustainable farming practices, and revenue-sharing arrangements that ensured tourism benefited the communities as well as the reserve.

"Many of our most effective anti-poaching rangers come from local communities," he noted. "Their tracking skills often exceed what can be taught in formal training, and their local connections provide invaluable intelligence about potential threats."

As the sun began its descent toward the horizon, casting the landscape in golden light perfect for photography, Pieter directed the convoy toward a particularly scenic overlook for the traditional safari sundowner experience. Staff prepared a small setup with drinks and light refreshments, positioned to maximize the views across the reserve.

While the tourists disembarked to enjoy this quintessential safari ritual, Pieter took the opportunity to share more technical conservation details with those particularly interested. He described their wildlife monitoring systems, which combined traditional tracking techniques with modern technology, including camera traps, drone surveillance, and GPS collars on key species.

"Our conservation management relies increasingly on obtaining data," he explained to Nkosi and Jack, who'd expressed particular interest. "We track vegetation changes, animal movements, water quality, and dozens of other metrics to guide our actions."

He outlined Kariega's approach to adaptive management. He explained how they used real-time information to adjust conservation strategies as conditions changed. "The ultimate goal isn't just to restore what was here historically," Pieter concluded as the group prepared to return to the vehicles for their drive back to the lodge. "It's to create resilient ecosystems capable of adapting to changing climate conditions and human pressures. Conservation isn't about freezing ecosystems in time—it's about enabling their continued evolution under challenging circumstances."

As twilight descended and they began their journey back to the lodge, the evidence of Kariega's successful conservation efforts surrounded them—herds of animals visible on distant hillsides, the chorus of birds settling for the evening, and the tangible sense of ecological health that permeated the landscape.

"What you're experiencing here," Pieter noted as they approached the lodge, its lights now visible in the gathering darkness, "is conservation in active progress rather than a finished state. Despite our successes, we're maybe thirty years into a hundred-year restoration process. Each generation builds on the work of the previous one."

This perspective clearly impressed the group. As they disembarked at the lodge, the runners shared their feelings about the animals and the conservation mission.

For Sheryl, observing these interactions reinforced the value of their visit to this specific reserve. The wildlife trafficking they'd inadvertently stumbled into threatened not just individual animals but the entire restoration effort Pieter had so eloquently described—a multi-decade investment in ecological healing that poaching could damage in a single night of violence.

Later that evening, as the group gathered around the lodge's central firepit to share stories from their first safari experience, the conversation repeatedly returned to Kariega's restoration story. Something about this narrative of ecological redemption had captured their imagination more powerfully than individual animal sightings.

"It's the hope in it," Madeline observed thoughtfully, watching the flames dance in the traditional boma fireplace. "So much environmental news is negative. But here, we're literally watching healing happen."

Pieter, who'd joined the evening gathering, nodded in appreciation for her insight. "That's exactly why we share our history so openly. Kariega isn't just about spectacular wildlife viewing, though we certainly offer that. It's about demonstrating that meaningful restoration is possible when our commitment extends beyond individual human lifespans."

As stars emerged in spectacular profusion above the reserve—far from urban light pollution—the conversation gradually quieted into contemplative silence. The rhythmic sounds of the African night provided the perfect soundtrack to this moment of connection with the surrounding landscape.

CHAPTER 33

TRESPASSERS

The pre-dawn darkness at Kariega Game Reserve carried a distinctive chill — that uniquely African morning coolness that would surrender to heat as the day progressed. By 6:15 a.m., the Global Runners group had assembled at the main lodge's entrance, fortified with quick coffee and rusks but saving proper breakfast for after their early game drive. Excitement overcame any lingering sleep deprivation as they climbed aboard the three open Land Rovers for their safari experience.

"Morning, everyone," Pieter greeted the guests assigned to his vehicle. His Land Rover carried a diverse subset of the tour group — Sheryl in the front passenger seat as tour leader, with Wanda, Joan, and Margaret occupying the middle row.

Nkosi and the Alvarez brothers filled the rear bench. Each vehicle was similarly filled with a driver, guide, and two rows of tourists.

Pieter explained the plans for the remaining safari drives. "We'll be taking the entire group out at the same time. But once we clear the resort area, each vehicle will go in a different direction. With a single vehicle, we disturb the animals less, and you get a more private experience. Don't worry, every vehicle will visit each area and its animals, just in a different order."

Heads nodded, realizing the advantages of this approach.

Dawn was just beginning to paint the eastern horizon with delicate watercolor strokes of pink and gold as the small convoy departed. The vehicles moved at a deliberately slow pace along dirt tracks that wound through the reserve, headlights illuminating the path ahead while the spotlights mounted on each side allowed guides to scan the surrounding bush for reflective animal eyes.

"Early morning offers our best viewing opportunities," Pieter explained as they traveled. "Many species are most active during these cooler hours, especially in spring. We'll begin at Elephant Dam, a reliable gathering point for multiple species."

The transition from night to day unfolded around them as they drove—the gradual illumination of the landscape revealing details that darkness had concealed. African dawn happened with remarkable swiftness, the sun breaching the horizon and climbing with purpose, unlike the languid sunrises of higher latitudes.

"Look left," Pieter instructed quietly. He slowed the vehicle down even more and directed his spotlight toward a thicket where movement had caught his attention. The beam revealed a pair of bat-eared foxes returning from their nocturnal hunting. They were delicate creatures with improbably large ears that swiveled like radar dishes. They paused briefly, assessing the vehicle, before trotting into denser vegetation and disappearing from sight.

"Extraordinary hearing," Pieter noted as they continued. "They can detect insect larvae moving underground. Most of their diet comprises termites and beetles, which they locate by sound rather than sight."

This initial sighting energized the group. Cameras emerged from protective bags as the growing light made photography increasingly viable. The vehicle followed a winding route through diverse habitats—open grassland, acacia savanna, and denser thickets that characterized the Eastern Cape's valley bushveld ecosystem.

As they approached Elephant Dam—a large, artificial water source created during the reserve's development—Pieter reduced speed once more, approaching with deliberate quietness.

"We'll stop just before the clearing," he whispered, then cut the engine and allowed the car's momentum to carry them to an ideal viewing position at the edge of the open area surrounding the dam. "Perfect timing."

A small family group of white rhinoceros stood at the water's edge, their armored bodies silhouetted against the reflected sunrise. Nearby, giraffes maintained vigilant observation while drinking—their splayed legs creating the characteristic vulnerable posture required to reach the water. The periphery hosted some smaller players—a herd of impalas, several majestic kudu bulls with their spectacular spiral horns, and a pair of warthogs who knelt on their front legs to drink.

"Look, multiple species gathered together," Wanda whispered, already filming with her camera.

The group maintained respectful silence, the only sounds the soft clicks of camera shutters and occasional whispered questions directed to Pieter. The guide provided context in hushed tones, explaining how different species listened to each other's alarm signals, creating a collective security perimeter against predators.

"The impalas function as the alarm system," he explained. "Their eyesight and hearing are exceptional. When they startle, everyone else pays attention, too."

For nearly twenty minutes, they observed this natural gathering as the morning light strengthened—the perfect introduction to Africa's wildlife in a single tableau. Eventually, the animals began departing in small groups, their morning hydration needs satisfied as the day's heat began building.

"We'll continue deeper into the reserve," Pieter announced once the clearing had emptied. "I want to show you some of our more secluded habitats where we sometimes find leopards and specialized antelope species."

The vehicle resumed its journey, following narrower tracks that penetrated more remote sections of the reserve. The landscape grew increasingly rugged. Rocky outcroppings created distinctive microclimates, while deeper valleys supported denser vegetation fed by seasonal watercourses. All the while, Pieter provided ongoing commentary about the visible ecology—pointing out particular plant species, explaining geological features, and identifying birds that rested in the treetops.

About an hour into their drive, they approached what appeared to be a human-made structure partially visible through the bush—sections of high fence forming a large enclosure.

"This is one of our acclimation bomas," Pieter began explaining as they approached. "When we introduce new animals to the reserve, particularly predators like leopards or even certain herbivores like some antelope species, we keep them confined initially to allow them time to adjust to their new environment before fully releasing them."

The Land Rover rounded a bend in the track, bringing the enclosure into clearer view. "Our most recent residents were a pair of leopards relocated from a conflict zone in the Limpopo Province. They've been successfully released and are establishing territories in our eastern section. The boma's currently empty, awaiting—"

Pieter's narrative halted abruptly as the enclosure came fully into view. His expression shifted from casual tour guide to intense professional concern in an instant. "That's not right," he stated tersely, accelerating slightly to reach the fence line faster.

As they pulled alongside the enclosure, the cause of his concern became immediately apparent. Inside the supposedly empty acclimation boma stood a dozen kudus—magnificent spiral-horned antelope looking confused and agitated within the confined space.

Pieter immediately reached for his radio, calling the other vehicles to join them while contacting the reserve's security team. "Control, this is Pieter. We've got an incident at the eastern acclimation boma. Unauthorized animal containment. Multiple kudus confined. Request immediate security response."

The crackling response confirmed that his message had been received and support had been dispatched. Turning to the increasingly concerned tourists, he provided the professional context his expression had already suggested.

"We're looking at poacher activity," he stated plainly. "What you're seeing here isn't part of our management operations. Someone deliberately captured these animals and contained them."

The other safari vehicles arrived within minutes, their guides equally disturbed by the discovery. After a brief conference with Pieter, a decision was made that would dramatically alter their planned safari experience.

"I need to investigate this situation immediately," Pieter informed the group. "Under normal circumstances, we'd continue your game drive along the planned route. However, given the significance of this discovery and the educational opportunity it presents, I'm offering you a choice."

He surveyed their faces, reading the mixture of concern and interest his announcement had generated. "Those who wish to continue with a traditional game drive can transfer to the other vehicles. Anyone interested in understanding the realities of our anti-poaching work is welcome to remain with me as I investigate. The latter will be less comfortable and potentially disturbing, but it will also be a unique educational experience."

The response was immediate and unanimous—no one volunteered to transfer. The discovery had transformed their tourist experience into something more meaningful, their collective indignation at the obvious poaching overriding any interest in conventional wildlife viewing.

"Very well," Pieter acknowledged. "Let me establish some safety rules first."

He conferred briefly with the other guides, arranging for them to maintain perimeter security while radioing again for additional anti-poaching personnel. With basic security established, he turned back to his group.

"We'll approach the enclosure on foot to examine any evidence we can find without creating additional vehicle tracks that might obscure what's already there. Please, stay together, and follow my instructions precisely."

The group disembarked, their cameras now repurposed from wildlife photography to evidence documentation. Pieter led them in careful formation toward the enclosure, pointing out details that his trained eye immediately recognized.

"Note these tire tracks," he indicated, kneeling beside distinct impressions in the sandy soil. "These aren't from reserve vehicles—wrong tread patterns. And here—" he said and pointed to a patch of disturbed earth near the enclosure gate, "—drag marks where they've forced the animals into the boma."

The tourists gathered around, their expressions reflecting a growing understanding of what they were witnessing. It wasn't an abstract concept of poaching from documentaries or news reports—it was an active wildlife crime occurring in real time.

"The kudus have been captured but not killed…yet," Pieter explained as they observed the confined animals. "That suggests the poachers were interrupted or planned to return at a later time. These animals are targeted primarily for the bushmeat trade—the horns have some value, but the meat is where the real money's at."

Joan, who'd been examining the ground with a fierce attention to detail, called from several meters away. "There are more tracks heading east," she noted, pointing toward a game trail that led away from the enclosure.

Pieter joined her immediately to examine the trail she'd identified. "Good eye," he confirmed. "Same vehicle pattern."

With radio confirmation that additional security personnel were en route, Pieter made a rapid decision. "We'll follow these tracks briefly to assess the extent of their operation. Stay close together, and be silent."

The group followed the trail for about two hundred meters, moving deeper into a wooded section of the reserve. The evidence of intrusion became increasingly apparent to even untrained observers—broken vegetation, discarded items including cigarette butts and an empty water bottle, and occasional boot prints distinct from the rangers' standard issue footwear.

The trail led them to a small clearing where Pieter suddenly raised his hand in the universal signal to stop. His posture changed instantly—tension visible in every line of his body as he surveyed what lay ahead.

In the clearing lay the carcass of a Cape buffalo—one of Africa's most formidable herbivores. The animal had been partially butchered, with its characteristic curved horns removed entirely, leaving a grotesque absence where they should have been.

"Remain here," Pieter instructed firmly. He approached the carcass alone to assess the scene while maintaining radio contact with security. After a brief examination, he rejoined the group, his expression grave.

"This animal was killed last night," he informed them. "Professional work—precise cuts to remove the horns and some prime meat sections. They were interrupted before completing their butchering. Likely the same group that captured the kudus."

The tourists' reactions reflected a genuine emotional impact—it wasn't the sanitized experience many safari operations carefully curated. Margaret pressed her hand to her mouth, visibly distressed by the mutilated animal. The Alvarez brothers exchanged looks of anger, while Wanda quietly documented the scene with her camera.

"Why would they take just the horns?" Sean asked.

"Cape buffalo horns fetch significant prices in certain Asian markets," Pieter explained. "They're carved into decorative items or ground for supposed medicinal properties. The meat is a secondary profit, sold locally in informal markets or transported to urban areas."

As they processed this information, radio communication from the security team alerted Pieter to additional discoveries. His expression darkened further as he listened to the report.

"They've found more," he informed the group. "We need to move quickly. This location is now an active crime scene and potentially still dangerous."

The group returned to their vehicle with new urgency, following Pieter's instructions without question. Their safari experience had transformed entirely—from wildlife observation to witnessing the front lines of conservation's most challenging battle.

They followed the security team's directions to another location about one kilometer away. There, the evidence of poaching took an even more disturbing form—a white rhinoceros lay on its side, alive but immobilized, breathing in a labored pattern seen in large mammals who had been tranquilized.

"They were scared away before they could remove the horn," Pieter explained, and his voice was tight with controlled anger as they observed from a safe distance. "Likely by our night patrol—we maintain twenty-four-hour coverage in rhino zones."

He immediately radioed for the reserve's veterinary team, providing precise coordinates and a status assessment. "We've got a darted white rhino, adult female, about six years old. Breathing is stable, but she's in a compromised position. Require immediate veterinary response and recovery team."

The tourists watched in somber silence as Pieter coordinated the emergency response. When Pieter returned to address them, his professional demeanor remained intact, but the emotional undercurrent was unmistakable.

"The vet team's twenty minutes out," he informed them. "They'll administer a reversal agent for the tranquilizer and monitor her recovery. I think we found her just in the nick of time, so she should make a full recovery."

He surveyed their faces to see how they were handling the things they had seen thus far. "This is the reality we face daily. Last night, we interrupted at least one poaching team that managed to capture kudus, kill a buffalo, and tranquilize a rhino before being driven off. They'll return—if not tonight, then soon."

The group remained with the rhino until the veterinary team arrived—a specially equipped vehicle carrying two veterinarians and additional rangers. They watched as professionals efficiently assessed the animal's condition, administered medication, and positioned it more favorably for breathing while its recovery began.

"We'll need to maintain observation until she's fully mobile," the lead veterinarian explained after the initial treatment was complete. "The greatest risk now is if she has any physical complications from prolonged immobility—the biggest threats are respiratory issues, circulation problems, or muscle damage."

With the rhino receiving proper care, Pieter determined that it was time to return to the lodge. The morning's events had exhausted their scheduled game drive time, and the group needed some time to reflect and recharge after the unexpected intensity of their experience.

As they drove back toward the main lodge, the conversation in the vehicle reflected what a profound impact the morning had on them. Today wasn't the idealized safari experience of perfect wildlife photographs and sundowner drinks. It was a raw, disturbing reality—the daily struggle between conservation and exploitation playing out in real time before their eyes.

"How often does this happen?" Joan asked, breaking a lengthy silence as they approached the lodge.

"More often than we publicly acknowledge," Pieter admitted. "We typically document three to four incursion attempts a week. Most are intercepted before animals are taken, but we lose some battles. Every reserve in South Africa faces similar challenges."

"Why don't more people know about this?" Margaret wondered aloud, still visibly affected by what they'd witnessed based on the severe frown she wore and how red her eyes appeared.

"Tourism and conservation exist in a complex balance," Pieter explained. "People come to Africa expecting to see magnificent wildlife and beautiful landscapes. The violent reality of poaching disrupts that narrative. Most reserves choose to shield guests from these ugly details."

"That seems counterproductive," Wanda observed. "How can people care about solving a problem they don't fully understand or know exists?"

Pieter nodded appreciatively at her insight. "Exactly why I decided to include you today. Authentic understanding sometimes requires confronting uncomfortable truths."

As they pulled into the lodge's entrance, the contrast between the manicured environment and the raw conservation battlefield they'd just experienced seemed particularly stark. Other guests lounged by the pool or enjoyed a late breakfast on the viewing deck, their safari experience conforming to the expected scenes of wildlife viewing and comfortable luxury.

"We'll have a proper debrief after breakfast," Pieter informed them as they disembarked. "For now, take some time to process what you've seen and restore yourselves. This wasn't the morning experience you anticipated, but it was valuable, nonetheless."

The group dispersed toward the breakfast area, their conversations subdued but intense — comparing observations, processing emotions, and already beginning to formulate questions about what could be done. They'd crossed an invisible boundary between tourist and witness. Their relationship with Kariega and its wildlife was fundamentally transformed by direct exposure to the front lines of South Africa's conservation efforts.

Recognizing the significance of what they'd discovered, Sheryl remained briefly with Pieter as the others moved ahead. "Is this one of Malanga's operations? The one he's been warning us away from?" she asked quietly.

"Probably," he confirmed in a low voice. "The scale of what occurred last night suggests he's getting more aggressive. Three separate incidents in one night suggests multiple teams."

With a nod of understanding, they separated — Pieter to coordinate the ongoing security response, Sheryl to join her group for breakfast. The morning's events had changed their position, converting possible risk into an immediate reality.

The Global Runners group was scattered across multiple tables, their conversation focused on what they'd witnessed

rather than the typical safari excitement of comparing wildlife photographs.

As Sheryl joined them, she recognized something significant had shifted in their collective dynamic. They were no
longer simply adventure tourists consuming an experience,
but engaged witnesses to a genuine conservation crisis. The
shock and anger visible in their expressions suggested this shift
wouldn't be temporary. They wouldn't just forget what they
had seen or learned.

What had begun as a standard morning game drive had
evolved into something far more consequential — not just for
their personal experiences, but potentially for Kariega's battle
against the poaching that threatened its remarkable conservation achievements.

CHAPTER 34

THE WAITING GAME

The late morning sun had reached its full intensity by the time the group finished their delayed breakfast. Most tourists had dispersed to their accommodations for the traditional midday rest period. Animals retreated to shady patches under trees during peak temperatures; humans, likewise, sought respite before their afternoon activities resumed.

Pieter, however, showed no signs of relaxation as he convened an impromptu security meeting, well away from guest areas. The discovery of multiple poaching incidents had triggered a full response that defined the day's priorities. Sheryl joined this gathering at Pieter's request; her dual role as tour leader, an American park ranger, as well as her run-in with Malanga made her input valuable.

"Based on the evidence, we're dealing with at least two teams," Pieter explained to the assembled group. A map of Kariega was spread across the table before them, with markers indicating the morning's discoveries. "The captured kudus, dead buffalo, and drugged rhino show different techniques but similar timing. They killed the buffalo, but only tranqued the rhino, probably because it was quicker, quieter, and more reliable."

"They'll likely return for the kudus tonight," suggested one of the senior rangers, a man who had introduced himself to Sheryl as Simon. "Too much effort invested to abandon that catch."

Pieter nodded his agreement. "We've relocated most of the kudus for their safety, but left a few in the pen. That pen's the best bait we have for these poachers."

When the tactical planning concluded, Sheryl raised the question most relevant to her responsibilities. "What's your assessment regarding our tourist activities? Should we cancel our scheduled evening game drive?"

Pieter considered this question carefully, weighing guest security against guest satisfaction. "We should maintain a normal appearance to avoid alerting the poachers," he reasoned. "Canceling scheduled activities signals that we expect them to come back."

He turned to the map again, indicating different sectors of the reserve. "Your evening drive was planned for the northern section, focusing on the elephant herd currently moving through that area. That's quite distant from our poaching hotspots."

His finger traced the considerable distance between the marked incidents and the planned safari route. "I'll put our most experienced armed guides in your group's vehicles. They've got military backgrounds and extensive anti-poaching experience, as well as excellent tourism skills."

"So, you think the scheduled drive's still safe?" Sheryl clarified.

"Yes," Pieter confirmed. "The poachers target specific areas with particular species. They've avoided our elephant zones—too dangerous and too visible. Your group should see nothing more threatening than an irritable bull elephant, which Archie's equipped to handle."

With the plan finalized, the meeting adjourned so everyone could prepare for the evening's event.

As Sheryl exited the meeting room, she found Luke waiting in the garden, his expression revealing his awareness of the events. Clearly, his brother had shared the details of what they had found earlier.

"Pieter told me about your morning drive," he confirmed as they walked together toward the main lodge. "Remarkable that our group stumbled onto all three incidents. Coincidence?"

"Or not," Sheryl replied quietly. "Why would Malanga's men be so aggressive while we're here?"

Luke considered this possibility. "I doubt his people in the field know or care about us and our runners."

"Possibly. But we disrupted his diamond smuggling. Maybe he's afraid we'll do something similar to his poaching here."

Their conversation paused as they reached the lodge's main deck, where several guests lounged in the dappled shade of acacia trees. The contrast between the security briefing's intensity and this tranquil scene was jarring—guests reading books, sipping cold drinks, and occasionally raising binoculars to observe wildlife at the distant waterhole.

"I'm comfortable with the plan," Luke stated. "Archie's excellent. Your group will be in capable hands."

With the day's plans established, Sheryl took advantage of the midday lull to check on everyone, circulating through the property to ensure that they were comfortable and processing the morning's unexpected experiences well. Most had retreated to their individual accommodations.

She found Margaret and Sabrina Chu sharing a conversation on their private deck. Their vehicle on the morning game drive had followed the planned route after Pieter's group separated to investigate the poaching incidents.

"We saw hippos and a baby giraffe," Sabrina reported, her expression showing her excitement. "But everyone's talking about what your vehicle discovered. Is it true you found poachers?"

"Evidence of poaching, not the poachers themselves," Sheryl clarified. "Unfortunately, it's an ongoing challenge for all African reserves."

"What you found today was awful," Margaret commented. "After hearing Pieter's presentation about their conservation efforts, it seems particularly tragic."

Sheryl agreed, and after making sure that Margaret would be fine on her own until their evening drive, she left to continue her rounds. Sheryl encountered several other guests with similar reactions—concern about the poaching tempered by an appreciation for the reserve's transparent handling of the situation. Rather than diminishing their experience, the raw glimpse into the conservation team's challenges had deepened their connection to Kariega's mission.

A burst of excited chatter from the Wilsons' chalet drew her attention when she was leaving Professor Nkosi's place. She arrived to find them photographing a troop of baboons that had invaded their private plunge pool — three monkeys of various ages drinking and splashing with evident enjoyment in the small water feature.

"They just appeared from nowhere," Emma explained while filming the impromptu pool party. "The little one's pretty timid."

"They're regular visitors, according to what Pieter told me," Sheryl explained, maintaining a respectful distance from the wild primates. "Attracted to water during the heat of the day. Perfectly safe if you don't approach them or offer them any food."

Emma looked down at the banana she held, then back at Sheryl. She placed it back in the bowl on the table.

These lighter moments provided a good balance to the morning's darkness — reminders that the daily rhythms of African wildlife continued, despite all the human drama that plagued it.

When she completed her circuit of the chalets, Sheryl returned to the main lodge to find Wanda and Joan seated at a corner table on the viewing deck, engaged in an intense conversation that paused as she approached.

"We were just discussing this morning's discoveries," Wanda explained, gesturing for Sheryl to join them. "Joan's got some interesting perspectives."

"Every criminal activity eventually connects to money," Joan confirmed. "What we saw this morning wasn't opportunistic poaching. The techniques, equipment, and targets suggest a professional operation with established distribution channels."

Her assessment aligned perfectly with what Sheryl already knew about Malanga's operation, though Joan had reached these conclusions independently based on her experiences in the finance industry.

"The kudus are bulk protein with local market value," Joan continued. "The buffalo horns target specific Asian luxury markets. The rhino horn would be the highest value product by weight. The diversity suggests a sophisticated network for collecting, transporting, and selling all kinds of products."

Their conversation paused as Luke approached, carrying site maps for the evening's planned game drive. "Thought you might want to preview our route for tonight," he explained, spreading the materials on their table.

The four of them examined the planned journey—a looping path through Kariega's northern section, where the elephant herd had recently been tracked. The route deliberately avoided the eastern areas where the morning's poaching evidence had been discovered.

"These elephants," Wanda inquired, indicating the herd's marked location, "are they rescued or born here?"

"Both," Luke explained. "The original breeding pair was relocated from Kruger during the reserve's early days. Several calves have been born here since then. They're one of our conservation success stories."

As they discussed the evening plans, Sheryl noticed Joan's attention repeatedly drawn to the landscape off the viewing deck—the vast expanse of African bush stretching toward distant hills, occasionally animated by wildlife near the waterhole below.

"Something caught your interest?" Sheryl inquired when Luke and Wanda became engaged in a discussion about camera settings for nocturnal wildlife photography.

Joan hesitated before responding. "The beauty of this place. The animals, the terrain, the vegetation. It's protected because of money. And it's threatened because of money," she said quietly. "I've spent decades chasing financial crimes from a comfortable office. Seeing the physical reality of what those transactions actually mean—the buffalo, the rhino, the kudus— it's kind of upsetting."

Sheryl remained silent, at a loss for a response.

As midday transitioned to late afternoon, guests began reemerging for tea service on the main deck—a safari tradition that bridged the gap between lunch and dinner while providing energy for the evening game drive. Conversation naturally centered on the anticipated wildlife.

"Will we see the elephants for certain?" Nkosi asked Luke. "I'm particularly interested in their nocturnal behavior."

"The herd was near Acacia Dam this morning," Luke confirmed. "They typically remain in that area for several days when water is plentiful. Our chances are excellent."

As the group dispersed to prepare for their evening excursion, Sheryl noticed Joan and Wanda remaining at their table, apparently content to continue their observation of the waterhole below. The two women presented an interesting study in contrasts—Wanda's extroverted stuntwoman personality alongside Joan's more reserved presence—yet, they seemed to have formed an unexpected connection through just a few days of adventure.

Curious about their friendship, Sheryl approached their table again before departing for her own preparations.

"Anything interesting happening?" she inquired, noting they'd transitioned from tea to wine as the afternoon progressed.

"Just some informal surveillance," Wanda replied with a smile that didn't entirely mask her seriousness.

Joan nodded, her attention still focused on the landscape below. "We've been logging all wildlife appearances and movements."

She held up a notepad where she had, indeed, created a methodical record of sightings—species, numbers, duration of the sightings, and behavior patterns recorded with professional precision. Besides these observations, she had sketched a simple map of the routes the animals followed when approaching and departing the waterhole.

"We're probably being excessively vigilant," Joan acknowledged with slight self-consciousness. "But it's better than sitting idle all afternoon."

"Not excessive at all," Sheryl assured her. "This kind of observation is what the staff here do all the time. Most visitors focus on dramatic sightings rather than those regular patterns."

The harsh midday sun was yielding to the golden hour that photographers prized for its warm illumination. The changing light revealed new dimensions in the landscape—shadows lengthening, colors intensifying, and wildlife beginning to stir from heat-induced lethargy.

The late afternoon unfolded with practiced safari rhythms. Guests prepared camera equipment, applied insect repellent, and donned light jackets for the cool evening temperatures. By 4:30 p.m., they'd gathered at the vehicle assembly point, excitement building for their sunset wildlife experience.

Archie, their specific group's assigned guide, appeared. He was tall and powerfully built, and he looked the part of both soldier and conservation ranger. "Welcome, everyone," he announced as they boarded the modified Land Rover designed for wildlife viewing. "Tonight, we search for the elephant herd that's been moving through our northern section. Along the way, we'll likely encounter other species emerging as the temperatures drop."

Their vehicle departed, following the planned route toward areas where the elephants had recently been tracked. Archie provided ongoing commentary about visible wildlife and ecosystem features, his extensive knowledge delivered with engaging storytelling skill.

From the lodge's main deck, now empty of guests, Pieter watched their departure with professional interest. Once the safari vehicles disappeared beyond the nearest ridge, he keyed his radio to coordinate the security teams positioned strategically throughout the eastern reserve.

"Tourist vehicles proceeding as planned to northern sector," he confirmed. "Anti-poaching units maintain position and communication. Expect contact after full darkness."

As twilight deepened toward night, two parallel operations unfolded across Kariega's vast expanse — the tourist game drive proceeded northward in search of elephants, and the anti-poaching teams converged silently on areas where evidence suggested poachers would return. Between these deliberate movements, the wildlife continued their typical patterns. Predators began their nocturnal hunts, herbivores sought safety in numbers, and countless unseen interactions played out beneath the emerging stars of the African night.

CHAPTER 35

THE SHADOW OF DEATH

The evening game drive began with the tranquil beauty characteristic of African dusk. Archie guided their Land Rover along winding dirt tracks through Kariega's northern sector, his experienced eyes scanning constantly for wildlife among the lengthening shadows. The mood among the Global Runners group had lightened somewhat since that morning—the shock of discovering poaching now tempered by an appreciation for the reserve's active response.

"We're entering prime elephant habitat," Archie explained as they crested a gentle rise overlooking a broad valley. "This area features several types of vegetation they prefer, particularly the acacia trees whose bark contains minerals they crave."

The landscape opened before them—a sweeping vista of grassland interspersed with umbrella-shaped acacia trees, their distinctive silhouettes iconic against the sunset. A narrow waterway wound through the valley floor; its banks lined with denser vegetation that provided both food and shelter for numerous species.

"There." Archie pointed, his voice dropping to the hushed tone safari guides naturally adopted when approaching wildlife. "Just beyond that large acacia. Our elephant family."

Cameras emerged as the group spotted what Archie had already seen—the unmistakable gray forms of African elephants moving with surprising grace for creatures of such size. The vehicle slowed, approaching with deliberate care to avoid disturbing the herd.

"We currently have seventeen elephants in this family group," Archie explained as they drew closer. "Led by the matriarch we call Indlovu. She's approximately forty-eight years old. You can identify her by the distinctive notch in her right ear."

The Land Rover came to a complete stop at a respectful distance, positioned for clear viewing without intruding on the elephants' space. As the engine fell silent, the natural sounds of the African evening emerged—distant bird calls, the rustle of grass in the gentle breeze, and the surprisingly delicate sounds of the elephants feeding.

"They're aware of our presence, but not concerned," Archie noted, observing the relaxed body language of the herd. "We've been consistently non-threatening during our encounters, so they've learned to accept the vehicles as neutral elements in their environment."

The scene unfolding before them transported the group back to their expected safari experience—the magical encounters with Africa's iconic wildlife that had drawn them to Kariega. For this moment, at least, the harsh realities of poaching were forgotten as they absorbed the peaceful sight of elephants going about their evening activities.

Several young calves moved between the protective adults, their playful antics drawing delighted reactions from the observers. A juvenile male practiced his intimidation display against a small tree, mock-charging it with his ears spread wide before stopping short of actual contact.

"Young bulls begin practicing dominance behaviors years before they're actually capable of competing for mates," Archie explained. "It's essentially play that develops the skills they'll need later in life."

Time seemed suspended as they observed the herd. Before long, however, the magical golden light of sunset gave way to the deeper hues of dusk. Archie eventually started the engine again, moving the vehicle to follow as the elephants slowly moved across the valley.

"We'll follow at a distance for a little longer," he explained. "Then, we'll find a suitable spot for our sundowner drinks before continuing with the spotlights on to look for some of the more nocturnal species."

The Land Rover paralleled the elephants' movements for another twenty minutes, maintaining a sufficient enough distance to avoid interfering with their natural behavior. The fading light created increasingly dramatic photo conditions. The elephants' silhouettes against the remnants of sunset, the distinctive shapes of trunks raised to test the air, and the slow-motion choreography of the herd's movement across the terrain.

Eventually, Archie moved the vehicle to a small promontory overlooking the valley where the elephants had disappeared into denser vegetation. This natural viewpoint provided the perfect location for the traditional safari sundowner.

"We'll dismount here," he announced, retrieving the container of refreshments that had been loaded before departure. "The perfect spot to toast the African sunset before we begin our nocturnal wildlife viewing."

The group disembarked, stretching their legs after the confined seating of the vehicle. Archie raised the small portable table on the bumper, with both alcoholic and non-alcoholic drinks, alongside safari snacks of biltong, dried fruit, and savory crackers.

"To successful conservation," Joan proposed as they raised glasses, the connection to this morning's discoveries clear in her choice of toast.

As they enjoyed this peaceful interlude, darkness claimed the landscape with characteristic swiftness. Stars emerged, the southern hemisphere constellations unfamiliar to most American visitors, creating a celestial display undiminished by light pollution.

"We should see the Southern Cross just above that ridge," Nkosi noted, his academic knowledge extending to astronomy as he pointed toward the distinctive constellation.

They had just identified several celestial landmarks when the peaceful evening shattered—three distinct gunshots echoed across the valley, the sound unmistakable in the quiet night.

Archie's demeanor transformed instantly from relaxed guide to alert security professional. "Everyone back in the vehicle immediately," he instructed. His tone left no room for questions.

The group responded with commendable urgency, abandoning drinks and quickly reboarding the Land Rover. Archie secured the refreshment supplies before taking his position behind the wheel, his expression showing calculated assessment rather than fear.

"Those shots came from nearby," he explained once everyone was safely aboard. "But probably a few kilometers from our position. We're going to return to the lodge via the main road rather than continuing our planned route."

He started the engine and began a careful three-point turn to orient them toward the main track. The headlights swept across the landscape, revealing nothing beyond the expected terrain features—acacia trees, grassy verges, and the occasional startled antelope reflecting momentary eyeshine before bounding away.

"Are we in danger?" Margaret asked, voicing the concern evident on several faces.

"I don't think so," Archie assured her with professional calm. "The gunfire was not close, and any poacher will attempt to avoid our vehicles. They want to come and go invisibly, which means avoiding rangers and tourists alike."

The Land Rover proceeded at a measured pace along the dirt track leading toward the main reserve road—fast enough for an efficient exit, but controlled enough to remain safe on the uneven surface. Archie keyed his radio, speaking in quiet tones to the security team while focusing on his driving.

They'd covered perhaps two kilometers when the vehicle rounded a bend, and Archie abruptly cut the engine, allowing the car's momentum to carry them forward as he simultaneously dimmed the headlights. His raised hand signaled for immediate silence as the Land Rover rolled to a stop.

"Vehicles ahead," he whispered, indicating a faint glow of lights visible through vegetation approximately a hundred meters forward on the track.

The distant illumination moved erratically—flashlight beams rather than vehicle headlights, sweeping across the ground in patterns suggesting purposeful activity. Muffled voices carried on the night air, too distant for words to be distinguished but clearly human where none outside of those on the game drive should exist at this hour.

Archie restarted the engine with minimal noise and engaged the transmission, clearly intending to reverse their direction without approaching the intruders any more than they already had. Before they could retreat, however, a vehicle engine started ahead of them, its headlights suddenly blazing to life and illuminating the road in their direction.

"Hold on," Archie instructed tensely, accelerating forward since they'd been discovered. As they flashed past the pickup truck, the tourists could see a large animal carcass on the ground with one man struggling to load it and his partner at the wheel of the truck.

Time compressed into a single moment of mutual shock—the safari vehicle's occupants confronting clear evidence of wildlife poaching. The animal's distinctive mane was unmistakable, even in the chaotic lighting, its lifeless form a gut-wrenching sight for the conservationist-minded tourists.

The poachers recovered from their surprise—shouting and scrambling into their pickup.

"They're pursuing," Sheryl observed with calm assessment as lights appeared behind them, rapidly closing distance on the narrow track.

"Everyone, stay low in your seats," Archie instructed, his voice steady, despite the tension. "I know this terrain intimately."

He extinguished their headlights completely, driving now by moonlight and memory along the dirt track. The pursuing vehicle maintained an aggressive pace, its headlights creating elongated shadows that raced alongside the Land Rover like malevolent spirits.

When they reached a particular section where dense bush grew close to the road's edge, Archie made a sudden, decisive turn—swerving sharply off the track into what appeared to be impenetrable vegetation but proved to be a narrow game trail barely wide enough for their vehicle.

"Absolute silence now," he whispered as he cut the engine again, allowing the Land Rover to roll to a stop in the concealing bush. "They'll pass by, searching for us on the main track."

The group maintained commendable discipline, even as the pursuing vehicle slowed audibly on the main road—its occupants clearly aware they had lost contact with the safari vehicle. Flashlight beams probed the vegetation along both sides of the road, sweeping across the bush mere meters from their hiding place without penetrating deeply enough to reveal their position.

For several tense minutes, the poachers continued their search, voices occasionally carrying to the hidden safari group, though specific words remained indistinct. Then came a new escalation—three deliberate rifle shots fired into the dense bush on the opposite side of the track, clearly intended to flush out anyone hiding there.

"They're attempting to provoke movement or sound," Archie whispered. "Remain absolutely still."

The poachers waited briefly after their intimidation tactic, then fired again—this time directing shots into the bush much closer to the Land Rover's actual position. One bullet audibly impacted a tree trunk uncomfortably close to their location.

"We need some cover," Archie decided, his professional assessment recognizing the escalating danger. "Everyone, exit quietly on the far side of the vehicle, away from the road. Use the Land Rover as cover and stay low."

With remarkable composure given the circumstances, the tourists complied—silently sliding over the side away from the road and positioning themselves behind the protective bulk of the Land Rover. Archie joined them, carrying what appeared to be a compact rifle retrieved from a locked compartment beneath his seat.

"Standard security protocol," he explained in barely audible tones, noting Sheryl's recognition of the weapon. "For wildlife defense primarily, but useful here if absolutely necessary."

Another volley of shots tore through the vegetation alarmingly close to their position, followed by the sound of vehicle doors opening and footsteps on the dirt track. The poachers had apparently decided to conduct a more thorough search on foot.

In the darkness behind the Land Rover, Sheryl made eye contact with Wanda, a silent communication passing between them. Both women had positioned themselves slightly apart from the main group, their postures suggesting readiness rather than fear. With minimal gestures, they signaled a flanking approach — moving through the bush to circle behind the searching poachers.

Archie noticed their intended movement and gave a slight head shake of disapproval, but Sheryl's determined expression and subtle hand signals conveying her professional capability gave him pause. After a moment's assessment, he gave an almost imperceptible nod, focusing his attention on protecting the remaining tourists while the two women disappeared silently into the darkness.

Sheryl moved with practiced stealth, her ranger background evident in how efficiently she navigated the bush without creating noise. Wanda matched her movement with surprising competence — her stunt work apparently included skills that were useful in the bush. They separated slightly, creating a pincer approach toward the road where flashlight beams gave the poachers' positions.

The night provided the perfect cover, the quarter moon offering just enough illumination to navigate by while shadows concealed their locations. They could now distinguish two distinct poachers on foot, both carrying rifles and systematically searching the roadside vegetation. The poachers' attention remained focused on the area where they had fired their shots, unaware of the flanking movement behind them.

Reaching the road's edge, Sheryl and Wanda paused, silently coordinating their approach. The poachers had reunited near their vehicle, conferring in low voices about their next move. That created the perfect opportunity, as both targets were in proximity, temporarily distracted, with their backs to the approaching threat.

Sheryl signaled the initiation with three fingers—a silent countdown that Wanda acknowledged with focused readiness. *Three. Two. One.*

They burst out of hiding with synchronized precision, covering the short distance to their targets before the poachers registered their approach. Sheryl targeted the larger man, driving her shoulder into his lower back while simultaneously grasping his rifle barrel and forcing it upward. The weapon discharged harmlessly into the night sky as the impact sent both of them sprawling onto the dirt track.

Simultaneously, Wanda executed a flying tackle that caught the second poacher mid-turn, her momentum carrying both of them to the ground with sufficient force to dislodge his grip on his weapon. The rifle clattered away across the dirt as they grappled in the moonlight.

Sheryl found herself wrestling a powerfully built man whose initial shock quickly gave way to desperate resistance. He attempted to swing the rifle like a club, but her grip on the barrel prevented him from doing anything effective. She delivered a powerful knee strike to his solar plexus, stopping his breathing momentarily and allowing her to twist the weapon from his grasp.

Casting the rifle aside, she trapped his wrist and applied a joint lock that produced immediate compliance, accompanied by a pained shout.

"Don't break it, don't break it!" he gasped as the armbar hyper-extended his elbow to the edge of its range.

"Stop fighting, and I won't have to," Sheryl responded, maintaining the pressure and placing a knee in the middle of his back.

Nearby, Wanda was demonstrating that stunt combat training was effective in a real fight as well. After the initial tackle, her opponent had attempted to use his size advantage, but found himself facing a competitor with exceptional training and strength. She countered his attempt to regain his footing with a leg sweep that returned him forcefully to the ground.

When he reached for a knife at his belt, Wanda trapped his arm with theatrical flair. The poacher bucked desperately, attempting to dislodge her, but succeeded only in providing better positioning for Wanda to secure a submission hold.

"The more you struggle, the more it'll hurt," she informed him calmly, despite the intensity of their conflict. "It's your choice how this ends."

A particularly unwise twist to get away resulted in an audible pop from the man's shoulder joint, his agonized yelp suggesting it was now dislocated. The injury immediately stopped his struggles as Wanda secured his remaining functional arm.

With both poachers subdued, Sheryl called toward the bush where the Land Rover remained hidden. "Archie! We have them. But we need some restraints."

Immediately, Archie emerged with his rifle at the ready. Behind him, the remaining tourists followed with expressions ranging from shock to relief.

"Well done," he acknowledged, producing zip ties from his vest. "Though, your actions went completely against the reserve's security procedures."

"But effective," Wanda noted.

Archie zipped both poachers' wrists securely behind their backs, checking for additional weapons during the process and removing knives and a secondary firearm. Once restrained, the captives were seated on the ground against their own vehicle's tire.

"I've radioed Pieter and our security teams," Archie informed the group. "They'll handle the prisoners and all of this," he said, waving at the vehicle and the lion.

With the threat neutralized, the Global Runners gathered in the moonlight, processing what had just happened. Their safari had transformed into a terrifying nightmare, illustrating the true cost of the battle between conservation and poaching.

"Is everyone all right?" Sheryl asked, scanning the group for any signs of injury or distress.

"Better than all right," Joan responded with unexpected vigor. "Tonight was more meaningful than any tourist activity I've ever experienced."

Others nodded in agreement. There was a palpable sense of purpose that transcended a conventional vacation.

The captured poachers sat in sullen silence, occasionally testing their restraints but finding no way out. The injured man supported his dislocated shoulder as best he could, given his bound wrists, while his companion glared with undisguised hostility at their captors.

"The lion," Margaret asked quietly, her voice tight with emotion. "Is it…"

"Dead, yes," Archie confirmed after checking the pickup's bed. "Adult male, likely from our western pride. A significant trophy specimen for someone."

That sobered the group's momentary sense of accomplishment—their intervention had come too late for the magnificent animal whose lifeless form lay partially covered in the vehicle. The victory of capturing poachers was tempered by the permanent loss to Kariega's ecosystem.

Headlights appeared in the distance, approaching rapidly along the dirt track. Archie positioned himself protectively between the tourists and the incoming vehicles, rifle at the ready.

"It's our anti-poaching team," he announced with evident relief as the distinctive vehicles came into view.

Three specialized vehicles surrounded the scene, discharging rangers in tactical gear who immediately took custody of the captured poachers. Pieter emerged from the lead vehicle, his expression stern as he surveyed the situation.

"Everyone okay?" he asked immediately, prioritizing the safety of their guests.

"We're fine," Sheryl assured him. "Two poachers captured, unfortunately one lion lost."

Pieter nodded grimly, approaching the pickup to examine its cargo. His face tightened with controlled anger as he confirmed the lion's identity. "Skukuza," he stated quietly. "Our dominant western male. Magnificent animal."

The name humanized the loss, transforming an abstract wildlife crime into the death of a specific, known individual. Several tourists visibly reacted to this personalization, tears forming in their eyes as they turned away.

Pieter's radio crackled with new information, drawing his attention momentarily. After a brief conversation, he turned back to the group with updated intelligence.

"The team at the eastern boma captured another poaching group," he reported. "They were returning for the kudus, as we expected. Three more arrests, no injuries on either side."

This additional success provided some balance to the loss of Skukuza—not complete consolation, but a relief that this threat had been eliminated. For now, at least.

"We need to return you to the lodge now," Pieter continued. "Archie will drive you back with a security escort."

As they prepared to board their Land Rover for the return journey, Sheryl paused alongside Pieter for a private exchange.

"Malanga's people?" she inquired quietly.

"Almost certainly," he confirmed.

She nodded, having reached the same conclusion. "The captured poachers—potential for information on his operations?"

"We'll see. Local teams usually know very little about the broader operation. But every captured link helps us construct a chain of evidence."

The tourists reboarded their vehicle, now flanked by a security team that would ensure their safe passage back to the lodge. As they departed the scene, leaving the anti-poaching unit to complete their evidence collection and transport the captured poachers, a complex mixture of emotions characterized the group—satisfaction at having contributed to the conservation mission, sorrow for the lost lion, and a deeper understanding of the ongoing battle between preservation and exploitation.

The convoy proceeded carefully back toward the lodge, their car's headlights illuminating the path ahead while armed rangers maintained a vigilant watch for any additional threats in their own vehicles. The African night continued around them with stars wheeling overhead, distant animal calls punctuating the darkness, and somewhere across the vast reserve, other wild animals continuing their lives unaware of the drama that had unfolded in their midst.

CHAPTER 36

FURIOUS

The safe house outside Port Elizabeth presented an unremarkable façade—a modest farmhouse set back from the road, its weathered exterior suggesting nothing more significant than agricultural decline. Inside, however, the atmosphere crackled with dangerous energy as Malanga paced the worn linoleum floor of the kitchen, a phone pressed to his ear.

"Repeat that," he demanded, his voice deadly quiet, despite the rage evident in his rigid posture. "Exactly what happened?"

The caller's voice emerged tinnily from the small device, barely audible to Botha, who maintained a respectful distance near the doorway. The mercenary's face revealed nothing, though his hand rested casually near the holstered weapon at his hip—a recent addition after his run-in with Jack Hunter.

"Both teams? Captured?" Malanga's question carried dangerous incredulity. "By a tourist safari vehicle?"

Whatever details the caller provided next visibly intensified Malanga's anger. His free hand clenched into a white-knuckled fist, the tendons standing out like steel cables beneath his skin.

"Names. I want names," he demanded after listening further. "Particularly the tourists involved."

The subsequent information apparently provided insufficient detail, judging by Malanga's expression of cold frustration. "Find out more. Use your access to the booking records. I need to know exactly who's on that tour."

He terminated the call with savage abruptness, dropping the phone onto the kitchen table with controlled violence that suggested he wished to destroy something but retained just enough self-control to preserve valuable equipment.

"Police have both teams," he informed Botha, breaking his silence with precisely enunciated words. "Kudu operation and lion operation. Five men in total."

Botha absorbed this information with a neutral expression. "The eastern team? The ones at the holding pen?"

"Yes. Ambushed by reserve security." Malanga moved to the window, staring into the darkness beyond the glass as though seeking visible enemies. "But the lion team was intercepted by a tourist safari vehicle. Tourists, Botha. Not rangers. Not police. Tourists."

The incongruity clearly intensified his rage—his team taken down by amateur safari-goers. That was an embarrassment even beyond the material losses.

"My contact says two women from the tour group physically subdued Thabiso and Dirk while the others hid behind their Land Rover." His voice carried venomous disbelief. "Two women overpowered armed men who've worked in the bush for years."

Botha's expression shifted slightly. "Unusual actions for tourists."

"Exactly." Malanga turned from the window, his composure reasserting itself as analytical thought emerged from his rage. "First Cape Town, then Knysna, now Kariega. We know who this is—all of it."

He moved to a worn, leather briefcase resting on a side table, extracting a folder containing papers. "Remember this? The itinerary Reggie acquired before his unfortunate encounter in the Knysna offices."

The folder opened to reveal the detailed Global Runners tour documentation—daily schedules, accommodation listings, and personnel information, including a short description of the leaders.

"Global Runners adventure tourism," he continued, tapping the company logo with one manicured finger. "Specialty tours for running enthusiasts. No, it's a cover for police, security—someone who's out to destroy us."

Botha moved closer. "The warehouse in Cape Town," he noted. "The diamonds in Knysna. Now the poaching teams at Kariega."

Malanga extracted a specific page containing staff profiles, focusing on one particular entry. "Sheryl Diego, Lead Tour Guide. Former American park ranger, competitive ultra-marathon runner, extensive global tour experience. She's the key. We warned her, but she just kept coming. She didn't get the message from the snake. She didn't listen at the bridge. She has to go."

"And the big soldier, too," Botha added. His shoulder was still sore from their fight in the office corridor. "Jack Hunter."

Malanga continued, "And the security woman from De Beers. She was definitely sent to track those two fools with the diamonds." He closed the folder with a deliberate movement, his initial rage now channeled into cold calculation.

He returned to pacing, though now with measured strides reflecting strategic planning rather than uncontrolled anger. "They've disrupted three of our missions."

Botha said, "We've got that Asian buyer expecting rhino horn next week."

"Yes. Which is why we've got to take care of this problem now. We can't afford to lose that rhino contract, too." Malanga stopped pacing, his decision evidently reached. "We've got to go to Kariega ourselves."

Botha recognized the shift in his employer's demeanor—the transition from angry businessman to the calculating predator that had established his reputation across the entire country. This was Malanga at his most dangerous—cold, strategic, and utterly without restraint.

"They think they're hunting us," Malanga stated with quiet finality. "So, we're hunting them instead."

Botha processed this plan. "Kariega's secured territory. Multiple anti-poaching teams are active there, especially after tonight's incidents."

"Which creates an opportunity for us," Malanga countered. "They're watching the animals. We're after the people. They believe they've won. But while they're looking outward, we'll strike inward."

He turned from the window with renewed purpose. "You still have contacts among the seasonal rangers at Kariega? The ones who supplement security during peak periods?"

"Two reliable men," Botha confirmed. "Currently, they're on perimeter patrol duties."

"Perfect. We need internal intelligence about the tour group's scheduled activities, their room locations, when they'll be at the lodge."

Malanga moved to a map of the Eastern Cape spread across a side table. Its surface was marked with annotations indicating animal zones and lodge accommodations. His finger traced the boundaries of Kariega Game Reserve with predatory precision.

"I want a Kariega vehicle."

Botha nodded. "When?"

"Tomorrow evening," Malanga decided. "When everyone goes out on the evening game drive, we're going into the lodge compound. They're looking for us in the bush. We'll be in their house."

"Just the three targets?" Botha inquired, seeking tactical clarification rather than moral questioning.

"Extraction and elimination," Malanga stated with clinical detachment. "Diego. The De Beers agent. The security muscle. Collateral tourist casualties are acceptable but not necessary."

He traced potential approach routes on the map, identifying security vulnerabilities where an insider could let them through the fence undetected.

"Four-person team," he continued. "You and me, plus Luzuko and Kobus. Small enough for stealth."

Botha raised a single eyebrow—the only indication of surprise at Malanga's personal involvement. Typically, the businessman maintained his distance, delegating direct action to expendables while preserving his own plausible deniability.

Botha acknowledged the decision with a slight nod, his mind already processing the necessary steps. "I'll contact our guys in Kariega immediately. We'll be ready by morning."

"Excellent." Malanga returned his attention to the maps to study the layout of the chalets in the lodge compound. "Tomorrow night, we hunt."

CHAPTER 37

RUNNING WILD

The breakfast buffet at Kariega Main Lodge was plentiful, as usual. Yet, despite the offering, conversation at the Global Runners tables focused exclusively on the previous night's dramatic events.

"I still can't believe what happened," Margaret said, absently stirring her untouched coffee. "One moment we're watching elephants, the next we're in some wildlife crime thriller."

"With our very own action heroes," Stanley added, nodding toward Sheryl and Wanda, who sat together at the end of the table. The previous night's confrontation had cemented an unexpected bond between the two women.

Wanda shifted uncomfortably under the attention, her usual confident demeanor tempered by morning-after reflection. "It wasn't exactly a planned response," she admitted. "More like a survival instinct."

"Very effective instinct," Professor Nkosi noted. "Though statistically speaking, confronting armed poachers doesn't usually turn out this well."

"Tell me about it," Wanda agreed, rubbing her shoulder where the muscle stiffness testified to the previous night's exertions. "I've choreographed plenty of fights for the camera, but the real thing hits harder."

Sheryl nodded in understanding. Despite her ranger background, the confrontation had pushed beyond her typical experiences. "There's a reason I switched to tourism," she said with a wry smile. "The wildlife rarely shoots back."

Their honest vulnerability—acknowledging the fear and risk inherent in their actions—seemed to resonate more deeply with the group than any false bravado might have. These weren't hardened soldiers unfazed by danger, but ordinary people who'd found courage when the circumstances demanded it.

"What happens to the poachers now?" Joan asked.

"They're in police custody," Sheryl explained. "Pieter messaged this morning that formal charges have been filed— illegal hunting, trespassing in protected areas, possession of unregistered firearms, and animal cruelty. Significant penalties if convicted."

"And the lion?" Margaret's voice quieted with genuine sorrow.

"Being properly honored," Sheryl replied gently. "Kariega has procedures for wildlife lost to poaching—ceremonial burial and commemoration. Skukuza's line will continue through his offspring in the pride."

A thoughtful silence settled over the table, eventually broken by Wanda's characteristic pragmatism. "So, what's the plan for today? More poacher hunting or something less life-threatening?"

This question successfully lightened the mood, drawing appreciative chuckles from around the table. Sheryl seized the opportunity to reiterate the day's scheduled activities.

"Actually, we're going running," she announced, pulling up the morning's itinerary on her tablet. "A specially designed three-mile trail through one of Kariega's herbivore-rich sections. Perfect terrain, spectacular wildlife viewing, and absolutely no predators to worry about—either four-legged or two-legged."

"Running in actual game territory?" Tyler perked up immediately, his spirit evidently undimmed by recent events. "That's a first."

"Ranger-escorted, obviously," Sheryl clarified. "The route follows game trails through savanna and woodland sections, offering close-but-safe viewing of giraffe, various antelope species, and other non-predatory wildlife."

"Will we see springboks?" Nkosi asked with unexpected enthusiasm. "Always wanted to see South Africa's national animal in its natural habitat."

"Highly likely," Luke confirmed, joining the conversation. "They favor the open grassland sections we'll be traversing. Perfect springbok territory."

The prospect of this unique running experience seemed to energize the group, shifting the focus from the previous night's drama toward their next highly anticipated adventure. As breakfast concluded, they dispersed to their accommodations to change into running attire, the mood noticeably lighter than when they'd arrived.

❂ ❂ ❂

An hour later, two safari vehicles transported the running group to the trail's starting point—a picturesque clearing within sight of a small watering hole where several giraffes were currently engaged in their signature splayed-leg drinking posture. The runners disembarked amid excited chatter.

"Welcome to Herbivore Heaven," announced Pieter, who'd personally joined them for this activity. "This three-mile trail was specifically designed to showcase Kariega's non-predatory species in their natural habitats while providing beautiful hiking or running conditions."

He gestured toward the path visible behind him—a well-maintained dirt track winding between acacia trees toward distant rolling hills. "You can run or hike at your own pace. Two rangers will be on the trail as well—one leading, one trailing—ensuring your safety and pointing out wildlife."

The runners completed their warm-up routines, though many remained distracted by the wildlife visible even before they began—giraffes continuing their elegant movements near the water, a small herd of impalas watching curiously from beneath an acacia tree, and warthogs trotting purposefully along their own mysterious errands.

"Remember," Pieter continued as they prepared to depart, "we're guests in their habitat. We keep a steady pace without sudden directional changes. If you encounter animals on the trail, wait for them to pass or wait for other runners to catch up to you. The animals are used to people. They'll gracefully avoid letting you get too close."

With these guidelines established, the group formed up behind the lead ranger—a tall woman introduced as Anathi, whose impressive running physique suggested she could easily outpace most of their group if necessary. Pieter positioned himself in the middle of the group, while another ranger named David took a trailing position.

"Ready for the most wildlife you'll ever see on a trail run?" Sheryl asked, joining the front section alongside Tyler and Emma, who predictably had positioned themselves for a competitive pace.

"Beats dodging traffic in Denver," Tyler replied with a grin as Anathi signaled their departure.

The group moved forward at a comfortable pace—quick enough for legitimate exercise but controlled enough for wildlife observation and photography. The initial section followed the edge of an open grassland area, providing excellent visibility across the landscape, where various antelope species could be seen grazing in distinct social groupings.

"On the left," Anathi called, indicating a magnificent kudu bull watching their progress from about fifty meters away. His horns traced elegant curves against the blue sky, the distinctive white stripes on his flanks visible, even at this distance.

"That's about five years of growth," Pieter explained. "Kudu horns grow throughout their lifetime, with each spiral representing roughly one year."

They continued along the trail as it curved gently through increasingly varied terrain. The running surface remained excellent—packed earth with minimal technical challenge, allowing the runners to focus on the surrounding wildlife rather than their footing.

"Blesbucks ahead," Anathi announced as they approached a small herd of distinctive antelopes with prominent, white facial markings. The animals raised their heads in synchronized awareness but showed no alarm at the approaching runners.

"Why are they called blesbucks?" Tyler asked between controlled breaths, his running form remarkably efficient, despite the distraction of the wildlife.

"The name comes from Afrikaans," Luke explained, running alongside him. "'Bles' refers to the white blazes on their faces—similar to what you might call a blaze on a horse's forehead. So, literally 'blaze buck' or 'marked antelope.'"

"Our Dutch ancestors were more practical than creative when assigning names to the animals," Pieter observed. "See distinctive feature, name accordingly."

"Much South African wildlife naming follows that pattern," Anathi agreed. "Wildebeest means 'wild cattle.' Hartebeest translates roughly as 'hart beast' or 'stag animal.' Very descriptive approach to taxonomy."

As they completed the first mile, the trail entered a section of more enclosed woodland, the canopy providing welcome shade while changing the character of their wildlife encounters. Here, the animals appeared more suddenly and at closer range—nyalas browsing delicately on low-hanging foliage, bushbucks blending almost invisibly with dappled shadows until movement revealed their presence.

"This feels surreal," Madeline commented as they maintained a steady pace through this enchanted environment. "Like running through a nature documentary."

"Better than any treadmill run I've ever had," Stanley agreed, his characteristic humor emerging, despite the exertion he felt. "Though, I'd appreciate it if the warthogs stopped judging my form. They look so disapproving."

This observation drew appreciative laughter as they passed a family of warthogs who, indeed, seemed to watch their progress with porcine skepticism, their tails held vertically like judgmental scorecards.

"They're not judging," Wanda countered with mock seriousness. "They're taking notes. 'Dear Diary: Today, I observed strange two-legged creatures moving inefficiently across the terrain. Unlike sensible animals, they appeared to derive pleasure from unnecessary exertion.'"

The trail emerged from the woodland into another open section, this one featuring expansive grassland punctuated by occasional acacia trees, creating the classic African savanna landscape immortalized in countless wildlife documentaries. Here, several distinct antelope species could be seen simultaneously, demonstrating evolution's remarkable specialization within similar ecological niches.

"Springboks at two o'clock," Anathi called, indicating a sizeable herd about two hundred meters away. The distinctive antelopes—medium-sized with characteristic white faces and brown lateral stripes—moved with the elegant, bouncing gait that gave them their name.

Nkosi's expression brightened visibly at this sighting. "The springboks! South Africa's pride."

"You're a rugby fan?" Luke asked, noting his enthusiasm.

"Absolutely. Been following since university." Nkosi's running pace increased slightly with his excitement. "Four-time World Cup champions now. Remarkable achievement for a country this size."

"The 2023 victory was particularly sweet," Luke acknowledged, his own national pride evident in his voice. "Back-to-back titles, matching New Zealand's record. The whole country celebrated for days."

"The springbok's 'pronking' behavior gave both the animal and the rugby team their name," Pieter added, joining their conversation. "That distinctive leap where all four feet leave the ground simultaneously requires both agility and power."

"Perfect sporting emblem," Nkosi agreed. "Though, I notice that the actual springboks seem considerably more graceful than some of the rugby players."

"Slightly fewer collisions in their daily routine," Luke said with a laugh. "Then again, rutting season might give a rugby scrum fair competition for intensity."

As if responding to this discussion, several younger springboks in the distant herd began demonstrating the very behavior under discussion—launching into gravity-defying vertical leaps that seemed to defy both physics and purpose.

"Are they actually accomplishing anything with that jumping?" Wanda asked, observing the seemingly pointless acrobatics.

"Multiple things," Pieter explained. "Predator detection—gaining height to see further. Predator deterrence—

demonstrating fitness to potential threats. And social signaling within the herd."

"So, basically, showing off," Joan translated. "The animal kingdom's version of a gym selfie."

This unexpected quip from the usually reserved woman generated appreciative laughter throughout the group, the shared physical exertion and wildlife encounters creating a natural camaraderie that bound them together.

As they approached the midpoint of their route, the trail curved alongside a small seasonal waterway. Giraffes browsed on acacia trees, their impossibly long necks making the upper foliage accessible, while various antelope species munched on the lower vegetation.

"Natural resources support multiple species through differentiated adaptation," Nkosi observed with academic precision. "Vertical stratification of feeding zones."

"Big animals eat high leaves, smaller animals eat low leaves," Wanda translated with a grin. "Nature's buffet line with height requirements."

"Exactly!" Nkosi agreed, appreciating the humor.

Their pace adjusted naturally as they observed particularly compelling wildlife scenes, sometimes slowing to appreciate the animals before resuming a normal running rhythm. Throughout, the rangers maintained a vigilant awareness of their surroundings.

"Halfway point ahead," Anathi announced as they approached a scenic overlook positioned on a small rise. "Brief rest stop for water and photos."

The designated midpoint provided spectacular vistas across Kariega's landscape—rolling hills covered in different vegetation, the distant glint of river systems, and wildlife visible in every direction. The runners gathered at this panoramic viewpoint, catching their breath while absorbing the remarkable scene.

"This puts our local park run into perspective," Emma commented as she sipped from her water bottle. "Way more impressive than dodging dog walkers."

"Though fewer water stations," her husband, Tyler, observed with mock seriousness. "I've counted exactly zero volunteers offering sports drinks."

"The giraffes were supposed to handle hydration support," Sheryl played along. "Budget cuts forced us to scale back."

This lighthearted exchange reflected the group's improving spirits—the combination of physical exercise, spectacular scenery, and wildlife encounters gradually displacing lingering tension from the previous night's adventure.

After a brief rest, they continued along the second half of the trail. This section traversed more open grassland, allowing observation of animals at greater distances while providing faster running conditions.

"Is that a zebra?" Margaret called, indicating movement near a distant tree line.

"Good spot," Pieter confirmed. "Small family group—stallion, three mares, and two foals born this season."

The distinctive black and white patterns became more visible as the zebras moved into clearer view, their coloration stark against the natural background.

"They look like they're wearing prison uniforms," Rogerio observed with characteristic directness. "Nature's convicts."

"Their stripes are actually a sophisticated evolutionary adaptation," Pieter explained, smiling at the comparison. "The pattern disrupts outline recognition for predators and creates optical confusion for biting insects, particularly tsetse flies."

"Plus, excellent group identification," Wanda added. "Can't lose your friends at a crowded watering hole when everyone's wearing the same jumpsuits."

"One mile remaining," Anathi announced as they reached another gentle rise in the landscape. "Primarily downhill and flat terrain to finish."

This final section offered perhaps the most spectacular wildlife density of their entire route—a broad, open area where multiple species had gathered in the cooler morning hours. Wildebeest, zebras, impalas, and springboks created a living diorama of African savanna life, different species keeping their social groupings while sharing the productive grassland.

"It's like running through the opening scene of *The Lion King*," Wanda observed.

"Just missing the musical soundtrack," Joan agreed. "Though, I'm not volunteering to sing."

"Tyler could handle the percussion," Emma suggested mischievously. "His breathing's loud enough."

"I wasn't aware that me trying my best to get enough oxygen was providing you with entertainment," Tyler responded good-naturedly, his competitive runner's breathing indeed more pronounced than the others.

"Multi-tasking," Wanda explained. "Running, wildlife viewing, and unintentional beatboxing. Impressive skills."

The trail's final quarter-mile featured a gentle descent toward their finish line. As they approached this conclusion, a family of warthogs crossed their path, trotting in characteristic single-file formation with their tails held vertically.

"Nature's exclamation points," Stanley observed, indicating the perfectly upright tails. "Always seem so enthusiastic about their destinations."

"They maintain that posture so they can find each other when moving through high grass," Pieter explained.

"Still looks like they're perpetually surprised by everything," Stanley insisted. "Like they can't believe they're actually going somewhere."

This imagery proved irresistibly amusing as they watched the warthogs' distinctive running style.

The group completed their run where the ever-present refreshments had been arranged beneath some trees.

"That was absolutely spectacular," Nkosi declared, his earlier excitement about the springbok sightings having expanded to appreciation for the entire experience. "Nothing in thirty years of running compares to that."

Others nodded in agreement, each processing their favorite moments from the morning's adventure.

"The lodge staff have prepared lunch for our return," Sheryl announced as they rehydrated and stretched. "We should head back soon to keep to our afternoon schedule."

"What's on the agenda?" Joan asked.

"Something special," Luke replied with evident anticipation. "We're visiting the local school supported by the Kariega Foundation. It's an encounter with the culture that you won't want to miss."

As the safari vehicles departed, retracing their route back toward the main lodge, the running trail returned to its natural state—temporary human visitors departed, leaving the landscape to its permanent residents.

CHAPTER 38

FUTURE FOUNDATIONS

The midday sun blazed overhead as the Global Runners group boarded their tour bus for their afternoon excursion. The morning's unique trail run had energized rather than exhausted them, creating a buoyant mood as they settled into their seats for the short journey to the local school.

"This afternoon, we're visiting Ekuphumleni Primary School," Luke explained once everyone was aboard. "It's one of several educational institutions supported by the Kariega Foundation—the reserve's community outreach program that channels tourism revenue into local development projects."

He gestured toward a young woman seated at the front of the bus who'd joined them for this particular excursion. "You met Anathi on this morning's run. She also coordinates educational partnerships between Kariega and local communities. She'll get you started with some local culture before we arrive."

Anathi stood and turned to face the group with a warm smile. She wore the typical khaki uniform of the game reserve staff.

"*Molweni, nonke!*" she greeted them with evident enthusiasm. "That's Xhosa for 'hello, everyone!' Today, you'll experience something different from wildlife viewing—you'll meet some of our most precious resources, the children of the Eastern Cape."

As the bus departed the reserve, following a paved road toward the nearby community, Anathi continued her introduction. "The school we're visiting serves about 1,400 students from ages six to thirteen. Many come from challenging economic circumstances, but you'll find them among the most joyful, intelligent, and engaging children you've ever met."

She moved into the aisle to better engage with the entire group. "Since we've got about twenty minutes before our arrival, I thought we might use this time for a quick introduction to isiXhosa—the predominant language in this region. Would that interest you?"

The response was immediate and positive, with several tourists expressing particular enthusiasm for this cultural opportunity.

"Perfect!" Anathi smile widened. "Let's start with basic greetings. The most common greeting's '*molo*' for one person or '*molweni*' for a group."

She demonstrated the pronunciation with careful emphasis, then encouraged the group to repeat after her. "*Molo.*"

The tourists echoed the greeting with varying degrees of accuracy, some struggling with the distinctive tonality of Xhosa pronunciation.

"Good effort!" Anathi encouraged them. "Now, to ask 'How are you?' we say, '*Unjani?*'"

This phrase proved more challenging, with several amusing mispronunciations that Anathi corrected with patience. "The 'nj' sounds like the 'ny' in 'canyon' but slightly different. Let's try again…*un-JA-ni.*"

Margaret asked about the clicking sounds they'd heard earlier. "Are those not part of these basic phrases?"

"Excellent question," Anathi acknowledged. "The three main click consonants appear in many Xhosa words, but not in these particular greetings. We'll encounter some clicks in our next phrase—'*enkosi,*' which means 'thank you.'"

She demonstrated this word with particular care, the lateral X-click sound appearing subtly in the natural flow of the word. "*En-KO-si,*" she repeated, encouraging them to attempt the pronunciation.

The group made valiant attempts, producing a range of approximations from surprisingly accurate to completely click-free versions that drew good-natured laughter from everyone, including Anathi herself.

"Learning a new language requires fearlessness," she encouraged them. "Better to try and miss than never to try at all."

For the remainder of the journey, she guided them through constructing simple conversational exchanges, combining the phrases they'd learned into basic dialogue patterns.

"If someone greets you with '*molo*,' you respond with '*molo*' as well," she explained. "Then, they might ask, '*Unjani?*' You can answer, '*Ndiphilile, enkosi*,' which means, 'I am fine, thank you.'"

By the time the bus turned onto a dirt road leading toward a modest compound of single-story buildings, many of the tourists were attempting simple exchanges with each other, their enthusiasm for immersing themselves in the local culture outweighing their concerns about perfect pronunciation.

"We've arrived," Luke announced as the school came into full view—a collection of cream-colored buildings with green trim arranged around a central courtyard, with sports fields visible across the street. Children in daily casual clothes were visible in the courtyard, apparently awaiting their visitors with barely contained excitement.

"Remember," Anathi said as they prepared to disembark, "the greatest gift you can offer these children is genuine engagement. They're eager to practice English with native speakers and share their own culture with you."

As the group descended from the bus, they were greeted by an explosion of joyful energy—dozens of children offering enthusiastic waves, bright smiles, and a chorus of "*molo!*" that immediately put their language practice to practical use. Several tourists responded with their newly learned Xhosa greetings, eliciting delighted reactions from the children.

A woman in her early fifties stepped forward from the school entrance, her professional attire and confident bearing identifying her as an administrator before introductions were even made.

"Welcome to Ekuphumleni Primary," she greeted them warmly. "I am Ms. Thandeka Mabaso, the school principal. We're honored by your visit and grateful for your support through the Kariega Foundation."

After brief welcoming remarks, Ms. Mabaso organized the children into their respective classes, creating more manageable groups for the upcoming tour and activities. "We'll begin with a tour of our facilities," she explained, "particularly focusing on the developments made possible through the foundation's support."

The main school building revealed both challenges that still needed to be solved and progress that had already been made. The group saw classrooms equipped with basic necessities but showed signs of careful maintenance and thoughtful organization, despite the school's limited resources. Colorful educational posters, many handmade by teachers, covered the walls alongside student artwork that demonstrated remarkable creativity.

"Our student-teacher ratio remains higher than ideal," Ms. Mabaso informed everyone as they observed a classroom where about forty children were engaged in a mathematics lesson. "But we've reduced it from sixty-to-one five years ago to forty-to-one currently—significant progress made possible through foundation-funded teaching positions."

The tour continued through various facilities—a small library with carefully maintained books and a modest science lab where equipment was clearly precious and well-preserved.

The highlight of the tour came when they reached a recently constructed building at the rear of the campus—a structure with enhanced security and climate control systems not evident in the other buildings.

"Our newest pride," Ms. Mabaso announced as she unlocked the door with obvious satisfaction. "The BBD Computer Center, completed just eight months ago."

Inside, the contrast with other facilities was immediately apparent—twenty modern laptop computers arranged in a thoughtfully designed learning space, with appropriate furniture, and reliable electrical infrastructure.

"This is a transformational opportunity for our community and our students," the principal explained as they explored the facility. "Digital literacy is no longer optional for meaningful economic participation. Without these resources, our community would face insurmountable disadvantages in pursuing higher education or employment opportunities. This lab is accessible to both the local population and the students in the school."

A young woman in her mid-twenties emerged from a small office adjacent to the main computer room.

"This is Zintle Makalima, our IT coordinator," Ms. Mabaso introduced her with pride. "Zintle was once a student here at Ekuphumleni. Through the Kariega Foundation's scholarship program, she completed both secondary education and university studies in computer science."

Zintle stepped forward with a confident poise tempered by genuine warmth. "I graduated from Rhodes University three years ago," she explained. "I could've taken positions in Cape Town or Johannesburg, but I chose to return here because I understand exactly what access to technology means for these children."

Her personal connection to the school created an immediate impact among the visitors, the concrete example of an educational investment yielding meaningful outcomes clearly resonating with the group.

Zintle explained, "These children have potential that's limited only by access to resources and opportunities. My role isn't just technical support—it's showing them a possible future they might not otherwise envision."

As they explored the facility, several older students showed current projects—digital presentations about local ecology, basic programming exercises, and research projects that included offline educational resources specifically designed for limited-connectivity environments.

"Internet access remains our greatest challenge," Zintle acknowledged. "We've got a satellite connection, but bandwidth limitations and cost concerns restrict usage to essential educational applications. We've developed creative solutions—offline resource libraries, local network applications, and scheduled online access for specific projects."

The technical challenges clearly hadn't diminished the students' enthusiasm, however. The children demonstrating their computer skills showed remarkable adaptability and creative problem-solving capabilities that impressed even the more tech-savvy tourists.

"They maximize what they have," Joan observed with professional appreciation. "Innovation from scarcity, rather than from abundance."

As the facility tour concluded, Ms. Mabaso consulted her watch. "Now for what the children have been most eagerly anticipating—sports activities!"

The group followed her outside to where the school's modest sports facilities awaited—a grass soccer field marked with white lines and equipped with goal posts, alongside a netball court with recently painted boundaries. Children had already organized themselves into teams, their excitement barely contained as they awaited their visitors.

"We'll divide into two activities," Ms. Mabaso explained. "Soccer on the field, and netball on the court. Our students will coach you through the rules."

The runners separated according to interest, with Tyler and Emma predictably gravitating toward the soccer field alongside several other tourists with clear experience. The remaining visitors approached the netball court with curious interest, most admitting complete ignorance of the sport.

"Netball?" Stanley inquired as they approached the court where children in basic sports clothes waited eagerly. "Is that like basketball?"

"Barely. There's a hoop," Luke explained. "It's enormously popular throughout the Commonwealth, particularly in schools. Let the children teach you."

The boys and girls took charge with surprising confidence, assigning positions to the visiting adults and explaining rules with patient enthusiasm that occasionally dissolved into giggles when their instructions were misunderstood or clumsily executed.

"No moving with the ball," a serious-faced girl of about eight explained to Joan, who'd instinctively begun dribbling like a basketball player. "You must pass or shoot from where you catch it."

"No men in this position," another child informed Rogerio when he wandered into the wrong court section. "You must stay in the center third only."

"Why?" he asked, genuinely curious about the gender-based restriction.

"Because those are the rules," the girl replied with the perfect certainty of a child reciting established truth, before adding with unexpected wit, "And because you're too tall and it wouldn't be fair."

On the soccer field, a similar cultural exchange unfolded as the local children demonstrated technical skills that occasionally surprised their adult visitors. Despite playing on uneven grass rather than manicured turf, several boys displayed remarkable ball control and tactical coordination.

"Where'd you learn that move?" Wanda asked after a particularly impressive dribbling display from a boy who couldn't have been more than ten.

"Watching Bafana Bafana and Mamelodi Sundowns," he replied, referencing South Africa's national team and a popular club team. "And practicing every day after school."

The games proceeded with increasing integration as adults adapted to the children's guidance and children accommodated the adults' limitations with diplomatic politeness occasionally punctuated by irrepressible laughter when particularly awkward moments occurred.

"You kick like a rhino," one boy informed Stanley after a spectacularly missed penalty shot, before immediately adding with perfect politeness, "but your trying's very good."

On the netball court, similar honesty prevailed. "Your catching's like my grandmother," a girl informed Joan after a missed pass, "but she's eighty-three years, so she's got an excuse."

What might have seemed impertinent in another context was delivered with such genuine good humor and followed by such earnest encouragement that it created a connection rather than an offense. The children's unfiltered observations, combined with their obvious joy in the interaction, created a uniquely refreshing dynamic.

As the games continued, Sheryl observed from the sidelines alongside Ms. Mabaso, appreciating this rare opportunity for her tour group to engage directly with the local community beyond the typical tourist experiences.

"They'll remember this more vividly than many wildlife encounters," she noted to the principal. "Your children will create the most lasting impressions."

"And for our children, these interactions expand their understanding of the world," Ms. Mabaso replied. "Many've never traveled beyond our local district. Meeting people from different countries broadens their horizons in ways formal education alone can't achieve."

Eventually, a whistle signaled the conclusion of the activities, much to the disappointment of both children and adults who'd become thoroughly engaged in their respective games. The visitors gathered their belongings, many exchanging high-fives and taking selfies with their young teammates.

Before their departure, Ms. Mabaso organized a brief ceremony in the central courtyard, where students joined in chorus a traditional song of welcome and gratitude.

"We extend our genuine gratitude," she explained as the song ended. "Your contributions directly support these children's educational opportunities and future prospects."

The moment carried real emotional weight for the American visitors. It was a concrete connection between their tourism activities and a meaningful community benefit. Several of the runners were visibly moved as they waved good-bye to their impromptu teammates. As they prepared to board their bus for their return to the lodge, many attempted their newly learned Xhosa phrases in farewell, drawing delighted responses from the children who enthusiastically corrected pronunciation with the natural confidence of native speakers guiding well-meaning beginners.

"*Enkosi!*" the visitors called as they departed, the thank-you phrase they'd practiced now carrying deeper significance after experiencing the joy and kindness of the children.

Once the bus was underway, Anathi moved to the front again to encourage reflection on their experience. The mood had shifted noticeably—the lighthearted anticipation of their outward journey replaced by a thoughtful consideration of the encounter.

"Questions about what you saw today?" she invited, creating space for people to speak up.

"The children seem so happy and engaged, despite what appear to be challenging circumstances," Margaret noted. "Is that representative of the entire community?"

Anathi nodded, acknowledging both the observation and its underlying question. "Children show remarkable resilience and capacity for joy, regardless of their material circumstances.

But yes, there are significant challenges beyond what was visible during your brief visit."

She paused, considering how to frame the complex socio-economic realities without overwhelming the positive aspects of their experience. "South Africa currently faces about 40% unemployment nationwide, with even higher rates in rural areas like ours."

This statistic clearly shocked many of the tourists, their expressions registering disbelief at such an extreme economic challenge.

"How's that possible?" Joan asked, her financial background engaging with this economic anomaly. "That's depression-level unemployment, yet we've seen functioning businesses, infrastructure, and services."

"The simplest explanation is demographic," Anathi replied. "Our population's grown significantly faster than economic development. When apartheid ended in 1994, new opportunities emerged, but not at a sufficient enough scale to absorb rapid population growth, especially among young people entering the workforce."

She continued with the measured tone of someone explaining difficult realities without surrendering to either false optimism or unproductive despair. "Educational advancement helps individuals compete for existing opportunities, but it can't alone create the volume of employment needed. That requires broader economic policy reforms, business development initiatives, and infrastructure investment beyond what's currently occurring."

The bus traveled in thoughtful silence for several moments as the tourists processed this sobering context for the school visit that they'd just experienced.

"Yet, despite these challenges, we witnessed remarkable commitment to educational excellence," Nkosi observed. "Investing in future potential even without guaranteed outcomes."

"Precisely," Anathi agreed. "We continue building foundations for possible futures. The children you met today face obstacles, but they also possess opportunities that their parents never had, like access to technology, quality education, and connection to global networks."

This perspective seemed to resonate with the group. Their questions shifted toward specific ways their continued engagement might support the school and broader community beyond their brief visit.

"Kariega and other foundations provide ongoing support," Luke explained in response to these inquiries. "Including scholarship funds, infrastructure development, and teacher training initiatives. We can provide information to those interested in continued involvement."

As the bus approached the reserve's entrance, Anathi offered a final observation that effectively contextualized their experience. "Today, you witnessed both joy and challenges, potential and obstacles. That complexity is South Africa's reality—a nation of extraordinary possibility still addressing historical inequities and economic difficulties."

She smiled with genuine warmth as she concluded, "But most importantly, you connected with children who'll remember your visit long after you've returned home. That human exchange matters beyond any material support, though both are valuable."

The bus passed through Kariega's main gate, returning them to the carefully maintained safari environment that contrasted markedly with the more modest facilities they'd just visited. Yet, rather than creating a disconnection, this transition seemed to highlight the interdependence between conservation success and community development—each supporting the other through mutually beneficial relationships.

As they disembarked at the main lodge, preparing for the evening activities and dinner, the conversations among the tourists reflected a deeper engagement with South Africa beyond the wildlife and beautiful environment. Their schedule for tomorrow would return to safari experiences, but today's school visit had provided the essential insight for understanding the complete ecosystem—both natural and human—that made these conservation efforts meaningful.

CHAPTER 39

INFILTRATION

The afternoon sun cast lengthening shadows across Kariega Main Lodge as a reserve maintenance vehicle passed through the service entrance without drawing particular attention. The driver—a seasonal ranger whose financial needs had proven greater than his professional ethics—maintained a casual conversation with the gate security guard, who waved them through with only cursory verification.

"Supply delivery for the maintenance shed," the driver explained, gesturing toward the covered truck bed. "Got that broken water pump replaced—finally."

The security guard nodded without suspicion. Vehicle movements between lodge areas and maintenance facilities occurred regularly, particularly during late afternoon when the service would be invisible to the guests.

Once out of sight of the security gate, the vehicle diverted from the main road toward a rarely used maintenance building located conveniently between staff quarters and guest accommodations. The structure's strategic location provided both concealment and access to the lodge's luxury chalets without crossing high-traffic areas.

The driver parked alongside the building, killing the engine before rapping twice on the partition separating the cab from the cargo area. "We're clear," he announced tersely.

The truck's rear canvas lifted, revealing Malanga and Botha. Two additional men—the hardened operatives, Luzuko and Kobus—followed, all four moving silently into the building.

"The tourists are still off-property at the school visit," the driver informed them, checking his watch. "Should be back around six. Then, they'll probably head straight to dinner."

Malanga nodded. "What about lodge security?"

"Not much inside the guest area," the driver confirmed. "Most security's out at the reserve perimeters and poaching hotspots after last night. They're looking in all the wrong places."

"Guest chalet assignments still accurate?" Malanga inquired, consulting a small notebook containing the lodge layout diagrams.

"Yeah. Diego's in Chalet 7, Hunter's in 12, and the De Beers woman is in 8," the driver replied. "Got it from today's housekeeping schedule."

Malanga's expression revealed cold satisfaction as he surveyed the layout once more. The luxury accommodations were arranged along the central road and surrounded by native trees and landscaping for privacy—design choices that now suited their plan perfectly.

The driver hesitated momentarily, his moral discomfort briefly visible. "No one gets hurt beyond the three targets, right? That's what we agreed."

"Exactly as discussed," Malanga assured him with practiced smoothness that conveyed certainty without being entirely convincing. "This is a targeted removal of specific problems."

Whether persuaded or simply unwilling to acknowledge his complicity further, the driver nodded before departing, leaving the four men to finalize their preparations in the maintenance building's concealing shadow.

"Luzuko and Kobus, secure the woman in Chalet 8 first. Botha and I'll get Diego in 7. Once both are secured, I'll message you to bring her to us."

"What about Hunter?" Botha inquired, his wounded pride eager for payback.

"Final phase," Malanga confirmed. "Once we've got the women, we'll use Diego to draw him in. That way, we don't have to fight him."

The group conducted final equipment checks of their communication devices, restraints, and weapons. The arsenal revealed their approach—primarily non-firearms to maximize stealth. Knives, rope, duct tape—all silent but potentially deadly.

"Remember," Malanga emphasized as they concluded their preparations, "these aren't typical tourists. Both women have already shown that they can fight. Expect resistance—don't hesitate to get rough."

With roles confirmed and equipment prepared, they settled into silent waiting.

❊ ❊ ❊

The distant sound of returning vehicles eventually broke the silence—the tourist group arriving from their school visit, voices carrying intermittently across the property as they disembarked and proceeded to dinner. Through narrow window slats, Malanga observed their targets among the returning group—Sheryl directing the group with characteristic cheerfulness, the De Beers woman walking alongside another tourist, and Hunter's distinctive physical presence bringing up the rear.

"Visual confirmation of all three targets," he noted quietly to Botha. "We'll proceed as planned. They'll be busy with dinner for about ninety minutes. We move right after."

The waiting resumed as afternoon yielded to evening and the characteristically swift African sunset transformed the landscape. The lodge lighting systems came on automatically, illuminating pathways with a gentle, indirect glow that preserved the natural atmosphere while ensuring guest safety.

At precisely 8:30 p.m., they departed their hiding place with practiced stealth, using lodge service pathways to avoid the main guest routes. Their movements remained unhurried and purposeful—resembling staff activities rather than intruders, a technique that was more effective than attempting complete invisibility.

Luzuko and Kobus reached their position, using a staff access key provided by their inside contact to enter Chalet 8.

They positioned themselves in the darkened interior—Luzuko concealed himself beside the entrance, Kobus deeper within the living area, where shadows provided the perfect cover.

Simultaneously, Malanga and Botha entered Chalet 7, concealing themselves to intercept Diego upon her return. The waiting resumed.

Across the property in the main dining area, the Global Runners group was concluding dinner service. The atmosphere was relaxed and engaging, with no indication that three of their members had been targeted by deadly professionals now waiting in their rooms.

"Early start tomorrow," Sheryl reminded the group as dessert service concluded. "Our final game drive starts at 5:30 a.m. to catch the best dawn wildlife."

This announcement prompted varied reactions—enthusiasm from some, good-natured groans from others, and the inevitable questions from those who needed to plan every detail.

"A light breakfast will be packed and ready on the vehicles," Luke clarified in response to these inquiries. "Full breakfast when we get back around nine."

As coffee service completed the meal, guests began departing in their typical staggered fashion—some lingering over conversations while others headed directly to their chalets, creating the natural flow of tourists on vacation.

Anika was among the early departures, excusing herself with the mention of catching up on some work before bed. Her professional focus had remained consistent throughout the tour, balancing the tourist experience with the underlying investigation that had brought her to South Africa in the first place.

She followed the illuminated pathway toward her chalet, appreciating the evening symphony of nocturnal insects and distant animal calls of the African night. The security of the lodge perimeter allowed guests to walk unescorted between facilities—a feature about to be weaponized against her.

Reaching her chalet, Anika unlocked the door and stepped inside, reaching for the light switch. Before her hand could complete the motion, a powerful arm closed around her throat from behind while another slapped duct tape over her mouth, preventing any sound beyond muffled protests.

Her immediate struggle—testament to better-than-expected fighting skills—proved ineffective against Luzuko's professional restraint. Kobus secured her wrists with practiced efficiency while maintaining minimal noise throughout the encounter.

Within thirty seconds, the struggle was over—her captors returning to their concealed positions in the darkened chalet. Their portion of the operation had proceeded exactly according to plan.

Luzuko messaged Malanga: "Package secured."

The main dinner gathering continued its natural dissolution, with Sheryl among the last departures. Her responsibilities included ensuring all guests understood the next morning's plan before she could retire for the evening. Jack remained similarly engaged, sharing military stories with Archie.

By the time Sheryl finally departed the main lodge, most guests had already reached their accommodations. She followed the now-quiet pathway toward her chalet, noting the peaceful evening atmosphere that suggested everything was normal on the property.

Reaching Chalet 7, she unlocked the door and stepped inside, securing it behind her out of automatic habit. The interior remained dark—she hadn't left any lights on when departing that morning—and she reached for the nearby switch while mentally reviewing tomorrow's plan.

Before her hand found the switch, powerful arms seized her from behind—one encircling her waist while another clamped across her mouth. Sheryl's response was immediate. She drove her elbow backward with force, connecting solidly with Botha's eye socket and producing a muffled grunt that confirmed impact.

The momentary advantage was insufficient against the man's substantial size and strength. He maintained control over her despite the painful strike, forcing her to the floor with controlled violence that minimized noise while maximizing dominance. Malanga joined in quickly when it looked like Botha had the woman under control, applying restraints with clinical efficiency, despite Sheryl's continued resistance.

"Impressive," Malanga commented quietly as they secured her. "You've been quite the thorn in my side, Ms. Diego."

Once properly restrained and gagged, Sheryl was positioned in one of the chalet's chairs with Botha's hand holding her firmly in place. Only then did Malanga allow his phone screen to illuminate his face—enough for her to recognize him without being seen in case anyone else was walking outside.

"We've got a lot to discuss," he informed her with cold detachment. "Starting with your remarkable talent for screwing up my business dealings across this entire country."

Sheryl's eyes conveyed defiance rather than fear, assessment rather than panic—cataloging her captors, evaluating the restraints, calculating potential escape routes. This type of reaction confirmed Malanga's suspicions about her non-tourist status.

"You infiltrated my Cape Town warehouse," he continued conversationally while Botha stood silent. "Intercepted my Knysna diamond deal. Captured my poachers. Pretty remarkable coincidences following your tour group's movements, don't you think?"

Unable to respond verbally, Sheryl maintained a neutral expression, despite the damning accuracy of his summary. Her eyes continued their methodical assessment of the situation, revealing a competent opponent rather than a frightened captive.

Malanga messaged Luzuko: "Bring her."

Within minutes, a soft knock at the door signaled Luzuko and Kobus's arrival with their package.

Anika's eyes widened upon seeing Sheryl similarly restrained, the full situation becoming immediately apparent. Like Sheryl, her response reflected preparation rather than panic.

"Excellent," Malanga observed as both women were settled within the chalet. "Now, we're just missing one key player in our little talk."

He retrieved Sheryl's phone from her belongings, pointing it at her face to unlock it. With this access secured, he composed a message while showing the screen to Sheryl so she understood exactly what trap was being laid.

To Jack Hunter, he typed: "Need to discuss something important. Can you stop by my chalet?"

The message sent, Malanga returned his attention to his captives. "Mr. Hunter's arrival will complete our gathering. Then, we'll head somewhere more private where we can discuss your interesting activities…in detail."

The response came almost immediately: "Be there in five."

"Perfect timing," Malanga noted with cold satisfaction. "Let's go," he instructed his team. "Our vehicle's waiting outside."

The entire group moved silently to the safari vehicle parked beside the chalet. Minutes passed before they heard the crunch of gravel as footsteps approached.

As Jack walked to the door, Malanga called out softly from the shadows. "Good evening, Mr. Hunter." The unexpected voice caused Jack to freeze momentarily—a critical hesitation that allowed Malanga to reveal the blade pressed firmly against Sheryl's throat.

"Easy now," Malanga continued smoothly. "Your colleagues' well-being depends entirely on your cooperation. We're taking a short drive together."

Jack's expression shifted from surprise to anger to detached assessment. He decided that compliance now could create survival possibilities later.

"Eastern service road," Malanga directed the driver once Jack had boarded, Botha holding a pistol to the back of his dangerous captive's seat. "Just take it easy until we're clear of the lodge's perimeter."

The vehicle began moving slowly — nothing suggesting anything out of the ordinary. It followed service roadways before connecting to the main reserve's access route, lights illuminating the path ahead while darkness concealed the true nature of its occupants.

As the vehicle disappeared into the night, Wanda and Joan were returning to their chalets after lingering longer at dinner than most guests. Their conversation about the day's school visit paused briefly as the vehicle's headlights illuminated their path.

"Kind of late for a game drive," Joan observed casually as the vehicle passed, its occupants indistinguishable in the darkness.

"Probably just staff heading to their quarters," Wanda suggested without particular concern.

Their conversation resumed as they continued toward their accommodations, unaware that the vehicle carried their colleagues under deadly threat.

As the vehicle passed beyond the lodge's lighting into the darkness of the reserve proper, Malanga allowed himself momentary satisfaction at the operation's successful execution thus far. Three targets secured, clean extraction accomplished, and no alarm raised to interrupt their departure.

"Now," he addressed his captives with cold professionalism, "we'll head to a location where we can discuss your remarkable talent for interfering with my business. I expect that conversation will prove quite enlightening for all involved."

The vehicle continued into the African night, its headlights illuminating only the immediate path ahead while darkness enveloped everything beyond—an apt metaphor for the captives' circumstances as they were transported away from safety into unknown territory, where natural predators were far less dangerous than the humans who held them.

Behind them, Kariega Lodge continued its normal evening activities—guests retiring to their comfortable accommodations, staff completing their duties, and security maintaining their vigilance against threats beyond the perimeter rather than those who had already infiltrated the reserve.

CHAPTER 40

INTO THE DARKNESS

The safari vehicle penetrated deeper into the reserve, deliberately avoiding established game drive routes in favor of seldom-used maintenance tracks.

Inside, the forced silence created palpable tension. Jack maintained a controlled stillness in the front passenger seat, his posture revealing neither panic nor resignation but tactical patience—waiting for circumstances to change. Behind him, Botha remained vigilant, his pistol positioned at Jack's back, ready for any unauthorized move.

In the middle row, Sheryl sat with apparent submission, her bound hands resting in her lap beneath a light blanket Malanga had casually tossed over her—not from compassion but to conceal evidence of captivity should they encounter another vehicle. This inadvertent concealment provided perfect cover as her fingers worked methodically at the pocketknife she had extracted from her waistband. The blade worked steadily against the restraints, her movements imperceptible beneath the blanket.

Anika occupied the rear seat under Luzuko's guard. Her eyes continually tracked their route and surroundings, cataloging landmarks and terrain features with precision, despite the limited visibility.

"You've caused some pretty remarkable disruptions to my well-oiled operations," Malanga observed, breaking the extended silence with a conversational tone that heightened rather than diminished the underlying menace of the situation. "I'm curious which agency actually employs you. You're definitely not just a tourist guide."

No one responded, Sheryl and Anika with their mouths taped and Jack with no intention of sharing information.

"Doesn't matter," he continued after a bit of silence. "Just curiosity. Your interference ends tonight, regardless."

The vehicle turned onto an even narrower track that had increasingly uneven terrain. They penetrated an area deliberately avoided by standard game drives. The habitat transition was evident, even in darkness—denser vegetation created claustrophobic corridors on either side of the car, and branches occasionally scraped against the vehicle's sides.

"Perfect location," Malanga noted as they entered a small clearing. "The map says this area's got three lion prides with overlapping territories, plus hyena clans looking for scavenging opportunities. Nature will erase all evidence by morning."

The vehicle stopped in the clearing's center, headlights illuminating a wall of bush beyond which darkness concealed whatever wildlife might be observing these human intruders. The engine fell silent, allowing the nighttime sounds of the African bush to emerge—distant calls of nocturnal animals punctuating the insect chorus that formed the soundtrack of the wilderness.

"We're here," Malanga announced unnecessarily. "Everyone out."

At his direction, Luzuko and Kobus exited first, establishing perimeter security with efficiency, despite their evident discomfort with the location. Their flashlight beams probed the surrounding vegetation for potential threats.

"Clear for now," Kobus reported tersely. "But we should finish this quickly. This area's active predator territory after dark."

Under Botha's unwavering direction, Jack exited first, moving with deliberate compliance that revealed neither fear nor reckless defiance. His eyes continuously scanned their surroundings, cataloging details, despite the limited visibility provided by vehicle lights and scattered flashlight beams.

Sheryl followed, maintaining the appearance of secured restraints while her nearly severed bonds were ready to snap. Her expression revealed nothing of this advantage as she joined Jack in the clearing, positioned where Botha could maintain visual coverage of both simultaneously.

Luzuko approached the rear seats to extract Anika from her position. He lifted and pulled the small woman over the side and onto the ground. She stood momentarily beside the vehicle, seemingly resigned to the unfolding situation as the group focused primarily on Jack and Sheryl—the targets they assumed to be the greatest threats.

This momentary lapse provided the catalyst for everything that followed.

Without warning or preparatory movement, Anika exploded into action—not toward her captors, but away from the vehicle, directly into the surrounding darkness. Her movement carried such unexpected decisiveness that she covered nearly ten meters before Luzuko reacted.

"She's running!" he shouted, his flashlight beam swinging wildly in attempted pursuit, illuminating only glimpses of movement before the bush swallowed her completely.

The sudden disruption was exactly the diversion Jack had been waiting for. With Botha momentarily distracted by Anika's escape, Jack launched into explosive motion—not a desperate lunge, but a precisely calculated kick targeting the weapon rather than the man. His foot connected with Botha's wrist, sending the pistol spinning from his grip.

The weapon discharged once as it left the man's hand—a single round firing harmlessly into the night as the pistol tumbled into tall grass, immediately lost in the darkness. The gunshot seemed supernaturally loud in the previously quiet clearing, momentarily silencing even the insects' chorus as its echo dissipated across the landscape.

Simultaneously, Sheryl snapped her restraints, ripped the tape from her mouth, and launched directly toward Malanga. Her attack carried the aggressive precision of her ranger training.

One fist smashed into Malanga's diaphragm, eliminating both his breath and vocal capacity for the moment. As he instinctively bent forward, her elbow connected with devastating precision against his temple, sending him sprawling backward onto the ground.

The attack created only seconds of advantage—not victory, but an opening. Jack recognized this narrow window immediately. He threw one powerful arm around her waist and pulled her toward the concealing bush. Realizing his purpose, Sheryl moved with him, leaving their captors stunned in their wake.

They plunged into the bush together, Jack's knowledge of wilderness navigation immediately evident in his choices—moving purposefully rather than randomly, selecting routes that minimized sound while maximizing their distance from the clearing. Within seconds, the vehicle's lights were lost behind them, the surrounding darkness becoming an ally rather than an obstacle as they moved deeper into the bush.

Back in the clearing, Botha recovered from his initial surprise quickly, ignoring his lost weapon to attend first to Malanga's condition—evidence of his personal loyalty to his boss.

"Sir?" he inquired tersely, kneeling beside his employer while watching the bushes close behind their captives.

Malanga regained his composure with remarkable speed, considering the blows he'd absorbed, waving away assistance as he returned to his feet. A trickle of blood from his temple and his slightly unsteady movement revealed the significant effect of Sheryl's strikes.

"Find them," he ordered, cold fury replacing his previous detachment. "All of them."

These orders sparked immediate action from Luzuko and Kobus, though their response carried visible reluctance as they retrieved additional flashlights from the vehicle. The prospect of pursuing targets through predator-filled territory was clearly not something they wanted to do.

"They're headed in different directions," Luzuko noted, indicating the divergent escape routes. "We should stick together rather than split up."

"Afraid of the dark?" Malanga questioned with dangerous quietness. "You've hunted this reserve countless times. Suddenly the wildlife scares you?"

"Poaching's different from man-hunting," Kobus responded with surprising directness. "We shoot from the protection of a vehicle. We don't stumble through the dark where the animals can see us, but we can't see them."

Malanga's expression hardened further at this resistance. "Your concern's noted. Now, your compliance is required. Find them before they get any further."

Recognizing the futility of further objection, the two men nodded.

"Luzuko, go after the woman you let get away," Botha directed, establishing his leadership to compensate for Malanga's injured status. "Kobus, you're with us after the other two."

Malanga dabbed at the blood on his temple. "That woman's more capable than I expected," he noted with grudging admiration. "Treat her with the same care you'd give Hunter."

"Will do," Botha confirmed.

"The outcome's still the same," Malanga stated with cold certainty. "They're on foot in predator-filled territory with no phones, no weapons, and no vehicles. Time is on our side, regardless of where they run."

This fact set the tone of their approach—controlled pursuit rather than panicked reaction, methodical pressure rather than desperate searching. They would win in the end.

"I particularly want the Diego woman," Malanga added, rubbing his bruised solar plexus.

Botha nodded in understanding before locating his sidearm in the grass.

"We'll move together," Botha said as they departed the vehicle's illuminated perimeter, their flashlight beams joining the others already probing the surrounding wilderness. Behind them, the empty safari vehicle's headlights remained on—a beacon marking their return point in a landscape otherwise claimed by absolute darkness.

The African night enfolded them all—pursuer and pursued alike—its vastness diminishing their movements and concerns. Whatever daylight might eventually reveal, the coming hours belonged to darkness, and only those best adapted to its concealing embrace would survive.

CHAPTER 41

PREDATORS

Darkness engulfed Jack and Sheryl as they moved deeper into the bush, the vehicle's headlights quickly lost behind them. They moved with purpose — not panicked flight but deliberate evasion, each step placed carefully to minimize noise.

"We need to find Anika," Sheryl whispered once they'd established some distance. Her voice barely carried the few inches between them.

Jack nodded, invisible in the darkness but sensed through proximity. "Can't leave her out here alone. No weapons, no phone."

They paused briefly, allowing their eyes to adjust to the darkness. The star-filled sky provided minimal light — enough to see basic shapes and avoid large obstacles, but little else. The moon remained low, not yet high enough to help.

"Which direction?" Jack asked, deferring to Sheryl's ranger background.

"She ran northeast from the vehicle," Sheryl said, mentally reconstructing their separation. "Smart move—away from the lodge but toward higher ground where she can see the terrain and any pursuers."

Jack considered this information briefly. "Let's move thirty degrees to the right. Go parallel rather than direct."

They changed course, adopting a careful rhythm—they took ten steps and paused, listened, observed, then continued. This pattern minimized noise while maximizing awareness, essential in territory where human pursuers weren't the only threat they faced.

The surrounding bush was filled with nighttime sounds— insects providing constant background noise, punctuated by occasional calls from birds and distant mammals. Most concerning was the low, rumbling growls that occasionally carried through the darkness.

"Lions," Sheryl said quietly. "Not close, but they're active in the area."

"Malanga chose his spot well," Jack noted grimly. "Dangerous, even if we escaped."

They continued their careful advance, senses heightened by the combination of danger and darkness. Each sound registered clearly, each shadow demanded instant attention, each step required careful placement.

After about fifteen minutes, they registered subtle movements ahead—not the deliberate sweep of searchers with flashlights, but the natural movement of wildlife or possibly another person trying to hide.

They froze simultaneously, no communication needed between them. The movement ahead stopped for several seconds, then resumed with slightly greater urgency—suggesting human rather than animal behavior.

Sheryl signaled their approach with light pressure against Jack's arm, indicating they should flank rather than approach directly. He acknowledged with a barely perceptible nod, then separated slightly to create better coverage.

They advanced cautiously, closing the distance slowly. When they were near, Sheryl deliberately created small noises—just enough to trigger a reaction without revealing their exact position.

The response came with explosive suddenness—not a retreat, but an attack. A low sweeping impact connected with Sheryl's legs, executing a perfect takedown that dropped her to the ground. Before she could respond, a human form was on top of her, using its body weight to pin her down.

"Anika, it's me. Stop," Sheryl whispered urgently, recognizing the figure above her.

The pressure immediately relaxed, though she wasn't released, possibly from caution before being certain of her captive.

"It's us," she confirmed, keeping her voice barely audible. "Let me get those bindings off of you."

Jack kept watch while Sheryl freed Anika, her sharp blade making quick work of the restraints. The tape came last, Anika controlling her breathing as the restrictive material was removed.

"Thank God, it's you," she whispered once able to speak, and the relief was evident in her voice. "Are we free? Can we run?"

Already orienting away from the flashlight beams now visible behind them, Jack confirmed tersely, "We're moving. Together, minimal sound."

They formed a tight group, each keeping physical contact with at least one of the others to prevent them from getting separated in the darkness. Their movements adjusted to move more efficiently as a pack—slightly slower but more secure, ensuring that no one was left behind.

The sounds behind them continued to approach, and occasional voices carried further than their owners likely realized. The searchers appeared to be moving in a loose formation rather than wandering carelessly.

"Higher ground," Sheryl directed, guiding them toward the elevated terrain. "Better defensive position."

They increased their pace as much as the darkness and vegetation allowed, navigating through increasingly uneven terrain. The rising moon began providing marginal help—not yet direct light, but gradual brightening of the eastern sky that improved visibility.

A sound to their left froze the group—movement through vegetation without accompanying flashlight or human voices. The distinctive yipping call that followed confirmed what they feared.

"Hyena," Anika whispered, her voice steady, despite the implications.

"They're hunting," Sheryl added. "Not targeting us yet, but they know something's in their territory."

This unwelcome development accelerated their progress toward the elevated ground ahead, compromising silence slightly in favor of reaching a better position. The terrain grew increasingly steep, eventually presenting a vertical embankment too sheer to climb—a natural barrier that changed their plan.

"Follow the base," Sheryl decided after a quick assessment. "Find a way up or someplace we can defend."

They proceeded along the embankment, searching. The rising moon soon provided measurable light, revealing their surroundings with increasing clarity while simultaneously exposing them to their pursuers.

After several hundred meters, they encountered a promising feature—a dense stand of trees growing against the embankment, their trunks and lower branches offering both climbing assistance and potential cover.

"We'll hold here," Jack directed, guiding them into the natural fortress created by the cluster of trees.

The position offered multiple advantages—a restricted approach so they couldn't be surrounded, elevated root systems creating natural barriers, and sufficient vegetation to break visual detection while maintaining their own views from within.

The pause allowed them to get a better assessment of their surroundings. They saw flashlight patterns indicating at least three pursuers, animal movement suggesting predator activity in response to the unusual human presence, and terrain that limited their evacuation routes.

"Which way's the lodge?" Anika asked.

"Southwest," Sheryl said and pointed with a minimal gesture. "About eight kilometers across rough terrain. No direct route from here."

This sobering fact settled on them—the reality of their situation sinking deeper. Even without being pursued, covering such distance through predator-filled territory in darkness was a significant survival challenge.

Before they could process their options, a distant sound shattered the silence—a human scream, clearly distinguishable from animal sounds. The scream carried unmistakable terror, followed by incoherent shouting. A flashlight beam, visible through distant vegetation, swung in frantic patterns, clearly showing someone in distress.

Then, silence. Absolute and sudden.

The distant flashlight extinguished mid-movement, darkness reclaiming the location with unsettling finality. No further sounds followed, no movement that suggested continued human activity in that area.

"Predator contact," Jack said flatly. "One searcher down."

"Luzuko or Kobus," Anika added. "The hired help."

This disruption triggered a change to the search pattern of the other flashlights. The lights moved directly away from the site of the animal attack. No one was rushing to investigate or help the fallen man.

The search patterns were now oriented more directly toward the fugitives' position.

"They're tracking us," Sheryl observed, noting the increasingly precise approach. "Something's giving us away."

"I think they're following the same embankment we did," Jack suggested.

Whatever the mechanism, the three remaining searchers were unmistakably closing the distance.

Sheryl extracted her pocket knife, the blade catching momentary moonlight as she considered its limited value. Four inches of steel represented little defense against either armed humans or natural predators, yet it was their only weapon.

"Take it," she directed, offering the knife to Jack.

The unspoken implication registered immediately with the others. Jack accepted the knife with a solemn acknowledgment of its meaning.

Without a word, Jack melted into the surrounding darkness, his movements immediately lost. His departure left Sheryl and Anika in their defensive positions, the modest protection of tree roots and trunks now seeming significantly less substantial as flashlight beams continued their inexorable approach. Each woman lifted a sturdy branch from the ground and tested its weight. It was the best they could do.

The African night continued its gradual transformation as the moonlight shining overhead strengthened. Natural shadows gained definition while hiding places diminished. Somewhere in the surrounding darkness, Jack moved with predatory purpose while unknown numbers of actual predators tracked the unusual human activity in their territory.

CHAPTER 42

STALKING

Jack moved through the darkness with precision, his footfalls virtually silent against the African soil. His eyes had fully adapted to the minimal light, the stars and rising moon providing just enough illumination to navigate the terrain. He circled wide of the women's position, placing himself between them and the approaching search party.

The pocketknife felt inadequate in his hand, but he'd worked with less. He tracked the approaching searchers by their flashlight beams and their careless sounds through the bush. Professional hunters in daylight, these men moved with surprising clumsiness in the dark, betraying their positions with every step.

One beam separated from the others, moving at an angle that would miss the women's position but inadvertently headed directly toward Jack's location. Perfect. Kobus judging by the silhouette and movement pattern. The man was alone, having spread out from the other two.

Jack remained perfectly still as the searcher approached, controlling his breathing to near-imperceptible levels. The flashlight beam swept across the brush five meters to his right, then pivoted to scan the area ahead. Jack waited for the moment when the light moved furthest from his position, plunging Kobus into temporary night blindness as he stared into the illuminated foliage.

Then, he pounced.

Three swift steps closed the distance before Kobus registered the approach. Jack struck from behind, one arm snaking around the man's throat while his other hand clamped over the flashlight, preventing it from signaling any distress to the others. Kobus reacted with surprising speed, driving his elbow backward into Jack's ribs.

The blow connected solidly, but Jack had expected resistance and adjusted his position to absorb rather than block the impact. He maintained control of the flashlight while shifting his chokehold to a less lethal but equally effective restraint position.

Kobus twisted violently, breaking Jack's grip enough to call out, "Bot—" before Jack's hand clamped over his mouth, cutting off the alarm mid-word. The scuffle intensified, both men fighting in near silence—one to escape and alert his companions, the other to neutralize without attracting attention from either human or animal predators.

Jack had significant advantages—better night vision from avoiding flashlight use, superior hand-to-hand training, and the element of surprise. Still, Kobus fought with the desperate strength of someone who understood exactly what failure meant in this environment.

The struggle took them to the ground, rolling through the brush with muffled impacts. Jack maintained focus on two priorities: prevent shouting and keep the knife. The blade remained folded in his pocket during the initial engagement—using it prematurely would escalate the confrontation unnecessarily.

Kobus managed to break Jack's grip momentarily, gasping for breath and reaching toward the knife at his hip. That movement justified Jack's next move. He extracted the knife, flicked it open with practiced efficiency, and slashed across Kobus's forearm.

The man hissed in pain, instinctively pulling back the injured limb. Blood glistened black in the moonlight, the cut deep enough to disable but designed to avoid major arterial damage.

"Run or die," Jack whispered, his voice carrying absolutely minimal distance but conveying deadly seriousness. "Your choice. Now."

Kobus registered his situation—isolated from his companions, injured, facing a clearly superior opponent in the darkness. Self-preservation overrode bravado as he scrambled backward, abandoning the flashlight in favor of a quick escape.

"The animals will find you," Kobus hissed as he retreated. "All of you."

"They'll find whoever bleeds more," Jack responded coldly, gesturing toward the man's wounded arm. "Keep moving."

Kobus made the rational choice, running roughly toward the clearing where they had parked the vehicle rather than deeper into the wilderness. Jack watched him go, certain that he'd prioritize his personal survival over rejoining the search, especially given the blood seeping from his arm.

Jack claimed the abandoned flashlight but kept it extinguished, preserving his night vision while securing a useful tool. He oriented himself quickly, trying to figure out where the other two hunters had gone since their flashlights were no longer visible.

* * *

Near the tree cluster where Sheryl and Anika had established their defensive positions, Malanga and Botha advanced with increasing confidence. Their flashlights probed the darkness methodically, sweeping across the terrain in a thorough pattern.

"They're close," Botha noted quietly, pointing out disturbed vegetation and subtle signs visible in his flashlight beam.

Malanga nodded, his earlier urbane manner completely replaced by predatory focus. The blood on his temple had dried to a dark crust, his designer clothes now disheveled and dirt-stained from the hunt. None of that appeared to concern him as they closed in on their prey's likely hiding spot.

"Kobus should've caught up by now," he observed, noting the extended silence from their third team member.

Both men instinctively moved closer together as a low, rumbling growl emanated from the brush behind them—not visible but close enough to register as a legitimate threat.

"We've got company," Botha noted unnecessarily, his flashlight beam sweeping toward the source of the sound but revealing nothing beyond gently swaying vegetation.

Something was tracking them through the darkness. Shadows shifted against other shadows, vegetation was disturbed in sequential patterns—all the subtle indicators of a large predator's stalking behavior.

"Keep looking," Malanga directed after a brief pause. "They'll be the meal tonight."

They proceeded toward the tree cluster cautiously, now splitting their attention between their human quarry and the potential animalistic threats. Their flashlight beams occasionally revealed glimpses of the natural fortress ahead—intertwined tree trunks growing against the embankment, creating a distinctive silhouette against the night sky.

Within the tree cluster, Sheryl and Anika reacted instantly to their discovery. Anika immediately began climbing higher into the protective branches, her smaller frame and natural athleticism allowing swift vertical movement, despite the challenging hand-holds.

Sheryl made a different decision, positioning herself behind the largest trunk for maximum protection—she waited silently.

"Keep climbing," she whispered to Anika, barely audible. "I'll stay low."

Their position suddenly seemed far less defensible as flashlight beams probed directly toward them. The searchers were now confident enough to advance more aggressively.

In the tree cluster, Anika reached a stable position four meters above ground-level, finding a notch where multiple branches created natural seating. Sheryl held her position behind the massive trunk, formulating a plan, despite their dire circumstances.

The standoff had reached its critical moment—the pursuers were closing in, the fugitives were cornered, and natural predators were circling the entire group. The conflict would unfold with the brutal efficiency of the African wilderness, where survival depended on split-second actions and reactions.

CHAPTER 43

BLOOD FURY

"We know you're there," Malanga called, his cultured voice carrying an edge of anticipation rather than anger. "Come out now, and we'll make it quick."

Silence answered him, and the tree cluster revealed nothing of its hidden occupants. Seeking any signs of movement, Botha's flashlight traced methodical patterns across the vegetation.

"Last chance," Malanga continued, moving closer with measured confidence. "The animals will make your ending considerably less pleasant than our plans for you."

Twenty meters from the largest trunk, Botha's light caught a brief flash of movement—subtle but unmistakable. He adjusted his aim quickly, the pistol rising in coordination with the flashlight beam.

"There," he confirmed quietly, illuminating the massive trunk where Sheryl was crouching.

Malanga nodded with satisfaction as they closed the distance with caution. The hunt was concluding exactly as he'd anticipated.

"Flush her," he directed while remaining slightly behind his enforcer's position.

Botha advanced with his weapon trained steadily on the trunk's edge, where he expected their prey to emerge. His focus was entirely in front of him, the fixation leaving him momentarily unaware of the threat developing from above.

The attack came with devastating suddenness—Anika dropping from an overhanging branch directly onto Botha's back. Her smaller frame belied remarkable strength as she locked her arms around his throat in a textbook chokehold, legs wrapping around his torso to secure herself against the inevitable counterattack.

Botha staggered under the impact, losing his gun as Anika's weight unbalanced him. Then the flashlight dropped from his grip, spinning across the ground and casting chaotic illumination across the scene as he reached backward with powerful arms to dislodge her.

At this exact moment, Sheryl exploded from her position behind the trunk, launching toward Malanga with released fury.

Malanga reacted with surprising speed, producing a knife from his belt with a practiced motion. The blade gleamed in the scattered light as he slashed in a defensive arc, forcing Sheryl to duck low.

"You've been a persistent problem," he hissed as he moved around her. "Now, that's over."

Sheryl matched his movements with predatory focus. Her eyes tracked the knife rather than his face. "You've threatened my people for the last time," she responded, her voice deadly calm, despite the circumstances.

They clashed in violent convergence, Malanga's knife slashing in defensive patterns while Sheryl evaded with minimal clearance—reading his attacks rather than reacting in fear.

On his third swipe, Sheryl created an opening, allowing the blade to pass undefended before trapping his wrist with both hands and applying a joint lock that spun him to his knees.

The knife dropped from nerveless fingers as Malanga's wrist bent beyond its natural range, ligaments stretching to their limits. Before he could escape, Sheryl switched to offensive strikes—not wild punches but deliberate hits to vulnerable spots.

Her elbow connected with his throat. As he folded forward to catch his breath, her knee rose to meet his descending face. The cartilage in his nose yielded with audible impact. Blood sprayed through the air and out of his nostrils as he staggered backward.

Sheryl pressed her advantage aggressively—a hooking strike to his floating ribs, a precise punch to the brachial plexus that temporarily deadened his right arm, then a fist to the temple that dropped him to the ground.

"You're finished," she stated with absolute certainty, securing a restraint hold that kept him immobilized and gasping in the dirt.

❀ ❀ ❀

While Sheryl systematically dismantled Malanga, a different battle unfolded meters away. Botha had recovered from the initial surprise of Anika's attack, his frame absorbing her blows while he easily remained standing, despite her weight on his shoulders.

He reached backward, finding purchase on Anika's smaller form and closing his massive hands on her arms. With a roar of effort, Botha broke her grip and used his considerable mass to slam her against the ground with stunning force. Anika hit hard, the impact driving the breath from her lungs and momentarily stunning her.

Botha loomed above her. Rage emanated from his face as he raised his boot to stomp down on her exposed ribcage. "Should've stayed in the jewelry business," he growled as his leg descended.

The impact never landed. Jack flew from the bushes, a missile of explosive force. His tackle caught Botha in a momentarily unbalanced position. Despite the enforcer's size advantage, physics favored the attack—Jack's full body weight connecting with the man's hips to send both of them crashing into the underbrush.

They separated with surprising speed, both fighters immediately ready as they assessed their opponent. Recognition flashed across Botha's face—not fear but the realization that this man before him was a serious threat.

"American military," Botha growled, circling with measured steps. "Special operations, I'd guess."

Jack offered no response, conserving energy rather than engaging in psychological banter. His stance revealed nothing while he prepared for everything.

Botha opened with a combination of strikes designed to test his opponent's skills. Jack deflected each, controlling his distance while making his own assessments.

The enforcer fought with brutal efficiency—no wasted motion, no telegraphed moves, each attack flowing into the next. His size and strength created a significant advantage, forcing Jack to maintain a perfect defense rather than attacking.

They exchanged blows for nearly a minute, neither gaining a decisive advantage but both accumulating damage. Botha's right eye was swelling from a precisely placed punch; Jack's lip had split from a glancing blow that could've been concussive if it had fully connected.

The next clash began with Botha pressing forward, using his aggression to force Jack onto uneven terrain that would compromise his mobility. Jack appeared to yield ground, seemingly pressured by the enforcer's superior mass and power.

But when Botha committed to a particularly aggressive move, Jack executed a perfect sweep, sidestepping his opponent's forward movement and using it to topple him into the brush as he passed by.

*** *** ***

Anika's head cleared, finding herself lying on the ground. The sounds of two separate battles registered through her receding disorientation. She pushed herself upright, finding herself bruised but functional, nothing broken, despite the jarring impact.

Her first priority was figuring out how to help either fight. Sheryl appeared to have complete control of her situation, systematically dismantling Malanga with professional thoroughness. Jack and Botha remained locked in a more even contest, neither having a decisive advantage over the other.

Movement in her peripheral vision drew her sudden attention—not a human form but something larger, moving with predatory stealth through the vegetation. The shadow resolved into a distinctive silhouette as it approached their position, moonlight glinting from the forward-facing eyes that tracked the human conflict hungrily.

Anika froze momentarily, primal recognition overwhelming her as she identified this deadly threat. The lioness was tracking the most active fight—Jack and Botha's battle creating the most distinctive visual and auditory signatures.

The fight reached a critical point, both men now showing signs of exhaustion but maintaining their professional focus. Jack executed a perfectly timed counter to Botha's latest attack, creating a momentary advantage that he exploited with a precise kick to the larger man's knee.

The impact forced Botha backward, disrupting his balance. He staggered toward the darker vegetation, unaware of the predator that was waiting.

The attack came immediately—130 kilograms of apex predator launching from her hiding place with explosive force. The lioness materialized in the moonlight with supernatural suddenness, powerful forelegs extended to secure a grip on her prey while her massive canines closed around his shoulder.

Botha's scream contained primitive terror beyond human language—a recognition of absolute vulnerability against nature's perfect killing machine. The lioness maintained its crushing grip while powerful hind legs pulled her prey toward denser vegetation.

Botha's struggles ended with shocking rapidity, his movements becoming uncoordinated within seconds of the initial bite. His last sounds faded as the lioness dragged him deeper into the concealing bush.

The entire sequence from her initial attack to Botha's disappearance occurred in seconds.

Jack stood momentarily frozen. His composure temporarily forgotten in his own primitive fear of the big cats he now knew for a fact were out there.

Anika's voice finally broke the stunned silence. "Lions! Several of them!" she called, pointing to movement in the surrounding vegetation. "We need cover!"

This warning galvanized Jack, who moved toward Sheryl's position, where she had full control over the now thoroughly subdued Malanga. "Sheryl, lions!" he shouted as he pulled at her shoulder.

The group retreated toward the natural fortress, Sheryl dragging Malanga along with them. Their defensive position offered them marginal protection at best, the trees potentially climbable, but it was all they had available.

The surrounding darkness seemed alive with predators, multiple sets of reflective eyes now visible in the moonlight as the lions recognized vulnerable prey.

Just as the lions began closing the distance, the night erupted with a mechanical roar approaching with surprising speed through the surrounding vegetation. Headlights suddenly illuminated the scene, a safari vehicle bursting through the brush with dramatic impact.

The vehicle skidded to a stop just meters from their position, powerful spotlights sweeping the entire area. Two rangers leaped from the vehicle with a sense of urgency. Their rifles were raised into a defensive position as they scanned the area.

"Where are the threats?" Pieter called, his weapon tracking every sound he heard.

"Multiple lions," Jack shouted back. "One person dead behind you."

The vehicle's sudden arrival had scattered the lions, the combination of mechanical noise, artificial light, and human numbers creating sufficient commotion to drive them away. The reflective eyes disappeared into the surrounding vegetation.

"Jack! Sheryl!" Familiar voices called from the vehicle's interior, where two figures now stood visible in the moonlight.

"Wanda? Joan?" Sheryl responded with disbelieving recognition. "How did you—"

"Later," the lead ranger interrupted. "Get everyone in the vehicle now. We'll figure this out when everyone's safe."

His orders spurred immediate compliance. Sheryl dragged Malanga toward the vehicle, Jack and Anika following behind them. The second ranger helped drag the semi-conscious criminal into the vehicle's protected interior.

"The other one's over there," Jack reported, pointing to where Botha had disappeared.

Pieter nodded grimly. "You stay here. Alex and I will get him." Together, the two rangers stepped into the bush with both their rifles and flashlights ready. They returned within minutes carrying the lifeless body of Botha between them. They wrestled him into the rear row of seats in the vehicle.

Within minutes, all the humans were secured within the vehicle's protective frame. The driver executed a tight turn, orienting the vehicle back toward the road.

Jack turned to Pieter, "There are two more poachers out here somewhere. One was attacked by animals, and I had a tussle with the other one."

Pieter nodded and spoke into his radio to relay this information. Then, responding to Jack, "The security teams will find them."

As they pulled away from the battle site, the emotional reality of survival began to sink in for all of them. Wanda and Joan embraced Sheryl and Anika with tearful relief, the intensity of their reunion reflecting their genuine fear they might never have seen them alive again.

"We thought we'd lost you," Joan managed through uncharacteristic emotion. "When we realized what had happened—"

"How'd you find us?" Anika asked, the logical question coming through her evident exhaustion and relief.

"Later," the ranger interrupted again, maintaining his focus. "We all need to hear those details when we're somewhere safe."

This professional reminder set their priorities straight—survival first, debriefing later.

In the vehicle's middle seat, Malanga sat in restraints—bloodied, defeated, but alive, despite the night's events. His expression revealed a seething anger beneath the physical damage and exhaustion he felt. Unlike his enforcer, he would survive to face human justice rather than nature's more immediate version.

The African night continued around them as the vehicle pushed toward the lodge, the brief human drama already fading into a distant memory. The natural predators of this territory had demonstrated the relative position of humans in the natural hierarchy.

CHAPTER 44

CELEBRATION

The safari vehicle's headlights carved a path through the predawn darkness as it followed the reserve's maintenance roads back toward Kariega Main Lodge. Inside, the atmosphere hung heavy with exhausted silence—the adrenaline that had sustained them through the night's ordeal gradually yielding to profound fatigue.

Sheryl sat with composed dignity, despite her disheveled appearance. Dirt and blood stained her clothes, and bruises were already darkening her exposed skin. Beside her, Anika maintained a similar demeanor, though occasional tremors betrayed the physical and emotional toll of their experience. Jack occupied the seat in front of them, his vigilance undiminished, despite his fatigue. His eyes still scanned their surroundings for danger.

Wanda and Joan flanked the trio. Their eyes were filled with quiet concern for their friends. In the front seat, Pieter was on the radio, efficiently summarizing the situation for lodge security.

"Police are on their way," he reported after concluding his communication. "And our medical team's standing by when we arrive."

In the vehicle's rear compartment, Malanga sat under the second ranger's watchful eye. Despite his battered condition, he maintained a defiant sense of dignity, his eyes showing anger rather than defeat at his capture.

As they approached the lodge's perimeter, security lighting revealed their first glimpse of civilization after the primal wilderness experience—the carefully maintained grounds and buildings appearing surreally normal compared to the night's savage reality. Staff members emerged from the main building as the vehicle pulled to a stop, their expressions revealing genuine concern.

"Medical assessment first," the lead ranger directed as they disembarked. "Then, debriefing."

This order structured their immediate activities, with medical staff conducting preliminary evaluations. The group remained tightly together, reluctant to separate after their shared ordeal.

Before security could remove him to isolated containment, Malanga locked eyes with Sheryl across the reception area. "This changes nothing," he stated with disturbing certainty, despite his current position. "The system can't hold me. We both know that."

Sheryl met his gaze without flinching, her composure revealing neither fear nor bravado. "You've lost," she responded simply. "Your business is exposed. Your enforcer's dead. This changes everything."

Malanga's expression didn't change. Like all professional criminals of his caliber, he was certain that he could beat the system with bribes and threats delivered in the right places.

After medical exams confirmed no life-threatening injuries, the ranger directed Sheryl, Jack, Anika, Wanda, and Joan toward a private sitting room adjacent to the main lodge. The space offered both privacy and security—comfortable seating arranged around a central coffee table, large windows providing natural light as dawn gradually brightened the eastern horizon.

They'd barely settled when a uniformed police officer entered, accompanied by the lodge's chief security officer. Introductions were brief and professional, establishing plans for formal statement collection while respecting the trauma the group had experienced.

"We need comprehensive statements while the events are fresh in your minds," the officer explained, then activated his recording equipment. "Starting with a chronological sequence of events, beginning with your abduction."

Sheryl took the lead, detailing how she had returned to her chalet after dinner, the ambush upon entry, and her subsequent transportation deep into the reserve. Her description had a professional detachment, despite the personal nature of the attack, focusing on important details rather than her emotional reaction to what she had gone through.

Jack followed with similar efficiency, his statement corroborating Sheryl's timeline while adding tactical observations that revealed his unique background without explicitly stating it. His description of vehicles, personnel, and operational methods provided invaluable details for prosecuting Malanga.

Anika completed the abduction narrative with her own experience.

Throughout these accounts, the police officer took notes without interrupting, recognizing the value of unbroken narrative flow. Only after all three had completed their abduction stories did he ask clarifying questions about specific details and timing.

"We were lucky to have friends who noticed our absence quickly," Sheryl concluded, turning toward Wanda and Joan with open gratitude.

"That's where we come in," Wanda interjected, leaning forward with characteristic directness. "Something felt wrong from the moment we saw that vehicle leaving after dark."

Joan nodded in agreement. "We were heading back to our chalets after dinner when we saw a safari vehicle leaving the lodge area around 8:45."

"At first, we figured it was an anti-poaching patrol after yesterday's incidents," Wanda continued. "But when we got to the chalets, everything changed."

Joan's expression tightened at the memory. "I was rooming with Anika. I went in and found some of our gear scattered around. Furniture was knocked over. Anika's phone and backpack were on the sofa, but she was nowhere to be seen."

"I knew right away something was wrong," Joan continued. "I immediately went to find Sheryl, hoping she'd know where Anika was."

"But when I got to Sheryl's chalet," Wanda picked up the narrative, "it was the same thing—signs of a struggle, abandoned personal items, and no answer when I called out. After yesterday's poachers, we had a bad feeling."

"We went straight to ranger headquarters," Joan explained. "We described the mess in the rooms, the missing women, and that suspicious vehicle leaving just before we discovered that Anika and Sheryl were gone."

The police officer nodded encouragement as their accounts continued.

"The rangers mobilized immediately," Wanda acknowledged with obvious respect. "Multiple search teams went out within twenty minutes."

"But how'd you actually find us?" Sheryl asked, the question that she had wanted to ask since their rescue. "The reserve covers thousands of hectares. Finding us in that darkness seems almost impossible."

Joan and Wanda exchanged glances before Joan explained. "Partly good search patterns, and partly luck," she admitted.

"We were with the eastern search team when we heard a gunshot," Wanda continued. "From our position on a ridgeline, we could see distant vehicle headlights that'd been sitting still for several minutes. That wasn't normal for ranger patrols."

"As we got closer, we could see flashlights moving around in the bush," Joan added. "So, the rangers crept through the vegetation toward the lights."

"And then, we heard the screaming and another gunshot," Wanda concluded grimly. "That really got things moving. The rangers floored it to get to you as fast as they could."

This explanation of their rescue created a momentary silence as the group realized how close their survival had been to an entirely different outcome. The margin between life and death had been minutes and meters, their rescue dependent on events that could easily have failed at multiple points.

The debriefing continued for another hour, each person adding details to the narrative while the police officer constructed a coherent timeline of events. As formal statements concluded, the eastern windows displayed full daylight—the African morning proceeding with indifferent beauty, despite the night's violent events.

"We'll need additional statements later," the officer said as he gathered his materials. "But these initial ones will give us enough for immediate charges. Mr. Malanga will be transferred to regional holding facilities for formal processing."

After the officials departed, the group remained in the sitting room, reluctant to separate, despite their exhaustion. The shared trauma had created a connection that transcended their previous relationships, binding them together through an experience that outsiders could never fully comprehend.

"I need a shower and about forty hours of sleep," Sheryl finally acknowledged, rising from her seat with visible stiffness. "But I'm not sure I want to go back to that chalet just yet."

"We'll go together," Wanda decided immediately, her protective instincts kicking in. "All of us."

This suggestion received immediate agreement. The group gravitated toward Sheryl's accommodation, not from practical necessity but from emotional solidarity. Her private pool was an additional incentive.

The morning sun had risen fully as they walked through the lodge grounds, casting golden light across the landscape that seemed surreally beautiful against their recent wilderness terror. Staff members they passed offered respectful acknowledgment without intrusive engagement, word of the night's events having clearly spread throughout the property.

Sheryl's chalet had been thoroughly cleaned, all evidence of the previous night's struggle removed by efficient housekeeping. Despite this surface-level restoration, she hesitated momentarily at the threshold, the psychological impact of the violation not so easily erased.

"I'll check it first," Jack offered quietly.

After confirming the space was secure, they entered together, immediately moving toward the private pool area.

They settled into loungers positioned around the pool, the simple act of horizontal rest triggering immediate physical relaxation. The adrenaline that had sustained them through the night's ordeal drained away, leaving profound fatigue in its wake.

"I should feel triumphant," Sheryl observed quietly, staring at the pool's tranquil surface. "We survived. We stopped him. But all I feel is…"

"Shaken," Anika completed when Sheryl's voice trailed off. "It's normal. We've been through a lot."

Jack nodded in agreement but remained silent, his expression revealing the compartmentalization of someone accustomed to processing these kinds of events. He closed his eyes to deal with the trauma in his own way.

They remained in companionable silence for some time, each processing the experience differently.

Their tranquility was interrupted by a gentle knock at the garden gate, followed by Luke's concerned voice. "Can we come in? The others are worried."

Sheryl roused herself with visible effort. "Yeah, come through."

The gate opened to reveal Luke and Margaret, carrying a thermos of coffee and a basket of fresh pastries. "We thought you might need these," Margaret explained, setting the offerings on a nearby table with motherly concern.

This initial visit broke the invisible barrier between the survivors and the wider tour group. Within the hour, other runners began arriving in small groups—Nkosi and the Alvarez brothers bringing fresh fruit, the Wilsons contributing bottles of water and sports drinks, Stanley and Madeline appearing with cushions and blankets.

Each visitor expressed genuine concern without demanding detailed accounts, respecting the survivors' need for recovery while demonstrating their care. Their presence gradually reintegrated the night's victims into a communal experience rather than leaving them isolated with their trauma.

By mid-morning, the impromptu gathering had evolved into a celebration—not of the danger, but of their survival and all the support they'd received. Lodge staff, recognizing the spontaneous event, arrived with brunch provisions and beverages—champagne for mimosas, vodka and tomato juice for Bloody Marys, and pitchers of Van der Hum Tangerine Fizz, a distinctively South African cocktail made with local citrus liqueur.

"A toast," Luke announced, raising his glass once everyone had been served. "To Sheryl, Jack, and Anika—who showed remarkable courage under circumstances no tourist should ever face."

Glasses raised in unanimous support; the genuine warmth of the group created a momentary emotional wave among the survivors. Before the moment could become awkward, Wanda stepped forward.

"And to Joan," she added, raising her glass toward her unexpected partner, "who proved that accountants can be badass rescuers when necessary."

This lighter toast broke the emotional tension perfectly. Joan blushed at the recognition but accepted it with quiet dignity, her usual reserve softened by the group's genuine appreciation.

The impromptu party continued through late morning. Conversations flowed with increasing naturalness as the traumatic edge gradually dulled through shared support. The survivors participated with growing animation, each finding their way back toward normal interactions at their own pace.

No one mentioned departure schedules or tour plans. Instead, the conversation focused on immediate comforts, shared experiences from earlier days of the tour, and gentle humor that acknowledged their ordeal without dwelling on its darkest aspects.

As afternoon arrived, observers noted the gradual quieting of the three central characters. Sheryl, Jack, and Anika gradually succumbed to their accumulated exhaustion, despite their best efforts to remain engaged. Margaret nudged

Madeline, pointing to Anika's relaxed form in her lounge chair. It was obvious that she was sound asleep, despite the surrounding activity.

Within minutes of each other, all three had surrendered to exhaustion. The group around them recognized the shift and their conversations quieted to whispers before Tyler gestured toward the gate.

"Let them rest," he suggested softly. "We'll check back later."

The gathering dispersed with remarkable consideration, a few placing soft kisses on Anika's or Sheryl's forehead as they exited. Joan and Wanda withdrew into the chalet, arranging themselves in nearby chairs with tacit agreement to maintain their protective presence while their friends slept.

As the afternoon sun traced its path across the African sky, the three survivors slept undisturbed—their minds processing the night's events through whatever subconscious mechanisms evolution had provided for such experiences.

Around them, lodge operations continued with professional precision. But in the private pool of Sheryl's chalet, none of these activities penetrated the survivors' exhausted sleep. Protected by friends and warmed by the African sunshine, they enjoyed the simplest and most essential form of recovery before more complex healing could begin.

CHAPTER 45

WALKING WITH NATURE

The golden morning light bathed the savanna in warm hues as the Global Runners group gathered for their final excursion. After days of viewing Africa from the elevated perspective of safari vehicles, they would experience the landscape on its own terms—on foot, at eye level with the creatures that called it home.

Everyone was acutely aware of the harrowing events of the night before. Runners and rangers alike cast glances at the central figures of the ordeal—Sheryl, Jack, and Anika—who stood in the crowd, ready to embark on the outing. Each had insisted that they were rested and preferred an active day to sitting idly with their thoughts.

"Today, we walk with the land rather than passing over it," explained Archie, the senior ranger who would lead their expedition. "This is how humans experienced this territory for thousands of years before vehicles."

Luke distributed water bottles while Archie outlined safety procedures. "Each ranger will carry a rifle. These are required by national law," he explained, patting the weathered stock of his .375 H&H Magnum. "But we won't need them. The large predators are resting during these hours, and the herbivores are used to seeing humans on foot. They'll give us plenty of space."

Sheryl nodded agreement. "Trust the rangers," she told her runners.

The group set out in single file, following a clear game trail that meandered toward the central watering hole. After days of shared adventures—both planned excursions and unexpected dangers—they all fell into synchronized formation.

A family of impalas grazed nearby, the dominant male raising his magnificent lyre-shaped horns to assess the approaching humans before returning to his breakfast with obvious indifference. The group passed within thirty meters, close enough to hear the soft tearing sounds as the animals plucked grass from the ground.

"Notice how calmly they're reacting to us now," Margaret whispered with wonder. "On our first drive, they seemed so skittish."

"They're reading our energy," Archie explained. "Animals sense when we're comfortable versus when we're tense. You've gotten used to the bush—you move like you belong here now."

This observation resonated deeply with the runners. Their initial days had been characterized by constant startling, gasping, and pointing at every animal sighting. Now, they walked with measured appreciation, their excitement no less genuine but expressed through quiet observation rather than disruptive exclamations.

The trail curved around acacia trees, revealing three giraffes browsing on the highest foliage. Unlike their previous vehicle encounters, where the tall creatures maintained their distance, today, they allowed their visitors to move closer before stepping casually away.

"Twenty meters is their comfort zone with humans on foot," Archie explained. "They know we're not a threat at this distance, but instinct tells them to keep some separation."

Tyler knelt to photograph the scene, his movements deliberately slow and predictable. "I've never felt so…intimate before," he observed quietly. "In the vehicle, we were observers. Now, we're almost like residents."

This sentiment settled on the group as they continued their walk. The distinction between observing nature and existing within it permeated their awareness. Their footfalls settled into a natural rhythm, their breathing synchronized with the gentle breeze, their senses expanding to absorb the landscape's complex texture rather than just isolated highlights.

For most of the group, this connection produced profound contentment. The constant connectivity demands of civilization—emails, messages, schedules, deadlines—had faded into irrelevance against the immediate presence of the African bush. Here, life operated on different principles.

"I feel so present," Joan remarked as they paused to observe a small herd of nyalas moving through dappled shade. "No past regrets, no future anxieties. Just here in this moment."

Wanda nodded in agreement. "Life at home's so distracting. Everything's transactional rather than experiential."

Yet, for Jack, Sheryl, and Anika, this immersion carried additional layers after their recent ordeal. As the group continued their walk, Sheryl unconsciously scanned the tree lines and identifying potential cover positions—a practice heightened by her recent experience. She noticed Jack doing the same, his relaxed stride belying the awareness in his eyes.

"Feels different after being prey, doesn't it?" she remarked quietly when they briefly fell to the rear of the formation.

Jack nodded, understanding immediately. "I'm still wound up, ready to spring."

"Exactly," Sheryl agreed. "I feel at peace right now, but I know how quickly that could change."

This paradox defined their experience—the deep appreciation of nature's beauty inseparable from recognition of its fundamental brutality. Their recent night as prey had connected them to an ancient human experience largely forgotten in modern life—the knowledge that darkness transformed the landscape from a nurturing sanctuary to a hunting ground.

"It's more honest this way," Jack observed after thoughtful consideration. "Most people see only half the reality."

Sheryl nodded. "The light without the shadow. The beauty without the danger."

This exchange, brief but profound, captured their shared perspective—neither diminishing nature's wonder, nor ignoring its fundamental harshness. Their experience hadn't created fear but a deeper understanding of the complete cycle rather than only its comfortable side.

The group continued along the path until Archie halted beside a massive earthen structure rising nearly two meters from the surrounding terrain. The towering mound, hardened to a concrete-like consistency by the elements, stood as a testament to the architectural capabilities of its tiny builders.

"Termite cathedral," Archie announced, removing a small, collapsible shovel from his pack. "One of the bush's most important engineering marvels."

With careful precision, he opened a small section of the mound's outer wall, revealing intricate chambers and tunnels teeming with industrious insects. The group gathered around, their fascination overcoming any initial discomfort they may have felt as they observed the complex social structure within.

"Each mound houses millions of individuals working together," Archie explained, pointing out different paths through the exposed sections. "Workers, soldiers, the reproductive queen deep inside. They're a single superorganism with a kind of collective intelligence."

He indicated the surrounding vegetation, which showed distinctive patterns of health and vigor. "These mounds cultivate the soil structure for hundreds of meters in every direction. They create microenvironments that support entire ecosystems, improve water penetration during rains, and recycle nutrients that'd otherwise remain locked in dead vegetation."

Stanley leaned closer. His initial aversion to insects yielded to fascination. "So, these tiny creatures shape the entire landscape?"

"Exactly," Archie confirmed. "In terms of ecological impact, they're as significant as elephants or any large mammal. They're the invisible engineers that make everything else possible."

After allowing sufficient observation, Archie carefully resealed the opening. "They'll repair this damage within hours. They're remarkably efficient."

As they continued their walk, the trail led them past evidence of nature's recycling systems in progressive stages. First came the bleached skeleton of a water buffalo, its massive, curved horns and substantial bone structure having resisted decomposition long after soft tissues had returned to the soil.

"Final stage of return," Archie noted and invited the group to observe the weathered remains. "Even these bones will eventually dissolve into calcium and minerals that feed the grasses, which feed the herbivores, which feed the predators. Nothing's wasted."

The pristine whiteness of the bones against the red soil created a hauntingly beautiful picture of death being transformed into a sculpture by time and the elements. Several group members photographed the arrangement, appreciating its stark aesthetic without the emotional response that fresher remains might provoke.

A hundred meters further, that contrast became evident as they encountered much more recent evidence of predation—an impala carcass partially consumed during the previous night's hunting activities. Unlike the sanitized skeleton, this scene contained a raw immediacy—torn hide, exposed muscle tissue, the metallic scent of blood mingling with the sweet decay of the beginning stages of decomposition.

Several group members instinctively stepped back, their civilized sensibilities overwhelmed by nature's unfiltered reality. Jack moved closer, however, his expression revealing curiosity rather than discomfort.

"Lion kill," he guessed, pointing to the pattern of consumption. "Maybe a young female, judging by the bite radius."

Archie nodded in confirmation. "Good observation. She'll return tonight to claim what's left, though jackals and vultures take bits of it during daylight hours."

Jack studied the scene with particular intensity, his thoughts evidently extending beyond the immediate evidence. The partially consumed impala provided a visceral reminder of what awaited any creature claimed by predators—including humans who ventured into this environment unprepared.

"Botha would've looked similar," he observed quietly to Sheryl, who had joined his inspection. "If we hadn't recovered his body immediately."

Sheryl shuddered slightly. "I wouldn't want that for anyone, even for him."

Finally, their walk brought them to a slight elevation that offered a panoramic view across the surrounding savanna. Archie selected this location deliberately, providing a natural amphitheater where the group could rest while absorbing the landscape around them.

From this vantage point, the interconnected nature of the ecosystem became visually apparent—patches of different vegetation creating a mosaic that supported diverse herbivore populations, which, in turn, sustained the predators. Waterways wove through the landscape like arteries, connecting distinct habitats into a functioning whole.

"Everything you see exists in balance," Archie explained as they settled onto sun-warmed rocks. "Predator and prey, grass and grazer, decomposer and new life—all parts of a single system that's evolved over millions of years."

The group remained silent, each processing the scene from a different perspective. For some, the beauty they witnessed dominated everything else. Golden light illuminated acacia silhouettes against an azure sky, the distant movement of animals creating a living tapestry across the landscape. For others, the integration of seemingly contradictory elements resonated more strongly—the harmony emerging from competition, cooperation existing alongside predation.

Margaret expressed this paradox perfectly by saying, "It's brutal and beautiful at the same time, isn't it? No pretense, no artifice—just life doing what it does."

"The brutality's part of the beauty," Nkosi observed thoughtfully. "Without the predators, the herbivores would overgraze, destroying the vegetation that supports everything. The harshness creates the harmony."

Sheryl nodded in appreciation of this insight. "That's what most visitors never fully grasp. They want the beauty without the brutality, but the system requires both to function."

"Worth it?" Jack asked quietly, the question encompassing their entire journey from its planned adventures to the unexpected dangers.

Sheryl considered briefly before nodding. "Completely. You can't truly understand a system until you've experienced all its facets."

As they prepared to return to the lodge for their final evening, Anika said, "We came here seeking adventure, but we found connections instead. To this place, to each other, and to something more fundamental that we've lost in our regular lives."

The walk back proceeded in thoughtful silence. Unlike their arrival when the landscape had seemed alien and intimidating, they now moved through it with a sense of belonging—not ownership, but participation.

As the lodge buildings came into view, Sheryl paused for a moment of reflection, her gaze sweeping across the landscape they were leaving. "Sometimes brutal," she acknowledged quietly, "but always beautiful and enduring."

This simple observation captured the essential truth they had discovered—not just about the African wilderness but about existence itself in its most honest form. They would carry this understanding back to their civilized lives, forever changed by having walked, however briefly, in nature's unfiltered reality.

That evening, the group gathered for dinner on the main lodge terrace. Conversation flowed naturally around the table—tomorrow's departure logistics, favorite moments from the tour, exchange of contact information for future reunions.

Margaret watched the three survivors with grandmotherly attention, noting the subtle signs of recovery. Sheryl participated actively but maintained a constant awareness of her surroundings. Anika engaged more freely than she had during the early days of the tour, accepting invitations and contributing to discussions. Jack remained vigilant but relaxed, his military bearing melting more smoothly into social interactions.

"They're not unaffected," Margaret murmured to Joan, "but they're unbroken. That's the best outcome anyone could hope for."

As the evening wound down and guests began retiring to their chalets, the three survivors lingered on the terrace. The African night surrounded them. The sounds of insects and distant animal calls made the perfect soundtrack.

"Tomorrow, we fly home," Sheryl said, the statement carrying weight beyond mere travel logistics.

"Different flights, different destinations," Anika added. "Back to our separate lives."

"But we're connected now," Jack concluded. "What we went through together—that doesn't just disappear when we board our own planes."

They sat quietly for a few more minutes, each recognizing that this moment marked a transition. The intensity of shared trauma was giving way to the slower process of individual healing, but the bonds forged in those terrifying hours would endure.

"We should stay in touch," Sheryl suggested.

"Definitely," Anika agreed.

Jack simply nodded, the gesture carrying his full commitment.

As they finally rose to return to their chalets, each carried the knowledge that they had not merely survived their ordeal—they had been transformed by it. The incident had become part of their respective life narratives rather than disrupting those narratives entirely.

The African night continued around them, vast and indifferent, but no longer threatening. They had faced its darkest possibilities and emerged with new understandings of their own resilience and the unexpected strength found in human connection during times of crisis.

Tomorrow would bring their departure back to their daily lives and the beginning of longer-term recovery. Tonight, they were simply grateful survivors, blessed with friendship and the promise of morning.

THE END

AI DISCLOSURE

The text of this novel was written by the human author. I used GPT-4 and Claude as research tools to collect cultural, historical, geographical, and geological information on South Africa.

ABOUT R.D.D. SMITH

R.D.D. Smith writes science-fiction, medical thriller novels featuring advanced surgical devices, AI, telesurgery, simulation, and speculative diseases; and global travel adventures that follow running tourists through exotic countries. The medical series is inspired by his career in healthcare and experience with robotic surgery devices. The travel novels are inspired by his actual vacations in the countries featured in the books.

He holds a doctorate and MBA from the University of Maryland, a master's from Texas Tech University, and a bachelor's from Colorado State University.

He lives with his wife, dogs, and cats in sunny Florida, frequently escaping to cooler climes during the beastly Florida summers.

STAY IN TOUCH

Review:
Please leave a review of this book on Amazon or
your favorite book site.

Join Us:
Join our community of readers to receive fascinating news
related to the story.

www.rddsmith.com/free

ACKNOWLEDGMENTS

As an author, I am infinitely grateful to my readers who invest their time, money, and imaginations in following my stories and characters through their challenges, failures, and transformations.

First, to my wife and children, who have endured decades of fanatic immersion into whatever my latest passion is, most recently, these novels. Your patience, dedication, and love are appreciated every day.

For this adventure story, I am indebted to Vacation Races Global Adventures (USA) and Runcation (South Africa) for organizing the fantastic trip that inspired the events in this novel. Special thanks to Cheri Santiego, Zoe Calcott, and Salem Stanley for creating a business, an adventure, a community, and a family all in one. Thank you to my fellow vacationers and runners for your enthusiastic encouragement as we created and discovered each chapter of this book together.

For my editor Kaitlin Travis, book layout artist Adina Cucicov, and the many advisors who made this book far better than I could have accomplished alone.

REAL GLOBAL TRAVEL ADVENTURES

If you're looking for running adventure travel:

Vacation Races Global Adventures
https://www.vacationraces.com/global-adventures/

Runcation (South Africa)
https://www.runcation.co.za/

And a pair of non-profits working with these organizations:

Kariega Foundation
https://kariegafoundation.com/

Be Moved Collective
https://bemovedcollective.org/

Photo Credit: Barbara Cole, Used with Permission from Vacation Races
www.barbaracolephoto.com

www.ingramcontent.com/pod-product-compliance
Lightning Source LLC
Chambersburg PA
CBHW050606170726
48283CB00001B/126